great sporting moments

great Sporting moments

The best of *Sport* magazine 1988–2004
Edited by Damien Wilkins

VICTORIA UNIVERSITY PRESS

VICTORIA UNIVERSITY PRESS
Victoria University of Wellington
PO Box 600 Wellington

http://www.vuw.ac.nz/vup
http://www.sportmagazine.org
http://www.nzetc.org/tm/scholarly/tei-corpus-Sport.html

National Library of New Zealand Cataloguing-in-Publication Data

Great sporting moments : the best of Sport magazine, 1988-2004
/ edited by Damien Wilkins.
Includes bibliographical references.
ISBN 0-86473-515-4
1. New Zealand literature—21st century. I. Wilkins, Damien,
1963- II. Sport (Wellington, N.Z.)
NZ820.8—dc 22

Acknowledgements
Grateful thanks to Morgan Lawrence-Bach and Emma Turner,
Whitireia Publishing students, for their hard work on this volume;
and to Creative New Zealand for consistent financial support
for *Sport* through the years.

Printed in Singapore

Contents

Introduction

Is there a less suggestive way of saying this? *Sport* was born in the back of my yellow Ford Escort as we were rounding the Basin Reserve some time in mid-1988. I was driving. Fergus Barrowman and Elizabeth Knox were in the backseat. This was a period in which on important occasions I was—rather oddly it now seems—their chauffeur. Several months later I was to drive Fergus and Elizabeth home in the same vehicle after their wedding. Neither could drive; it gave them great power.

'I think we should do the magazine,' said Fergus, 'and I think it should be called Sport.'

'Sport,' I said. 'Mmn.' Well, has anyone loved the name on first hearing it? (In his only editorial for the magazine—please see *Sport* 3—Fergus ponders gloomily the notion that the gender imbalance in that issue might be connected to the name, with its 'blokeish self-satisfaction'. 'This,' says FJB, 'is certainly not intended.')

Elizabeth spoke from the back of the car. 'He's going to do it too.'

'It's not settled,' said Fergus.

'It is,' said Elizabeth. She leaned forward. 'He's doing it.'

'Good,' I said.

The reconstruction is naturally imperfect. It's also disingenuous on my part. I sound rather cool about the whole thing. I was probably in that moment dreaming wild dreams of paradigm shifts—and thinking with deep pleasure that I could now get some of my own stories published. We'd been talking up the idea of a literary magazine for a while. These conversations, like many we had around literature, were satisfyingly high-flown, full of pitiless assessments of others' failings, and wonderfully free of resolution. Nothing was any good—and that was enough for us. *Landfall* seemed less and less interested in stories and poems. Robin Dudding's excellent *Islands* appeared to be lost. The inspiring guerilla raid of *Rambling Jack* was complete. It's hard now to say why the decisive moment for action came in the car. Fergus had the name—and maybe that was sufficient.

The written record of the time—supplied chiefly by us—doesn't entirely support my picture of bruising confidence. We sound assertively mild in public. We speak of 'good writing' and avoiding the 'unproductively prescriptive' oppositions of 'simplicity or artifice, postmodernism or not'. (The terms sound quaint; they were becoming so even at the time.) There is mention of 'fun'. Fergus sees *Sport* in the 'entirely appropriate image of a traditional literary magazine.'

Our third issue had not just FJB's note but another editorial, from 'EFK'. Elizabeth's version upgrades her husband's sober ambition: 'In producing our magazine we could fancy ourselves as Baptists, making strait the way.' I recall something of this fervour attaching itself to our near-daily visits to Unity Books where another member of the editorial team, Nigel Cox, standing behind the counter, would urge us on with wise, insightful, frequently libelous statements about the book trade. Now, Nigel pressed, is the hour. It was also around this time that Barbara Anderson, when visiting VUP, used to tell friends, 'I'm just off to see the baby-faced killers.' I remember Janet Paul, the artist, visiting the office to talk about the use of one of her paintings on the cover of Barbara's first book. Another visitor was there at the same time, and he was wearing a bright shirt. Janet said, 'It's so wonderful to see men wearing colourful clothes!' Then she turned sadly to look at Fergus and me, dressed in our dull, dark shirts. But here I'm reminded of that character in Anthony Powell's novel *Temporary Kings* who blacks out at a party in which he's come across people and stories from his past. When he revives he considers the likelihood that he's literally dying of nostalgia.

Of course a literary magazine usually needs more than hostility to what's around it to keep going. Fortunately we had some writing.

I'd recently joined Victoria University Press as Fergus's assistant. We were publishing Jenny Bornholdt's first book, Anne Kennedy's first book. Barbara Anderson had begun to win short story competitions. Dinah Hawken had won a Commonwealth

Writers' Prize for her first book the year before. Forbes Williams was a recent graduate of Bill Manhire's creative writing course. (The course crucially fed both VUP and the magazine; Fergus has been an external examiner for more than twenty years.) Bill himself was publishing short fiction for the first time. Nigel had published his second novel the previous year, which was also the year of Elizabeth Knox's debut. Alan Brunton was back in the country after a decade away. Vincent O'Sullivan had just been given a chair at Victoria. Ian Wedde was working on his next big novel. Things were happening. Nor is it only in retrospect that all this activity seemed important. The great rolling weight of excellence pushed at our backs. Many of these writers were in regular contact with Fergus through VUP. The first issue—an all-fiction affair—more or less picked itself.

Fergus was the editor and publisher and designer. This was still the time of slicing and waxing galleys, where a good part of our day was used up pleasantly bent over the lightbox, fixing the typesetting in place. Fergus would sometimes greet an author at the door of our prefab office with a scalpel in his hand. The first three issues were done in this manner, literally cut and paste. Fergus also drew the cover image, after Picasso. And he hit on interested parties for the start-up funds. Andrew Mason, then literary editor at the *Listener*, gave money, as did Alan Preston, owner of Unity Books. Bill Manhire and Nigel Cox also helped. A couple of these loans to this day remain outstanding, giving a nice sense perhaps of the way obligations of this sort sometimes never quite disappear. As in most businesses, the creation of stationery and the taking of a private box were highlights— for me, even end-points. I remember the shock of reading the copy on the back cover when the first issue came back from the printer's, which stated—in an alarming present tense—that the magazine 'is published twice-yearly, in October and April'. It was October. I was ready to retire.

A quick study of the newspaper photo of that moment reveals our foolish, unchecked joy. Perhaps only Fergus held back—was everything in place? was the spine straight? was the binding solid? had we spelled everyone's name correctly?—but only then for a few moments. We'd each flicked to our own pieces.

'I think it looks pretty convincing, don't you?' he said. In the photo we look capable of eating the thing. Indeed a version had been consumed a few weeks before when Nigel, together with Marion McLeod, had organised a cake for Fergus and Elizabeth's engagement party. The cover appeared in lurid green icing with the message 'Give Marriage a Sporting Chance'.

In some ways the first issue is strangely misshapen, a memorial to abandoned projects and interrupted careers. The lead-off piece comes from Forbes Williams, who did publish a book of stories and from whom the odd brilliant noise issues, but who hasn't, as they say, 'gone on'. Nigel's chapter comes from a novel which never appeared, and he wouldn't publish another book for thirteen years. Miro Bilbrough's prose poem sequence was never finished and she's now a filmmaker based in Sydney. Keri Hulme's contribution finally ended up in a book sixteen years later. Wendy Pond's rather beautiful story 'High Line', which narrowly missed selection here, appears to have been her last. Poets Bill Manhire and Jenny Bornholdt get in with prose—Jenny has not yet found a place in her seven books for 'The China Theory of Life'—and novelist Elizabeth Knox is represented by an essay she originally wrote for an English Honours paper, also as yet uncollected.

An odd bunch of things then; less emphatic perhaps than my nostalgic sense of the period had allowed—and yet, totally in line with the usual parameters of a literary magazine. (Here Fergus was proved right.) There are the classics—'*from* Motel View', is one of these. There's also work of absolute accomplishment which is not followed up on—a category of peculiar poignancy. Then there are major writers in a minor mode perhaps, minor writers writing up, off-cuts, dead-ends, surprises, jokes—oh, and failures. The literary magazine always has space for these.

The second issue has always belonged in my mind to a single author, the Australian Gerald Murnane, whose 20-page story 'When the Mice Failed to Arrive' should be here except for an irregular selection policy with regard to overseas writers. (Paul Durcan makes it but James Fenton's deserving 'Here Come the Drum Majorettes!' doesn't. Something to do with New Zealand references, relative availability of said work and other mumbled excuses.) Most of the 'foreigners' were guests of the International Arts Festival; publication in the magazine being seen as useful exposure ahead of in-person appearances. Murnane was not in this group. He believes that flying is 'an insult to the earth'. Fergus and I thought he was simply the most exciting fiction writer around and we wrote a begging letter. We commissioned Catherine Bagnall to draw the cover based on the Murnane piece. I'm surprised—and delighted—to see that this issue's centerpiece is, in fact, J.H. Macdonald's 45-page debut, a novella which was to grow into his novel *The Free World*. We also secured a chunk of that Wedde novel, which promptly disappeared for another sixteen years and counting. Is there a relationship, *pace* J.H. Macdonald and R. Carl Shuker, between excerpting a novel-in-progress and said novel's demise? For pedants, the bits we got from Maurice Shadbolt's *Monday's Warriors* (*Sport* 3) and Maurice Gee's *The Burning Boy* (5) don't affect the result since both were completed at the time of magazine publication. Shadbolt's piece appeared—at the author's specific request—with a © attached; sign perhaps that our credibility had not been fully established.

Poetry also broke through in this issue, with classic Bornholdt and Hawken and Les Murray. I'm sure there was an attempt originally to keep poetry out of *Sport*. What were we thinking? I believe we were thinking *Granta*. The quarantine broke easily once we saw how little we had in prose reserves, and how strong the poetry was. We also said no reviews, and only relented when the occasion looked momentous. If Douglas Standring, in the third issue, seemed to be hedging in his piece on some short story collections ('They are homogenous in their diversity.'), Stephen Stratford, reviewing the *Penguin Book of Contemporary New Zealand Short Stories* in the next issue, gave his feelings away in the title: 'Is Your Book Really Necessary?' Much later, Andrew Johnston also had things to say about Mark Pirie's *New Zealand Writing: The NeXt Wave*: 'a self-contradicting, ill-informed and ill-conceived production that misreads and misrepresents recent writing by young New Zealanders'—a few subscriptions might have been lost that day, and perhaps a few gained. (For the record, the subscription base hit its level almost immediately—at around 250—and has stayed near there ever since. *Sport* has always relied on bookshop sales more than subscribers.) When Alan Brunton was commissioned to review the *Penguin Book of Contemporary New Zealand Poetry*, he turned in fourteen pages mainly of quotations from the anthology and other sources, including a 'want list' found in a library book.

Survey pieces and critical commentary appeared from time to time: the UK critic Michael Hulse looked at some recent NZ poetry. ('[Gregory] O'Brien, for a start, doesn't seem to have been to God's funeral.') Vincent O'Sullivan wrote about Owen Marshall. Gregory O'Brien fired in an appreciation of the Australian poet Ken Bolton in *Sport* 16. ('If the amount of annoyance Bolton's poems have caused is any indication then he's a very effective poet indeed.') A sizeable section of *Sport* 23 was given over to pieces about the sale by Victoria University of Colin McCahon's painting 'Storm Warning' and O'Brien again wrote the memorably fierce lead essay: 'Colin McCahon's belief in art as "a means of conquering spiritual death" must sound like mumbo-jumbo to the post-humanists and those sainted individuals bold enough to describe themselves as "skilled in reading the visual". How could they cope with McCahon's stated objective "to make a painting beat like, and with, a human heart"?'

The personal essay or memoir quickly became an important part of the magazine's appeal. In addition to the terrific pieces here—many of which have yet to be collected in book form—there were notable contributions through the years from Iain Sharp ('Green Viva' 21), Murray Bail ('Killing an Elephant' 4), James Meffan ('Lie of the Land' 14), Elizabeth Knox ('On Being Picked Up' 24), Nigel Cox ('On the Way to the Jewish Museum Berlin' 28 and 'Eva from the Tyre Factory' 29), Laura Kroetsch ('Moby Dick on Darwin Harbour' 29), Tim Corballis ('Taking Root' 29), and Elizabeth Smither ('Head or Hat' 9). Bill Manhire's account of his trip to Kuala Lumpur in 'Wings of Gold: A Week Among Poets' (6) is the greatest of these and can be readily located in his essay collection, *Doubtful Sounds*.

As if announcing a new initiative, there are two interviews

in *Sport* 5—with visiting poet James Fenton, and with Maurice Gee—and despite good intentions, this form wasn't revisited until fourteen years later when I interviewed Geoff Cochrane (*Sport* 31). More reliably, the magazine has featured substantial photographic work by Peter Black (twice), Bruce Connew, Bill Culbert, Mary Macpherson, Bruce Foster, Alan Knowles and Andrew Ross.

There's also probably an essay to be written on *Sport* covers, which have featured commissioned work by artists such as Julian Dashper, Nigel Brown, Ruth Watson, Ronnie van Hout and Brendan O'Brien, as well as forgiveable appearances by Jack, the editor's son, as a baby, and by his sister-in-law as a figure in a worrying re-enactment of a violent scene from a Caravaggio painting. When Jack Barrowman was five, he illustrated the cover of *Sport* 21 with a drawing of 'Mummy and Daddy' as horned devils with tridents and tails. Daddy has cloven feet and a large belly button; Mummy on the whole looks happier. This image was made into a teeshirt as part of the 21st celebrations, which were also marked by *Sport*'s first subscriber giveaway, a limited edition book by Dinah Hawken called 'The Little Book of Bitching', one of the harshest, most invigorating birthday presents ever dispensed.

My own direct involvement in the magazine ended when I went overseas in 1990. And though *Sport* has remained Fergus's baby, several others have helped out—even saved the baby on occasions. James Brown has been vital to the magazine from number 11 onwards. For more than a decade *Sport* has largely worked up its contents list from decent on-going arguments between James and Fergus. James also gave this anthology its title. The other principal influence on the shape of the magazine has been Bill Manhire, most obviously in the number of writers who came to the magazine via his creative writing class; less publicly in the twenty-year conversation Bill and Fergus have carried on around literature. A week at VUP when I worked there was somehow incomplete if Bill didn't drop in for a chat. I've no reason to think anything's changed.

Greg O'Brien also deserves credit in this story since the Peter

Black issues, as well as the aforementioned 'Storm Warning' feature, were driven by him. Andrew Johnston was another important ally and member of the editorial team for several years, while Kate Camp, Catherine Chidgey and Sara Knox have acted as guest editors. Jenny Bornholdt instigated and oversaw the Bill Culbert issue. Like all survivors, Fergus has never surrendered, but he's always been available for capture.

In reading through thirty-two issues I was struck by how much I'd missed first time around. I'm not sure whether my ignorance simply suggests a personal laziness—well, of course it does—or whether it speaks of any writer's self-regard, the small fortress one erects around one's work. To my shame, I paid little attention to Annora Gollop, Emma Lew, Chris Pigott, Adam Shelton, Alex Scobie. Had I properly read Dennis McEldowney's autobiographical pieces? I seemed to have passed over Cilla McQueen's 'Map', Frankie McMillan's 'Marshmallow', Rhian Gallagher's 'First Sailing'. This job has been as much about discovery as recovery.

It's not a defence but over the years I've tended to read *Sport* erratically, temperamentally, unfairly. And while it would be stupid to consecrate this as 'the writer's way of reading', I do think writers tend to respond to things which seem to have 'relevance'; that is, things which connect with what they themselves are currently engaged in. Is this any different from the woman thinking of leaving her husband, or the man thinking of exploring China by motorbike, seeking out those books which feature such figures and scenarios? Not really. Except there's an expectation that writers, since they're in the business, might read each other, might keep up. They don't. I know writers who won't read novels in the first person, or which feature angels. Poets who won't read poems in which pets appear, or the moon. There's a writer, represented here, who burned a copy of one of my novels because it didn't furnish him with 'a sufficient sense of redemption'. Though some of us, as Elizabeth suggested in her editorial, may be Baptists, we are none of us saints.

To push further into the mire, is there something about a literary magazine that is less than compelling, a sort of limited, compromised essence? The literary magazine has a documentary function as well as a literary one. It stops time—excitingly for a moment, a week, a month—before time moves on. A writer friend once commented that he always shudders when he sees on anyone's shelf a line of old *Landfall*s. The reaction seems reasonable to me. Old issues of *London Magazine* have a similar effect, of *Paris Review*, of *Meanjin* and *Scripsi*. The sense that one is looking at a lost world can be unpleasant. Who were all these poets and short story writers? All these bios which run, 'He spent three years at university but it did him no good'?

To anthologise such a venture might seem then a dubious undertaking. A literary magazine lives in the currents of its time, swept along by the culture which makes it and which it tries to make, victim finally of the mailbox and of the commissioning energies of the editor. In a way, *Great Sporting Moments* runs counter to this movement. It aims, I suppose, to make a good book, to do the Best Of. It has trouble with what Ian Wedde, writing about the 'profoundly humbling' experience of editing the *Penguin Book of New Zealand Verse*, calls 'the immense emotional force of the collective minor'. I hope not to confuse *Sport*'s little life with that of a national literature; nevertheless the collective minor, if it lives anywhere, it's within the pages of just such a journal. Scholars of that bent will need to go further than the present volume to find out whether what appeared individual to those writing it was in fact part of something happening not just to them but to us as well.

When we showed the contents list to James Brown, an editor more familiar with the material than I am, he commented that an alternate selection could probably be made that would look just as convincing. That's true. But right now, I like this stuff the most. (The selection criterion was no more sophisticated than that.) It's about ten per cent of everything that appeared in the magazine. There are many more great sporting moments out there. And nearly all of the magazine will in due course be readable in cyberspace as one of the New Zealand Electronic Text Centre's on-going ventures.

Heading into the project I feared two things: that I'd reject the past, and that I'd reject the present. Acts of apostasy and of humbuggery are equally tempting here. To say I gave in to neither might suggest I reached some cosy and accepting middle-ground, where everything looked persuasive. I did not—and it did not. Discussions with Fergus—and I must thank him and acknowledge his guidance—were punctuated with statements such as, 'Why on earth did you publish *that*?' Being a literary publisher—in my book, the best—he was rather used to, and even fond of, such attacks. 'Ah, yes,' he'd say, rubbing his face. There are more than five thousand pages of *Sport* in the world, over four hundred writers represented. What I haven't asked its publisher is how he feels, looking back over this bulk. If I were him, adding up the fine writers who have been allowed to use the magazine to grow under his editorship, I would feel deep satisfaction; I might even feel vindicated—though that seems a small emotion for the largeness of the achievement. This sampling from the five thousand can only hint at what's been done over seventeen years. And of course there is the next issue to think about. Fergus has been saying for years that this one will be the last. We've all stopped believing him—because of course it's in our interest to do so.

Despite the seminal drive in the Ford Escort, where something was decided, and the first few issues, I know I've had little to do with all this extraordinary writing. The task of choosing the best has nevertheless filled me with a strange pride. I feel a bit like the billionaire owner of a great soccer club—somehow in a position to take whomever I like and put them on my side, have them perform their wonders, and make me look good. What can I say? Here's the team then. Look at them run onto the field. Play, you devils, play!

Damien Wilkins

To Robin Dudding

BARBARA ANDERSON

Day Out

About three times a year my friend Ruth and I drive over the Rimutaka Hill to see our friend Lindsay, who lives in the Wairarapa. We would like to make it more often and so would Lindsay, she says, but you would be surprised to find how difficult it is to get three women organised for the same day, same time, weather permitting.

This is because we are busy. We are not proud of this fact. When people ask us how we are we do not reply, 'Busy.' Busy is not how you are. Busy is what you do with days.

Nevertheless, we are.

One of the reasons Ruth is busy is because she and Tom are good grandparents and either she is visiting grandchildren to the north, or the south, or locally, or they are coming to stay.

Ruth and Tom like this and know how lucky they are. Ruth is also an ace cook and hospitable as well. Twenty-four for Christmas dinner, you know the type. Her daughter cooked the turkey this year. But even so.

Ruth also does good by stealth and is funny with it.

When I say weather permitting, I mean it. Who would want to drive over that hill in a force ten gale? I don't enjoy it in fair weather with a following wind, but Ruth likes driving, which is lucky for me. I'm not bad at the wheel, I have never had an accident but don't quote me. It's just that either you're keen or you're not. I've never been a bags-I-drive kind of girl. Or indeed bags-I-anything much.

Our friend Lindsay is also a busy woman. She cooks and sews and reaps and hoes and her husband, John, is not getting any younger. Lindsay also has grandchildren; older, busier, coming and going they frequent her days. Her daughters are busy too. Astonishingly busy. Lindsay doesn't how they do it, and nor do I. Most people in the Wairarapa are busy. There is not much ambling or rambling—except, of course, on the Wine Trail.

Ruth tucks two or three cushions underneath her so she can

see over the wheel, and we're away. We cruise along beside the Hutt River. We note the debris from the last flood, the broken branches, the silt piled against the willow trunks. Goodness, we say. We talk all through Upper Hutt, which, as always, goes on for longer than you would expect. We sail over the first group of small hills which is a preliminary hurdle before the five-bar of the Rimutaka itself.

I realise I am exaggerating. There's nothing wrong with the Rimutaka Hill and it's better than it was. I know a young woman who drives a twenty-six-wheel articulated truck over it twice a day and loves every minute. During the First World War when the men had finished their training in Featherston they marched, in full kit, up and over the Rimutakas to Wellington.

Nevertheless, I still don't like it. It is covered in bush and scrub. 'Its cliffs are sombre and its defiles mysterious', but the road is too near to both.

Ruth is unperturbed. Before long we are up and over, have passed through Featherston which is the Gateway to the Wairarapa and are creaming down the straights towards Masterton. The power lines are singing along beside us and we are still talking.

To our left lie the mountains, but Ruth can only glance.

Shadowed with clouds and wreathed in mist, their leviathan shapes, blues, greys and purples, roll on forever. They are mysterious and unknown, and likely to remain so.

We agree with the psalmist who wrote, 'I will up lift mine eyes unto the hills, from whence cometh my help.' We nod our heads in unison. However, we are not convinced that our help cometh from the Lord, let alone that He made Heaven and Earth.

Ruth adjusts one of her cushions with a quick heave and says that if the help which cometh from the hills doesn't come from the Lord, where does it come from? That we can't have it both ways.

I say that's not the point. We say we can get a sense of numinous awe from the sublime wonders of Nature without . . .

'What's numinous?'

'Spiritual, awe inspiring.'

'Like God.'

'Well, a local deity, perhaps. Small g.'

'Like the Maoris?'

'No, but . . .' I see the sign in the nick of time. 'Mushrooms!' I shout, and we turn onto the side road and head for the farm.

'How do you feel,' I say later when we get back to Ruth's car with our five-dollar trays of mushrooms and what good value, 'how do you feel about us lending fifty-seven million dollars to help bail out the financially embattled South Korean Government?'

Ruth resettles a large, fresh, pink-gilled mushroom. Mushrooms are fragile and she does not want any to spill or spoil before we get home. She gives a smaller darker one a reassuring pat before getting back into the driver's seat. She snaps her safety belt, plumps her cushions. 'I can see why it makes sense,' she says. '"Major New Zealand trading partner, fifth largest market, vested interest in its recovery." All that. But . . .'

'The Minister of Finance says that the chances of getting the loan back are "very high".'

'"Very high",' says Ruth, 'is not high enough.'

We are silent as we drive through Carterton, which goes on longer than the previous village, Greytown. One is considered more desirable than the other but I can never remember which.

'The Accident and Emergency Department,' says Ruth suddenly, 'is so run down there are holes in the linoleum.'

'I know.'

'However, my main problem at the moment,' she says after a pause, 'is my funeral.'

I give her profile one startled glance, then calm down. Ruth, her eyes focused on the road ahead, is not thinking about the immediate future. Ruth is onto abstracts, the practicalities of these abstracts are giving her concern.

'In what way?'

'You know.' Ruth says you know quite often, and pokes you for emphasis, though not at the moment. 'Being Jewish, going to an Anglican boarding school, marrying a Welshman. I feel I've lost my roots.'

I take a quick peek over my shoulder to check the mushrooms. 'What's that got to do with your funeral?'

'Everything,' says Ruth. 'Who's going to do it?'

'You don't have to have anyone now. Not a professional. You can get a coordinator. A sort of MC.'

'Who?' says Ruth, staring sourly at the straight black asphalt unrolling before her and not another soul in sight.

'Anyone. A family friend. Marriage celebrant. Some vicars don't mind no God now.'

'But which *sort* of vicar.'

'What about a Rabbi?'

Her glance withers. 'I don't belong to the Jewish faith. I never have. How can I start at this stage?'

'You could read it up.'

'*Read it up.*'

I know what she means. I had a T-shirt once. *So many books, so little time.*

'And anyway,' she says. 'I don't know that I want to.'

'Then why fuss?'

Ruth sighs. 'There're some peppermints,' she says, 'in the glove box.'

They are large peppermints, dusted with soft sugar; good of their kind, but cumbersome.

We take one each, suck in silence. 'It's because,' she says eventually, 'I'm scared of death.'

'I can't see for the life of me how the sort of funeral you have is going to help that,' I say. 'You're putting the cart before the horse.'

'Well, they'll have to do something,' she says. 'Won't they?'

'Yes, but why should it worry you? You'll be the last person on earth to be taking an interest.'

'It's all very well for you,' says Ruth.

This is true. As with everything, death only matters if you care. I am rather a chucklehead in this regard, but again, don't quote me. I try harder.

'How about the Salvation Army?' I say. 'You've always been a great supporter.'

'You can't just bail up a uniformed officer and ask him or her to take over your funeral. You're no help.'

'Well, then, try your local talent. The clergy.'

'I don't even know who they are.'

'Then find out. Patti, you know Patti?'

'Yes, indeed.'

'She tracked one down. Nice man. Quite young. She asked him round for a cup of tea and explained her position frankly, and asked him if he would be prepared to take her funeral service at a later date. He said certainly, that was his job, or one of them, and that it would be a pleasure, or words to that effect. They had quite a merry time, Patti said, working things out, choosing this and that, getting the whole thing teed up and a rough draft down on paper, and then he had a sherry and a few nuts and departed. Patti was delighted, so pleased to have the whole thing organised. It had been hanging over her, she said.'

Ruth laughs and laughs. 'You have to hand it to Patti.'

'Yes. Except the poor man dropped dead next week.'

'How *terrible*. What?'

'Coronary.'

'So then what?'

'I'm not sure. I think Patti sort of lost heart.'

'Tt,' sighs Ruth. 'What an awful story.'

'Yes.' We are silent for a moment or two.

'I don't like those ones, do you,' I say, 'when the congregation are invited to come up and share their own memories of dear old Ralph?'

'Not much. Not when they talk to the box.'

'You can see why, though. It's all a matter of personal preference.'

'Yes,' says Ruth bleakly.

I have been tactless. 'You'll be all right,' I say quickly. 'Why don't you have one of those no God ones and a family friend coordinating and a few people asked to speak. And beautiful music. You're musical. Some of those ones are lovely. You could decide the music now. That'd be something done.'

'So could you.'

'No. The Cow Cow Boogie wouldn't get me anywhere.' I

think about it for a while then perk up. 'There's the hymns though. And those wonderful old prayers, psalms, the old words. Glorious. Restore your faith in anything. You can't beat them, really. I've been to some inspirational funerals with God and hymns and the old words.'

Ruth turns into Lindsay's carport and switches off the ignition.

'*Which God?*' she snaps.

Lindsay comes to greet us. She is pleased to see us and vice versa. She declines mushrooms. No, no. She can get them any time. She stands beside Ruth and tells me she is half an inch taller than her, though this is a moot point.

If you boiled the three of us down you would get three average-sized women, happy to be together again.

'What've you been talking about?' says Lindsay as we walk into her house, which is filled with light and warmth and welcome.

'We've been working,' I say, 'on our funerals.'

'Oh good,' says Lindsay. 'Where've you got to? Which sort? Let's have a glass of wine.'

Ruth shakes her head. 'Not for me, thank you,' she says sadly. 'I'm driving.'

Peppermint Frogs

I'm glad you asked me about my 21st. It's not a topic which crops up often, in fact I don't think it ever has before.

21st birthday recollections don't have the starkness, the where-were-you-when-it-happened impact of global tragedies—that day in Dallas, that car crash.

Nevertheless, memories surface, and strangely vivid they are too. Looking back I see the day itself, and more especially the day before I came of age, with detachment. This was not so at the time.

My father used to say that one of the pleasures of his old age was the sudden reappearance of long forgotten memories. A glimpse so sharp it startled him, of, for example, he and his brother fly fishing in Taranaki streams 60 years before. He could feel the sun on his back, see the silver-pink irridescence of the newly-caught fresh-run hen at his feet. The birds, even the birds, he could hear.

I told him I would look forward to such pleasures and he replied, his virtually blind eyes leaking with mirth, that he wished me luck.

I cannot include memories of my 21st among such joys. The celebrations were muted but emotions ran high.

At the age of 20 I was teaching Science at a Girl's Boarding School. I was, in fact, Head of Science. Science, in that school, was me.

As well as teaching Forms Three to Seven I had, like all the residential staff, extra-curricular responsibilities. These were a mixed bag and revolved mainly around the Boarders: House Duties with the Boarders, Dining Room Duties with the Boarders, Prep Supervision with the Boarders, Church Attendance with the Boarders, and, finally, Lights Out for the Boarders. Yippee—but softly. The Staff House held perils of its own.

A responsibility which was mine alone was the restocking of

the Science Cupboard. This stood at the back of the laboratory
where I taught, secured for safety yet still threatening, like
some large and famished animal snarling for food. I did toss it
some copper sulphate occasionally ('Chile, girls, is virtually a
mountain of copper') but remember little else.

For some reason this task alarmed me more than most.
More than Full Day Sunday Supervision with the Boarders
which included Ballroom Dancing with the Seniors in the
Hall after tea. Not more, certainly, but almost as much as the
importunate clamour of my alarm clock each morning and the
strictly hierarchical queue for the geyser-equipped bathroom in
the Staff House.

I can still see the dressing gowns: the plaids, the camels, the
florals and the sad. And the sponge bags creaking in the hands
of First Assistant, English, Maths, French and so on down the
line. Physical Education and Science tossed for second to last.

There were power cuts that year I began teaching. I had bought
a radio shaped like a miniature caravan with my first pay
cheque, and listened each morning to Morrie Power's session
on 2ZB. Morrie was a cheerful man, or appeared to be so, and
I would like to take this opportunity of thanking him for my
morning laugh. At 8.30 each morning he would intone, 'Ladies
and gentlemen. On behalf of my brother, Vital Electric, please
turn off your radios.' I thought this very funny indeed and so
did Val.

Val (Phys Ed) was 21 and blonde. She danced and leapt about
the school, glowing with health and easy on the eye. I can
remember thinking at the time that working in an all girls'
school seemed rather a waste of Val's more obvious attributes.
Our other friend, Woody (Beryl Woodhouse, Geography), had
been teaching for years. Val and I took her breakfast in bed on
her 30th birthday. Woody, attractive warm-hearted Woody, sat
up in her bed and wailed, 'I don't *want* to be 30.'

Val and I stared at her. What could we say, what could we
possibly say to our friend Woody who was 30, still teaching,
still living in the Staff House, and not married.

We came to, prattled on: 'Look Woody, bacon *and* fried bread. Presents! And your favourites, peppermint frogs. And we're taking you to *The Best Years of Our Lives* tonight. And The Green Parrot after. We've got it all worked out.'

We had, hadn't we? Yes, we had indeed.

Val's boyfriend was now working in Auckland. Mine had left university unexpectedly and was mustering in the High Country. I still find that phrase deeply romantic. As one of Janet Frame's characters says, 'I should like to have lived in a house whose tall windows face the mountains.' Or think I should. I enjoyed Stephen's letters and his tall tales from the hills. Also words of affection and praise were more than welcome in the chilly atmosphere of the Staff Room.

However, I realised that I no longer loved their writer. Stephen, wrote to tell me he was coming up for my 21st. We would, he told me, paint the town red. I wrote to him immediately, saying, 'Don't come. It's over,' though more kindly and with grateful thanks. I still remember the relief. I practically levitated about the Staff House singing Val my new song, which I had set to the tune of an extremely indelicate tramping song about a maid in a mountain glen and a fountain pen.

'I'm out of love, so let's all cheer.
The turtle dove has shot through here.'

My birthday coincided with Easter Monday that year. Val and I, mostly Val, had organised an overnight tramp in the Tararuas with the left-over Boarders. Most girls and staff high-tailed as soon as the appropriate bell had tolled on Maundy Thursday. There were 12 stragglers left, girls ranging in age from 13 to 17, who, for various reasons, were stuck at school. The Headmistress and the cook were delighted with Val's enterprise and we set off, like Belloc's firemen, with courage high and hearts aglow.

Val was an experienced tramper and had access to one of the huts. The weather was fine, the beech trees sparkling in the sun and the girls delightful. My sense of freedom soared to euphoria.

The next day, appropriately tired but happy, we caught a nearby bus back to school. Val, I remember, taught me the words of 'The Martins and the Caugheys, those reckless mountain boys' *en route*.

We handed over our charges to the French mistress who was Sunday House Duties and thus also pleased with us, trailed back to the virtually empty Staff House and sat on the verandah, drinking tea and counting the treats in our working lives. We came up with three. A cup of tea, a hot bath (if and when the geyser behaved itself) and the Sunday Request Session.

'Well, we've got that later,' said Val, pushing back the hank of blonde hair which fell across her left eye. I asked her once why she didn't cut it off. She replied that the boys liked it. I understood immediately.

'And there won't be a queue for the bath,' I said. 'Toss you.'

Val won the toss and I went to my room which was small and dark and much loved. There was mail from home and, lying on top, a note from the Headmistress. 'Dear Miss Wright. Please come and see me in my study as soon as you return.'

Why on earth? I changed into a skirt, brushed hair, washed hands and set off. The Headmistress was working. She never stopped working. There are many types and conditions of women whom I admire but headmistresses of girl's schools, particularly boarding schools, come high on the list.

Miss Grainger looked up, smiled her anxious gentle smile, asked for details of our expedition, then corrected herself. She would speak to Miss Rowland and me after Assembly on Tuesday morning and hear all the details. She was glad it had been such a success. The girls had been very fortunate and the school was grateful.

She stopped, looked at me even more anxiously. She had a message for me. From a young man named Stephen something.

'Bamber!'

'Yes. He has been trying to contact you all weekend.'

'Where?'

'Here, of course. He seemed very surprised you weren't here. Very,' she murmured to her fingernails.

'But I wrote to him. Ages ago.'

The Headmistress's hands moved quickly. She didn't want to hear the details. Anything but. She handed me a piece of paper between thumb and forefinger. 'He's in a hotel in town. Here's the number. Perhaps,' said the Headmistress, 'you might care to contact him.'

'Yes, yes I will. Thank you, Miss Grainger.'

'Not at all.'

I rang Stephen. I saw Stephen. Stephen told me he had never received my letter telling him that our romantic attachment was at an end. He showed me the ring he had brought up from the south. The ring he had hoped to place on my finger as a token of our everlasting affection and regard for each other. I stared at the high-domed blue-velvet-covered box, at the bright golden circle with a diamond winking from ruched white satin and burst into tears of shame and guilt. Stephen wept too. He asked me if there was any chance of my changing my mind. I said no.

He asked me if he could kiss me goodbye. It is always a mistake to ask and I bawled louder.

Finally, thank God, he got angry, told me what he thought of me, snapped his little box shut and departed.

He married a girl called Bobbie not long afterwards and lived happily ever after.

The next day was my 21st. Morrie Power wasn't on that morning. I sat up in bed and opened birthday presents from my family and friends. Val and Woody brought me breakfast in bed and sang Happy Birthday, dear Barbara, Happy Birthday to you.

They had booked tickets for *In Which We Serve*. And we would go to The Green Parrot afterwards. There were peppermint frogs.

I didn't tell them, of course, but in fact I preferred chocolate fish with pink insides. And still do.

NICK ASCROFT

The Badder & the Better

This is the new novel.
This is the new unprocessed & overwrought.
This is the new ugly;
This is the new empty.

This is the new hocus-pocus, new subprofound,
The new ham dressed up as lamb.

This is the new bastardisation.
This is the new backtrack of the pack mentality—

The new ham-fistedness, new awkward—
New: indelicate.

This is the new silence
Of the poxy orthodoxy.

This is the new anger, new doubt,
The new energy, new insipid & confessional.

This is the new righteous.
The new clarity of nonsense,

This is the new volcano of molten vomit.
This is the new neo,
The new nothing.
The new say-nothing.

This is the new *nothing to add*.

TUSIATA AVIA

Pa'u-stina

I am da devil pa'umuku kirl
I walk down da street shakeshake my susu
I chew gum an smile wif my gold teef flashing
I call out to da good womens
sitting sitting in deir house
Eh, ai kae! An I make dem see my arse.

I am da dog kirl wif da fire in my arse
Dey call me da woman not da kirl
My thighs rub together make da fire in deir house
My fat taro legs my fat taro belly my fat taro susu
I walk pas all da good womens
an laugh wif my white teef flashing.

I smell like da hot rain flashing
An all da good men are looking for my arse
All da good men are waiting for da back of deir womens
You are da good kirl da sexy kirl da lovelybeautiful kirl
Dey run like da dog I let dem lick my susu
Dey run in da back dey run to deir house.

I walk pas da high chief' house
I walk on da high-heel shoe like da spear flashingflashing
My bra tighttight so I have da 4 susu
Da whole chief' council look for my arse
An make da special fine for da pa'umuku kirl
I can hear da laughinglaughing da smiling of da womens.

My red toenails wavewave to da womens
My red toenails shineshine to da womens in deir house
I am da devil pa'umuku girl
An I laugh when dey fine me wif my red lips flashing

I pull my skirt up an show my fat taro arse
I laugh like da dog da volcano shake my susu.

I am drinking on da road and playing wif my susu
Dancing wif da dogmen running from deir womens
I am laughing at da dogmen licking at my arse
I am laughing at da dogmen away from deir house
I am laughing at da dogmen deir black arses flashing
We love you sexy kirl we love you beautiful kirl we love you
    lovely kirl.

I laugh like da dog like da volcano like da arse hole. Dey cry
    for me like susu
We want you hot rain kirl we have forgotten our womens
We will go to da house of Pulotu we will go wif our black
    arses flashing.

pa'umuku: slut
ai kai: eat shit
susu: breasts / milk
Pulotu: Samoan underworld

HINEMOANA BAKER

Liver

I hang out the washing
at night.

Each peg squeaks
into place.

You, in the kitchen light,
warming my back.

*

I'm worrying again
about your liver

as if it helps.
I feel around

on you—which side
is it? How big?

*

You have nightmares
and kick me in your sleep.

Sometimes
I kick you back.

PAOLA BILBROUGH

Membrane

1

I was a festival child.
Cherry-picking season
we endured
unwashed hair, scant meals.

My father was a puppeteer,
I remember sunken eyes,
bruised cheeks,
empty glove bodies.

In the front row
of *Punch and Judy*
I held a stranger's baby,
its heartbeat filling the whole head.

The fontanelle before
the bones knit:
a frog's throat
as it swallows.

Dancers knotted
up baling twine hair.
Rain. And mud warm
between the toes.

Seven-year-old
skin gossamer
between myself
and the world.

In Dublin, your mother
cooked Sunday roast,
her stretch-suit
vivid hydrangea pink.

Your father argued
about The Pope over tea.
All I knew of Ireland
was our plough horse, Connemara.

2

Rain, pale Irish skin,
the band screaming
'Insane in the membrane . . .'
You call me 'Homegirl',

America spread over you
like fake tan. I want to take
your head, smooth it off
with impatient thumb.

Later, the sheet curls
from a stained mattress.
Your bones move apart
sounding of a forest.

Trying to sleep
in a fluorescent-lit garage,
each of us consumed
by separate pasts.

GRAHAM BISHOP

Why Do Sonnets Have 14 Lines?

Once I wrote a poem called **Soot**. It was a sonnet, and was 'highly recommended' by the judges of a national poetry competition. What made it a special poem, however, although I didn't know it at the time, was it was the last poem I was to write for 500 days. I had been 'cured' and my poetry production centre had been decommissioned.

Soot
Thirty-seven patients died when Seacliff burned
destroying the evidence of their tortured brains
and leaving only soot
At Wakari fifty years on it's much the same, just a more
    sophisticated game
of uppers and downers except they forget to tell you
which is so easy when they all look the same
They lock you in and set fire to your mind
so you sabotage your life
with arrowed words and hopeless dreams and deeds bizarre
or let you roam wide and far
unable to see or tell left from right, hoping the end will come
    by bus or car
It doesn't matter if it hurts or you sleep night and day, too sick
    to eat, wasted and weak
but these ignorati know not the power of poetry and words
    and numbers
Of the hypotenuse and Ozymandias
or the binary code of Coleridge and Janet Frame
So help me God
Will I too soon be soot?

For the next 18 months I lived in a creative desert, until the following year, when fortunately the southern spring came early. On the 13th of August a daffodil in a windowbox was on the verge of unfurling. That day was also notable for an animated evening discussion when **Dehibernation** was born. Water had come to the desert.

We talked about tomatoes and skeletons
sea urchins and smut
the subject was symmetry
but the conversation wandered
as conversations do
exploring the boundaries of
easy places, like moa bones and
coloured stones and rabbit habits
words to put in poems
the difference between smooth and spiky mountains
When I went to bed
a million or two neurons held hands and
in the morning I woke and wrote

a daffodil and I agreed
after a winter of a thousand nights
the 14th day of August was the first of Spring.

My first poem for a year and a half. Strangely enough it was another sonnet—well at least it had 14 lines (I call them liberal sonnets)—but that was nothing to the fact I was back in production again. Five hundred days seems a peculiar period to be sterile, but at the time it felt twice as long.

The flood gates opened. I wrote 5 poems in the next two weeks; 10 in the next month; and now I average 8 a month and have done for nearly a year. Many of these poems have been sonnets, and of those that weren't, many were 7 lines (half sonnets) or 28 lines (double sonnets). In fact of 624 lines of poetry, half have been in poems with either 7, or a multiple of 7, lines.

There were stranger things to come. I began to sense a regularity about the production line. Fortunately I normally date my poems so I set up a spreadsheet and plotted them on it.

Initially it looked like it had been hit by a shotgun, except there was a distinct peak in production about the beginning and end of every month. The calendar date didn't seem a very likely control, but then I had a brain wave—and plotted on the start and end of the 28-day lunar month. Then I asked a statistician to look at it, and suddenly all was revealed.

During the first quarter of every month I don't write any poetry at all. However, during the second quarter my production climbs to 2.7 poems a week. As the full moon begins to wane, it slips back to 1.5, but then skyrockets up to 2.8 poems a week in the last quarter.

Clearly my production of poetry is somehow based on a seven-day cycle. A week has seven days, and our bodies are driven by Circadian rhythms—the day/night cycle that acts on the hypothalamus —the most deeply buried part of the brain. My hypothesis is that the hypothalamus is the region of the brain where poetry is assembled, and that poetry is a powerful response to the celestial forces acing upon us.

But that's not all. What about other poets? I turned to another source of dated poetry. Again there was no mistaking the pattern, but in this case the productive and sterile periods were shifted with respect to the phases of the moon. One of the great mysteries of life had been resolved—I had finally discovered the difference between men and women. Women write poems on the new moon, men write them on the full moon.

That still doesn't quite resolve the question of why do sonnets have 14 lines? Well think of the brain being one of those clocks with ball-bearings that run down inclined ramps. Imagine that each ball-bearing is a blank line so that every 24 hours, or day-night cycle, a new blank line is created and added to a brain-file called *Next Sonnet*. We all know that a week is not long enough for anything, which is why the poetic week is actually a fortnight. At the end of it there are 14 blank lines waiting in my hypothalamus, and countless images and memories from a lifetime of living stored elsewhere in my brain. Suddenly something triggers 'copy/paste', and behold the 14 blanks fill up with ordered images like a computer screen and another sonnet is born.

Some of my poems are only two lines long, because I don't have many ball-bearings. People who write long poems on the other hand have so many ball-bearings that they rattle when they walk.

PETER BLAND

Wellington 1955

Fucking—in print—hasn't been invented
and the clitoris is a rumour . . .
no one knows where it is. In
Newtown zoo the last orangutan
freezes to death in an open cage
with a sack pulled over its head.
Entrails from a Hutt Valley abattoir
foul summer beaches. The sea is red
with wounded Moby Dicks. Death's
rich: both priests and backstreet abortionists
lay down the ground rules for a life without sin.
Up on The Terrace escaped Nazis teach Nietzsche
while down in the harbour refugee ships
bring more walking wounded from exhausted Europe
to till fresh fields and play their violins.
(What's local has got a fist like an All Black
and downs ten jars between five and six.)
But the scent of something more than meanness
is blowing in with the Cook Strait wind:
poets are beginning to burn their soap-box
while girls with pony-tails kick their heels
to rhythms that are more than meek. In
fugged-up coffee bars 'the young and restless'
light black candles and plan their escape.

JENNY BORNHOLDT

The Man Dean Went to Photograph

The man Dean went to photograph
has the Easter Island statues on
either side of his back, the
pyramids in between, across the
top the Pyrénées and above them
the sky. In between is a gap
he is worried about. He plans the
Niagara Falls down one
side, the pink and white terraces
down the other. He likes things
big so you can see them. Like
when he climbs the Pyrénées and
sees the country displayed
before him like the sea
inviting pleasure craft to play
upon its surface—he finds enormous
satisfaction in this. Likewise, when
he gazes down on the plain and
sees his wife, the great wings
of the eagle spread across her back
impatient to rise.

Villanelle

That summer that wouldn't go
the light was far too bright.
We didn't want to know.

But then we did. Slow,
or fast, the fight?
That summer that wouldn't go.

We couldn't know.
One thing we learned, though, was how might
fails, and that, we didn't want to know.

But then we wanted it all, blow
by crushing blow. After all, it was our right,
that summer that wouldn't go.

And so we sat it out. The glow
of light sinking into a night
we didn't want to know.

But it was the one sure thing. The only
thing we knew. And it was wrong, not right.
That summer that wouldn't go.
That summer we didn't want to know.

WILLIAM BRANDT

His Father's Shoes

I spent all last winter I was walking around in a pair of those you know those kung fu shoes just made of flimsy cloth and all falling apart with a big hole in the toe and my feet would get soaked in all the puddles and all cold and wet.

I really needed a good pair of shoes. A good pair of leather shoes. Waterproof shoes, comfortable, hard wearing, that I can walk long distances in. That will protect my feet from the road, from sharp objects, from mud and cold.

And my father had this pair of old boat shoes. He didn't wear them on the boat any more, just for gardening. He's got a new pair for the boat. But these are just his old knock-about gardening shoes. He never gardens. They just sit around in the wash-house under the sink.

But they were just what I needed. Exactly what I needed. They fit me, they were well made and comfortable and waterproof.

So I made an approach to him at one time, if he would like to give me those shoes. I explained to him that I do a lot of walking and I needed some good leather shoes on my feet. I asked him politely and reasonably. I just quietly asked, or rather if you like I suggested, if I could possibly have or he might like to make a gift to me of those old gardening shoes down in the wash-house.

And his answer was no.

Which was typical for him. And so I asked him, quite politely and reasonably for his reason for refusing, and he said that they had sentimental value. His exact words were: 'I'd rather not, they have a certain sentimental value, you see.'

Sentimental value.

I decided to pursue this whole question of sentiment, of feeling, of emotional attachment, because I felt that I had a lot to say to him about this subject. There was a lot that I wanted to say to him. And what I wanted to suggest to him here was

44

that there might be, perhaps, a greater sentimental value to him in the act of giving his son something he needs, in giving him a pair of shoes, than in denying that son a pair of shoes just for the sake of having this old pair of worn-out boat shoes sitting around under the house.

But I did also want to make it clear to him that I wasn't angry or upset, that I was just picking up, pursuing this theme in the spirit of a spirited or you might even say a high-spirited or almost humorous although at the same time not entirely frivolous debate, but not at all acrimonious, just to say, just to point it out to him, so first of all to show that I was calm and not at all angry, to show that, I yawned slowly, three times, very deliberately, before continuing, to make that very clear that I was not at all excited or upset.

I then stated to him as I have said, that whatever sentimental value he might attach to an old pair of shoes, surely there would be more value to his sentimental feelings, his fatherly feelings, in the act of a gift to his son. Straightforward point, a valid point.

He absolutely refused to enter into any discussion of the matter whatsoever. He quite categorically refused to answer any of the subsequent questions I put to him at that time. He simply repeated his position without discussion again and again: 'I don't want to talk about it. I don't want to talk about it.' Those were his exact words.

You can't talk to the guy. This is typical of the sort of attitude he has. This is the sort of situation you get where I am trying to put my point of view to him, to express my feelings, and he just will not listen.

So I threw a glass ornament against the wall, and the glass ornament broke as a result of that, and completely shattered into very small pieces. I also hit the door very hard with my fist to show him how I felt. What I wanted to show him was that he won't allow me to express my point of view, and that was why I did those things, to express my frustration and anger. But he just walked out of the room. And this is the sort of thing that happens.

This—this gets really heavy. My mother—my mother was

standing at one end of the hallway begging me, actually literally begging me, to leave the house, to go. But he was just sitting in the lounge-room pretending to read the paper. But his hand was shaking.

I was shouting at my mother. I left the door open deliberately through to the lounge so he could hear what I was saying. I was saying it to my mother, but it was really for him to hear. I said how can I communicate all these things I have to say if he won't listen? He could hear, but he would not acknowledge that he could. This is how my father conducts himself. He uses his powerful connections and his cunning to deny me my personhood. It's quite common.

Now at this time it was mid-summer. My need for a pair of shoes was therefore not so urgent, so I let the matter rest. I went barefoot a lot of the time, or I would wear the kung fu shoes. I thought if he wants to refuse his son such a small thing which would do me so much good and him no harm, then he can go ahead and do it. Not my problem. Let him sweat it out.

But by the time winter was coming round I again thought that I really needed a pair of shoes. I mean, my feet man . . .

I did go at one time into Hannah's shoe store. I looked around and I did find a pair of leather shoes which fitted me OK. They were OK. They had a good hard-wearing rubber sole with leather uppers. They would have been OK. They cost $89.95. I had the money at that time and I did almost buy them but I didn't, I don't know why, I was about to buy them but then I just walked out of the shop. I had the shoes in my hand but I dropped them to the floor. I had to get out of there. The place was very uninspring.

So then I thought I'll give him one more chance. One more chance to do something for his son, a small thing, a small gesture of caring between father and son, the sort of thing that should happen without even thinking.

To make sure that he did actually understand the position I was in, and the full situation, just so he couldn't say later on he didn't know all the facts or hadn't been properly informed, I made a bit of polite conversation, creating an appropriate background or backdrop. Just talking about the weather, about the condition of the roads, about the condition of my current footwear and my feet.

I then asked him again, politely and reasonably, or rather if you like I offered to him the opportunity to give me the shoes. I'd seen them there that afternoon they were still there in the wash-house.

He said he would never give me his shoes. He said I should forget the whole matter, I should just forget it. He was very emphatic. He said there was absolutely no chance that he would change his mind later on, and although I offered him an opportunity just to think it over for a bit, wait till he cooled down a bit, he said no, he said his answer was final as of that moment.

So I made the obvious suggestion of the logical solution, which was a fair compromise. We would share the shoes.

I would wear the shoes. If he wished to do some gardening he had only to contact me the day before, giving a clear twenty-four hours notice (and I was willing to take full responsibility for making absolutely sure that I could always be contacted at any time of the day or night), and I would immediately see to it that the shoes were returned for his use in the garden, at my own expense. Unless I was out of the country. That would be at his expense.

He told me to get out. His exact words were: 'Just get out. Just get out.'

By now I no longer had any interest in my father at all. I did not consider myself then and I don't consider myself now, to be his son.

I therefore proposed to him that we settle the matter once and for all: that he settle on me there and then, as his rightful heir, the benefit of any inheritance or property that would rightfully be due to me on his death, and that I in return sign or execute any document or agreement he might require or suggest as proof that he had discharged any and all obligations under that head or any other. He would then formally and legalistically disown me as his son. We would then part forever. No correspondence would be entered into, and no further claims to be pursuable at any time by either party.

I was willing to take a cheque.

I then announced my intention of leaving the country. I would go to Germany where I held the intention to seek gainful employment as a roof builder. Germany is a highly organised industrial nation with a steadily growing population. The building industry is therefore buoyant, and I had no doubt that work would be easy to find. The German people, as a nation, are highly skilled and organised. They are clean, boisterous, and they know how to get the job done, working as a team. Also they are very pure people. I felt and feel that life under these conditions would appeal to me, and that I could make a new and happy and productive life for myself in Germany.

That was on the Friday. On the Saturday morning I decided to hitch down to Wellington. I got a bus as far as Manukau City and tried to hitch a ride from there. But after two hours I still hadn't got a ride. I was feeling quite discouraged, quite low, and I decided to take a meal break as I still had seven dollars fifty-five in my pocket.

After the meal break, I tried hitching again for a while, but it was starting to get dark and I still had no luck so I decided my chances of getting a ride were about nil for that night anyway. I walked back into town.

By now I was feeling very aimless, with no sense of direction, or no goal to aim for. There seemed to be nothing to pin my hopes on, in the immediate present outlook, or even for the coming days ahead. Everything had fallen through and I was frightened of the police. I began to feel very sad and depressed.

Also, I had stepped in a puddle while making my way across some muddy waste ground. My feet were cold and wet.

I tried to sleep on the front steps of a church, but it was not practicable. There was a cold wind and dead leaves were blowing around. I could not prevent the dead leaves from blowing against my face in a repulsive fashion.

It seemed a very meaningless way to carry on an existence.

So I decided to return to my father's house and ask my father if he had considered my proposition. I had nowhere else to go.

When I arrived the house was empty. I remembered that they were going sailing that weeked. I had lost my key so I couldn't get inside. But the door to the wash-house was unlocked. It didn't have a lock, in fact. I went into the wash-house, planning to rest and wait.

I turned on the light and I saw there my father's shoes. They were under the sink. I went over to them. I brushed the cobwebs off them.

And I slipped my right foot into the right shoe.

There it is. The right shoe. Feels good. Good leather shoe. And then I just slipped my left foot into the left shoe, and there it was. And there I was.

They're good shoes. I had no choice. I need shoes, man. He could have given them to me, but he wouldn't. It could have been a warm and giving thing between father and son, and instead he did what he has always done, he refused to give me what I asked, what I needed, what I wanted.

Want your shoes, Dad. Simple. Want your shoes.

JAMES BROWN

(damaged by water)

For years I had read of the poetry
not (illegible) getting any
quite right. So (damaged by water)
if only I were better at sports.

The man on the park bench sat
(blot)ing his (deleted) smile.
The pigeons were very (crossed out).
The pigeons were very cross.

And then the (scribble) of your first
'commercially viable' single moves you to
(grey haze). It is still too sad and too long and
too like the Velvet (heat/ light) in (unclear) places.

The (mildew?) comes in little puffy sniffs.
(smudged) the park bench, under the tall songs,
it's (indecipherable) how quickly
one's *pain au chocolat* is gone.

The Book of Sadness

If you were expecting a weighty tome,
you'll be disappointed.
The Book of Sadness is actually
quite small—a manky paperback, in fact,
that will fit snugly in a pocket.

Perusing a dim alcove of a second-hand shop,
I latched onto it immediately.
It had seen many owners.
I spied your name, inked
in your careful, considered hand
—and my own scrawl, of course,
lurching like a drunken spider.

I wondered what page you'd got up to,
but there were so many folded corners
and abandoned bookmarks
it was impossible to tell.

I opened one at random and, yes,
the passage was bleak beyond conscience;
after each sentence, I could feel
my slim allotment of hope
draining into sand.
Indeed, it would not take much
of such 'wrung consequence'
to leave one
'foetal in the well's zero'.

At the counter I offered five dollars,
as the soft-pencilled price indicated.
'I'm sorry, but it's actually ten,'
said old Mr P. 'You see, it's signed.'

'But,' I mumbled, 'I'm the author.'
'Good for you,' said old Mr P quietly,
'good for you.'

DAVID BURTON

A Mullet in Luxor

In 1941 L/Sgt Frederick Burton was swimming at a beach near Alexandria with a group of fellow soldiers from the 2nd New Zealand Expeditionary Force, when a tsunami appeared from nowhere, broke on the shore and sucked them all out to sea in its aftermath.

In a desperate rescue attempt, those left on shore linked arms and formed a human chain. The man on the end managed to grasp my father by his luxurious shock of hair, but lost his grip as the frail chain of flesh itself was broken and swept away.

Frederick swam, struggled, and trod water with steadily decreasing strength, until eventually it became hell to resist, and bliss simply to lie back and let the water pour down his throat. And yes, his life did flash before him, along with the thought that he would be leaving his five-year-old daughter an orphan on the other side of the world. He entered the clear white light of the Void and his body was washed ashore. It was laid on the beach in a line with some thirty others.

A group of Frederick's loyal friends immediately began the old Holgier Nelson style of resuscitation, propping him from behind, taking his arms and stretching them out like Christ crucified, then folding them together in front of him. It was an ungainly and inefficient method—mouth-to-mouth was yet to be invented.

An army medical officer, walking up and down the line of the drowned men, gave Frederick a cursory once-over, and advised the friends to give up, as he was a lost cause. They persisted, however, for another ten minutes until the medical officer passed by again and formally ordered them to stop. They ignored him and carried on for half an hour, until the officer appeared once more and threatened to have them charged with disobeying an order.

Frederick's body was bundled on to the back of a truck and taken off to a British army hospital in Alexandria.

On this journey to the morgue, Frederick partially regained consciousness. He was aware only of something thumping up hard against him as the truck turned corners, and having to fend it off with his arm. It was a corpse.

At the hospital gates, without regard for his having just returned from the Void, Frederick was ordered by a hard-boiled matron to climb down from the truck and walk, naked and unaided, through the wards to a bed.

Exactly two decades later, in 1961, the events of Frederick's life assumed a grim symmetry: desperately weak once more, he was again forced onto his feet by a nurse, this time for a walk which took him back into the Void forever.

He was dying of cancer. Having been flown over to Wellington for surgery, he was led across Wellington airport, wearing only a thin silk dressing gown and slippers, in a penetrating southerly gale.

He contracted pneumonia and died four days later.

As a nine-year-old, I began to jigsaw my father's past together with the pieces he had left around the house: a collection of bayonets, the head of a time bomb, an Italian anti-aircraft bullet; a gas mask; a scabrous black scorpion packed into a tobacco tin with its tail arched permanently into a stinging position; some captured Italian army insignia; shrapnel from a thermos bomb and an incendiary bomb, labelled for posterity in his minuscule handwriting; an Afrika Korps camouflage gun cover which we used as a ground sheet on our family picnics; his service medals and their miniatures, and the solar topee Frederick was wearing in the Western Desert the day a shell exploded in the breech of a howitzer and blew three fingers off his right hand.

His personality was not, however, so uncomplicatedly macho: he also left a minute mirrored silver perfume bottle, an Egyptian woman's veil, a tasselled fez, a scarab, a jewellery box exquisitely inlaid with ivory and mother-of-pearl, and an Egyptian clay water bottle, which maintains coolness by allowing water to evaporate gradually through its pores.

In our kitchen was a row of bottled eggplants, a rare sight in the New Zealand of 1961, which Frederick had grown and preserved himself. Hidden away in the top cupboard was a trove of tinned treasures: Perigord truffles, Burgundian escargots, frogs legs and Meredith Bros. shell-brand toheroas. There was Frederick's mayonnaise-making gadget, which he had doggedly cranked for half an hour at a time, and his library of cookery books, including a bound volume of hand-written recipes he had used in his post-War career as Nelson's leading caterer.

What captured my imagination most of all, however, was a collection of leather-bound photograph albums, which presented a picture of Cairo in 1940 as an elegant city possessing a mixture of both Deco and traditional Arabic architecture, neat cobbled streets, scrupulously clean and largely deserted, with woven wire litter bins at each lamppost, impeccably manicured public gardens, sidewalk cafés, exotic men in fez, turban and a caftan known as a jelabiya, women beneath the veil, lemonade sellers plying their trade, and itinerant bread sellers with hoops of bread looped around poles.

In another album we called his ditty book, were menus from bars, cafés and brasseries of the period: the Pam-Pam, Buffet & Bar 'Bristol', Nelson's Greek Shop, 'Splendid' Bar; Claridge Bar; Bar & Buffet 'Pole Nord', the Washington Restaurant Brasserie. Most of these reflected the tastes of the British colonial rulers, offering permutations of eggs, steak and chips.

At the Brasserie Britannia, however, one could dine on poisson mayonnaise, riz à la financière, tripes à la venetienne, escaloppe à la viennoise, gâteau praline, tartlette au fraise, and finish off with roquefort and gruyère.

At the Brasserie Restaurant Finish, on June 22, 1940, Frederick had been able to choose from porc en gelée, pommes vapeur; crevettes, sauce remoulade; poisson à la Grecque; jambon, sauce madère et épinards; and crème caramel.

At Groppi, still in existence today, one could even sip, at a price, vintage Veuve Clicquot and pick at pressed beluga caviar.

It was a sophisticated, cosmopolitan society, where wealthy Europeans of every nationality held garden parties for the troops in their leafy garden suburbs, in expensive villas surrounded by date palms.

In the intervening half century before I reached Egypt,

however, a generation of fellaheen had sat at the cinema, and later reclined on the straw beds of their mudbrick huts in front of television, and had had their minds filled with hitherto undreamed luxuries of England and America; the consequence today is that they have all come to Cairo in search of them, and in the process, strained every facility to bursting point. Sewage now spews out onto those neat cobbled streets, pock-marked with unfinished road-works. Tides of humanity are forced to spill from the footpath out onto the road, ignoring the horns of impatient taxi drivers trying to cut a swathe through them.

Accommodation has become impossibly tight, with the result that in the tourist season, from November through to March, it can be a problem finding a room of any sort.

This we were to discover, arriving in the city at the end of the day, having been detained for half an afternoon by Egyptian immigration at Cairo Airport, for entering the country without the visa the Egyptian embassy in London had insisted we would not need.

After trying four hotels and finding them all full, we arrived at the Pension Suisse. Its owners might well have benefited from a lesson in Swiss hygiene. The winds which blow in daily from the Sahara had caked the entire foyer—walls, floor and ceiling—with a film of brown dust. This should have been sufficient warning in itself, but we entered the rickety 1940s lift nevertheless. It dropped several centimetres as we stepped in.

At reception, four young Egyptian men were reclined on a large sofa in a writhing knot. One was sitting in the lap of another, who was fondling his crotch. At the sight of us, they simultaneously leapt up and came running. Fresh prey.

They led us off to show us a room. Down the hallway an Englishman complained his shower wasn't working. Nor was the toilet in our room: the bowl was full of faeces and the cistern was broken. The wooden floor was grey with dirt. There were brown, unidentifiable stains over the walls; a few scattered flakes of silver backing a pane of glass on the bathroom wall denoted it had once been a mirror. They showed us three rooms and they all stank equally of shit, stale sweat and unwashed sheets.

The Goden Hotel and the Hotel Tulip were much the same.

As darkness fell we were on the streets once more with our baggage.

'Can I help you?' asked a young Egyptian, a pretty boy in his early twenties, with huge almond eyes, slanting down into each other. They roamed every inch of Kate's body, his thick lids flickering slightly, before resting inscrutably on me. 'You need accommodation? I know a place I could show you.'

'Are you a commission agent for the place?' I asked.

His face fell. He seemed genuinely offended. No, he'd have us know he was completing an MA in history at Cairo University. He didn't care at all if we didn't see the pension, he was only trying to help us.

And indeed he was. The Pension Roma was a haven: spotlessly polished wooden floors, ensuite bathroom, hot water, freshly ironed sheets and an ornately carved wardrobe, £8.50 with breakfast included. From our sixth-storey room, I surveyed what we had just escaped: a dismal landscape below of flat roofs, each and every one covered with a metre deep pile of rubbish.

The next morning, dutiful tourists, we took a jolty trot atop a camel around the Giza pyramids to the sad mouldering mound which is all 20th-century air pollution has left us of the Sphinx.

We then decided to ferry down the Nile to see Old Cairo.

The ticket box had once been painted blue, but it now bore what I was soon to realise was the Egyptian trademark for public hatches: an accretion for perhaps 15 cm all around the frame of solid shiny brownish-black grime, from generations of clamouring hands. There was a layer of rubbish over the floor of the waiting area, and the seats were either broken or had split coverings, with the stuffing spilling out.

The ferry itself was even more disgusting. It was a late model, no more than ten years old, but it had never been cleaned. The friction of bums had ensured the plastic bucket seats had remained orange on one side, but their backs were like the ticket hatch—coated solid with shiny black grime. A sheet of canvas had once covered the floor, its brown and grey ragged remains long since trampled under. The portholes were so streaked and splotched that we could barely see where we were going.

The ferry moved in a painfully slow zig-zag from one side of the bank to the other, stopping all the way, until we reached what an elderly passenger told us was Old Cairo.

Our visit lasted approximately five minutes. A stench of donkey dung and human excrement assailed my nostrils as I viewed a scene of desolation: streets of crumbling mud buildings, not a leaf or a twig in sight, and an ankle-deep layer of rubbish everywhere—frayed remains of plastic bags, scraps of cardboard packaging, bits of yellowed newspaper. A group of dirty children played and wallowed in the midst of this, obviously knowing nothing else.

Stepping back aboard the ferry, we were accosted by a commission agent who invited me to see his 'father's' perfume shop. Father my foot, I thought, but I followed him in any case.

We were not sorry, for the Thousand and One Nights Perfume Shop proved to be everything that Old Cairo should have been. Pushing aside the beaded glass curtain over the doorway, we entered a dimly lit room which was the embodiment of a 19th-century Orientalist painter's fantasy: a silk canopy was suspended from the ceiling, finely woven kilims covered the floor with a riot of colourful patterns, and around the walls were richly carved cabinets containing jars of perfume, the scent of which pervaded the whole shop.

We were ushered to chairs inlaid with mother-of-pearl while the tout's 'father' launched into a well-polished spiel: what is sold in the West as French perfume, he claimed, is made at Grasse from a much diluted base of Egyptian oil, distilled from flowers grown in vast commercial crops in the Nile Valley. Once home in New Zealand, I could dilute his Chanel No. 9 or Opium base nine times with ethyl alcohol, and end up with French perfume. Whatever the truth of this, his oils certainly smelled wonderful, and with a black market exchange for my US dollars at twice the official rate, his prices were unbelievably cheap.

Our deal haggled over and successfully concluded, the merchant sent his shop boy out on an errand. Several minutes later he arrived back with glasses of heavily sweetened mint tea and a plate of scented semolina and coconut cakes, simple but very delicious:

Basboosa

Boil together 1 1/2 cups sugar and 1/2 cup water for 8 minutes, until the syrup is thick enough to coat the back of a spoon. Stir in the juice of 1/2 a lemon, and 1/2 tsp rose essence. Allow to cool.

Melt 125g butter and add 2 cups semolina, 1/2 cup plain white flour, 1 cup castor sugar, 1 cup desiccated coconut, 1 tsp baking powder, and 1 tsp ground cinnamon. Pour in 2/3 cup milk and stir until you have a smooth batter. Spread it about 1 cm thick over a greased baking dish. Bake at 180°C for 30–40 minutes, until golden brown and crisp on top. Remove from the oven and immediately cut into diamonds. Pour over the reserved syrup and serve hot or cold.

*

Despite our misgivings about Said, our unofficial dragoman whose salacious glances Kate had not failed to detect, we felt beholden to him and, out of guilt, agreed to meet him at his favourite haunt for lunch that day.

His hangout was a despicably filthy little outdoor café down an alley. Fag ends, bottle tops and scraps of paper littered the ground, providing wayside distractions for flies doing the rounds of improperly wiped table tops.

Kate sat down gingerly, her mouth set like a disapproving memsahib. No thank you, she didn't want anything to eat or drink. Nor did I, but out of politeness to Said, I ordered a casserole. This was promptly brought down from the first storey kitchen in a crude, lopsided black dish by a grimy waiter, clutching a handful of pitta breads in his other hand. These he slapped down onto the bare tabletop. I made a mental note not to eat the bottom piece; not that it would have made any difference.

The outside of the dish was coated with lumpy patches of an unidentifiable black substance which I was able to scrape off with my fingernail. Thrice cooked grease perhaps. Inside was a mixture of mutton, green fava beans, tomato paste and broth.

The vessel was an aquarium of unseen amoeba and bacteria, with the mutton no doubt a particularly genial host. Setting my face as bravely as I could, I scraped together a spoonful of the beans. Swallowing it, I had an urge to order some water, but thought better of it.

The state of the kitchen preyed on my mind until finally I arose, walked up the stairs, and poked my head through the door. The kitchen was stained black with smoke and decayed food scraps. A squalid figure was huddled over, 'washing' glasses—rubbing them with his fingers in a basin of cold water, its shade of grey matching his filthy splotched jelabiya. Around the inside of his collar, the ribbing of the linen was accentuated by a row of shiny black knobs of dirt. He wore a skull cap and a hurt expression on his wrinkled face, from which sprouted a grey four-day growth.

I walked back to the table feeling sick.

At adjoining tables men were sitting around smoking hookahs and playing backgammon and cards. A wild-eyed young man appeared at the table. Said introduced him as Mohammed, his friend. But he didn't seem particularly friendly; standing there, glaring, he began firing questions at me: country? name? profession?

'Journalist,' I replied, thinking, who is this guy? A cop? 'Do you understand what I mean?'

'Of course I understand. I speak English, not double Dutch.'

He moved over to the next table and sat down by himself. Calling for a hookah, he produced a small dark brown lump and began crumbling it.

Hashish? Here in public? I turned to Said for an explanation.

'Oh, everybody smokes hashish in Cairo,' he laughed. 'It's always been this way, even in my grandfather's day. It's almost unknown for us to get arrested. And Mohammed's certainly okay. He's a policeman. But no problem even for you in some parts of the town. Come with me tonight, and I'll show you some Cairo nightlife.'

We began soon after nightfall in another little grot hole off Kemal Ataturk, with more men sitting around smoking hookahs and playing backgammon and cards. I was captivated by the dramatic gestures of the men; their self-important expressions were so unintentionally comic, as they slapped the cards down on the table, that I found it difficult not to laugh.

I was introduced to another student friend of Said's, a rather imperious young chap who positively glowed as he was introduced as a descendant of King Farouk. With a few niceties, a stroke of his fingers through his beard and a flick of his shoulder length hair, he excused himself and went back to his backgammon: he had an audience, and he was winning. Up, up into the air went each counter, and then bang! slap down on to triangles which had all but been eclipsed by wear and grime.

He later joined us in a taxi ride across town to the Khan Khalli market, where we alighted and walked through a maze of narrow, unsealed dirt streets. Out of doorways men and boys hissed 'Hashish?' at us as we passed.

Finally we stopped at a doorway where Said had to strike a match to show the way upstairs to a room. More accurately, it was the remains of a room, since the roof and part of one wall were missing.

A group of men were sitting in a circle, one old man in turban and jelabiya reclined on a bed.

It was only when I saw the hookah, and beside it a custom-built tray filled with neat rows of prepared bowls, that I realised I had been brought to a hash den. Each bowl had a little crumbed brown hashish mixed with a few strands of jet black Egyptian tobacco, shining with glycerine.

Smoking the hookah was a well defined ritual. First some lumps of charcoal had to be fired over a gas stove. A hollow tin was placed over them to act as a chimney, and a piece of cardboard used to fan them. After they had flamed and begun glowing, the live bits were broken off and placed in a small sieve, which was then swayed violently from side to side to make it glow all the better. A prepared bowl was taken from the tray, covered with live coals, which were then patted down as the smoker drew in, taking it very gently.

When it came to my turn I impressed them with my ability, though the first pipe had no effect. Then came the second, and the third pipe. Still nothing. Well, I thought to myself, either hashish is vastly overrated, or this is a really dumb way to smoke it.

It certainly seemed to have affected the others however, as they seemed to find unlimited hilarity at a little game I was having with the old fellow on the bed beside me. He would say 'Saida' (good morning) and I would echo the Arabic word back to him. Then the same for 'good night', 'go to sleep', 'go to hell', etc.

After the fourth pipe an anvil descended from the cosmos and landed upon my skull. I was rendered speechless and sat there, catatonic, until 15 minutes later I managed to move myself in slow motion through the gap in the wall in time to vomit over a rubbish pile conveniently sited outside.

Said immediately took on the role of nurse, and sent out for some basboosa, which he assured me would settle my stomach. As he fed it to me, he began questioning me about my relationship with Kate. Ha! I thought, so he is finally going to come out and reveal his ulterior motive.

I assured him Kate and I were very close and there was no question of her sleeping with other men.

He laughed: 'But I'm not at all interested in Kate . . . don't you see? I want you!'

*

The GPO in Cairo is not signposted. As we stood outside, parcel in hand, wondering if it could indeed be the same building marked on our map, an Egyptian man of around 40 stopped beside us and asked if we needed any assistance. We explained.

'I am a lecturer at an agricultural college near here, and this is my lunch hour. You are in luck.'

Indeed we were, I mistakenly thought, as we entered a courtyard lined with a Kafkaesque series of counters.

Each counter was marked with elegant swirly Arabic calligraphy. Unlike every other sign I saw in Cairo, whether it be for a street, a softdrink or a shop, these did not have English translations.

The lecturer enquired at one counter, then another, then at a third, where we waited for 18 minutes in a queue, only to be told we were required to go to a separate office to get permission to send a parcel out of the country.

We walked around the building and delicately sidled around a giant puddle which filled an entire courtyard. 'Drainage problems,' the lecturer explained, as we clambered over a mound of deserted earthworks.

The 'office' in question I mistook for a derelict warehouse. We opened the barn-sized doors to reveal a group of youths in berets and patched black woollen uniforms, lounging around on the floor. One of them was absentmindedly drawing doodles in the dust of the floor with the muzzle of his rifle, a World War I vintage Lee Enfield. They eyed us curiously as we passed.

As we turned to mount the stairs, we were greeted by what I at first took to be a monumental modern sculpture, but then realised was a four-metre high pile of debris: wheels, engine parts, some bent and twisted rods, bald tyres, the whole mélange coated with brown dust.

So thick and even was the icing of dust over the windows beside the stairwell, that at first I thought they had been painted out. I ran the tip of my finger over one to make sure.

At the top of the stairs was a wooden room, devoid of furniture or decoration. This in turn led to the 'office'—another room, bare except for a trestle table, behind which sat two women. We were fifth in the queue and waited for 15 minutes.

Was our parcel above or below five kilos?

'By sea or by air?' By sea.

'Write your name, address and passport number here, and here, and here,' ordered the younger of the two, handing me a form in triplicate, without any carbon paper.

In the meantime, a youth appeared and wrapped my parcel for a small fee. One of the women pasted on a stamp, wrote on the parcel and collected another fee.

'Now,' the lecturer explained, 'we must apply for permission to send the parcel out of the country.'

'I thought we just had.'

'Oh no, that was just to get it registered and weighed.'

Back down the stairs, over the pond, and down the street for half a block, was another similarly barren office, only with three rather grander desks with men seated behind them. At the central table sat a middle-aged man with pebble glasses and an open-necked shirt in a hideous riot of greens, yellows and browns.

Two more forms were to be completed, one of which came with an English translation, headed 'Application for the Viewing of Printed Material Leaving the UAR'.

So, he was an official censor. He ordered me to open the parcel so meticulously wrapped half an hour earlier. I showed him the dangerously seditious galley proofs for my cookbook.

The censor didn't speak a word of English, let alone read it, so for all he knew the manuscript could have been details of Egyptian troop movements bound for the Israeli secret service. He beckoned a minion leaning against the door post, dressed in a jelabiya and turban, who took the parcel away and returned a quarter of an hour later with it done up with a cobweb of thick brown string, sealed at irregular intervals with blobs of tarry pitch. I grabbed the parcel impatiently and strode out, elated, to the counters in the courtyard where we had started out an hour and a half earlier.

While our friendly Egyptian flipped over the wad of documentation one by one and explained the details through the grille, I pulled out my wallet in eager anticipation.

The exchange went on for several minutes, until finally the lecturer turned to me and said the clerk had just told him there was no sea connection between Egypt and New Zealand. The parcel would have to go by air and our documents were thus invalid. We would have to repeat the whole process from beginning to end, in order to have this amendment entered on all five forms.

By this stage Kate was in tears. I sincerely thanked the lecturer for his help but explained I would dump the parcel in the nearest rubbish bin. So it was that *Delectable Fruits Cookery for New Zealanders* went to print uncorrected.

＊

Our first truly edible meal was served us in the most unlikely of places, aboard the Cairo–Luxor train: roast chicken; an excellent pilaff, sliced aubergines baked in a thick, egg-enriched béchamel; and a truly delicious cumin-tinged yoghurt and cucumber salad, variations of which are to be found in just about every cuisine of the Middle East from the Balkans to India. Another pan-Arab favourite followed: a very sweet, gluggy rice pudding, sprinkled with coconut and sultanas, served with that symbol of US gastronomic imperialism, a can of Pepsi Cola.

By Cairo standards, our First Class carriage was clean: the now familiar patches of black grease were confined to the edges of the thick plastic seat coverings, and the canvas laid down over the carpet still showed some white.

Even more cheering was the succession of small mudbrick villages flashing past our window, free of rubbish piles and raucous signs and hoardings. Housewives in headscarves and three-quarter-length dresses chatted while their children played a popular game using an old tyre as a hoop, darting in and out amongst a stream of donkeys, horses and carts, and the odd camel.

Here was the Nile valley scene of popular imagination: in the foreground fields in lush bright shades of green, divided by neat hoed lines into a patchwork of smaller squares. Within each square were rows of miniature irrigation channels, some of bare soil, others in full crop, still others lying fallow. Set among clumps of much darker green palms were one- or two-storied, flat-roofed farmhouses. Then behind, the Sahara loomed up abruptly in the distance as a knobbly line of barren yellow hills, etched with rambling ravines, silhouetted against a clear blue sky.

Birdlife abounded: scores of a cheeky bird which resembled a stork hit with a mallet, a reddish-brown kingfisher, and swallows which flew up quite near to the windows of our carriage, veering up and back more deftly than any jet fighter to expose a shiny midnight blue belly turning iridescent green in the sunlight.

A number of late model tractors were at work, but equally there were plenty of water buffaloes, paired up in teams and pulling an ancient Egyptian plough held by men in turbans and jelabiya.

They were tending cabbage, cotton and field after field of melokhia (*Corchorus olitorius*), a mucilaginous green leaf which goes into Egypt's national soup. The making of it is thought to be depicted in Pharaoic tomb paintings. At its coarsest level, the leaves are simply boiled with a vegetable stock and taken out as lunch to the men in the fields.

Melokhia soup, however, has today become a sort of self-conscious symbol of Egyptian nationalism, a rustic dish in reaction to the cosmopolitan, decadent cuisine associated with King Farouk and the old regime. The chastened middle class now prepare melokhia soup also, albeit in a gentrified form, with meat stock as a base and flavoured with garlic and perhaps even the odd meatball.

Nearer Luxor, the sugar plantations began; as sunset approached, they turned an electric lime green.

Safely ensconced that evening at the Pension Riviera, we drank rum mixed with the local cane juice, a vile-looking murky brown liquid, cranked out on the street between the rollers of ancient wringers.

The label on the rum bottle read 'Better than Egyptian rum'. It is distilled and bottled in Alexandria.

*

Luxor, home to a host of famous Pharaoic temples and tombs, is a charming town provided you realise the locals have been catering to tourists for the past four thousand years. It has obviously taught them not to underestimate our stupidity.

'Psst, sir!' hissed a stall owner from behind a table of tacky souvenirs, carved from snot-yellow alabaster. He looked theatrically back and forth, then from under the folds of his jelabiya produced a badly focused photograph of a tomb painting, set into a broken plaque fashioned from bandages and plaster of paris.

'Robbed from a mummy in the Valley of Kings. How much you want to pay?'

The Pharaoic tombs in the Valley of the Kings and the Valley of the Queens are indeed the two sights truly worth seeing at

Luxor. Those who linger at demolition sites in New Zealand cities may appreciate the ruins of Luxor Temple, Karnak Temple and the Ramaseum, bearing in mind, of course, that these particular mountains of broken rubble lack the added interest of bulldozers at work.

A handful of burial chambers in the Valley of the Kings are, however, almost miraculously intact, with blue painted ceilings, gold leaf motifs around the walls, and figures of Horus, Isis and Ra in colours as vivid as if they had been painted yesterday.

The side rooms of one tomb featured scenes from the royal kitchen. They were in poor condition, but I managed nevertheless to make out a cook stirring a cauldron, and his assistant sitting over a group of smaller pots.

In another tomb a mural depicted a team of bakers. They would, indeed, have been very busy, as some thirty distinct varieties of bread were known to the ancient Egyptians: some raised, some flat, some with mashed dates mixed into the dough, some with milk, honey or eggs, plaited, made into cones, or into the shapes of bulls and geese.

The crudest type of flatbread, known as ta, was sold at street stalls as early as the 12th century BC, and together with beer and onions, formed the basic diet of the peasantry.

The rich and lordly, however, would hold three-day feasts, at which whole oxen would be spit roasted and served by dancing girls naked to the waist. Mullet caviar would be washed down with wine served in gold goblets, preceded by a good portion of boiled cabbage, which would, they wishfully believed, prevent drunkenness. Mushrooms were reserved for the Pharaoh himself, but the court partook also of cheese, stewed figs, fresh berries and pastries.

The Egyptians persisted for many centuries with attempts to breed and domesticate such wild beasts as the gazelle, antelope, ibex and oryx. Around 2200 BC, however, they gave up in disgust and went back to hunting and gathering the spoils of the marshes: berries, lotus root, fish and birds.

Ducks, quails and all kinds of small birds were hunted, some of which, according to Herodotus, were pickled in brine for a few days and then eaten raw. And Hipparchus, in the second century BC, noted disdainfully that the Egyptians were 'forever plucking quails and slimy magpies'.

Among the food remains excavated from a third century BC tomb was the remains of a pigeon stew, a dish still enormously popular in Egypt today. Given its reputation as the rat of the sky, I was not willing to eat pigeon reared in the urban filth of Cairo. In the relative cleanliness of the countryside around Luxor, however, they are to be seen everywhere, flying in and out of the elaborate spires into which they are enticed to breed, a clay pot set on its side into the mud wall for each family. At the tender age of four weeks, they are considered ready to eat.

Tender they certainly are too. I first got to taste this ancient delicacy in a sterile post-modern restaurant above a shopping arcade on the outskirts of Luxor. A small pile of the birds was brought on a platter. They had been simply halved, grilled, and sprinkled with lemon juice and chopped chervil, but needed nothing more: they were full of flavour, and tasted more like beef or lamb than any game bird or poultry.

Another taste from ancient Egypt was the mullet served at the Chez Farouk, a restaurant on the bank overlooking the Nile, done out with rusticated ceilings and walls of rush matting.

A tweedy Englishman whom we had invited to join us at the table pointed out the sights, including a 1920s steamboat berthed at the water's edge, the very one used in filming Agatha Christie's *Death on the Nile*.

Over a bottle of rude Egyptian Three Cats vodka ('Winner of International Exposition, Brussels, 1938–39') he told us he had been a teacher at a minor public school, but had taken early retirement after learning that 67 was the average life expectancy for a male who saw his full teaching career out. His time was now divided between Kent, Luxor and Aswan.

He recounted the tale of an elderly Englishwoman who lived in Aswan and proclaimed herself as the reincarnation of an ancient Egyptian queen. 'Perhaps the locals believed her, because after she died in 1981 they preserved her home as a shrine, just as she left it, with a bookcase with a few Agatha Christie and Daphne Du Maurier novels, and a tin of Nescafé on the kitchen table.'

Oh holy Nescafé.

He told us how the ancient Egyptian priests had worshipped the eel—to the point of encrusting certain live specimens with precious gems. They, of course never touched the flesh, but the laity commonly ate them, along with mullet, carp, perch and tigerfish.

As the feluccas with their prehistoric triangular sails paraded down the Nile at sunset, the mullet on the menu seemed the obvious choice.

'Oh, by all means order the mullet!' urged the Englishman. 'That is, of course, if you actually enjoy a little dice with The Grim Reaper. You know what happened to Peter Ustinov the morning after he ate the mullet here, don't you? Seriously, the Nile is really one great river of poison these days. Truly, you mustn't even dip your hands in—there are millions of parasites ready to permeate your skin and turn your liver into Swiss cheese.'

He unsteadily emptied the bottle of vodka and ordered another.

The mullet, grilled and served with a tarator sauce, was delicious, and *my* liver remains intact.

Tarator sauce

Set a food processor with the metal blade running and drop in 2 cloves garlic one by one and pulverise. Add 250 g pine nuts, almonds or walnuts, and grind them to a powder. Now add 2 slices white bread, the juice of 2 lemons, salt to taste, and any liquid left after the fish has been baked or grilled. With the machine still going, add sufficient water to make a smooth paste.

Spread over a whole grilled or baked fish before sending to the table, and garnish with lemon slices and green pickles.

RACHEL BUSH

What People Want

I have read some of your stories says my aunt Elspeth who is crocheting a blanket in cream wool for her first grandchild. Cream not blue or pink because at this stage they can't tell whether it will be a little boy or a little girl. In a way, she says, I feel quite proud. You know I always wanted to be an authoress myself. Your mother was beautiful, no doubt who had the beauty in our family; Rodney had the brains but I had imagination. You have imagination too. But I must tell you I don't honestly care for what you're writing at the moment. They're just little bits. Now is that what people want? I don't think so. What people want is a good story and they want characters they can believe in. That's what I could do, characters and a good story. Not just little snippets in the middle of nowhere about people that are well frankly peculiar. Sometimes, she says, I wish I'd done this in blue. Blue is okay for either and I really don't think it gets so dirty. You know with a little baby you're washing all the time, every day. It gets you down in the end. Especially when it rains. It's the smell gets to you. Damp things draped round all over the place.

No, I wish you'd write something about a woman lawyer. Women should get a good education. It's the in thing for a woman to have a career. She doesn't have to be beautiful. Nowadays personality is what counts. She could have a perfect creamy complexion and long slender fingers, but maybe her nose just a centimetre, no maybe five millimetres too long for regular beauty. Now the trouble with you is that you'll do something dreadful like give her a nasty red hickey—I mean zit—I know what hickies means nowadays—a nasty red zit just to the right of and above her upper lip with a little pale head about to burst and she can't resist squeezing it so it goes splat on the mirror in the Ladies' Room at court where she is defending a poor solo mother of four lovely kiddies who got so desperate for money to feed them, they were hungry poor things; she was caught trying to smuggle out $118.95 worth of groceries concealed under this enormously baggy coat she'd bought that morning from the Methodist op shop, you know the one, in Collingwood Street, especially for that purpose. And also in an old Supervalue bag she had been given there the last time she had gone to buy her groceries in that supermarket. The funny thing is she'd have got away with it except a packer at the checkout saw her reach for four Bounty bars, you know what they are, one for each of her kiddies just as she was standing in the queue. They keep bars and stuff up by the counter. She slipped them into a sleeve and then kept her arm bent, pretending to scratch her neck. Some people are desperate you know. It's too easy to get caught up in your own little world and forget about what happens to anyone else. That's where imagination comes into it. People like me can't forget even when we try, just to give ourselves a break.

I do like cream, even if it's not as practical as blue. I'm only going round once more and then I'll probably do a shell pattern.

Anyway I'm getting away from what I wanted to say although come to think of it there's a whole book waiting to be written about that poor woman with her four kiddies and only a two-bedroom flat with an outside toilet and the youngest one an asthmatic and needing constant medication. So there's this young woman lawyer. Wearing the sort of clothes they wear. I can't think of the designer's name, it's not Caroline Sills, it'll come to me. Like a very well cut navy suit with a pure silk shirt underneath and no jewellery. The jacket doesn't do up, no buttons, but there's that kind of embroidery where you'd expect there to be lapels, you know what I mean, it's the same colour as the suit itself. Well maybe a little jewellery, like one brooch which is an heirloom on her shirt. Very small with seed pearls round a rather lovely moonstone. I think elegant is the word for her, but at the same time there is something very touching about her, almost something childlike in her smooth brow and wide set grey eyes. It is perhaps that as well as her amazing eloquence, it is so rare to find a woman who can speak with real confidence, which draws the attention of young Doctor Jennings. Richard is his name. He is also in court because he is concerned with the accused in a professional capacity and is very anxious that not just the welfare of her children but even her sanity itself may be jeopardised by the humiliation of the court case, the trauma of it. He has come to offer her what little support he can and sits in the court a somewhat solitary figure, resting his chin in one hand. His brow is furrowed. I thought at first a chiselled jawline, but I think you can overdo that sort of thing. Not that he's a chinless wonder; I don't like men with no chin. He believes in justice, wants justice to be done for this woman who is so poor and defenceless. One of the things you notice immediately about him is how his eyes are creased at the corners. It's very noticeable because mostly the skin on his face is so brown, bronzed really. He's wearing, well it's hard to say—it's not so important in a man, but there's something very casual about the way he wears his suit, not grubby mind you, no spots of melted butter off his breakfast toast on his fine wool trousers. Anyway he eats muesli and yoghurt or if he's in a hurry as he often is and not looking after himself properly because he cares so much about his sick patients, then he just grabs a cup of coffee, percolated coffee, not instant and rushes down to his surgery or out to make his house calls.

Then there's all the bit about the court case and the accused standing there and witnesses swearing to tell the truth, the whole truth et cetera, and the judge who is widely known for his resistance to women lawyers, though generally fair-minded, but he does give women a hard time. But the part I want you to get to is where their eyes meet, well in fact their eyes lock for one instant, and then he looks away, disturbed because he has this understanding with a woman with dark lustrous eyes and a full sensual mouth but also of low reputation who is a successful ceramic artist working from a studio in Parnell. Masha her name is, but they say it *ma chère* as in the French, it means my dear. She is a very independent woman who wears incredibly large dangly earrings, and trousers to almost everything. She gets her shoes from a shop in Parnell, a sort of shoe boutique where they cost anything, maybe six or seven hundred dollars a pair. She has to have the very best. She frequents particular little galleries and there is an article about her in a recent *Metro*. Investors snap up her every piece and hostesses, these are the ones that make up the Auckland jet set, are desperate to have her at their dinner parties. So as they say, the course of true love never runs smooth and at first she, I haven't named her yet, maybe Louise or Laura, at first she mistakes the reason for his interest in the court case and assumes there may be some entanglement with the mother of four who has a worn and haggard grace about her, and he too has misunderstandings about her, Laura or Louise, thinking she must be just another high-flying career girl for all the vulnerability of her face which could be just surface.

I'm going to go round this again before I do a border, scallops. You know, like shells, just to finish it off. Only sometimes when I get near the end like this, I think how it's all just one long thread really and if I slipped the hook out I could just unravel and unravel it right back to the knot I started with. Of course I never would, not after all this work.

The trouble is I never seem to get any time for writing these days. But you can use it, if you like, the whole thing. Will you put them in a story? It's what people want.

EDMUND CAKE

My father's speakers

I worked a nightshift at the BP service station on Junction Rd
in New Lynn. I remember driving home one night and 'Round
Midnight', the Thelonius Monk version, came on the car radio.
It was very moving. A guy I worked with named Pete always had
lots of pot and after we had locked up the place we would stand
in the automated carwash and smoke a joint. One night it was
incredibly foggy and I drove home very stoned. I hardly knew
where I was, the fog was so thick and I ran over traffic islands
and up curbs when I missed corners. The afternoon my sister
called me at work to tell me Dad was dead, Pete was working
too. He came to see me at my flat in Dominion Rd a couple of
weeks later. I think we got stoned.

He told me he would wake up
with his wife giving him a blow job
I told him my Dad was dead
I nearly fell over
I cried in my boss's office
where I'd smoked cigarettes in the dark

The dead industrial zone at night
with the orange street lights
We smoked pot in the sleeping carwash
and drove home in the thick fog
over traffic islands and kerbs

I galloped around the forecourt
on an office chair with wheels
Years later I put a microphone in front of
the rattling wheels of a similar chair and recorded it

then slowed the tape right down on playback
It sounded like a busy port with ships and seagulls

He came and visited me a couple of weeks later
we got stoned, it was a kind gesture
I thought about my Father's stereo speakers
My Father used to think about his Father's radiogram

Pete got a new job at a plumbing supply shop
in Onehunga
Back at work, I found the security cameras
oriented toward the staff behind the till
The BP area manager sat me down
and issued me with a written warning
for spending an hour and a half of work time
crawling around in the roof and making insulting gestures
at the camera
He told me 'You've changed'
So I told him my Father suicided a few weeks ago
That shut him up.

KATE CAMP

The spine gives up its saddest stories

I pay a man to manipulate me.

He lays out a sheet of clean tissue
cradles my head and says
from behind a Swiss moustache
have you had accidents before?

Oh yes, I want to say,
I am the very devil for injury
I disguise myself
as a white line and live on the road.

I do not say this, I lie
prone in a curtain room
the William Tell overture
plays at quiet volume

his chest is warm on my back
my head is heavy in his hands
there are tiny clicks happening inside me
that even he doesn't know about:

the secret language of the spine.

CHARLES CAUSLEY

Birthday Photograph, 1989

An evening sea swims in
To re-arrange the shore.
Swallows a thousand stones.
Comes back for more.

The young photographer
Sprints to high ground.
Stay there, he signals; moves
Half-circle round.

Draws with an easy care
In falling sun
Bead after bead, as though
He held a gun.

I stand, uncertain, on
A mince of shells and scree.
Tireless, behind my back
Hurls the long sea.

A talismanic Celt,
I fear, and I know why,
The thieving look that's in
The camera's eye.

From my house to the shore
Ten miles are spread.
All through the night the tide
Turns in my head.

Time, eager as the sea,
Dispatches one more day;
Lies, patient, at my side
And will not go away.

CATHERINE CHIDGEY

The Craters of the Moon

By the time they reach the lake it is dark; as they drive around it they can't even see the water. Jim wonders if it is really still there at all. He keeps glancing at the black space where it should be.

'For God's sake, keep your eyes on the road,' says Felicity. 'We don't need to crash ten minutes before we get there.'

'Holiday Road Toll Reaches Unexpected High,' says Aidan from the back seat.

'Shut up, Aidan.'

When they climb out of the car at the bach, though, they can hear the water. Jim would like to stand in the garden for a while and listen, just to be sure, but the others are keen to get inside and unpacked after five hours in the car. He unlocks the back door and they step into the kitchen.

Suzanne makes for the bedrooms. 'A water bed!' she calls, belly-flopping on to the daisy-print eiderdown, staking a claim. 'Hey, Aidan, there's a water bed!'

Felicity eyes the net curtains, the flamboyant linoleum, the marbled carpet.

'I told you it wasn't pretty,' says Jim.

She fingers a macramé owl. 'Into brown are they?'

Jim blows the dust from a free-standing globe that dominates one corner of the lounge like a television. He twirls it gently on its axis, closes his eyes and points. Chile.

'Everything that nobody wants any more ends up here,' he says. 'Want a drink?'

Felicity peers at the globe. 'Christ, that's ugly. Even the water's brown.'

'My aunt and uncle are the kindest people.'

'I hate this sort of velvet,' says Felicity, squirming on the arm of a tasselled easychair. 'You always stick to it. Got any gin?'

Jim unhooks a latch on the side of the globe and the northern hemisphere lifts back. Inside—cradled in the southern hemisphere—are bottles, grouped around a set of glasses. Felicity screams with laughter.

'God,' she apologises between gasps. 'God, sorry. It's just so—sorry.'

Jim can hear them through the walls of the lounge, grunting. They declined a night swim with him and Felicity; they were tired after the long drive, said Aidan, and the lake wasn't going anywhere, was it? Suzanne smiled across the table then, and Jim felt her long dress brush his shin, raising the hairs, as her bare foot searched for Aidan's under the table.

Now there is a thump from their bedroom that makes the bars of the heater sing, followed by suppressed giggling. After a moment or two the grunting starts again.

Jim tries to focus on his game of chess, but after considering his move for at least quarter of an hour he gives up. He shuts the lid of his computer, slips it back into its case—the amount of sand that could be trailed into the bach concerns him—and wonders if, out of politeness to Aidan and Suzanne, he should put some music on.

Beside him, Felicity seems unaware of the noise and is running her finger along the map, calculating the best route to take the next day. Jim watches her follow the course of the river, trace around the lake. Her hand spans mountains.

'We used to play games here,' he says. 'When it was raining.'

'Mmhmm,' says Felicity, fingertips still moving, along State Highway 1 now. She is almost at Rotorua.

'Scrabble.'

'Oh God!' Aidan groans through the wall.

'Monopoly, Trouble, Cluedo. Snakes and Ladders.'

Felicity folds the map away, along its original creases. Jim can never do that.

'I think we should do the mountain tomorrow,' she says. 'We can fit in the hot pools any time. It might be too foggy if we leave it till later.'

'Oh God!' groans Aidan. 'Ohgodohgodohgod!'

*

The pumice is cool underfoot as Felicity and Jim head for the water. She didn't really want to go swimming so late at night—she is uneasy about lowering herself into a lake she cannot see—but Jim insisted. Okay okay, she said, too subdued by the gin from the globe cabinet to argue, but I'm keeping my togs on.

'She's a bit of an idiot, isn't she?' she says now. 'Suzanne. Not really Aidan's type.'

'She likes you,' says Jim. 'She thinks you're terribly independent.'

'My mother said that at Christmas-time.' Felicity kicks to stay afloat. She moves her hands back and forth through the water; twigs, leaves, tiny discs of pumice pass through her spread fingers.

Jim is silent on the way back to the bach. Felicity wants to get things organised, discuss the order in which they will see the local attractions. She is worried that the whole trip will be spent at the lake, and decides it was a wise idea to get one swim out of the way so early in the piece.

'The Craters of the Moon,' she says, and Jim cranes his head back. 'The volcanic area, stupid. I want to go.'

'Oh. Okay.'

He is still scanning the sky. Felicity sighs.

'Lamppost,' she says. 'Tree.'

They push the single beds together. Felicity seizes a musty double sheet and raises her arms as if to incite a crowd. For a moment the fabric fills the air between them and suddenly Jim feels like jumping underneath it the way he used to and letting the soft cotton settle.

'Where's Jim gone?' his mother would say, looking under the pillow, behind the curtains. 'He was here a moment ago . . . I wonder where he could have got to?' Her searching would become more thorough—the wardrobe, the toy chest—while Jim lay absolutely silent. This was never a problem. 'Is he behind the pot plant? In this vase, perhaps? Should I ring the police?'

Jim wants Felicity to slide under the pale flannelette with him now, and hide. But already the sheet is sinking, taking on the solid shape of the bed—the beds—and Felicity is pulling the edge towards herself, trying to tuck it in.

'Aren't there any queensize ones?' she says. 'And why did they have to get the double bed?'

'They're guests.'

'I see.' She shakes a pillow into its case. 'What does that make me?'

Jim does not sleep well. At one point he wakes up wedged between the two beds, wrapped tightly in the bottom sheet. The other one is bunched underneath Felicity.

She will have lines all over the backs of her legs, he thinks groggily, hoisting himself back on to the shiny, bare mattress.

'Snow!' says Suzanne. 'Can we stop? Please?'

'It's better higher up.'

'Just for a minute?'

'Can you stop whining? Just for a minute?'

Suzanne stares at Aidan as if she can't believe what he's just said. She twists the fringing on her long, long scarf. It matches her hat.

'I just want to get out of the car for a bit, that's all,' she says.

Jim glances in the rear-view mirror at her. 'Are you going to be sick?'

'No, I am not going to be sick.' She exhales heavily.

'I think I am,' mutters Felicity.

'I just wanted to see the snow,' Suzanne says quietly. 'I've never seen it before, okay?'

Nothing is said for the next fifteen minutes or so. They seem to be passing plenty of perfect places to stop, Felicity thinks, but Jim drives on, further and further up the mountain.

'Here,' he finally says, and jolts the car to a stop, throwing everyone forward in their seats. Felicity doesn't feel much like getting out of the car; if everyone is going to argue she would rather stay where she is and finish off the Minties that are scattered in the glove box.

But Jim is saying come on, it won't take long, and is pushing her jacket at her, and Suzanne and Aidan are already leaping out, and there is a rush of brittle snow air that smells a lot better than the inside of the car. So she zips herself into her jacket, the one that makes her feel she cannot bend her elbows and so must walk around like some undead creature or sleepwalker, and she grabs her sunglasses from the glove box, sprinkling Minties on the sandy car floor, and then she's outside with the other three on the cool bright mountain.

'Hey, guys, over here!' calls Aidan. 'It's like carpet!' He is jumping up and down on a stretch of wiry moss. The others run towards him, trying to land on patches of rock that have not been covered by snow, and then they are all leaping around on the springy moss. Suzanne and Felicity collide and fall back into the snow, laughing.

'Aidan,' says Jim, 'do you see what I see?'

'Horizontal females?'

'Over there.' He points to a rise in the ground, a smooth slope of snow.

The two of them make their way across to it, walking in a dead straight line this time, not bothering to aim for rock. Small plants snap beneath their feet.

'What the hell are they doing?' says Felicity, sitting up.

Suzanne hands her a thick dark leaf. 'Here, sniff this. It smells like apricots.'

'I claim this land for the Queen,' calls Aidan. Then he and Jim undo their jeans and in a moment Felicity can make out two arcs of piss against the snow.

'Feel free to join in,' calls Jim.

On the way back to the car Felicity feels a bit drunk. 'Too much nature is bad for a person,' she mumbles. She wipes her nose with the back of her fist, and finds she is still clutching Suzanne's leaf, which does smell like apricots.

As Jim is turning the car around, a jeep drives by, slowing as it passes. The two men inside, dressed in dark green uniforms, scrutinise the car.

'I think we should get moving,' says Suzanne. 'Look.'

At the edge of the road, right beside where they have been running around, is a sign: Native plant regeneration area. Please keep off.

'Shit.'

'Well, it's not a very big sign, is it? And there's no fence or anything.'

'And not many plants now. Shit.'

'Just drive.'

So although the jeep has gone, and no one is following them, Jim puts his foot down hard and they have soon left the snow behind. Felicity washes her hands when she gets home, but for the rest of the day she can smell apricots.

'Guys,' says Suzanne one evening, after they have all been for a swim, 'we've decided it's not fair you've had to sleep in the single beds every night, so you can have the waterbed.'

'Only for the last two nights, though,' Felicity says after they have swapped sheets and she and Jim are lying in the dark.

'They meant well,' says Jim, although he had become accustomed to the single beds, and wouldn't have minded staying put. In the bedside rubbish bin, which Jim's aunt has decorated with wallpaper and rows of bunched lace, there are condom wrappers.

The waterbed is a relatively old one, one of the first. They're very *gimmicky*, Jim's father said when his brother Ted first bought it. Jim's parents had not approved of the bach, either. Such a waste of money, they said, standing empty eleven months out of the year. And they still have to pay the phone and the rates and everything else for the full year. Jim had not liked to point out that the bach was an investment, that it was on a prime piece of real estate, that it would pay for itself many times over if it were sold. His parents don't understand business.

He can't fall asleep now, and wonders if he should move to the more solid couch. Felicity seems restless, flinging her arms about and kicking in her sleep. Jim can hear water every time she moves. She flails, thrashes, trying to escape from something, or to save herself.

I should move to the lounge, thinks Jim, or put up the camp bed, like we used to. He thinks it's in the wardrobe; he knows he saw it somewhere. Possibly the garage.

In the morning he is woken up by the sound of water. In his

half-awake state he thinks their bed—in which he seems to have
remained—is leaking, but it is only rain at the windows and on
the corrugated iron roof.

'You be Miss Scarlet,' says Aidan, handing Suzanne the red
plastic figure. 'The slutty one.'

Suzanne giggles. 'Only if you're Reverend Green.'

'I really wanted to do the mud pools today,' says Felicity,
staring out the window. 'Do you think it's clearing up?'

'It's nearly your turn. You're Mrs White. Jim's idea.'

'Captain Peacock to you.'

Felicity pours herself a drink from the globe cabinet, which
now stands permanently open, and slides on to the fourth vinyl
chair at the table.

'Three, four, five.' Aidan places his plastic figure on top of
Suzanne's.

'Hey, you can't do that! Only one person per square.'

'Now you wouldn't refuse a man of the cloth, would you, my
child?' Aidan wiggles Reverend Green on top of Miss Scarlet.

Jim sighs. 'Must everything be about your crotch?'

'Pretty much.'

'You threw a six, you know.' Felicity holds the dice under
Aidan's nose.

'Aha! The good Reverend may enter the conservatory!'

Aidan checks his Detective Notes, shielding the paper on
either side with his palms.

'I think it was Colonel Mustard, in the conservatory, with
Miss Scarlet. And Reverend Green was watching.'

'A weapon, Aidan. You have to choose a murder weapon.
We've explained this to you before.' Felicity closes her eyes.
'Miss Scarlet is not a weapon.'

'You haven't seen her in a cocktail dress.'

'I need another drink,' says Felicity. As she stands up, she
knocks the board off the table with her glass.

'Great,' says Jim. 'Now we don't even get to find out who the
murderer is.'

'Just look at the cards, idiot.'

'It's not the same.'

'The globe's nearly empty,' says Suzanne, peering sadly inside the cabinet.

'Well, the southern hemisphere,' says Felicity.

Aidan stretches out on the couch. 'I blame London.'

'Shit,' says Jim. 'We'll have to replace it, you know.'

Aidan rolls his eyes. 'Just stick some water in, they'll never notice the difference. How old are they?'

'That stuff's been there since the sixties anyway,' says Suzanne. 'They won't mind.'

'I haven't done any work the whole time we've been here,' says Jim, taking his laptop from the formica dressing table.

'No point starting now then, is there?' says Felicity, climbing into the waterbed. 'Why do they always have these barrier things on the sides? It's such a pain getting in and out.'

'I should at least do a thank-you letter.'

'Actually, they don't have them on the new ones, do they?' She folds the thin pillow underneath her cheek and closes her eyes. Jim can hear the bath being run, and Suzanne and Aidan giggling.

Dear Aunty May and Uncle Ted, he types. A quick note to say thank you for the use of your wonderful bach. My friend Felicity—you might remember her from Aunty Peg's funeral—says she's never felt so relaxed. My two other friends also enjoyed themselves. I know you said not to worry about the electricity or the phone bill, but I wanted to give you a little something as a thank you present. Hope you like these—I know Aunty May has always had a sweet tooth!

Jim pauses, wondering if he should mention the depleted globe. Beside him, Felicity is probably already asleep. He can hear splashing coming from the bathroom.

After a while his letter disappears from the screen, and is replaced with rushing stars. He knows the effect is just the result of a binary code, a particular combination of the numbers one and two, but he watches the screen for a while, holding his hand very still over the mouse, and tries to imagine himself rushing through space. Then Felicity moves in her sleep, nudging his hand, and for a moment, before his letter reappears on the screen, the stars freeze.

INGA CLENDINNEN

Big Louis

Big Louis is dead. I found out only yesterday, because the last time I went to the Clinic I didn't meet any of the people who might have told me, which can happen when you're down to three-monthly visits. He might have died as long as five months ago. It is odd to discover you have been orphaned for months without knowing it. Louis was the first person to receive a liver transplant at the Unit when it started at the Austin Hospital here in Melbourne in 1988. Units were already working in Brisbane and Adelaide, but he was our first. They'd tried transplanting livers long before that but everybody used to die, so they gave up for a while, but in the early eighties they began again. What had changed the odds were better operating techniques and yet another miracle drug, this one called 'Cyclosporin'. Cyclosporin controlled rejection without too much damaging the patient. It came into use only in 1989, so Louis must have survived his first few months without it. The Unit people must have been proud of him.

So Louis was Number One. The last one, operated on about a week ago, is Number 301. I am Number 108, from April 1994. We write our history in the old-fashioned way here. Dates and numbers matter in this long, thin, accidental family I have joined. We care about lines of descent, too, so Louis was our grandfather. He was a big, slow-moving Frenchman or Belgian in his late sixties who couldn't or wouldn't speak English. He would sit peaceably in the waiting room on his too-small chair, one large hand on each knee, and exude the mild benignity of an elephant, or perhaps a bishop. It was good to see him slowly moving up the corridor ahead or lying back in the padded chair for the routine blood test. He was our talisman against the fates, and we took comfort from his being.

The family has no politics or class, and prior relationships are erased on entry. Class is officially erased too. Because humans happen to be endowed with two kidneys and only one is

86

necessary for life, a friend or kinsman might surrender the other to a specified donor, as Kerry Packer's helicopter pilot recently did in a blare of ambiguous publicity, but even our richest man couldn't buy himself a liver. 'Living cadaver' transplants, as they are called—liver, heart, lungs—are done democratically, in designated public hospitals, with public patients queued in accordance with need. We are nonetheless selective. There are no honorary members. The only way into the family is by way of the operation. People on the waiting list don't even meet us post-transplant people except for one person selected by the Unit to be their counsellor or 'next friend'. This segregation might be no more than a way of ordering the doctors' time, with some days being allocated to a string of individual pre-transplant interviews, and some to the crush of the post-transplant clinics with people being called into the offices one by one, but I suspect it is also policy. People on the waiting list panic easily. They need to know some things, but not others, and they haven't yet learnt to trust the medicos, who naturally want to control the information-flow so that no one gets muddled or demoralised. However, we sometimes meet. Before my transplant I had seen my doctor and was waiting by the Unit's lift, shaking, yellow, cradling my distended belly with my arms (with advanced liver disease the abdomen swells grotesquely) when a slender sari-wrapped Indian lady standing in the corridor was suddenly beside me, holding my shaking hand in her steady warm ones and saying, 'You'll be all right. I promise you, you will be all right. It is only three months for me and look, already so well!' She smiled into my eyes like a loving little sister. 'And today I am off to Sydney to be with my husband! They are letting me go to Sydney!' The lift doors opened, she pulled my head down and kissed me firmly on the forehead, pushed me inside, and I saw her blessing me through the closing crack as I slid through the floor.

I was startled by this emotional surge from a delicately scented stranger, but I was also warmed by it. Months later, after my own transplant, I felt the same surge of affection for a yellow, wasted man trying to cradle his swollen belly in exactly the same place: the little hall by the lift outside the Liver

Transplant Unit's offices. I shared her impulse but lacked her courage. I didn't speak. Guilt lived with me until I came across the man in the surgical ward after his transplant, transformed back to his original form of a small tough Scot with a spiky ginger moustache, and cheerfully remembering 'the little Asian-looking fella' he had once been.

A handful of pre-transplant people are terrified or suspicious or downright paranoid about the whole business, which can seem surreal, and then someone who has been through it is allocated to them to calm them. One woman I was sent to see sat huddled in a blanket in her hospital bed, persuaded that the doctors had not the least concern for her welfare and were intent on experimenting on her body. Another woman, startlingly beautiful even in her flattened state, was incandescent with rage at the unseemly eruption of the physical melodrama which had plucked her from the world and sequestered her in a tiny blue-curtained tent (she kept her bed curtains furiously drawn). She had festooned the tent with what looked to be hundreds of cards, communiques from her lost life. She finally acquiesced, I think largely because I described the process of the alternative death. Then she died anyway. Most people on the waiting list die. Australia has a very low donor rate, one of the lowest in the world, which used to surprise me. I thought a bunch of secular humanist hedonists like us would be easy givers, and suspected that the influx of migrant families with strong religious backgrounds explained the low rate. That seems not to be the case: provided the correct rituals are followed (naked candles in Intensive Care if required), those families tend to be generous. Perhaps the hedonism is the problem. Perhaps we refuse to think about death exactly because we believe it is the end, and there can be no previous discussion, with everyone being agreed they will live forever. Then families lurching under the brutal impact of grief are asked to allow a loved one's body to be, as they think of it, pillaged. That is why the recent scandals in Britain about the unauthorised taking of organs for research distress me. They will make people even less ready to think about the simple realities, so even more people will die.

For we lucky few who enter the family the benefits are

multiple. For example: the worst thing about being seriously ill is the loneliness. You know that nobody, neither your doctor nor your husband nor your best friend, can imagine what it feels like, especially in its more trivial manifestation: how your left calf will clench and tremble for no reason, how dread comes sliding smoothly out from behind the water jug. Your new family knows. They will say, 'It was my right leg used to do that, quiver like a mad thing. And in the small of your back, like a big vibrator buried in your spine, do you get that?' and you say, with relief, 'Yes I do', and the loneliness is less lonely, and you also know there will be someone eager to listen when you need to talk about fluttering muscles, inexplicable tastes in the mouth, inexplicable tears. The doctors might give you a brisk explanation as to the why of it, but they can't help you find the words to describe how it feels.

In the Clinic I also found again the radiantly chaotic social world I thought I had lost when I left primary school and began a lifetime of picking and choosing friends and associates. The studious egalitarianism of the Australian national health system serves up a marvellous mix of genders, ages, classes and ethnic origins. As it turns out—as my betters have told me but I never really learned—the greatest of these is class. People I would never have met, never glanced at, never even seen in my ordinary life as a middle-class academic of Anglo ancestry, were now sitting next to me for a couple or more hours at a time, waiting our turn. I realised the privilege of coming to know, for example, Gloria. She would be up by 4.30 a.m. on clinic days to come in to Clinic by public transport from her distant outer suburb, where I had never been, its name no more than a sociological tag for deprivation and disorder. She didn't have to leave quite so early, but she dreaded being late and seeming less than grateful. She would get home again by mid afternoon, to deal with her two small children and her superbly uncooperative husband. The drugs had happened to work in her to produce a soft flow of surplus flesh. Most of us had had our adventures with our protean bodies, but no one else billowed with flesh as she did. She had also become chronically breathless and uncertain of her balance, and now she was a diabetic, which sometimes happens. You can't fool with bodies without some unintended consequences. Gloria would sit with her pretty hands in her matron's lap and the face of a pretty girl lost somewhere in her wide one, and when she saw me she would direct a vague smile somewhere past my right shoulder and pat the seat she had been keeping beside her. As far as I could discover (she spoke little and softly) she was at once desperately shy and shamed by her shyness and shamed by her flesh. She was also determined to be stoical, which is why she needed a friendly presence beside her. Some husbands and wives always came to the clinic with their spouses and acted as talking chiefs for them, thereby re-enacting a way of being married I had forgotten about, but she had to get through everything alone. She was fiercely grateful to the Unit's doctors, and fiercely obedient to their instructions. We all were—we knew what we owed them—but we would moan and groan and trade jokes about them. Gloria never did. These people had chosen her and cared for her, as I think no one had done before.

Pat wasn't shy, just scary. He looked as if he had been rough-carved over a chunk end of redgum; a long bristle of red hair ran right down the middle of his big bare skull; and his arms, and for all we knew all of him, were blue with tattoos, most of an embarrassingly intimate nature. No one was game to talk to him for a while, but I thought he could scarcely turn on a grey-haired old granny, or not in the Unit's waiting room, and one day sat next to him. He had been, as he looked and in his own description, 'a very bad lad', deeply into illegal substances, violence, motor bikes and alcohol. Then at 28 he discovered he had ruined his liver and that he might well die soon and unpleasantly, and immediately after that some well-spoken strangers in white coats were ready to try to give him another chance provided he mended his ways. So he did. He gave up drink, drugs, even smoking, and now when he went to the pub to see his mates he drank lemon squashes. He'd also sold his motorbike: if he wanted to go anywhere he walked or rode his pushbike or took a train. (He lived in a suburb where train-travel was quite peaceful, provided you were built like a tree.) He was translucently proud that his thirteen-year-old son was building his first machine in the garage—he'd done the same when he was thirteen—but he himself was through with them. Motorcycles were too dangerous, now that his body didn't belong exclusively to him. He had tried to throw his life away, and it had been given back to him. He would not throw it away again. What was most noticeable about Pat—what I privately thought rare and noble about him—was his refusal to moralise from his experience. He was utterly free from the middle-class urge to preach. This had been his personal lesson, and he had learnt from it. He's still going well.

Most arguments against transplants make me angry, like those made by fastidious people who do not suffer from a terminal disease and who find the notion of brain death too complicated or the whole idea of transplantation of organs too aesthetically distasteful to be contemplated, while here we are in our various bodies, walking around enjoying ourselves. We are the argument for it. Of course our situation is a touch precarious. Given the chronic shortage of donors, what being accepted on to the waiting list for a transplant most feels like is being snatched out of a turbulent river and hoisted up onto a rickety suspension bridge. You know you would surely have died in the water, but you still don't feel too safe. But soon the people ahead of you on the bridge are turning to hug you, cheering you on, and telling you the quivering and rocking is normal, the vertigo is normal, everything is normal and you will be, indeed you already are, fine. Over the next few weeks or months you meet more of your new family, and sooner or later they'll point to a slow-moving shape up ahead, and say, 'That's Louis. He's Number One.' And now Louis is gone and we turn and clutch each other, because without his weight the bridge is trembling.

GEOFF COCHRANE

Pile Diary

Day One

There's disorder down there.
Tenacious muscles
pleat and pucker and pop.
Axiomatic too
that if I want to adjust
there's an Arab in the car park.
I go for Doctor Unguent
and ride home in a cab
with forty dollars' worth of Xylocaine.
The sky's a dish of creamy lime delight
forecasting needles, blades . . .

Day Three

'What can you tell me
about X?' she asks.

It's Sunday. I'm in pain.
I have to sit in a certain position.
'He was once in the navy,' I say.

'He uses *little* words.
He asked me to suck him off.
I'd like him to fuck me
without a condom,' she says.

In the absence of God and soul
and any afterlife,
sex itself becomes holy.

Day Five

Tomorrow, the op.
I'm frozen in the act
of giving birth to grapes;
as the hours pass,
they tarnish and dry.

The clues of the crossword
make a surreal poem.
I'm a cast baboon
presenting her bulging vulva.

The Boiler-House

1972. The longer your hair, the sexier. Sandals and flared jeans, that's me. I speak with a special accent acquired in the Duke of Edinburgh Hotel, a chaotic dive.

'Please Respect the Privacy of Patients.' I register the place in terms of roses and tennis-courts, asphalt paths and beamed ceilings. From a window at the back of Rutherford, one can see a little mortuary.

'Do you dream about drinking?' Sir Charles Burns asked. I did and do and now there's something wrong with my heart. A drink would fix my heart; a drink is not exactly contra-indicated.

I'm learning to polish floors with a machine. Tilting the handles gets you traction and momentum. Calm, surcease, belonging. The rocking swing and *shush* of the polisher. I'm nonetheless the thirstiest man in Australasia.

As my father and I approached Rutherford, a man came out to meet us. 'I'm the Ward Host.' He shook my father's hand. 'Welcome to Queen Mary, Mr Cochrane.'

'You've got the wrong bloke,' my father said.

A diffuse rain fell, wafting down like steam. On my first night in Hanmer, scents sulphurous and piney. From the tables in the hall came a clacking of balls. The light in the boiler-house suggested a course of action: when my treatment was over, I'd get a job shovelling coal. Faulkner had had his post office, I'd have my boiler-house.

Dr Maling is as leggy as a flamingo. 'Has it ever occurred to you that drinking is a sort of petulance?'

'?'

'A way of saying I *want it all*?'

It has and does but now there's something wrong with my heart. I put away my polisher and go to breakfast. Sunlight fills the dining-room. The surly Belfast man offers to trim my hair. When I go to his room later in the morning, I see that he's equipped like a proper barber—all that's lacking is a barber's big mirror. I sit in a chair and submit to his ministrations; the touch of his scissors is light and professional. At length he hands me a pocket mirror. 'I've given you a choice of styles,' he says. 'Tell me which you prefer, Paddy,' he says.

One side of my head retains its brown curls, the other has been almost completely denuded.

It's a glorious day in February. I feel big-eared and stark. Warmth and clarity, the odour of mown grass—and now I look like everybody else. I sport travesty: my shorn condition seems to represent compromise and moral slippage. A man in his sixties tells me, 'An ignorant sort of prick, that Belfast sod.'

The lunch bell rings. One's place at table is dictated by a seating plan. A bag of toffees and a telegram have been left beside my knife. 'BEST WISHES ON YOUR TWENTY-FIRST LOVE MUM AND DAD.' The telegram read and internalised, there remains the mystery of the sweets, the provocation of the toffees.

GLENN COLQUHOUN

An Explanation of Poetry to My Father

To my Mum
And to my Dad
Who made me good
And made me bad

An apology

I was not a son to take the Word
of God to the whole world.

I was not a son to spot a fine
cow at auction.

I was not a son who was able to
fix the inside of dark engines.

I did not win the game
in its final minute.

I was not a son to sweat all day
on the end of a shovel.

I was not a son to remain calm
at the sight of my own blood.

I was not a son to capture the
hearts of beautiful women.

I did not save for a rainy day.

I was not a son to discover
the cures to rare illnesses.

I was not a son to bear you
a generation of fine children.

I was a son who believed
in the making of poetry.

Which is, I suppose, in the end,
pretty much the same thing.

The first lesson

Now are you going to listen or not? There's nothing tricky
about a poem. It's just a collection of words like one of those
bunches of grapes that used to hang in the backyard, how every
one had a particular shape depending on the way it grew, or
like one of those macramé pot-holders Aunty Jean used to make
except the words are the knots and at each one you can change
direction, or like when mum cooks and some words are like
mince and cheap and easy to fill you up with and contain most
of what's good for you and those are the ones she uses a lot
and some words are spicy so she only uses them a little bit and
like some words look so good she uses them for colour and
others act differently under heat, cheese for example, to melt
all through a poem which is great unless you don't like cheese.
Some bits might stick in your teeth for days unless you brush
them and I know you don't always do that. Maybe if you think
of words like cars on a motorway, how if they are speeding or
not being driven carefully they can easily lose control and cause
an accident and then another car will hit them and then a truck
and before you know it there is a huge pile-up with everyone
tut-tutting, well the pile-up can be a poem too. Sometimes you'll
even find poems like grandad did with that piece of driftwood
which looked like a woman with her legs crossed and if you're
lucky no one else has pinched it so you can pick it up off the

ground and put your name on it and the ladies at church will wonder why on earth you have that in the garden. It can even be like when you're laying cobblestones and every word fits neatly into the next so that sometimes there's a pattern if you stand back far enough, or if you're laying bricks, how you have to knock words in half to fit them into the end of sentences so the next layer has something to build onto and all you do all day is look at bricks and when you put your head up there's a whole wall or a house with windows and corners that you're surprised is there and while we're talking about bricks sometimes you can put words together because of the way they look, brown bricks or red bricks or rough bricks or smooth bricks so people can enjoy them like when we go for a drive through Howick and mum likes the colour of the houses, and sometimes you can put them together because they hold things up and are strong and have a use even if no one sees them, bricks don't really have a sound unless you drop them on your foot and then they make a sound that sounds like bloody hell, and sometimes when you read a poem you feel like it doesn't even belong on the paper or that you've seen it before somewhere or should have seen it before or always meant to make one just like it and so if you turn around it will move behind your back, sometimes it's like a child who makes you drop him off up the road from school so his mates won't see you kiss him goodbye and then shoos you away as if to say 'don't make such a fuss' but the way I like to think of poems the most is that they are like a lolly for your mind or an argument with a clever person who is always trying to put words into your mouth and then spends the rest of the day trying to take them back out again.

The Page Three Girl

1. In the beginning was the word. And the word was with God. And the word was God. Then the word became flesh and dwelt among us.

2. At first the word was a German housewife. Simon the mechanic said she reminded him of *A History of the World in Eight Volumes*. He left her sitting on the shelf.

3. Next the word was a nun. Barry the Gib-stopper was as interested in her as he was in reading the Bible.

4. Then the word became a solo mother with three kids who had just been left by a troubled husband found spying on his boss for a foreign government until he ran away with her. Dave the cabinet-maker said she was as complicated as a novel.

5. Next the word was an actress. Dick the electrician fell asleep when he found out there were no car chases in her script.

6. Later the word was a barmaid. Vic the bricklayer quickly made off with her as though she was a Sunday newspaper tucked firmly underneath his arm.

7. At last the word appeared as naked as a poem. Mum found her hiding underneath my mattress. I said heavens. She said hell. You said Jesus, Mary and Joseph. And all Jeff the plumber ever said was God!

The shape of words

A is the shape of a tin roof on an old church.

B is the bottom of a fat man.

C is a crab scuttling along the beach.

X is the shape of butterfly wings.

hallelujah is the shape of righteous people sitting closely together in church.

abracadabra is a caterpillar crawling along its leaf.

bubbling is the shape of water boiling.

higgledypiggledy is a collection of flowers dripping out of their windowboxes.

daddy-long-legs are small carts unloading suitcases from the back of an aeroplane.

orange is the shape of a round fruit hanging from a tree, a young woman reaching out to pick it, a kitten chasing after its own tail, an old woman weeding her garden, a small boy fishing from a pond, the sun setting over a smooth beach.

smoke is a lazy snake crawling towards the sun, two large clouds billowing, a round mouth coughing, a small bird singing in a tree, the eye of a tired child falling asleep.

love is one leg planted firmly on the ground, a spare washer for a dripping tap, that beautiful bird flying towards me or away, a broken eggshell opened on the floor.

The sound of words

A–B–C–D–E–F–G–H–I–J–K–L–M–N–O–P
Rain falling on a tin roof.

One–Two–Three–Four–Five–Six–Seven–Eight
The feet of marching girls as precise as tape.

She Sells Sea Shells by the Sea Shore
Cars passing cautiously along wet roads at night.

Ka mate Ka mate Ka ora Ka ora
Morepork calling inside a dark forest.

Old MacDonald had a farm E–I–E–I–O
A round ball rolling off the end of the front porch.

Bee–bop–a–loo–baa–a–wop–bam–boom
A can of paint falling down a ladder.

Romeo Romeo Wherefore art thou Romeo
A man revving his motorcycle outside a woman's house.

Etcetera–Etcetera–Etcetera–Etcetera
Crickets warming themselves underneath a drying sun.

**Ourfatherwhoartinheavenhallowedbethynamethy
kingdomcomethywillbedoneonearthasitisinheaven**
A bee trapped uncomfortably inside a closed room.

The meaning of words

1. *Either*

```
T  T  S  A  L  I  T  P  T  I  P  N
H  H  H  N  I  T  O  A  H  N  R  O
E  E  O  D  K  W  F  U  E  G  E  T
C  R  U  D  E  O  O  S  S  O  C  H
H  I  L  O  L  U  R  E  P  F  A  I
I  G  D  W  A  L  G  F  E  B  R  N
N  H  B  N  D  D  E  O  C  A  I  G
E  T  E  I  D  B  T  R  T  L  O  B
S  I  W  N  E  E  W  A  A  A  U  U
E  D  R  A  R  D  H  B  C  N  S  T
H  E  I  R  S  I  E  R  U  C  L  T
A  A  T  O  T  F  N  E  L  I  Y  H
V  W  T  W  H  F  W  A  A  N  O  I
E  O  E     E  I  E  T  R  G  V  N
   R  N     N  C     H  F     E  A
   D  U        U        E     R  I
   S  P        L        E        R
               T        E
                        L
```

2. *Or*

Words are halfbacks.
They don't scrum.
They don't ruck.
They don't maul.
They don't jump.
They don't throw into lineouts.
They don't carry oranges at half-time.
They don't argue with the referee.
They just pass—
Ideas as quick as bullets.

God help you
if you drop them!
Poetry is a game
But so is footy
And we all know how serious that is.

The word as a wrapping

It would help if you think of words as wrappings

That plain brown paper a butcher uses to surround steak

The newsprint announcing your fish and chips

A patterned cloth spread over the kitchen table like butter on a
slice of bread

All circles: such as the letter O, open mouths, diamond rings,
key-rings, keyholes, portholes, plugholes, life-savers, lipstick
stains, washers for taps, the rim of soap left around a bath
when the water is let out

All containers: such as cups and saucers, salad bowls, hot-
water bottles, pot-plant holders, schoolbags, jam-jars, fruit
tins, ashtrays, woven baskets, plastic milk bottles and hollows
in the stumps of trees

All pipes: such as drainpipes, downpipes, sewer pipes, exhaust
pipes, spouting, U-bends, gutters, stormwater drains, inner
tubes, brandy snaps and hydroslides

Eggshells
             Seashells
        Cigarette papers
                       Soap holders
        Cellophane
                              Raincoats
            Fur coats
                    Wrap-around skirts
     Hot air balloons
                Soap bubbles

Sunglasses worn by a particular friend you cannot recognise
without them

Brightly patterned lolly papers picked up by the wind and
bounced against the concrete-coloured pavement of the sky.

The word as a means of communication

Above everything else
the word is an attempt
to end isolation

Fingertips of heroes
clinging defiantly
to ledges

Small boats
sailed fearlessly
on wide oceans

That grass
which grows from
the armpits of concrete

Those temporary footsteps
at regular intervals
of Captain Scott
disappearing in the snow.

The word as a memory

Not everyone agrees that blue
is the correct word for a fine sky.

For parents of children who have drowned
in deep water blue is the colour of dying.

For lovers undressed silently by the light
of the moon blue is the colour of desire.

For travellers who wander the edges of
mountains blue is the colour of horizons.

For the lonely left aching by scandalous
lovers blue is the colour of music.

For soldiers who have died in defence
of their flag blue is the colour of glory.

For children raised on a street of brick houses
blue is the colour of rebellion.

For thieves who have been asked to empty
their pockets blue is the colour of policemen.

For women who love men with indigo eyes
blue is the colour of swimming.

For undertakers who apply lipstick to the
mouths of the dead blue is the colour of ice.

For dogs who have been fed from blue plastic
bowls blue is the colour of a full stomach.

The word as a tool

Language is as full of tools as the inside of a hardware store.

Nouns are everything you can make something out of, four-by-twos, six-by-twos, three-by-one-and-a-halves, weatherboards, ceiling battens, PVC, Gib-board, aluminium windows, bricks, doors, tiles, carpet, concrete reinforcing rods and all types of spouting.

Articles are builders' pencils, used for making marks, drawing arrows, stirring tea or placing behind an ear when you're working.

It is no coincidence that **commas** come in the shape of chisels perfect for breaking up that overlong sentence with too many words which no one can stop because one thought leads into another and then into another again until you have forgotten how it all started anyway and now it won't fit into the back of the ute.

Verbs are Estwing hammers, 20-ounce, full metal shaft, comfortable plastic composite handles with a non-slip grip and claw head. Ideal for putting some whack into a sentence. They come in black and blue and have a good feel hung from a leather pouch firm against your thigh.

Rhyme is the ratchet on a socket, two steps forward and one step back. Use it to draw words as tight as wire against their fenceposts.

Ellipses are screwdriver sets—Philips, slotheads, Allen keys in a full range of sizes. They can be used to increase the torque inside a poem.

Rhythm is a tape measure, one of those ones that rolls up into a case, or a ruler that folds out and then folds out again so you can lay it down beside a sentence and mark off the metres.

Conjunctions are all screws (roundheads, countersunk, self-tappers), nails (flatheads, jolts, galvanised and bright), clouts, staples, PVA glue or Polyfilla and whatever else you use to cover up the gaps between words.

Alliteration / Consonance / Assonance are grades of sandpaper—for obtaining that extra-smooth finish. The trick is to make everyone think you haven't used them.

Similes and **Metaphors** are rolled-up sets of plans carried underneath your armpit or in the back seat of the truck that someone else has spilt their coffee on. A place where what you are putting together has already been put together, or if that doesn't make sense, it's what you meant when you always said after taking the nail off your thumb with a blunt hammer that the mongrel bled like a stuck pig.

Tyger Tyger, burning bright,
In the forests of the night:
What immortal hand or eye
Could frame thy fearful symmetry?

—the word as a member of the local community

Poems are small villages occupied by words.

Tyger is, by the sound of it, a local cat,

Immortal a priest dying of cirrhosis.

Fearful is a housewife whose husband ignores her.
She never likes to leave the house.

Symmetry is her partner. His body is sculptured from working out at the gym. He is notoriously unfaithful.

Of and **Or** are sisters. One forms dependent relation-ships. The other can never seem to make up her mind.

What is a schoolteacher
who always has an answer to everything.

Hand props up the local bar.

In is the publican. She is buxom and blonde.

Mr **Burning** is a fireman, a hero during the war.
He drives an ice-cream van on weekends.

Bright is his deputy who is dull.

The is the milkman who always seems
to show up everywhere.

Thy is his father who is retired
but still does the odd delivery.

Frame is a builder. He has played prop
for the local rugby team ever since he was a boy.

Forests is the gardener who knows
the names of trees.

Night is a burglar. He lives in an old house
at the far end of town.

Miss **Could** is a spinster who wonders what might have happened
if she had run away with the butcher's son when she was a girl.

Eye is their policeman watching through his window, round as
the moon in the middle of the night

rearranging pencils against the top of his desk

making sure everyone around him
is serving their sentence.

A set of instructions to be used when reading a poem

1. To begin with lift the poem carefully out of its paper.

2. Balance the poem in the palm of your hand.

3. Don't be afraid of the poem.

4. Run your fingers around the outside of the poem:

    a. Is it rough or smooth?
    b. Is it heavy or light?

5. Throw the poem up into the air. Does it float?

6. Put the poem into your mouth. Either:

    a. Squeeze a small amount onto
        your tongue like toothpaste.

    b. Enter the whole poem
        into your mouth like cake.

7. Remove the first word and the last word from the poem.
    Shake vigorously. Each word should fall out of line.

8. Place the words into your mouth and roll them around.
    Suck. Chew. Gargle. Hide the words in your cheeks. Spit
    them at people.

9. When you are finished put the words back where they
    belong.

10. Whisper the poem quietly to yourself.

11. Yell the poem out loud.

12. Recite the poem in broad daylight / in moonlight / with the lights on / with the lights off / in the bathroom / in the garden / underneath a tree.

13. Recite the poem on fine days / on rainy days / on calm days / on windy days / on an empty stomach / with your mouth full.

14. Put the poem on blocks and lie underneath it. Tinker with the timing. Pack each word in grease. File off the engine numbers. Repaint the poem.

15. Eat breakfast on the poem. Stain the poem with coffee.

16. Stand on the poem.

17. Water the poem.

18. Mix the poem in with the washing.

19. Carry the poem around in your pocket for a week.

20. Now the poem belongs to you.

To a man of few words

Old King, in the end
what I mean to say
is that a poem is just like you.

These obvious criteria:

> two arms, two legs
> a head, one belly
> warm blood, tough sinew
> wet tears, snot
> muscle and eyes.

Those hidden lines:

> unsaid, undone
> unfinished, unwound
> uncomfortable
> unexplained
> unspoken.

All that is not said

The riddle of you

That gap between us.

A place I sometimes come to
at the edge of my skin

like the lookout up on One Tree Hill
to stare across at Rangitoto

wondering how you can be both out
there and inside of me at the same time.

In other words

A poem is a way
of knowing you are alive

As shocking as fish
leaping out of deep water

As sharp as light stabbing
through a row of trees

As bold as opening up
your eyes during prayer

As simple as lying awake
in the middle of the night
listening to the sound
of people snoring

Every minute
of every day
of every life

is a full library

The last word

One day I saw
a bird flying

Without strings

Without wire

Without obvious attachment.

There were no instruments
to measure altitude

No fine pencil-marks made
by engineers when constructing
the elegance of machinery.

It was as though the sky
was not blue and empty
but filled by patterns

One of which was
cleaved like strong wind
by soft paper.

All I have wanted
is to ache for words
as clean as that.

TIM CORBALLIS

Efforts at Burial

Day 1:

The goldfish, which I have named Oliver North and Hugh Grant, are in a fishtank on the table in the kitchen. I have put a picture behind the fishtank and visible through it, of a lake set in native bush, and in the background is Mount C. The effect of this is that the goldfish appear to be swimming *above* the surface of the lake.

The goldfish were a present from my father—the first present he has ever given me which is not a book. At first I tried to read them.

At an Alpine Club meeting men and women in fleece and down jackets listened to a talk on the tendency for climbers to take less and less equipment when climbing a mountain. The speaker had slides of some of the Himalayan peaks, which he had climbed not only without bottled oxygen, but without ropes or ice tools. In fact, he had used *nothing but love*. At the top, he had cried for the loss of that love. He told his audience: if you love it enough to take it, make sure you hate it enough to lose it.

Afterwards, they argued about whether love was enough to climb a mountain safely. Jon was a new face there. He was unusual in his eloquence, and in the careful attention he paid to his clothing.

He said to me, 'Climbers talk about fear, and about love. I don't know if love is enough—perhaps you need the love of fear?'

I said, 'Sorry?'

He said, 'Perhaps you need to love fear, if you climb a mountain.'

I said, 'Well, a lot of people say that sort of thing. I suppose.' Then I said, 'I'm J, by the way.'

'Oh, yes, J. I'm Jon.' He was looking at me. 'Maybe what you need, then, is the fear of love.'

Jon was thin, of medium height. His hair was curly, his face glowed with enthusiasm for the minimalism of the mountains. Jon had climbed Mount A and Mount B, and by the end of the evening he and I had decided to make an attempt on Mount C, easy by comparison, later that winter.

People started to leave. 'I'll call you, then, and we should arrange some time to meet and talk things over,' I said.

He said, 'OK, J. Ciao then.'

I tell all this to the goldfish. And more: I tell them how Jon carried the spectrum around with him, but that in the alpine world the only colours are black and white.

It is my first day in this house, after a long absence. It has been empty for a long time—though it still belongs to the family, it has been almost forgotten. My grandfather built it in his twenties—which coincided with the twenties of this century— and added rooms throughout his life as they were needed. It sits in the middle of a lush, New Zealand landscape.

The house itself, however, is still-life. I am given a pen, and I try to write a painting.

Day 2:

The goldfish seem a little nervous in their new environment. I try to calm them with tales of my childhood visits here.

That guests came around, helped themselves to drinks, which the grandfather was always happy to give, provided he matched them drink for drink. There was an open fire, the guests stayed a little longer, and dinner, which the grandmother had cooked, was held up. The guests were invited to share it. More guests arrived, uninvited like the first. There was only enough dinner for a mouthful of food each. The children asked their grandmother for more. The grandmother said: 'In good time, in good time.'

The next night the situation was the same. Hundreds of friends and neighbours were hidden in a landscape that seemed

only to bear sheep and thistle. The children learned to do
without food. They dug an underground chamber, cooked mud
and rocks there, and managed to survive. The feet of the guests
muddied the paddocks and the grandmother's garden and lawn.
The church was demolished. Only the sheep, the thistles, and
the headstones remained.

And then, of course, there is the reason for coming to this house,
which is to discuss the accident.

The funeral took place within the strong lines and muted
colours of a McCahon, oil on canvas. I recognised a woman,
who met my eye and came to talk with me. It was Jan, my
personal banker. She is a middle-aged woman with a nervous
demeanour. Her eyes are tiny, like the tips of two ballpoint
pens.

Jan said, 'That's a very nice coffin.'

I was not sure what to say. Jan said, 'This will sound terrible.
I mean I know it's a sensitive topic, but I've seen such awful
things.'

I said, '. . . Yes . . .'

Jan said, 'I like to be as involved with my clients as possible.
Up to a point of course.'

I said, 'You were Jon's personal banker?'

She said, 'Oh yes yes. And really, Jon had the best cover
possible. Actually it's quite fortunate that I ran into you here.
I've got to talk to you. I mean, have you got a family yourself,
J?'

'No.'

She said, 'Well, phew! Ha, I mean, that's fine, that's OK,
that's easier. I know it's upsetting to talk about this, but have
you ever thought about, you know, what would happen if . . . A
funeral costs a lot of money. Three thousand dollars, *minimum*.
This would have cost a lot more, nice coffin like that, and all.
And his kids are well set up now. But as I say, he always insisted
on the best cover for everything, health, life, superannuation,
you name it.'

I said, 'Yes . . . ? Then, Jon had children?'

Jan said, 'Yes yes. Now, would your parents or loved ones,

say be able to afford a funeral? And, people get very upset. Oh really, some people really get upset when someone dies. Need counselling and all sorts of things. I've seen some awful stuff, families devastated by grief and so forth, and *not covered*, clients who just said, no thanks. I do my best, but it's their decision. I mean, it's *your* decision. With your income, as a, well you're a beneficiary aren't you? You can still afford basic life cover. You really should have that I think.'

I said, 'Yes. Or, well, my folks are fairly well off . . .'

Jan said, 'Good. Good! Really, I don't like to mention that. It's awful. Really rotten.'

I said, 'No, it's fine. You must understand that this isn't the best time?'

Jan said, 'Death is an economic event. And it makes me *so ashamed*. God. *So* ashamed. I mean I like to do my best for people, but it's all just . . . ah *God*. This is so sad.'

A few tears rolled upwards over her forehead, and fell up into the sky. As they fell, the drops turned to snow, then to cloud.

I said, 'Where are Jon's children? And his partner? That is, if . . .'

Jan smiled, then said, 'I can't tell you that. They're not here. I'm sorry I can't discuss the details of my other clients. I'm sorry, I really am, I mean, sorry. Here, take this—I worked this out for you. Basic life cover for just $3.85 per fortnight. Think about it.'

I said, 'Is there something wrong with Jon's children? He never mentioned them to me.'

She started to move away, making eye contact with a smartly dressed man.

She said, 'You should forget him, J. His account is fully balanced now.'

And she walked away.

The fish are casting looks upward. Towards the top of Mount C, behind them. Towards the lid of the fishtank.

Somewhere up there, an avalanche occurred. I witnessed the death of my friend Jon. Or: I witnessed an avalanche, and Jon disappeared underneath this. The avalanche was in the shape of an hourglass. From the slopes above, I watched myself walk over the moving surface of the avalanche, which bubbled like surf.

I dug holes in the avalanche looking for Jon. But since the avalanche was moving, the holes were also moving and it was difficult to keep track of them. As one hole moved past, I caught a glimpse of Jon's face, glowing with enthusiasm for the minimalism of the mountains. But it moved past too quickly. I kept searching for my friend.

I was right there. The avalanche was silent, for the sound took some time to reach me, like the hammer fall in the distance preceding the sound of its blows. The sound continues to travel, taking the long way around, and it still hasn't reached me.

Day 3:

There is a lean-to out the back where my grandmother made pottery. My grandmother was a cold woman—cold to the touch. The diagnosis was too much contact with earth, pottery and gardening—the warmth had flowed out through her hands, into soil and clay.

This was a present she gave to the children one Christmas: she agreed, straight-faced, to stay home from church for the first time in her life, so that her extended family could unwrap plastic toys, bottles of whisky and wine, clothes (trousers and socks), wooden puzzles, musical instruments, perfumes, candles and candleholders, recordings of Mozart symphonies.

If she said grace before meals it was quickly and quietly. If cancer came and took her away it was quickly and quietly.

I can only imagine my father's upbringing here. I imagine that his mother's gifts were all sacrifices. I imagine that his father's gifts were all demands. I imagine that he learned that gifts are either one or the other. His gifts are all books. What am I to do with the information contained in them?

But now, he has given me a pair of goldfish.

*

Hugh Grant says, 'It seems the more people you want to bury, the less holes you have to dig. This story is all about you. It might seem like it's about other people, but it's about you. No one will read it, for it will not be of interest to anyone else.'

I say, 'But there is history only if you know history. If you don't, there are only places. A house on a farm. A mountain. What else can I do?'

So I keep talking to them.

I walked down the mountain again, down a track past a skifield and out to the carpark. There were people waiting, as though they were waiting at the airport for a friend. I hoped that I might see someone holding a sign with my name on it. And it would be me holding the sign—I would have been waiting for myself, and holding the sign in case I didn't recognise myself.

They were the media. I was not sure how they found out about the accident, as I had been alone—there had been no one to tell about the death of my friend. I asked if the police or Search and Rescue had been contacted, and they said, 'No, we hadn't thought of that.' And some of them rushed off to interview the police and Search and Rescue.

I was interviewed by a woman in a down jacket. Her looks and hairdo were icy like the surroundings.

She said, 'You were on the mountain when the tragedy occurred? How was it up there?'

I said, 'Bad. Bad, not good at all.'

I noticed that the camera was remarkably small, and found it surprising that it would send my image to so many television sets.

She said, 'Has a body been found to your knowledge?'

I said, 'Not to my knowledge, no.'

She said, 'What would you say caused the accident?'

'Snow builds up on lee slopes. Windslab under tension can break and slide easily on an icy layer. It's just one of those things.'

She said, 'You were a friend of the victim?'

I said, 'Yes I was.'

She said, 'Would you say he was qualified to be where he was?'

I said, 'He had climbed Mts A and B, and he knew what he was doing.'

She said, 'But did he have *formal* qualifications or training?'

I said, 'I don't know, he had climbed a lot.'

She said, 'Tell us a little bit about him.'

I paused.

I said, 'He had climbed Mounts A and B. His face glowed with enthusiasm for the minimalism of the mountains.'

After the interview, I wondered who would watch it. Then I realised that I had my balaclava and hood on, and would probably be unrecognisable.

Day 4:

Oliver North says, 'Since we seem to have some sort of role in all of this, we'd like to ask a few questions. Firstly, we would like Jon's full name, age, height, weight, occupation. And how long did you know him?'

I say, 'I don't know any of that. He was Jon, and I have his phone number on a piece of paper. I knew him for a few months. That's all.'

Hugh Grant says, 'Family? Any other connections?'

I say, 'No one at the club seemed to know him but me. I talked to a man at his old phone number.'

I said, 'Hi, this is Jon's old number?'

The man said, 'Yes. What is it?'

I said, 'My name's J.'

The man said, 'Who are you with?'

I said, 'What?'

He said, 'Who are you? Newspaper, TV . . . How did you get this number?'

I said, '. . . I was with him, when he died.'

He said, 'Why are you calling?'

I said, 'I don't know. No, I do know!'

He said, 'You must understand that this isn't the best time?'

I said, 'I would like, maybe, to talk with his children?'

He laughed, 'Then this is *certainly* the wrong number! . . . You're the one who took him away climbing?'

I said, 'We went together. We both went.'

He said, 'Jon was terrified of climbing.'

I said, 'No. He had climbed Mount A, Mount B!'

He said, 'Yes! I was there. He had been going on at me to take him up Mt C too . . .'

I said, 'You climbed with Jon.'

He said, 'We needed next to nothing to climb those mountains. Look sorry I don't want to talk about this.'

I said, 'Jon was my friend! I want to know something about him!'

He laughed. Then coughed, or wheezed. 'Hang on, I'll just get someone else. Ciao.'

I could hear him move away from the phone, then say, 'Someone called J on the line. Can you talk to him?'

This time it was a woman's voice, 'Hi J. It's Jan.'

I said, 'Jan? Personal banker?'

Jan said, 'Yes.'

I said, 'What are you . . . ?'

Jan said, 'David says it's comforting to have me here because I only ask about finances and so on, keep my nose out of things. I guess I'm non-threatening, J. You know, I don't get appreciated like this much. But J, what are all your questions for?'

I said, 'His children?'

She said, 'They won't go near you. They only put up with me for much the same reasons David does. And there is money from Jon's estate. But you've got better things to worry about. You know, they're going to cut your benefit.'

I said, 'What?'

She said, 'Sorry, really.'

Then she hung up.

Hugh Grant says, 'Right. Dead end on the family and friends then. I guess the next question is, what are we doing here?'

I say, 'Um.'

Oliver North says, 'Or, to put it slightly differently, what are *we* doing *here*?'

I say, 'You were a present . . .'

Oliver North says, 'Nice! I like that, a present! I'm glad

we've enriched *your* life. And this *lovely* picture, just to give us an impression of what it would be like to have unlimited space. Goes well with the, well, Impenetrable Glass Walls, don't you think?'

Hugh Grant says, 'Um, I think the point here is that it's all very well for you to lock yourself away and all that . . .'

Oliver North says, '. . . and indulge in a good bit of grief . . .'

Hugh Grant says, '. . . but it actually doesn't really concern *us*. Look sorry, we really don't want to sound too, um . . .' He pauses.

Oliver North offers, '. . . cold-blooded?'

Hugh Grant nods.

Day 5:

After the removal and subsequent death of my grandfather, this house was forgotten by the family, or lingered in the subconscious like a letter which was never written. Out of sympathy and love for the old couple who were gone, their house and their farm, the locals have banded together to keep the farm running—mending the fences, shearing and dipping the sheep. There is no profit in it. The effort required brings the local community together in a way which it has not seen for years. They regard the farm as a work of art, a collaborative project which has value in its own right.

A neighbouring farmer comes with a bale wrapper. He wraps huge old trunks of macrocarpa and rusting farm machinery in black plastic.

Today, I wake up to find that the fish are gone. The lid of the fishtank has been forcibly removed from within, and lies in pieces on the ground.

I return to bed and lie there on my side. Soon, I think I feel two small shapes brush lightly against my cheek, but I do not open my eyes. Then they are gone.

NIGEL COX

Boys on Islands

New Zealand is an island country, and New Zealanders are islanders; which maybe explains why, as a boy, I was especially fascinated by books about boys living on islands. Certainly I grew up to write a novel about a man who wanted to live within view of an island; who painted pictures of islands; who proposed living on an island as some kind of solution; who maybe wanted to make an island of himself.

The first of these books I remember reading was a children's novel—or maybe it was just a story in the School Journal. Its title has escaped, but the elements of it are still with me: a boy, in this case a Tongan or Samoan boy, has been found wanting by his family and been exiled to a small island as a punishment. There he is frightened of the dark and the loneliness. He drops the knife he has been provided with into a deep dark pond and has to overcome his fear of the alien element to dive and reclaim it; the underwater world is, once entered, strangely comforting, brilliantly exotic. Then, in hunger, and almost by accident, he kills a pig. The pig is not a domesticated one, it is what is always called a 'wild pig', and in these stories it is invariably a pig with tusks, a boar—no puns allowed. The boy kills it, eats it, and, most importantly, cuts off its tusks and wears them, on a necklace woven from grass, round his neck. When his father, or the tribe, I can't recall which, comes to end his exile, there are his trophies bouncing on his chest, announcing his bravery, his independence. His manhood.*

Looking back now there are so many ways a text like that could be investigated. Tusk, for example, could be seen as a metaphor. But that wasn't how I read those stories then.

Of course I read lots of other things too: war comics, *Tarzan* comics, *The Phantom, Mandrake the Magician, Scrooge McDuck*, a series of comics that had *Moby Dick* and other Classics in it. This was New Zealand in the 1950s: there'd been a lot of educational hysteria about how comics destroyed children's ability to read properly and so in those days they were more or less forbidden in our house. But I would go round to other boys' places and sit in their bedrooms for hours, reading every comic they had. They thought I was a boring visitor. Back at home I read books, all kinds: on puppetry, on magic, on skindiving, *Famous Fives, The Moonmintrolls, Tom Sawyer, Animal Farm, Brave New World*, etc. But I was always on the lookout for Boys Stranded On Islands books. One in particular I read over and over again: *The Coral Island*, by R.M. Ballantyne. In this children's novel written in 1858 three boys are shipwrecked in the South Seas. Their names are Ralph, Peterkin and Jack, all names which will reappear here.

From *The Coral Island*:

> But now it occured to us, for the first time, that we had no means of making a fire.
>
> 'Ah, boys, I've got it!' exclaimed Jack, rising and cutting a branch from a neighbouring bush, which he stripped of its leaves. 'I recollect seeing this done once at home. Hand me the bit of whip-cord.' With the cord and branch Jack soon formed a bow. Then he cut a piece, about three inches long, off the end of a dead branch, which he pointed at the two ends. Round this he passed the cord of the bow, and placed one end against his chest, which was protected from its point by a chip of wood; the other point he placed against the bit of tinder, and then began to saw vigorously with the bow, just as a blacksmith does with his drill while boring a hole in a piece of iron. In a few seconds the tinder began to smoke; in less than a minute it caught fire, and in less than quarter of an hour we were drinking our lemonade and eating coconuts round a fire that would have roasted an entire sheep, while the smoke, flames and sparks flew up among the broad leaves of the overhanging palm trees, and cast a warm glow upon our leafy bower.

My friends and I tried this many times but it worked better in the book.

Apart from fire-making, the coral island boys hunt and kill pigs, make pets of the wild cats, go diving and are thrilled by the underwater world, fight sharks, escape pirates, save a mother and baby from cannibals and take part in a bloody battle with heathen natives, all adventures I could imagine myself enjoying.

At this age I was in no sense a serious or thoughtful reader. I just mowed through books, seeking escape. Looking back now, as I start to make the connections that link these books to my first novel, I suspect that what I really liked about the island stories, as opposed to the books set in America or England, was that they made the Wairarapa countryside seem filled with exotic possibility. I could imagine our bush as jungle, our nikau as palm trees. There were wild pigs in our hills and our family often visited Pukerua Bay where I rather timidly went skindiving. For savages, there were the local Maori; it was always Cowboys versus Indians, where it was possible to identify with whichever side you were on. But the sense I had that there were brown-skinned people who were different—it wasn't hard for me to think they were 'savage'—living in New Zealand around me fitted the sense of local excitement that reading these books gave me.

A few years ago I read Bill Pearson's *Rifled Sanctuaries: Some Views of the Pacific Islands in Western Literature*, where I learned that the Scotsman R.M. Ballantyne had never been to the Pacific and that *The Coral Island* is amongst other evils, a 'myth[s] of white supremacy in the form[s] of easy assumption of privilege or of domestication,' which of course it is.

I also read and re-read *Robinson Crusoe*, which Pearson describes as 'a myth of race relations'. My interest at that time was taken up mostly with the physical details of Robinson's survival, and with the sense of the exotic, the free world, close at hand, with no rules, no work, good fishing, swimming, sunbathing and company.

The *Swiss Family Robinson* I didn't like so much, probably, I suspect, because the Robinson parents survive the shipwreck.

I say that this exotic world was close at hand. But it was quite a while before I clearly understood that 'the South Seas' which is where all these stories were set was in fact the Pacific that I lived in.

I was obsessed with *Peter Pan*, whose story mostly takes place on vaguely located islands. Of course, *Peter Pan* is also a love story of sorts; in the primers my first girlfriend had been called Wendy, and for years I called myself Peter in childhood games.

I read *High Wind In Jamaica, The Old Man And The Sea, Tarzan of the Apes*, and found some of those elements I particularly liked in all of them.

Then when I was twelve I was first given (by a friend of my parents) a copy of William Golding's *Lord of the Flies*. At first I thought it was terrific—here were those same names, Ralph and Jack, echoing, and there was to be sunshine, no work or rules, the fascinating and bountiful ocean, and the promise of a pig hunt. I remember thinking, This is just like *The Coral Island*, and other people have thought it too: when in 1983 Golding won the Nobel Prize for Literature he was accused of having plagiarised Ballantyne's book. But the two novels have entirely different intentions; as I progressed with *Lord of the Flies* its story began to be blighted by reality. Pig-hunting took on a new meaning. The scene where Simon hides under the foliage and is talked to by the pig's head of the book's title scared me. My younger cousin was called Simon; I saw him in that part all through the novel, and was worried for him, and for me: what role might I fill in a story like this?

Lord of the Flies might have put me off Boys Stranded On Islands books for a bit; I don't remember reading any more of them, until fifteen years later, in 1974, when my wife and I were waiting on Paddington Station to go off on our honeymoon: I bought a copy of Ernest Hemingway's posthumously published novel *Islands in the Stream*. This, probably Hemingway's worst book, absolutely delighted me. It was set on islands in the Caribbean rather than in the Pacific, but all the familiar pleasures were in place—the seascapes, the underwater explorations, the heroic fishing sequences, the quaint natives, the characterful cats, etc. But I suspect that what I particularly liked was that the boys of my childhood books seemed to have grown up—and still there was no boring work to do. And now there were women around to be fought over, and art to argue about, and alcohol to exceed with. Even a war.

I had at this point already written what I liked to call a novel and was at work on a second. But *Islands in the Stream* sent me scurrying to my notebooks; and when my novel *Waiting for Einstein* was eventually published in 1984, it featured a painter living alone in a house by the sea, not in paid employment but keeping the dignity of work through disciplined sessions at the easel, with a cat to talk to, and a male friend to fight with over a woman, and many other elements straight out of *Islands in the Stream*. Its hero's name was Ralph, the friend was called Peter, and Ralph's alter ego, a man who is perhaps politically islanded, was named Robinson; I didn't use the name Jack, probably because it is my father's name. There's no pig hunting in the novel but many of the pig hunter's concerns were woven into *Waiting for Einstein*'s skindiving scene. The painter chose the house he lived in specifically because it had a view of an island; one of his paintings is called 'I island myself'.

These days *Waiting for Einstein* strikes me as a novel reduced by an innocence that might be called wishful thinking. It's looking for a reader who wishes that we were all still trying to make the dreams of the late 1960s real. It doesn't want to think what fiction is, or has been and might go on to be. It doesn't see the implications of its various mythologies.

I don't particularly want to knock the book; it has its strong points and has thus far sold quite a bit better than my second novel, which I think is more interesting. I introduce *Waiting for Einstein* because what catches my attention about the series of connections I've been attempting to make here is the way I was reluctant to see the New Zealand I was living in. One of the things fiction can offer is a lens to see through, a window, but as a boy I was simply not interested in reading anything written by a New Zealander or set in New Zealand. This lack of interest lasted almost until I had a novel of my own published. It wasn't that I didn't want to be here; what I suspect I wanted was for 'here' to be like the novels I felt I lived inside. It disappointed me when I realised that 'the South Seas' were the Pacific. Yet I always sought to make the escapes that I found in reading be grounded in everyday, in local reality. The insistence on connecting characters by name to members of my family, the sense that *The Coral Island* was fascinating because it might be set in the Wairarapa . . . this wasn't only reading to escape.

It was also a determination to drag the exciting world I was convinced was 'over there' back here. To stay in that 'over there' world until it arrived; to not be in non-fictional here.

Having that first novel published was meant to achieve all that. Surprise, surprise, it didn't. The wishful thinking meant that the novel wasn't really set anywhere that could be lived in, and at the same time it was not much of an escape, either; because it was hell-bent on making that wishful thinking 'real' it didn't have enough sense of itself as a game, as a source of pleasure. 'Well,' as Philip Larkin says, 'useful to get that learnt.'

When I look back over this strand of my reading, I sense that what I've been trying to describe is an innocence. Of course New Zealand has never been an innocent country. But I suspect we've been a country determined not to know that innocence has simply never been possible here.

These days, my reading habits have changed. I haven't re-read any of those old books for years, nor even properly remembered them until I started to work on this piece. I've never yet managed to read *Waiting for Einstein* all the way through. Not that there aren't books about boys alone on islands to read now. Michel Tournier's novel *Friday or The Other Island* is a superb reworking of *Robinson Crusoe*. Ian Wedde's *Symmes Hole* examines the same ocean of material. Albert Wendt's fictions are all set on islands in the Pacific . . .

And, like many other New Zealanders, these days I'm spending more time reading books written here, by choice, for pleasure, for entertainment. I wouldn't say I've exactly found that novel I've looked for, the one that brings the 'over there' world of fiction to the immediate 'here' of everyday New Zealand without a sense of strain, of willed arrival—but maybe that's not what I'm looking for anymore, either . . .

---

* Elizabeth Knox suggested that this book might be *The Boy Who Was Afraid* by Armstrong Sperry, and to my delight she was right. 'There in submarine gloom a boy fought for his life with the most dreaded monster of the deep.' I have left the plot as I remembered it, but in fact there are several discrepancies. The boy in the book exiles himself, and is never comfortable in the underwater world; he has to lose two knives (to the ocean rather than a pond) before he works up the nerve to dive and retrieve one.

Alan Preston

*Alan Preston, founder and owner of Unity Books, was also one
of the founders of Sport. Without his generosity, the magazine
would not exist.*

*Alan died in Wellington on 2 September 2004, and is sadly
missed. Nigel Cox is presently living in Berlin, and when he
realised that he would not be able to attend Alan's funeral, he
wrote this to be read by Jo McColl, with whom he worked in
the shop for a decade. Jo is presently the owner of Unity Books
Auckland.*

I don't have to be there to be sure that there are people from
everywhere, with immensely varied interests, gathered here for
Alan. My point is, this is what Alan was all about. He said
it often: books were how people connected. That is what he
wanted his bookshop to do.

I worked closely with Alan for a decade. What I mean is,
for a particular period. Everybody who knew him or worked
in the bookshop for a spell will have their own view of him,
and of the shop—of course. But only Alan was there all the
way through. The shop expressed what was essential about
Alan in an extraordinary and public way. Which is remarkable,
really, given what a private man he was. But that's how I see his
shop—as the public expression of him—he stood behind every
book in the place.

I originally met him as a customer. Unity was, during the late
1960s, one of the institutions which made me feel that the ideas
I was excited by were shared by others. Shopping there, you
were aware of someone who was around, not watching exactly,
not presiding over, but there—behind all this. Someone you
could talk to—I remember talking to him, even back then—this
was in the shop at 42 Willis Street—I guess I would have been
nineteen. Alan talked to everyone.

He was some talker. Talk was always serious with Alan—he

took everything you said to the highest level. In his own talk
there were phrases that kept coming up and which I will always
associate with him. 'I seem to shed more heat than light on
these occasions' was an Alan favourite. 'What I have to keep
telling myself is . . .'; 'I would be the last to know.' Hear there
the steady base of self-deprecation. But it was the themes of
his conversation that mattered. He was always talking about
the search for the new thing—'that's what quickens me,' he'd
say. And you knew that he meant it. Yes, it was important that
the bookshop be financially successful. But more important was
the way that it carried ideas—'that it's *relevant*,' he would say.
These ideas were important not to somebody else—of course,
to them too—but to him. Some books were so important to
him—'*hugely* important', as he would have put it—for instance,
Paul Fussell's *The Great War And Modern Memory*. He must
have talked to me about that book a hundred times.

That will always be my strongest memory of him—standing
in the aisle at 42 Willis Street, talking—the immensely firm
man wearing what I once called 'the trouser-coloured trousers'.
Alan's Viyella shirts, his polished brown shoes, the soft green
ties—these will go on forever. The glasses the shape of old TV
sets, and in them milky eyes full of what I can only call mild
intensity, if that makes sense. Leaning forward slightly, bending
sharply from the waist when particularly engaged. Passionate—
absolutely shaking with passion at times—listening hard to what
you were saying and stroking his chin thoughtfully, eyes going
up, as he filed away what you'd said. The next day it would
come round again—he'd been thinking . . . In a certain way
he was a baton carrier. Someone would say something to him
and then one of the many people who saw Unity as a place they
should visit once a day would come in, and the baton would be
passed.

Everyone who worked for Alan will know how he gave his staff
the chance to do their all with his shop. This was extraordinary.
That he loved the shop so much, and yet he'd encourage you to
take hold of it and make something new of it. Take it further.
Each of us was given a chance to take the wheel, to offer what
we had, and then move on. It is a very, very hard place to leave

and, like so many others, I never really have—but that I think is
what we owe it to Alan to remember and get right—his legacy is
that spirit where the cast changes but the essence stays the same.
In this way he gave all of us—I guess I am speaking particularly
for myself here, but I imagine everyone shares this view—the
most extraordinary opportunity to experiment, to learn. It was
the making of me, working for Alan Preston.

He was just so supportive of writers. I think it's easy to
forget, now that the place of those who write has become more
or less part of everyday New Zealand life, that it was not always
so. But the Unity files are full of grateful letters from people
like Curnow and Glover (on the label of a gin bottle) and many
others, expressing the sense they have that someone is behind
them, on their side. Obviously, I loved this while I was working
at the shop. Alan created a world where writers and writing
mattered.

Forgive me if I climb onto my high horse for a moment and
try to say something about what his shop has meant to our
culture. We all have our fears and doubts about what the place
of books will be in the future. But something will endure. That
is because people like Alan have made it so. To me he made what
might be called a culture machine—something that generated
meaning. Obviously, everything generates meaning. So now
I have to talk about what might be called 'the good'. I don't
mean in the religious sense, though maybe the ghost of that is
in here. But Alan was always determined to make a bookshop
that promoted what was good in society. He talked about it
constantly. This was what he saw himself as trying to do.

I once asked Alan what it was he wanted, for himself. I had to
drag it out of him. He said, some recognition of this. I continue
to hope that it might be possible.

I did attempt at one time, with Fiona Kidman and Bill
Manhire, to have Alan awarded an honour at New Year. This
was unsuccessful. What I remember from that was the great
difficulty I had in trying to say why what had essentially been
the development and running of a successful retail business was
so culturally important. Phrases like 'he invested in stock rather
than taking profit' seemed not quite adequate. But I do think

that another aspect of what Alan did is to illustrate a model of a capitalist enterprise entirely governed by high ideals and yet capable of financial stability. And this in an industry that routinely complains how it would so like to sell better books, if only it could afford to . . .

He was not always an easy person to understand. Others will I'm sure make a better job of expressing how Alan had his own way of looking at everything, how what was obvious to you could be something quite different for him. What I'm trying to say here may be no more than that he was utterly distinctive, utterly himself. I always sensed in him a passionate longing to keep going—to keep going further. He was very brave, actually. He would tell you about his fears, and he would work on them.

He always described himself as ordinary. I don't think anyone here needs to be convinced that obviously he wasn't. But what he would never admit to was any lyricism. He applauded everything *you* ever put forward in this line, delighted in it. But to me *he* was the one who got right the hardest thing of all. There wasn't a day, working at Unity, that I didn't marvel at the absolute rightness of that name. It's the word I'll always most strongly connect with him—of course, in connection with the shop, which of course will go on forever. But also for the way it expressed, and will always express, the marvelous, generous, humanistic, public-spirited optimism of the man.

ALLEN CURNOW

Investigations at the Public Baths

At nine fifteen a.m.
on the first day of his eighty-
first year. Why don't I

first-person myself?
I was hoping nobody would ask
me that question

yet. The strong smell of
chlorine for one thing, one thing
at a time, please.

For instance, there's always
this file of exercyclists
riding the gallery

over the pool. Bums
on saddles, pommelled crotches.
The feet rotate, the

hands grip, or hang
free, or hold open a book,
demonstrating how

the mind is improved
without progression, if not without
rumbling noises and

lascivious absences.
How free-standing engines enjoy
their moving parts

privately mounted
overhead. There's also the deep
and the shallow end

between which the body
swims and the mind, totally
immersed, counts

and keeps count. I think
sixteen, touch tiles, turn again,
with underwater eyes

follow the black line.
Touch, thinking seventeen, turn
thinking eighteen

and enough. Whatever's
thinkable next or only the peg
where I last hang

my clothes. A destination.
The gallery rumble-trembles, the riders
always up there were

an abstraction blooded, a
frieze the wrong side of the urn.
One grins, catching

me looking, lifts
a tattooed hand. I wave back. So.
You know how it is.

LYNN DAVIDSON

Hunger

Before I met you
we (not you and I)
sat in a Catholic chapel
writing.
I looked around and saw
that at one station
or another, Jesus fell
and saw his mother
and fell again.
Such intimate details,
I thought—
falling over and mothers—
then I felt hungry,
Jesus, I thought,
I'm hungry. I could
eat you up.

But if I ever open my mouth
for the wafer,
it will be in grateful knowledge
that it was made by
IHC clients down at
St Vincent de Paul's.
I will not be reborn
or cleansed, just a bit
happier.
And I'll think, *how savage*
how panoramic
how big
this little life is.

STEPHANIE DE MONTALK

'Blokes can relate to concrete'

In the weeks before he laid the path
to the front door
and put in steps
from the side entrance to the basement

he went to the library and borrowed a manual
sat weekends at a website
and talked at length in his lunch hour
with others
who had made the journey before him.

'Concrete's a male thing,' he said
'we appreciate the details of durable materials
the comparative benefits of embedded metals

and the step-by-step techniques
by which reinforced steel
in the form of rods, bars, or wires
can be stretched and retracted
to predetermined limits

better than you do

blokes can relate to it
we have a sense of it

there's a lot more to concrete
than the bonding
of sand and water
with stone and cement

there's a history of structural form to consider
think of the lighthouse
after oil lamps, torches, and antiquity

I'm talking about isolated rocks
exposure to the sea
strength without mass

a slender tower
a spiral base
and a design which allows a cylinder
to be set in the sea

think of the way it sets
around the tautly drawn wire
in the curves
and reinforced spans
of the world's major bridges

think of the classical example
of the Colosseum
iron clamps in its joints
enclosed on all sides

and the small volume of poems
around 80 AD
which celebrated its construction.
There are correlations,' he murmured

'between concrete
cubism
and the visual construction of verse

you can make a poem
out of concrete items
like iron
or eggshells

in the case of rain
you can let the letters fall in long slanting lines

consider e.e. cummings
famous for his typographical eccentricities

or the visually innovative man
in his workshop

making goddesses for the garden
and gnomes
with knives in their backs
he is doing a similarly tangible thing
I'm told that his aliens
Mexicans
and tyre-marked opossums
are popular

that people have been known
to write the names of their pets
on the necks of the replicas
he makes for them

but perhaps I'm straying nearer to philosophy here—
concrete as distinct from abstract
it's an interesting area—

concrete as real life
concrete as a bird
balanced with precision
on the uppermost branch of a tree

as a boy riding a skateboard

as existential experience

as concrete as rigid paving

this could mean we are talking
vegetation clearing
earthmoving
graders and bulldozers

the size and weight of traffic using the highway

the possibility
of underground streams

a system by which we can carry rainwater
to shallow gutters
at the edge of the shoulder

and the likelihood of erosion
if the steps are cut
into the wrong sort of hillside

in which case
we'll need a building code
for the slope

and a plan of action
should ground water drain
down the back of the section

and the earth start to slip
in the absence
of a retaining wall.

Look at this diagram—
sub-base
compaction
and a layer of concrete—

it raises questions of
shrinkage
temperature control

and warping of the slab
due to moisture variations
between top and bottom

and means that
on a summer's day

hosing of the garden
or lawn
on either side of the pathway

or more particularly
the steps

could lead to
cracking
crumbling

and the undignified sight
of concrete
losing its grip on the hillside.'

*

His path to the front door
was an unqualified success.

Later, he built the steps
to the basement

and every one of them
was unique.

JOHN DOLAN

A Couple of Mongols

A couple of Mongols came by while the power was out
and we sat around talking about pain.
Getting hit, I said, showing off, getting hit
is nothing. Food poisoning or seasickness,
ever have really bad seasickness? That's pain.
See I knew they were landlocked.
Then the Mongols, some long story,
molten silver in the eyes and ears,
I laughed for politeness' sake.
I knew I should've gotten them
clotted mare's milk. Gave them tea,
got huffy when I put the nutrasweet in
without asking. Always acting tough.
Another long story
about the Turks of Kazan,
how they drove these Turks
into a smaller and smaller
circle like a herd of deer, bla bla . . .
blood puddles, ponds, brooks
that the ponies cantered through splashing crimson,
So that Subotai's boots and quiver
were dyed red forever after, etc . . .
You have to let them talk.

PAUL DURCAN

The Adoration of the Kings

after Gossaert

Jesus Christ is my name.
I was born in Belfast city
But I live in New Zealand,
In the city of Invercargill,
In Southland,
South of Dunedin,
Five miles from Bluff,
Last stop
Before the South Pole.

Back in Belfast
I was known in my time.
Won trophies for table tennis.
My father Joe was a fitter
In the Harland and Wolff shipyard,
A meek, hysterical man
Who always wore red,
Who always saw red;
My mother Mary was a charlady
Who always wore blue,
Always saw blue.

We lived in the gate lodge—one room—
'The Pits' it was called—
Of the ruins of a medieval fortress
In Friendly Street
On the banks of the River Lagan
Right in the city centre,
Five minutes' walk from City Hall.

Every Christmas the politicians used to converge on us—
'Everything that crawls must converge.'
They'd haul Mother out into the middle of the ruins
And plonking her down there with her latest pot-bellied babe
(There were seventeen of us)
They'd stage this elaborate, operatic photo call
With them all presenting her with gifts,
'Pressies' they'd croon,
Employing the folksy idiom.
Belfast was a dandy place for the folksy idiom.
They'd arrive dressed up in their folksiest clobber:
All turned out in the latest golfing gear.

And when it wasn't politicians
It was paramilitaries
And when it wasn't paramilitaries
It was press.
Press—I think they were the worst
For palaver. Convoluted bullshit.

Father and Mother were so compliant,
Civil, co-operative with these gaudy chancers,
Especially Mother and yet
Mother was imperturbable.
If your intentions were truly evil
You could not get to her or at her.

Mother was comprehensively insignificant
In the scheme of things in Belfast city.
She had no position on or in anything
Nor did she read newspapers
Except the odd tabloid or watch TV
Except for *Coronation Street*
Or go to poetry readings
Except when her friend Edna'd tell her
They were having Charles Bukowski up at Queens
She'd chuckle: a grand wee man, that Bukowski.
He's like my poor wee Joe, that Bukowski.

In the depths of winter and squalor,
Orgy, murder, universal pretentiousness,
Mother was radiance—a candle in water.
She was placid with a global temper.

These guys—the politicians, the paramilitaries, the press—
They'd go on and on and on and on and on at her
With words. That's what I detested
About them so much—the words—always
The words. Worse than guns words are.
But she'd never react, never.
She'd sit there in contemplation of her body.

Father was a horrible worrier—an armpit of *Angst*.
He'd cast up his eyes to the cameraman, screeching:
'If all these people turned up on your doorstep
When your wife was having a baby, how would you feel?
I need to be taken care of, put away for some time.'
Father knew that to them she was dirt
And that in fact she was dirt
And that she was the mother of God.
That was my father's attitude to women—
He was the sort of man to whom a woman
By definition is the mother of God.

Every Christmas would be the same old pantomime:
The Three Ugly Brothers, each with his hangers-on,
His back slappers, his blurb writers.
One would get down on his knees
Proffering his hands in prayer at Mother's knee
Giving her newborn babe—all navel and curl—
A chalice of coins to commune with.
He'd have a large invisible placard round his neck:
I am a politician, a paramilitary, a pressman
But I am also a man of prayer.

On Mother's right-hand side
There'd be this bonzo in orange suede boots
Who'd have just clapped on a tiara
So in love with himself
That although he'd be holding a gift
It would be to himself he'd be giving it.
He'd spout—never once looking at Mother.
He'd spout poetry—poetry backwards.
He'd awarded himself prizes for his Backwards Poetry.

Numero 3 was always the silent type,
The man of few words, the laconic bod
Wanting to get it over with,
Thinking ahead to the next appointment,
The ex-commis waiter balancing his gift in one hand,
Fancying his dexterity. He wrote poetry sideways.

Mind, we never minded the neighbours having a good gawk.
One who always stood opposite Father
Had the most beautiful face in Belfast city.
Nor the boys at the back of the church
Nor the dog rooting about in the broken tiles
Nor the other bitch having a piddle.
Nor Father's donkey. He always kept an ass—
An ass was his grip on reality.

Up in the sky the ubiquitous helicopters,
Crews dangling from them—women with wings
Chatting away on their walkie-talkies for all to hear:
'Do you think baby ought to go to bed?'
'Do you think we should put a stop to it?'
Father would be groaning away
'Don't cry for me, Enniskillen.'
And he'd say to me:
'Christ, get the hell out of here,
It's a slaughterhouse.
All these politicians, paramilitaries, press.
Butchers the lot of them.'

Like most sons
I did not take my father's advice
Until aged thirty-three
I was executed in a football stadium in the suburbs—
Ravenhill Park.

So now I live in New Zealand.
No matter
What my past life may hold
I will never
Go back to Belfast.
Speaking for myself
As Christ the son of Joe and Mary
Let the Kings adore themselves.
Count me out.

Not only do I never want to see
A White Christmas again,
I never want to see any Christmas again.
My own wife here—Mary also—
Maori girl—we live on the *marae* in Island Bay—
She confides in me:
Christ—Christmas is not for you,
Does not agree with you.
She's right.
Christmas is for politicians, paramilitaries, press.
A fairytale to keep butchers happy,
A fairytale to keep the blood flowing—
And the cabbage, the smackers, the tin, the spondulicks, the
tickle-tickle.

Jesus Christ is my name:
For me Christianity is not on.

FIONA FARRELL

The Inhabited Initial

A   **ϗ**   aleph: an ox

Boustrophedon

She draws the others after
dees worruf gnol eht nwod
dropped in dark trenches.
reh fo enil eht wollof eW
going to the fence and
.toof yvaeh yb toof kcab

B   **ꒀ**   beth: a house

This bivvy shelters all
our gods and treasures.
We huddle reading the
calligraphy of fitful
flame, in our tumbled
dreaming the murmur of
mothers like blood round
the belly and beyond the
open window the grunt and
howl of things we cannot
name.

C   **⌒**   gimel: a camel

It sways toward us sewn in a
secret pocket with strange

seeds and stones. A cup with
a foreign cut carried across
dry land.

D   ◿   daleth: a door

You open it and everything
pours in: new stuff, old
stuff, some for the dump.
You shut it fast but there's
always some small fist
hammering at the other side.

E   ⌒   he: lo!

Behold! The Word is striding
high in new shoes! The mark
of its heel is stone. The mark
of its toe is feather and the
skin of unborn lambs. The Word
spans the air-bridge with
curlicue and flourish. Make
straight the way! Make room!
Make a cake!

F   ⊐   vau: a hook

Meaning hangs like a silk dress,
a heavy coat. There. Behind the
door waiting the structure of
a breathing body to plump and
move.

G   gimel: a camel

Here it comes again from
another direction, dust
fluff at each footfall
and on to dots and
silence . . .

H   heth: an enclosure

Teeth drawn up a white
pallisade and through
the palings wag woof
and oink moo click
suck burp cluck and
yap yap yap yap yap.

I   yod: a hand

Finger or fist. Take that!
Take that! If you would
rule a people, first force
them to eat your words.

J   yod: a hand

On the one hand, chaos.
On the other, order.
And down the middle,
the jagged blast of
knowing.

K   ᗐ   kap: the palm of the hand

And here's the bird-print of
the goddess her creatures owl
and hedgehog bloody as birth
and spiked with sticky jiggy-
jig. She examines the pattern
on a new leaf and says: look,
look. See how the heart cuts
across the other lines.

L   **L**   lamed: a goad

You gotta move. You gotta
figure it all out. You
gotta go with the babble
of brook and creek and
out into the main current
where the flow is thunder
driving us all to the edge
and over. Raus! Raus!

M   ᗰ   mem: water

When a word is launched it
bobs about like a little
red boat under a proper sun
on the blue stripe of now.
Go, little boat. Go.

N   ᑎ   nun: a snake

This letter wriggles through
dry leaves slipping from
skin to skin.

O   **O**   cayin: the eye

I see you. Yes, I see it all
through your round window. The
well, the bubble, the tear. No
pupil. Just your perfect bowl
holding nothing but white water.

P   ▱   pe: the mouth

Her mouth a puckered kiss
breath popping like seed
from a dandelion to settle
on other hillsides, other
mouths soft and damp as
flowers with their roots
down deep.

Q   ⟶   qoph: a monkey

The tricky ones skip and mimic.
No wonder the bootmen are burning
books, clipping the square for
another winter. But on the fence
above their sweaty heads the
letters tease. Catch us, bootman!
Catch us if you can!

R   **9**   res: the head

You've got your head screwed
on backwards, looking over
your shoulder. You keep your
head though, under fire. You

growl. You bare your little
teeth. You say heads I win,
tails I win. You are strong
backwards or forwards.

S 7 shin: teeth

The word bites leaving a
ragged edge and a tiny bubble
of blood. It goes off to sit
in its box, tasting memory.

T + taw: a sign

What signs are these? Crossed
sticks pointing every way. Grass
bent in the direction of travel.
A man whose arms are spread like
a cormorant's wings to dry in
the blast of faith. And down here,
he's 4 her.
In red and black
by the railway track
he sets the old refrain:
I Am
I Love
to the clickety-clack
of every passing train.

U ⅂ vau: a hook

High five.
Up yours.
Come. Go.
Bless. Bash.

Some letters
hang on by
living hand
to mouth.

V   ⊐   vau: a hook

Snagged in the mouth by a sharp
hook we were lifted to flap about
growing legs on the bank. At brain
stem's root the memory that once
we drew a perfect wake across a
still morning when there was no
sound but air comparing notes with
water.

W   ⊐   vau: a hook

Waa waa baby cry.
Waa waa. Maa maa.
Daa daa.

X   ✕   samech: a prop

They hold us straight as a
row of beans. Without them
we'd flop and muddle. Futharc
and ogam on wooden stakes.
Majuscule, uncial and all
those clever bastards who
have spelled out our rattle
and marked the spot where we
were lying buried.

Y ⅂   vau: a hook

Here it is shaking above the
hidden spring. And here it
is split for two wishes. And
here it is wine flowering on
a slender stem. Break the
glass with a dancing foot.
Let the wine run.

Z **I**   zayin: lightning

In a flash all is made plain:
an ordinary tale passed breath
to breath, like living. We perch
claws caught in the skin of a
shining tree. We sing with our
heads tilted to the storm. We
sing the song that is known only
in this valley. We pass it on.

LAURENCE FEARNLEY

Only touch me with your eyes[1]

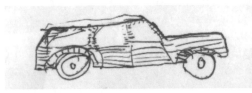

Only touch me with your eyes!

We began driving along a gravel road and through the rear-view mirror I watched the dust roll into a neat ploughed row behind us. It was a large car and there was no point in trying to move the driver's seat forward. It wouldn't budge and your fingers would just wind up touching something awful, something soft and damp, like a paper bag containing half a meat pie, if you groped down below the seat to find the release lever. So, whenever I drove I had to sit on the edge of the seat, my toes extended, ballet pointe, my arms straight, fixed ten to two on the steering wheel. When Jeff drove it was different. He was able to drive like anyone driving a Holden station wagon should: his elbow resting on the edge of the open window, his right hand loosely fingering the steering wheel as his left hand spidered across the shelf above the dashboard searching for a plastic animal, a small length of curved wire, or whatever else it was he wanted to show me. Jeff had a very particular way of driving. He would start at the left of the road, gaze through the windscreen at the view around him until the front wheels of the car were just over the white centre line, at which point he would jerk the car back to the left of the road before letting it drift once more to the right. I would keep my eyes fixed on the road straight ahead, not so much because I was scared we'd have a crash but because Jeff's driving made me carsick. So, I drove. The dust rising behind us, seeping into the car like poison gas in a scary film. When we arrived at where we were going and climbed out of the car there would be two perfectly formed circles on the bench seat, the only dust-free patches in the entire car. On the outside the dust would settle into the corrugations on the roof and bonnet, the same colour as the car itself.

This was his ordinary car. When you first look at it, it just looks like a hunk of rubbish[2]

Jeff's car was never empty. Perhaps, when he tried to sell it at Webb's auction in March 1993 or when he shipped it across to Australia in May of the same year, it might have been less full, but I never saw it empty. I never saw it empty and I never saw it without a tow ball—that's where Te Papa have got it most wrong.

The inside of the car was always dusty and throughout summer would smell of spilt milk and the cardboard pine-tree-shaped car deodorant which had been bought to cover the smell of the milk and had subsequently got lost amongst all the other things which filled the car.

It was impossible to get into the car without looking at your feet and first figuring out how you would arrange yourself around the cans of paint which were always on the floor on the passenger side. One of the last times I saw the car close up, I noticed that someone had knocked over a can of paint, and that the floor of the car was layered with yellow-soaked newspapers. On the concrete outside the car were yellow shoe prints which gradually faded as they walked from the car, across the car park, and up the stairs towards the entrance of the Dowse Art Museum.

The objects in Jeff's car could, I suppose, be divided into two categories: tools and other objects. Three categories if you included all his clothes—a clean set and a stick of deodorant would be stuffed into a bag somewhere in the car—and food. It seemed that he only ever ate food that came served in a thin white paper bag.

Besides the rolls of fencing wire, the things that were most noticeable to anyone travelling in the car were the small plastic animals and rivets. The animals served as models for many of his works. In the glove box, for example, was a small black plastic gorilla which served as the model for the corrugated iron King Kong which looms over an ice-cream shop on Napier's Marine Parade. The rivets covered most of the surfaces of the car— they were always on the seats; their spent tails, short sticks of metal, poked into your legs every time you shifted position. We had rivets in our knife-and-fork drawer in our flat on Talavera Terrace in Kelburn.

Jeff had an exhibition at the Bowen Gallery and arrived late one night from Napier with his trailer loaded with curved sheets of corrugated iron. The iron was stacked high, tied with lengths of yellow rope, ripped shreds of foam rubber placed under the rope at intervals so as to protect it from the sharp edges of the iron. He parked his car where I always parked my car: outside the neighbours' house, in the residents' car park. In the morning, tucked beneath the windscreen wiper, was a lavender-coloured envelope containing a folded sheet of thick lavender writing paper which read: Do not park this car (crossed out) thing here again.

That's the shit, that car[3]

Travelling in Jeff's car was like being on show. In my old car, a Toyota hatchback, I was as good as invisible—no one ever looked at me. In Jeff's car we were always being looked at. Even if you kept your face forward watching the car in front of you, you knew that to your side, the driver of the car next to you would be looking your way. It was even worse when you were towing something, like a large corrugated iron elephant, on the trailer behind you. Everything always took a little bit longer to do because there was always someone hanging around, waiting to ask the question that everyone else asked: How much does it weigh?[4]

We were standing outside a fish'n'chip shop in New Plymouth waiting for our order to be filled. It was a Friday night and a few other people were coming and going. They would go into the shop, place their order, come outside, look at the car, hit it with their fist and then ask Jeff, 'How much does it weigh—with all that iron on it?' Jeff would reply, 'The iron doesn't weigh all that much—about the same as an extra passenger, perhaps two at the most.' The person who had asked the question would nod and then lean back against the wall of the fish'n'chip shop and look some more at the car. The next person would come out of the shop and ask the same question. And then another. And now it wasn't Jeff who was answering the question but the first man who had asked it. It was always like that—except in Havelock North.[5]

I wasn't in the car, and I'm not sure that it happened, but Jeff told me that once he was driving down K'Road and had stopped at a set of traffic lights when the Front Lawn car, a car like his but covered in green astro-turf, pulled up alongside him. That must have made a few people laugh.

I love you now as much as I love a good sheet of rusty iron[6]

Jeff found the sheets of iron for the car at the rubbish dump. They came from the old Criterion Hotel in Napier, a building which had been gutted by fire. Jeff had a way of testing iron which he showed me. He would take the corner of a sheet of iron between his thumb and forefinger and bend it back and forward. If the corner snapped off, the iron was too brittle to use. If the corner didn't bend at all, it was too stiff. The corner of a good sheet of iron would fold back and forward without breaking. As each piece of iron passed the test he would lift it up onto the Holden, where it would lie snugly, its corrugations matching those of the roof of the car.

Jeff used to work in an old milk factory in Taradale in the Hawkes Bay and, if I was around, I would watch him. No matter how many times I saw it, I never tired of watching him cut a sheet of iron. He had a favourite pair of tin snips, yellow-handled with a footprint marked on the metal. He would rest the sheet of iron across his knee and simply cut it as if cutting a length of material with scissors. His hand and forearm seemed massive with strength and it was a beautiful thing to watch.

He wrote to me once about a visit he made to Don Driver's studio in New Plymouth: '. . . The galvanised objects I delivered from my local recycling depot in Napier were carefully untied

(from my trailer) and placed on the footpath from where Don carried them upstairs to his city studio. I managed to carry the last two pieces up and found Don had been arranging them on an aptly coloured greyish paint splattered tarpaulin—I placed my two things, he slightly changed the positioning and that was it—Sculpture finished (5 minutes) Found it really refreshing to see someone working so intuitively and spontaneous. Made me think of the many, many and many hours and a few more I put into individual works . . .'[7]

At night we used to drive the Holden into the studio and roll down the door behind it. When we did that, it always seemed to me to be like the part in Batman when the Batmobile returns to the Batcave. Everything suddenly seemed shadowy and calm and I would watch as, under floodlights, the sparks from Jeff's oxyacetylene torch sprayed off into the dark.

Today I'm about to start the first work for Sydney. CI, drainpipes, guttering etc. (still life wall relief). Studio clean and spacious—letters being typed for BHP and oz road safety people in Canberra—fax to Ray Hughes, trip to collect materials at recycling and letters to you and organisations in Melbourne . . . the car and container will leave for Sydney on the 20th

*May arriving early June. I look forward to our holiday and
venturing onto new ground*[8]

The day of the exhibition opening at the Ray Hughes Gallery
was the only time I saw the Holden in Australia. It was parked
in the entrance-way to the building and it looked out of place.
Jeff had made a new aerial for the car—a length of Number 8
wire bent into the shape of Australia (with Tasmania)—and we
had planned to leave for a three-week holiday straight after the
exhibition opened.

I had been reading the poems of Philip Hodgins and Laurie
Duggan and wanted to get out of Sydney, to see rural Australia
and Gippsland, before my annual leave was used up. The Holden,
though, wasn't roadworthy. It was rusty. It had sharp edges.
The steering wheel and the dashboard were cracked. The vinyl
covering the interior ceiling was ripped . . . and all around me,
on the night of the opening, I could hear people say, 'It's a lot
easier to get a warrant in Queensland. The Sydney authorities
are a pack of bastards . . .'

I never travelled in the Holden again. After the exhibition
opening I hired a white Datsun Sunny with 3650km on the
clock.

Only touch me with your eyes! If you want me to survive,
please just look at me

I was working in the Museum of New Zealand Project Office
in November 1994 so I knew the museum had bought Jeff's
car for its collection. Jeff and I were no longer living together. I
didn't really look at the car, stop and look at it, until a month
ago, during my last visit to Te Papa. For most of the hour I was
by myself, though from time to time a school group or a visitor
would come and stand next to me to look at the Holden. I've
worked in art museums and galleries and so it's been drilled
into me, the thing about not touching art objects unless you're
wearing white cotton gloves. It's just something I can't do—like
folding a page corner in a book or dropping litter. The people
who came and stood next to me had no such inhibitions. They
all touched the car, ran their hands over its corrugated iron
cladding, or knuckle-tapped its roof. I stood and looked at the
car, all the time wishing I could open the door and sit inside
and have a poke around in the glove box or run my fingers
down the back of the seats to see if any rivets were still stuck
in the upholstery. More than that, though, I wanted to run my
hand across the bonnet, to feel the warmth and roughness of the
metal, the texture, like skin on summer-cracked bare feet.

I couldn't touch the car though and I felt sad. Really sad.

Notes

1   Label attached to Jeff Thomson's corrugated iron-clad HQ Holden station
    wagon at Te Papa, Museum of New Zealand.
2   Tour guide. Te Papa. 2 December 1999.
3   Visitor comment. Te Papa. 2 December 1999.
4   I can remember that this was the first question I asked Jeff when I met
    him in 1991.
5   Jeff lived in the Hawkes Bay and spent a lot of time in Havelock North,
    Hastings and Napier. He moved down to Wellington in July 1993 and
    drove a Morris Minor which was partially clad in corrugated iron.
6   Letter from Jeff, December 1992.
7   Letter from Jeff, 22 November 1992.
8   Letter from Jeff, 31 March 1993. Jeff had an exhibition at the Ray Hughes
    Gallery in Sydney in June 1993 and then workshops in Melbourne until
    July.

Drawings by Jeff Thomson

CLIFF FELL

Ophelia

1.   *That moment*

There comes a moment
when you don't know where you end
and the creature in your arms begins.

The long rains.
Two years on from the accident
and the day after my sister left—
that day we knew we could be lovers no more
than sun and moon embrace the cradled earth.

I almost missed it in the market,
the monsoon slapping down,
but turned to see what I'd ignored:
wrapped in a faded, torn kikoy, a wriggle
and her hopeless eyes staring into me:

and all of Africa's anger and sex and wildness
were riding in there.

2.   *The price*

And there she was—
a baboon,
I said—
and not one of the blue baboons
you find upcountry
but a golden baboon from the coast,
a six-week-old Monroe blonde

who was already in my arms,
her little hands fast around the buttons of my shirt.

Unotoka wapi?
(Where d'you get her?)
I asked the Giriama—
one of the untouchable bushmen
of the coast—
                  he'd shot her mother,
drugged her with arrows to feed alive
to his pet python

and I bought her there and then,
for a ten bob cheque
written in pencil
                  which bounced.

3.   *Her name*

Why did I give her such a tragic name?
Perhaps it was the *Hamlet* I'd just done
but more to the point—at only fifteen
I guess I'd guessed what was to come;

and she as motherless as me
that when I stared into her eyes—
and it's this that I want to remember—
that look when you look into an animal

and see your own soul's country
deep in there, beyond the dark horizon.
And she brought me flowers, petals from the garden,
and her moon-coloured cries at night.

4.   *Food*

Whatever I ate, she ate—and from my bowl:
stone-sized chunks of aloneness
and whatever else my father's allowance allowed.
Sometimes an arm of grass, poured on a silver plate
from which her shining black fingers deftly sorted
all the seeds, which she ate
like a queen, buzzing away to herself,
while I lay on the sofa
smoking.

5.   *Tricks*

Tricks? Yes, she could do tricks:
she could outdrink anyone in the New Stanley,
pints of Elephant beer, though once
so drunk she jumped on Jack Block's head—
the owner deep in concentrated talk
trying to sell the place again.
Why him?
He banned us forever then.

And her noise a wonder in my bed at night.

But it wasn't her tricks so much
as just her being there:
at the chai kiosks and foodcarts of River Rd.
We ate African for free
sikuma wiki, posho, mukate maiyai—
for the punters we brought in.

And once, her first time on heat,
I woke in the dark to find her
gently
          sweetly
wanking us off—
both of us together.

6.   *Inner Child*

Stare into her eyes—
the fires and shining greens, the night's bright gems.
Do we reflect each other? Yes, we reflect each other—
but I want to enter that look and live in there forever
to know what the child inside her thinks of me
and this other country, this dream I've brought her to.

And we stared into each other's eyes—
        careless because we didn't care
        fearless because there was nothing to fear
        but the death we both inhabited

laughing as we waited for the final act—
        like I was her Player King
        and she my Player Queen.

7.   *Abuse*

But it wasn't all roses.
Have you ever tried
to house-train a baboon?

Shit everywhere. In our bed
at night, in the kitchen:
the houseboy fled after two days.

The old soliloquies of abuse:
I cursed her, I wished her gone—
away into the prayers and habits of

white silence.
                And was it physical abuse?
Yes, it was physical abuse:
I rubbed her face in it.

I beat her.
I locked her in the toilet

where Africa's tongue accused me,
screaming her wonderful noise.

8.   *A story*

My little put-put, my 50cc Yamaha—
that's how she travelled, riding pillion,
clinging to my waist, slipped inside my shirt.

Langata Rd, 4 a.m.—army roadblock:
spikes and chains, and cavalettis on the road
like a riding school.

The soldiers relax around me, smiling:
Habari aku, bwana? Pleasantries of the black night—
no matter this mzungu on a bike.

Then, her tail twitches and stands up
on the seat behind me—like a rod: *Shaitani!*
Shaitani! Devil! and their guns all cocked at me.

'Hey, whoa . . .' holding to the softness in my voice.
'It's only my baboon'—and as always in Africa
the childlike roar of laughter at ourselves

and friends for life, forever.

9.   *What was to come*

The Ministry of Wildlife was on to me.
My friends were on to me. My sister
was on to me, and the houseboys.

Through it all, Ophelia muttered at nothing.
She pickèd the lice from my hair.
She brought me avocados from high up the tree—

their dark jade glowing in her shiny black palms,
in the creases of her fingers.

10.   *Forever*

What is time to a baboon?

What did it mean to those eyes
that followed me from room to room,
or through the shantytowns
and Arab Quarter alleys
where children play soccer in the dust
and call for her, and follow her,
who followed me.

And even when she wasn't there,
when I locked her in the bathroom,
I could feel her gargoyle eyes on me,
the scrutiny that wildness grants—
to have this second sight with me.

But I don't know what time meant to her,
though if I had to guess
I'd say it meant simply this:
that we were there, together in that moment

and that the passing of each moment
was forever, or is forever
in the present simple tense to her.

11.   *Husband*

I had to do something.
A 'husband' must be found for her.
A born-free solution. After all,
this was Adamson Land.

I took her to a farm in Macharkos—
Eden Hill. For three weeks I climbed
through trees with her,
teaching her to swing through them—
to teach her to survive.

And then I betrayed her twice on paper:
I divorced her with my signature.
I gave up such rights as I was said to have
and read again my traitor's name—
printed in carbon on a BOAC ticket,

bound for England.

12.   *Bees*

Under the flyover, a council flat in Hammersmith,
where the letter came, falling like an autumn leaf,
wrapped in someone's white bandages.

It said that she'd been killed by bees,
stung to death,
trying to rob their honey.

I wept. I didn't want to believe.
I couldn't weep her out of me.
I wept her out of me.

13.   *Baboonery*

Time knows many ways of passing.

A yew tree in the graveyard at Stoke Gabriel—
green smoke of its branches
hangs above the tombs.
Its roots are said to feed in every grave.

Carvings on the church door.
The gargoyle style
                    they call baboonery—
how is it I forget you,
Ophelia,
for all of thirty years?

I look up at the stone faces:
a worn-out Herne the Hunter,
the wild hunt searching for souls—

and hold you as I come into myself,
feeding on that moment

where I don't know where I end

and the baboon in my arms begins.

RHIAN GALLAGHER

First Sailing

I rolled on and off the bunk.
My mother hung our coats on hangers,
everything went sideways.
I stretched my legs up
and clamped my feet to the ceiling.
Tea broke over the cup's lip
—we were out at sea.

Decks below the engines gurgled
in their grease, after that there was a skin
of metal and rivets that kept us from the water.
The water was dark, live, and so deep
that if you fell into it you would fall
and fall passing fish with neon eyes
—it would take days to reach the end.

My mother said 'get into your pyjamas
and brush your teeth' like it was home
—but no land was in view. It was all sea.
The water in my body
swished to and fro like the tea.

So in the morning I was amazed
that we had made it through the night.
I put my face to the porthole
to thank the fish and water for our lives
but a wave, coming sideways,
eyed me with its hollow. This was the sea.
It could swallow the whole ferry if it wanted to.

'Breakfast' my mother was saying, her voice
came from far away, everything balanced on a tray.

DAVID GEARY

Irene and Gaye

They stood in the middle of the road
and put straw hats on their bellies
and the wind just held them there.
I thought it was so cool
and they were so cool.
I wouldn't have minded being
those hats
pressed against their skin
with the wind as an
excuse.
It was down by the old butter factory. I think
in 1906, or something like that,
Rangiwahia won a prize for the best butter
in the World
but all we had now was girls who could keep hats on their
     bellies.
It was summer
and there was a mirage behind them as the road melted and
waved.
They had to explain that to me too.

ANNORA GOLLOP

To Mrs Bold from Little Gollop

I held that silver lizard until I mislaid it
and was covered in grief.

I held that silver lizard until the filigree of its memory
no longer matched the flattening detail of the silver.

I held that silver lizard until the silver lizard tail
bent and broke off and could not be kept
because the lizard became complete without it.

I held it until it lost its tail
I held it until its memory wore thin
I held it until it held within it death

And still I held it,
the gift of my childhood in silver.

JOSH GREENBERG

The Email Drought

They have just moved to a new town.

Aaron works at home—he is an investor and he is excited about the war, which has created an uneasy market. This means that when the market is no longer uneasy he will make some money. With this money he will buy fishing stuff.

Amy is a ballerina, but she is new in town and is looking for other ballerinas to dance with, or to teach. She works at the local café—it is the café where all the farmers go. The farmers at the café argue about clouds—it is a summer drought. Amy comes along with coffee and they drink the coffee and argue faster about clouds.

At eight every night, Amy gets one hour of computer time. This is when Aaron eats dinner. During this hour, Amy checks her email. Now that she has moved away from her friends, she has time to notice that she doesn't get a whole lot of email. Aaron thinks she is a birdwatcher in a forest of absent emails. He stands behind her, eating his macaroni and cheese, and ridicules her empty inbox.

'Jesus babe, you'd think that the server would send you some just to make you feel better,' he says. He does not see that she is crying. She stands and walks past him quickly. She disappears. Aaron shrugs and sits down to check his ThunderRoll stock (bowling balls) when he hears something of glass—a plate, a shooter, a figurine—smashed.

'What was that?' he asks loudly.

The door slams. Aaron shrugs. He gets back to business.

Over the next three days, Amy breaks a chair, a candleholder and a glass-encased photograph of their dog that was hit by a mail truck only a month before they moved. Aaron says nothing. He knows that he can't simply post her an email, as she detests his pity and would probably fling him through the window. He's worried about her breaking their things, because they don't have many things and sometimes he thinks they might run out of things if she doesn't receive an email.

'You don't understand,' she says. 'You get like forty emails a day. I don't get any except from that fucking sick shit,' she says. She is referring to the persistent messages from Rape187, which she immediately deletes. 'This can't be my life. My life is not unanswered. My life is too fragile for this.' She points at the computer. 'Deaf, blind and pissing me off.'

'You're crying over this? Jesus, Amy, there's wine to drink, or we could go for a walk. We could go to the river—it's always talking. Maybe it's talking about you today,' he says.

Amy reaches over, flicks the wooden Pinocchio off the desk, and stomps on it.

'Stop,' he says.

'I can't,' she says.

Amy talks in her sleep.

Aaron stays awake and listens for clues. 'Grandma make that molasses,' she says. 'I like sticky stuff in my toes,' she says. Aaron has always listened to her at night. His favorite poem is by Tennyson. His favorite poem is about the dog that hunts in dreams; it's his favourite poem because Amy dances in dreams and tells him about it. She is a person that sleep doesn't stop and that is why he married her. 'It's evolutionary,' he tells his market pals. 'I chose a mate that could raise my kids and still have energy for me.' This was balderdash, beer talk. And they can't afford kids.

'It's over there, over there by the pear,' Amy says. She smiles, her eyes closed. He used to think she was faking all this. She isn't.

'Come back!' she screams. 'Come back!'

'Thank you,' she says.

'Well it's easy at the supermarket,' she says.

Aaron has a plan. He slips out of bed. He doesn't turn on the light—this house is small and easily learned and is in his body. He uses her voice as a beacon, a lighthouse—a soundhouse, really—he orientates this way. Through the bedroom, negotiating the sofa, he sneaks into the other bedroom—what they call the study. He doesn't shut the door, just tilts it against the lock. As he positions his chair in front of the computer he steps painfully on a bit of Pinocchio. He grabs his foot, curses, but is determined: he awakes the computer. He logs on easily. Then he begins. He decides he'll do three. He chooses Excite and Yahoo and Hotmail. He opens accounts there under her friend's names: Anna Lime, Nicole Jackson, Sherry Thomas. Then he composes, addressed to her, as best he can. He closes his eyes and imagines what they would write. He thinks he is writing better messages than they would.

'Grab that cat!' Amy yells.

Then Aaron is done and he follows his wife's voice back to bed.

She is happy the next day, Sunday, though she doesn't check the email. He doesn't urge her. He thinks she is fragile now and if she were to find out what he'd done, she'd either break herself or break everything else.

She is happy when they go to the river, and he is happy to go to the river even if it is so low it's really more a stream. She will write poetry on the bank and he can fish.

She writes two poems, or one poem in two parts. It is hard to tell. They go like this:

Drought
He said, leave the faucet on, I'll need
It when I'm done
   Cutting
   Rubbing
   Baking
   Eating
Then I'll need it

He said, let's play in
Clouds. Let's play cloud
Angels. Let's play till
We're sweating. Then
I will kick out some kiwis—
We will play in the kiwis

These are the kind of poems she writes. They are the kind of poems she doesn't let him read. They are poems about him.

The next day, Monday, and they always say the Lord's Prayer before breakfast, and always eat the same breakfast (bananas and strawberry and cornflakes and soy milk). Then Aaron goes into the study for work. He thinks today is the day that she will check her email. Today is the day that she will be happy. But there is a problem.

'Babe,' he says. 'I can't get on the Internet.'

'I took care of that,' she calls from the kitchen. She is doing dishes but she stops and comes into the study. 'I took care of it this morning when you were in the shower.'

'What do you mean?'

'I mean, it's been taken care of. I mean, the Internet is gone.' She wipes her hands on her tights.

'Gone?'

'Gone,' she says. She spins, right there, in the study. She is a ballerina and dressed like a ballerina. He stands from the chair, shaking his head, but before he can figure out what to say she grabs his arm and spins him across the study. When he stops spinning, she casually puts her foot on his shoulder without bending her supporting leg.

She smiles. 'All the things we can do,' she says seductively.

'What do you mean, gone?' he asks. He does not remove the foot. He does not smile. He does nothing except reach into his pocket for a cigarette. He lights it and smokes next to her foot.

'This is good for the hamstrings,' she says.

'Gone,' he says. 'Did you check it? Did you check your email?'

'No,' she says. 'What's the point?'

'Gone,' he says. He shakes his head.

'It was bad for you, now it's good for you. Or,' she laughs, 'or, it was you for bad, now it's you for good.' She takes her foot off his shoulder—she has to go.

'Where?' he asks.

'I'm being screened to be a ballerina teacher,' she says.

'Where?'

'I found a place,' she says. 'Guess where I found out how to find it? At the library! I asked someone,' she says. 'Can you believe it? But now I have to go,' she says. She bustles about—it really is a small place—then she is dancing and twirling and leaping and gone.

He stands there, smoking, where she left him. Then he goes to the computer. Connect. Connect. Connect. There is a dial tone, then a car wreck within the computer. 'Jesus,' he says. He calls the server help number. There is a guy there—an engaging and confident guy who assures Aaron that everything is fine with their account. Okay, cheers then. Connect. Connect. Connect. ThunderRoll certainly needs monitoring. And Slickskin was falling and falling at last glance, and Aaron has been poised for the sudden turnaround. It is how he makes money. It is his life. Waiting and waiting and then the pounce! Timing. Connect. Connect. Connect.

'Fuck!' he screams. He throws his coffee mug against the wall.

'Amy, what did you do to the computer?' he asks when she returns.

'I made it,' she says. She spins and leaps. 'She said I was *over* qualified.'

'Yes, babe, but the computer? What did you do to it? What do you mean that it's gone?'

'I played with it,' she says.

'How so?'

'You know, screwed with it.'

'Changed the network settings?'

'No, like screwed with it. With a screwdriver,' she says. She is chewing on her index finger. She is nervous. He walks over and lifts the monitor off and sets it, carefully, beside the console. He lifts up the console.

The back wall is gone. The modem is there and green and hurt. The modem has been stabbed. They don't have much money. They don't have enough money. She giggles behind him.

'Amy,' he says quietly. 'Why did you do this?'

As an answer she puts a foot on his back, right behind the neck. He freezes when she does this. He always freezes, though sometimes he smokes. This time he doesn't. Today he's smoked enough.

'I'm losing money *right now*,' he says to her foot.

'Shhh,' she says. 'There's too much of that. Wednesday, at the café, a man called me a unit. Me, a unit. Not like that, but like this: he called his coffee a unit. He called everything a unit. He's the guy who does our fridges, and he's been doing it for so long everything is a unit. He would call you a unit. I have been dreaming in units,' she says.

'You have been dreaming about pears, Grandma, molasses, cats and supermarkets,' he says.

'Yes, and doing so *in units*,' she says. She takes her foot off but before he can move her other foot is on his back. 'Good. Now . . . listen. I'm thinking about a whole new way of our life,' she says. 'We'll live in this house. We'll change this house to the way we want it. We'll build it ourselves, the way we want it. We'll do it by hand. We'll dig a pool. We'll capture the rainwater. We'll heat bathwater on the stove. The farmers say we have good dirt. We can garden. The phone, of course, will be disconnected. Letters, handwritten, will be sent. Wood cut and gathered. I will teach ballet and write poetry. We have so much free time when we get rid of the things that make us wait.'

'What will I do?' he asks.

She switches feet again.

'Limitless,' she says. 'There are limitless things to do.'

'Anything?'

'Of course,' she says.

'I wouldn't mind fishing all the time,' he says. He laughs.

'Well there you go! What else?'

'I wouldn't mind making a movie about fishing,' he says.

'Good!'

'Well, I guess I could make my own fishing rods and sell them. And I could tie some flies. I could start a fly-shop. Probably write some books about fishing.'

'I could be a fishing guide,' he says. His eyes are closed.

'I could build fishing boats,' he says.

He is laughing. She can feel his laughter go from his brain to his belly to his spine, then up through her foot, through her leg, through her hips, through her abdomen, through her chest, through her throat and up into her brain, where it slowly loads.

'And nets,' he says. 'I could patch waders. And do photographic essays on different rivers. I could do fish studies in the mountains. I've done a little bit of that, remember? Back in the States? And I've been thinking about fishing expos, and then there's casting demonstrations, which is a whole 'nother kettle of fish, isn't it? And then promos and, yeah sure, Amy, I could even be a casting double for the movies, couldn't I?' He laughs and shakes his head. 'Ridiculous.'

She takes off her foot.

He doesn't see she is crying when she leaves the room; if he did, he would go after her. If he saw her crying he might take her out for drinks, or dinner and drinks, or even dinner and a movie and drinks. Later, when they returned, she might be drunk enough to read him her poems, or to dance to her own poetry, laughing at her stumbles. The living room is too small for her to dance in, especially when she is drunk. Then she will fall asleep and he will stay awake and listen to her talk in her sleep and he won't know what she's saying but somehow he will think he knows her better than any human in the world knows any other human in the world.

But he doesn't see her crying. So he sits in the computer chair and in his head tallies up how much a new modem will cost. There just isn't enough money.

The sudden explosion of glass surprises him.

BERNADETTE HALL

Go Easy, Sweetheart

Hydrangea clouds are loosed and floaty
on the black pool. She's making a hard job

of it, the little girl with the wooden spoon
creaming the butter and the sugar. Go easy,

sweetheart. Little bubbles exploding soft
like years later when he licks and licks and little

bomb blasts like pain that must be entered
into. Like delight. Her knuckles whiten,

her elbow is rigid with blessings: lavender shortbread
and honey ice-cream and all manner of berries.

*I can only understand you when you speak with an American
accent.* She's watched it all before—flower,

fruit and fall. Aha, so that's how it's done!
Still wondering how on earth it is to be done.

PETER HALL-JONES

Art Can't Smile

Art can't smile. That's his thing. He's crouched in front of the stereo in his chocolate-brown skivvy, playing with the volume and treble knobs, and 'Third Stone from the Sun' fills the room as if it is big, not loud. He's playing the whole song at 16rpm— playing his old copy, with a specially drilled off-centre hole in the record—and he is as happy as hell. But nobody would know it. In infancy the muscles around the lower part of Art's face never fully formed, and now the tightening around his lips makes it look as though he is doing his level best not to scowl.

He raises his head to look out the window. Nobody on the berm has noticed his added effects. Nor did they notice his treatment of the guitar solo in 'The Sailor's Tale'. Aunty Helen is talking and everybody else is either smiling or laughing. Everybody, that is, except his father. Irv has disappeared from view, along with that saddest of losers—Wayne Robinson.

Yma and Shireen Peato are chatting each other up. Who'd have seen that coming?

He looks across the room at the mirror above the mantelpiece and subtly snubs himself. Then he turns back to the little mixing desk he has rigged to his father's stereo. He adjusts the reverb and contemplates the pile of records he has brought out from his bedroom. What now? Pere Ubu? Nah. Can? Nah. Eugene Chadbourne? Nah. Os Mutantes? Nah. At the heart of his problem, if he can be said to have a problem, is the fact that he doesn't like his taste in music anymore. He can go to other people's houses and look through their CDs quite happily; he will always find something he wants to hear. And most of the time it's something he has at home but never plays. But what does it mean when you get 'Island Girl' stuck in your head for a whole week?

He has been looking much more closely at Country and Western recently, because he saw a busker singing 'The Long

Black Veil' down at the railway station. She had tears streaming
down her face—and then he had too; not because of the lyrics,
but because by some miracle she had got the phrasing exactly
right—maybe even better than Lefty's—and he suddenly
understood the Western part of the name. And the two of them
just stood there crying at each other until the song played out.

He passes wind enormously. Get on with the job. The Fall?
Nah. Robert Wyatt? Nah. Slapp Happy? Nah. John Cale or Mo
Tucker? Nah. Nick Drake? Fuck no! Why the fucking fuck had
he even brought that one out of his fucking bedroom?

'Third Stone from the Sun' finishes. As a filler he flicks over to
the tape deck, which he has cued to play weird old Yma Sumac.
At least his Dad will appreciate this one. Before the track can
begin there's a noise behind him. He spins around with fright.
It is his brother Yma.

Yma is smiling. He looks like shit.

'How are you, bro?'

Art says nothing. Yma knows the rules.

'Ah yes.'

Yma looks around and then picks a dried protea out of a
vase on the mantelpiece. Good one. He holds it to his mouth,
microphone-style, and the interview begins.

These are the rules. In 1968 Art became a rock star when Deep
Purple had a hit with 'Hush'—a song he'd written in the bath
earlier that week. Yma made the mistake of disbelieving him,
and the two of them argued even more than usual. Following
this they refused to talk to each other for a week. After that
Art decided that the only way he would ever accept any form of
communication from his brother was if it were delivered with
all due deference and by way of his rock-star persona.

'Hello, My name is Yma Martin and this is Wankers' World.
We're coming to you live tonight from Waitaki Bay, where we're
speaking with Art Martin (yes, yes, thank you, thank you), a
man whom I am sure needs no further introduction. Welcome
to the show, Art. It's good to have you back.'

Art straightens up and picks his sunglasses off the speaker
beside him. He puts them on and makes a strange face which

somehow pulls them up his nose. Then he runs his fingers
through his hair and says, in an unaffected voice:

'Hey thanks, Yma. Hey. It's really good to be here.'

'Now tell me, Art, how've you been passing your time since
I saw you last?'

'Well, much like kidney stones actually, Yma.'

'Oh, that's very good, Art. Let's just make sure the folks
at home got that one. Time passing like kidney stones! Yes,
yes, thank you, thank you. Okay, let's just take a quick break
while the applause dies away. Perhaps we'll have a word from
our sponsor.' Aside: 'In the meantime, hey Art, how have you
been?'

But Art is not to be fooled. He adjusts the volume on the
stereo for a moment and then looks up at the roof while he
drums his fingers on his knees, waiting for the ads to finish.

'Okay, okay, welcome back. Yes, come on people, please, we
have a show to do and limited time . . . Thank you. Now, tell
me, Art, it's been twenty years since we heard from you last.
Tell me, what have you been up to since then?'

'Well, you know, Yma, not a hell of a lot. I won't lie to you.
I'm on the sickness benefit, and I get $175 a week. Rent in town
is $130 minimum—that's enough for a shitty room in a shared
flat—so I live out here with Dad. But I tell you, it's fine. It's
actually really great. I enjoy margarine carving. In fact here's
a little tale the viewers might enjoy. Just yesterday morning
Dad found my mysteriously ironic homage to Jethro Tull in the
freezer and threw it out. You should have seen his conscience
chewing him up—God, I love it when he thinks he's been a
bastard.'

'That's terrific, Art. Now, look, we get a lot of letters to
Wankers' World asking about your current attachments. Since
your affair with Courtney Love became public property, and
pretty much wrecked your marriage to Cameron Diaz, has there
been anybody special in your life?'

'Hmmm, I think I might pass on that one, Yma.'

'Okay, well what about the future then, in that respect? Any
love interest on the horizon?'

'Well, Yma, if you insist on pursuing this line . . . there's a busker called Fat Duck who hangs out in the Pukeuri Mall. She's not the brightest crayon on the tray, but she's a fine musician after her own lights. I think if I were romantically inclined, well, let's just say I'd be brushing my teeth on a daily basis. But other than that, no, not really.'

'Still single, eh? That's hard to believe. Come on ladies, please, we're trying to conduct an interview here. Excuse me, Miss! I must ask you to return to your seat. Security! Thank you. Sorry about that, Art. And now tell me, what's the meaning of life, Art?'

'Well I'm glad you asked, Yma. You know, when I was twenty-three I took liberty caps and harmaline and spent a long night in bed thinking about stuff like that, and, you know, if you boil the question down and down and down, well, there's not a lot left in the pot. You know what I mean? I tell you, ever since that night I haven't paid too much attention to meaning. And I mean that in a good way.'

'That's deep, Art. And what about friends? I mean, what do you do for a social life?'

'Friends are wankers, actually. Except for old Mrs Duke up the road. I still go up there once a week and do her lawns and fix up little things around the house and shit.'

'Okay, well here's a few quick questions for the bubblegum set. What's your favourite song, Art?'

'Now that would have to be "Taboo" by the Fabulous Jokers. Even though it was a total fluke. Or do you mean that seriously?'

'Best book?'

'*The Lost Steps*, by Alejo Carpentier.'

'Greatest movie?'

'Oh, I think I'd have to go with *Tetsuo, Iron Man*. But ask me again in five minutes.'

'Congratulations, I haven't heard of any of them. You really have climbed a ladder up your arse, haven't you, Art? What I mean by that is, yes, thank you, Art, and now tell me, what's your favourite thing to do these days?'

'I like to go down to the railway station and wave goodbye to people.'

'Star sign?'

'Same as my politics—non-aligned.'

'Oh ho ho. Harmonica?'

'Rod Stewart in "My Boy Lollipop".'

There is a flicker of doubt on Yma's face. He doesn't believe that the harmonica solo on 'My Boy Lollipop' is played by Rod Stewart. Which reminds him, he still owes Art a million billion dollars if half of Led Zeppelin had their recording debut on 'Mrs Brown You've Got a Lovely Daughter'.

'Favourite instrument?'

'Theremin.'

Of course. It is the only musical instrument the house ever had—a souvenir of their father's trip to America in the 1950s. While other kids were learning to play recorder, piano and guitar, Art was mastering B-grade sound effects.

'Virgin?'

That one stops him dead. Art gawps. At the same time, he realises that his expression has given him away.

'Oh no way! You're joking?! Oh shit, Art, I was just kidding.'

'Moving right along.'

'Oh hell, back pedal, back pedal! Just forget I ever asked that, okay?'

'This interview is terminated. This is the kind of sensationalist muck-raking crap that the public has come to expect from you, Yma, and believe me, if this ever goes to air you'll never work in this town again.'

'Shit no. No way! You think I want it known around town that I've got a 45-year-old brother who's a long-haired bald virgin? And he is, isn't he? He bloody is!'

'You're getting in my face, Yma. Security!'

'Your mouth is saying "no no no", but your eyes are saying "yes yes yes".'

'Enough about me, let's talk about you.'

Yma stares into the dark glasses for a long moment, until the squirming has gone from his brother's manner, and then brings the protea up to his lips again.

'I heard from Mum.'

'What?'

Yma is shaking his head. He shouldn't have said that. He should NOT have said that. He should have had a long sleep first. He should have waited at least a week before he said anything about that.

'No, no, I was just kidding. I just said that to change the subject, so I could change it back again: when did you first discover you were a virgin? Come on people, please, show a little respect for our guest.'

The brothers look at each other in silence. Then the tape deck too falls silent.

When he finally realises that the music has stopped Art snaps his fingers loudly and repeatedly. He goes over to the jerry-built shelves and fishes about until he finds his prized French pressing of 'Memories'. Volume; volume. A volume of sound. Buying music by the volume. Playing with the volume. By the time the track begins he has regained his composure, and is able to speak. Yma does not hear, so he shouts.

'So what did she have to say?'

Yma takes a deep breath and shouts back. 'Can you turn that down a bit?'

'Don't be stupid.'

They can't bear to look at each other.

'She rang the day before I got out. She said sorry. She was crying her eyes out. Then she said: "Your father should have known." She said a whole lot of things—she was all over the place, and I was too surprised to take any of it in. Before I could get any real sense out of what she was saying, some guy picked up another line and started talking over her voice. I was trying to ask her where the fuck she was and then this guy started singing "It's a Small World After All".'

'No way. Then what?'

'Then I hung up.'

'Pardon?'

Yma shouts louder. 'I hung up. I just freaked out. No, no, that's right. Something else happened first. She asked the guy to get off the phone but he wouldn't. Then there was the sound of a door slamming, like she'd gone off to hunt him down. And it was just him and me on the phone, and he said: "Oh dear, she's going to waste a lot of time if she searches for me in the house." Then another phone got picked up, and Mum said: "Whatever you do, Yma, don't you listen to a word this man tells you. He is not himself." Then she put the phone down and I heard another door slam. The guy was just laughing at her.'

'So what did you say?'

'I didn't say anything. It's scary enough being set loose after three years in prison—I couldn't deal with this fucking insanity in my ear as well. I was trying to shout for her to call again later, but the guy started singing again; I don't even know if she was still there.'

'Shit!'

'I know.'

They stand there in silence, or, rather, in volume. Then Art crosses the room and slumps down deep into the old couch. He can't think. This just happens to be the worst song he could have chosen to play at this particular moment. It is a joke he chooses not to share with his studio audience.

Yma comes and stands beside him, and together they feel like crap. It is all over. Their mother is alive. She always has been.

Finally the music stops.

'We were never any good.'

Art says nothing. Then Yma brings the protea back up to his lips.

'Good evening folks. We're back in Waitaki Bay now, where Art Martin is looking kind of sick and weird. This is the end of your theory about Mum and the extra-terrestrial breeding programme, isn't it, Art? Hey?'

Art might have smiled if he could have, but either way he doesn't. He looks out the window. Bloody hell. She is alive and she hadn't even bothered to contact them, not once, in all that time. He almost preferred his sneaking doubts that their father had killed her.

'Are you all right?'

He turns the record over. Whichever of them it is who speaks, the other one does not answer. Art turns the volume down and still neither of them speaks. And then the air keeps filling with the sound of strange old Robert Wyatt yodelling into his preserving jar.

'Hey Art, do you remember what mum used to say whenever some kid in the neighbourhood did something wrong? She'd say: "Personally, I blame the parents".'

He doesn't reply. He takes off the dark glasses and rubs his eyes hard, until the colours come in flashes. He was fifteen when their mother disappeared. That was two thirds of his life ago.

'Do you remember the fairybread policemen?'

One year the family had gone on a holiday around the South Island. Honey had found a cookie cutter in a motorcamp kitchen. It was the shape of an English bobby, bent at the knees with an enormous truncheon protruding from behind his back. She brought it back home, totally embarrassed by her small act of theft, and for years afterwards, whenever there was a birthday or Christmas, or even just a good school report, she would churn out dozens of little bread figures sprinkled with hundreds and thousands.

'Good name for a band. The Fairybread Policemen,' says Art.

'Sure.'

They look at each other. Art wants to swear, but Yma's face puts him off. His eyes are the colour of morning sky on a crap day. Eyes like that on anybody else would signify an addiction to narcotics, but not on Yma. Even when he had been a junkie, Yma hadn't enjoyed pleasure.

'Tell me, Art, do they still call you Spacejunk?'

'They don't exist.'

He used to feel like this in the fifth form when everybody made his life worse and he couldn't see an end to it.

'I wish I didn't remember so much. Not that I do. Either I've forgotten all the good stuff or there never was any.'

'What stuff?'

'You know.'

'Yeah.'

'Do you remember old Werther?'

'The goldfish?'

'You remember what he looked like, eh? He was one of those see-through ones, where you can see the blood pumping around inside. When I was a kid I put his bowl in the freezer, just to see what would happen. I went back five minutes later to check but nothing much was going on—he was still just swimming around—so I left him a few minutes more, then checked again, then a few minutes more, then checked again. I must have gone back so many times that the freezer couldn't get properly cold, and then Mum came in and started making tea, so I had to go out to the lounge.

'All through tea nobody noticed that the bowl was gone. Then you and I got into a fight over something and I gave you a biff and got sent to bed. I woke up in the middle of the night and sneaked down to the kitchen and lifted the lid. It was awesome. These great clouds of cold air came out, and there in the middle of it all was old Werther. He wasn't see-through anymore, he had turned to bronze. He was stuck in the centre of this huge crystal, and all these cracks were radiating outwards from him to the edge. Man, he was heavy metal. He was totally beautiful.'

The record has finished and Art is almost whispering.

'Where are you going with this?'

'I put him back on the mantelpiece and went back to bed. And in the morning—it was a Saturday—there was Werther again, see-through again, swimming around as if nothing had happened.'

'Bullshit!'

'No, it's true. And you know what? I just worked it out. Mum must have gone out and got another one first thing in the morning. How simple is that? How come I never worked that out before?'

Art is shaking his head.

'Oh man—how much stuff don't we know? All the good stuff. All the good stuff.'

Yma smiles for both of them, and then brings the protea back to his lips.

'Ah, well, thanks for being with us tonight, Art. And thanks for joining us, people. You've been great. We'll be back tomorrow night, and we'll be keeping you up-to-date as more on this story comes to hand. Ladies and gentlemen, Art Martin. Give him a big hand.'

Art leans over towards the microphone and adds: 'We were never any good.'

What now? Yma puts the protea back in the vase. In the morning he will talk to his father, and together the three of them will decide whether or not to track her down. It would not be hard. Look how quickly the police had found him, once they had linked his name to the stolen credit cards. Perhaps she even wanted to be found.

Art goes back to his records. Yma watches as he starts sifting through the piles. There is no way of reading his mood. After a moment Yma goes back outside and sits on the front doorstep beside his father and Wayne Robinson. His mouth opens as his eyes close; it may not be sleep but it as close as his body can come.

Art closes the lounge door behind him.

Plastic People of the Universe? Nah. Carla Bley? Nah. Chambers Brothers? Nah. Shaggs? Nah. Bongo Joe? Thirteenth Floor Elevators? Stina Nordenstam? Henry Cow? Who ARE these people?!

Just as he is about to make do with The Count Five's first album he hears excited voices from out on the berm.

'Play one we all know!'

'Ginga chikk! Ginga chikk!!'

'. . . not Guy Lombardo!'

Is this some kind of popular uprising? He goes over to the window. They all have their backs turned on the house. There she is. People gather around Fat Duck as she settles back into the boll of the macrocarpa. In a flash she has tuned her guitar to an open chord and is taking a huge draught from the glass Aunty Helen has handed her. He watches as she drains it and grimaces comically. It's one of his father's martinis. Earlier that morning Irv asked Art to go onto the Internet and find the recipe . . . vermouth swilled around the rim of the glass then discarded; glass chilled then filled with vodka shaken over cracked ice . . . but at the last minute they had found that the olives at the back of the fridge were mouldy. Art suggested they substitute pickled onions. His father hadn't thought he was joking. And so it was.

A moment later Fat Duck is using the empty glass as a slide
on the neck of the guitar. She is a pop sensation. Perhaps the
small group on the berm doesn't see this as clearly as Art does.
They watch in awe, and acknowledge that her playing is better
than anything their imaginations could have come up with, but
Art just laughs out loud. He can do nothing until she finishes.
She is hunched over the guitar like some kind of prehistoric
predator, smiling and frowning at the same time, and making
little grimaces whenever she needs to affirm the rhythm. Old
Mrs Rose and Aunty Helen begin to clap. Then Shireen Peato
starts to whistle. Her whistle is a phenomenon in its own right—
the whistle of an elderly tradesman brought up on skiffle.

The blood drains from Art's face and his ears flatten back
against his skull. It is too late to get a tape and capture the
moment. And besides, it would be the wrong thing to do. It
would be just as wrong to go out to the lawn and stand there
watching. It would be wrong to put a flower in her guitar case.
It would be wrong to ask if she has an e-mail address. It would
be wrong to wait until she has finished and then play something
(anything) by Sam Cooke. It would be wrong to think that his
mother was still alive. It would be wrong to comb his hair. There
is, in fact, only one thing he can do.

A few minutes later Fat Duck is finishing her second martini
and wondering which of their requests she will play next. It is
not really a party, more like a family do, but the atmosphere is
nice enough. Then she hears a strange whimpering sound. At
first she assumes it is a ringing in her ear. She tunes her guitar
again—nothing fancy this time—and slashes at the six open
strings. The lost chord: 'A Hard Day's Night'. But she is only a
few lines into the song when the noise grows much louder; much
too loud to ignore. She stops playing.

'Unreal.'

'What is it?'

It is Aunty Helen who asks. Fat Duck knows already. There
is no mistaking that eerie wail. It is the sound of an approaching
alien space ship; the sound that underwrote a hundred low-
budget movies. Several of the group peer self-consciously up

into the evening sky, but its cauliflower folds reveal nothing. Fat Duck can hear her own breathing—deep and measured. She feels somebody shift beside her. At long last Shireen Peato breaks the silence.

'It's bloody him!'

It is. It is Art. He is standing in the lounge window behind an old wooden cabinet. A long thin rod extends from the top, and a long tubular loop comes out from the right. His hands are fluttering around these two protrusions as if they were aggressive snakes he is hoping to seize unharmed. The rest of his body is totally motionless. The flying saucer noise gives way to something that is clearly musical.

'Fuck me,' whispers Fat Duck. 'It's a theremin!'

Art is looking straight out at them now, but the light outside is fairly dim and all he can see is his own image reflected in the window. His eyes are focused somewhere far beyond this. It is the look of a juggler, struggling to expand his peripheral vision. At the limits of what he can see, both hands dance into and around the magnetic field, never quite touching the instrument.

The performance becomes more melodic, and at the same time sweeter, sadder, and strangely sarcastic. It might have been a number of things. It might have been a peasant's flute melody, played in the days before there was a consensus on scales; or it might have been the opening theme of some 1950s cult induction video; or perhaps a skit from some student revue, parodying the mawkishness of the violin.

Fat Duck is awestruck.

She takes up her guitar and, with her bottom jaw jutting forward and her brow knit ferociously, advances towards the window. Art does not see her approach, but he hears her guitar, and his face brightens. He shakes his arms and stretches his back, and the theremin dives wildly off-key for a moment. He resumes the playing position; in an instant his body is lifeless again, and his gaze has come unfixed. Even this emptying of facial expression alters the pitch.

'Don't encourage him,' hisses somebody.

But it is too late. Fat Duck is going into the house.

JOSEF HANZLIK

Mirror Poem

You must read this poem both of you before a mirror
so you may observe your eyes
and be convinced
that they are still alike
and still tremble
in the conch tones of anxiety and tenderness
read the word eyes
and read your own eyes above the white page
like opening flowers
like a pool in which flowers drown
search them for
the last shade of defenceless pigeon-grey
the last fragment of azure
the last flicker of emerald lightning
read your eyes
and long may you be happy
love each other
for it's not too late
it's never late for two people
who read a poem together

Translated by Jarmila and Ian Milner

DINAH HAWKEN

from **The Harbour Poems**

The harbour is hallucinating. It is rising
above itself, halfway up the great
blue hills. Every leaf of the kohuhu
is shining. Cicadas, this must be the day
of all days, the one around which
all the others are bound to gather.

The blue agapanthus, the yellow fennel, the white
butterfly, the blue harbour, the golden grass,
the white verandah post, the blue hills, the yellow
leaves, the white clouds, the blue
book, the yellow envelope, the white paper.
Here is the green verb, releasing everything.

Imagine behind these lines dozens and dozens
of tiny seed-heads whispering. They are a field
of mauve flowers. What they say is inexplicable
to us because they speak another language, not this one
written from left to right across them, made up of
distinct and very subtle, ready-to-burgeon sounds.

We need words to take us towards what words
reveal. But if words are ripped from their roots,
lose truth or become unloveable, how can we take their lift
      toward
what they could gracefully offer. Take fuck,
for example. Take intercourse. Take Him,
the all-powerful, single-minded, single-sexed god.

Having broken the argument down and down
we come to a place in the text—a clearing—
where a man and a woman have unexpectedly met.
We have been led to believe, remember, that one
will take advantage of the other, as we have been led
to believe that there is only one God.

How odd that there is no name for the place
above the poet's lovely upper lip
where fine stubble grows. He is wondering,
as his fingertips flicker across it, and as he
deftly clenches his broad brow, what else he can
say to his kind father and his kind uncles.

The plumbers have come. They're ripping iron off the roof.
They're tramping over her head with hammers.
Another hammer is sounding out in the valley,
striking a different material, a different note.
Inside she is living the oldest side of love, wiping soft
shit from the soft cracks of his little bum.

To examine her right breast with radiation
they are clamping it under pressure in a vice.
She wonders how on earth she let this happen.
And she let a stranger pierce her breast with a needle.
It's time to let herself sound out the longing,
and the knowledge in her soul of another way.

The path she's on is deserted. So is yours.
So are all the others which is wonderful.
To meet you'll have to wander off into the dense
bush where vines hang and soft ferns and mosses
cover the uneven ground. You won't know whose territory
you're in—if the wild-life's at home, or at large, there.

She's the fissure, the source where no-one has been,
the secret to be discovered. She may be too generous
for you, and too ruthless. Too fruitful, too fierce,
too gentle, too precise, too sensual, too naive. Of course
she hasn't let you in. She can't. There's a collage of passwords
to be found and learned and loved and spoken.

She is in an empty room. A curved bay window
fills a whole wall and each blind is drawn.
She has no clothes on her body. You are naked too.
Being sensual and strong and straightforward, you can
kiss her left breast, and then the rest
of her body while she—irrepressible—is exploring yours.

Turned away from the lecture on sexual economics
she goes down into the sexual garden, under its dark spread
and into its detail: ecstatically branching magnolia, tuberous
roots thrusting up huge leaves. Fuck the tulips in their damned
obedient rows. Stop. They're finally opening their throats!
They have dark purple stars! They have stigma! They have
    style!

DEBBIE HILL

Acrid

Over the border from Côte d'Ivoire into Ghana the bus stopped at a fruit market smelling richly of open sewers. Five big market women with twists of fabric on their heads stood around Laura. She was small, fair-haired and flaccid-armed.

'What you looking for?' the pineapple stall-holder asked Laura.

'Just looking.'

'So don't come here. We need money so if you window shopping go to the store.'

'I'm not allowed to look?' said Laura.

'No,' she said. 'Go away.'

The women waited.

'Well, I don't care what you think. I'm going to look.'

'Okay, carry on,' she said.

'Okay, give me one pineapple,' said Laura.

A man with a collarless white satin jacket laughed behind her. The market women looked at him admiringly.

'I am Innocent,' he said, offering Laura a pink palm.

He was wide-eyed with sharp cheek bones. Laura had seen him watching her when she was sitting on the back seat of the bus, soporific, between the bare, plump arms of two Ghanaian women.

Back on the bus they sat together, eating pineapple. The bus was airless and smelt of dead crab and escargot bought on the roadside in Cote d'Ivoire, mixed with the acrid odour of Innocent's deodorant on white satin.

Innocent told Laura he had come back to visit his family in Ghana after living in Paris for some years. At first he had slept in parks in Paris, then learnt French and was now getting regular acting work.

'And what brings you to Ghana, Laura?'

'Just looking,' she said, picking strands of pineapple from her teeth.

Innocent helped her find a taxi in the heat and red dust of Accra.

'Your hair is very fine, Laura, take care,' he said.

'You go fit be my wife, my fren, my sista?' the taxi driver asked.

'No, I don't want to be your wife, your fren, your sista. I just want go hotel,' said Laura.

He laughed out the open window, turned around and shook her hand, clicking her finger.

The hotel was on the sea front in the city centre and had once been fairly grand. It had a large empty swimming pool with deep cracks. The diving board was still there but the stairs leading to it had gone. The receptionist wore a black bouffant wig. One hand supported her cheek while she wrote Laura's name in a ledger.

'Where is my Exmas box?' she drawled.

'Where is your what?'

She leaned over and looked Laura in the eyes.

'Dash me some Christmas money.'

The roar and smell of the sea draped the bare white walls and louvre windows of her room.

In the morning Laura went down to the dirty beach in front of the hotel. She watched fishermen walking along the shore intrigued by a white woman with a taut brown body in a g-string bikini, doing scissor exercises. Laura had seen her the day before in the hotel restaurant, with a man who looked Lebanese, eating chicken and rice with a cigarette and coke. She had looked miserable.

Laura put her towel next to hers on the beach, keeping her T-shirt on and looking at her own white thighs spreading across the towel.

The woman said she was Adriana, from Italy, and had come back to find her boyfriend, a black American she had lived with in Accra. She couldn't stop thinking about him.

'He was fantastic in bed but what was I to do all day? I cook something then he goes out again. I was screaming with the boredom and then he kicked me out. I have to find him.'

Laura asked her about the Lebanese man.

'He says he will help me find him. He takes me here and there and we have a bit of sex.' She tutted. 'Promise me you won't tell anyone what I just told you.'

She took off her bikini top and lay on her stomach.

'Now I'm so tired. I like you Laura. You and me we should go out with two young black men and have some fun.'

Later Adriana went to get some barbecued chicken from a beach stall. Laura saw her talking to two Indian men and pointing at her.

'They're coming for us tonight. Come. Let's go, we can have some fun, they are born in Ghana, they'll take us around, clubs, dancing. You can have either one, I don't mind, for you only Laura.'

Laura liked the idea of being taken around by locals.

'Okay Adriana, only for you,' she said and cracked a molar on the chicken bone. 'I've broken my tooth.'

'Poor Laura.'

They met for dinner in the open-air restaurant before their dates arrived. Adriana wore a short pink skirt and a white crocheted top, her white bra and brown skin showing through the holes. Her long brown layered hair was freshly brushed and the pink lipstick made her look older, Laura thought. Her slip-on shoes clicked on the stained terrazzo floor. Laura had washed her hair and rubbed it at the roots to make it fuller. She wore dark pants and a grey T-shirt.

When the waiter finally came Laura ordered chicken with groundnut sauce.

'Sorry we have no chicken.'

The waiter looked out into the night behind their heads.

'But I really wanted chicken.'

The waiter paused.

'Okay, we have chicken.'

Sushil and Ranjit were smirking when they arrived. Their long-sleeved shirts were well-pressed and tucked in at the waist.

Ranjit was young with long black lashes. His family owned a small electrical shop in the city. Sushil, older with round cheeks, had an import-export business.

'Where are you from, Laura?' Ranjit asked.

'Australia.'

'Oh, very good.'

The conversation slumped into another silence.

'Come on, I'm bored here,' said Adriana.

They finished their drinks and left in an awkward line, Adriana leading. Laura hit her hip against the wooden arm of a chair as they left.

'Sorry,' said Sushil, behind her.

They drove to a beach with headless palm trees and Sushil passed around a joint. Two men stood at the black water's edge in some religious rite, one with arms outstretched, Christ-like, the other bent over and muttering.

'What are they doing?' Laura whispered to Ranjit.

'These Africans, Laura, they do some very, very strange stuff,' he said, waving his head from side to side.

The joint had made Laura's mouth dry and she couldn't find a way to sit. She locked her hands under her knees with her chin resting on top, her tongue exploring the broken molar. Ranjit had put his hand on Adriana's knee. He was talking in Hindi to Sushil and giggling.

'What's so funny?' Adriana asked, annoyed. 'You bring us here, it's no fun, me and Laura are wasting our time, I hate your stupid talk.'

Ranjit leaned over and whispered to her. She lit a cigarette and smiled. He laughed and said, 'You know, Laura, Sushil has a wife and two children.'

'Oh.' She coughed. 'Where are they?'

Ranjit laughed again.

'That is a very technical question,' Sushil replied.

He looked at her for a few moments.

'I see you have cried too much in your life.'

Ranjit's hand was creeping further up Adriana's skirt. He suddenly jumped up, shaking his hand in the air.

'She stubbed her cigarette on my hand! Bitch! Bitch!'

Adriana stood up.

'Come, Laura, we go!'

Ranjit grabbed Adriana's hand and pushed it hard back against the wrist. She pulled away from him and Laura followed her, the sand dune dragging down their knees and shoulders.

'Bok, bok, bok. You look like a chicken, Laura!' Sushil shouted.

They stood on the dusty edge of the road, unsure of where they were. A small white Toyota drove past then reversed back. Innocent got out of the car and laughed.

'I thought it was you. What are you doing here?'

He looked curiously at Adriana.

'Innocent, this is Adriana. I met her at the hotel.'

He asked where they wanted to go; Adriana wanted to go home.

'Please Adriana, I will take you home but first let me take you both for a drink.'

Laura saw a drinking bar called 'Don't Mind Your Wife' up ahead.

'There,' she said, pointing.

'No, no, Laura, not there I think. I know a better one.'

Laura looked at Innocent driving and saw the perfect line of his jaw meeting his neck. For a few moments the thumping of Hindi film music filled the car as Sushil and Ranjit sped past.

They sat at wet aluminium tables outside at the 'Time Heals' drinking bar. It had white-washed walls on three sides, an uneven concrete floor and no roof. Loud Ghanaian High Life music crackled through thin speakers and a man and a woman danced slowly in a small area clear of tables. Innocent had put on his white satin jacket. A waiter brought them three very cold beers.

Laura asked Innocent why the waiter was wearing yellow sunglasses.

'He has Apollo.'

'Huh?'

'When Apollo 11 landed on the moon there was an epidemic of conjunctivitis and so we call it Apollo.'

They both laughed.

'Why is Ghana so funny?' she asked.

'Because they do things for their own sake, not for a reason.'

Innocent went to buy some kebabs from the stall next to the bar.

'You like him Laura, don't you. You never tell me about him. Why?'

'I don't know, it didn't seem necessary.'

Adriana looked very tired.

'And, Laura, I tell you everything, everything! Is he your boyfriend?'

'No! Of course not. I just met him on a bus. Anyway I think he's gay, don't you?'

'He's very handsome. Why don't you go for him, Laura? Because he's black?'

Laura took a drink of beer and wiped the condensation off on her trousers. She thought of when she stabbed a guy in the hand with a broken glass in a bar, for no reason. That's when she'd left. She'd been quieter since.

'Didn't you feel better when you did that to Ranjit?' Laura said.

Adriana shook her head. Innocent came back to the table.

'I go now, Laura. You stay here,' Adriana said.

'No,' said Innocent. 'I promised to take you home. Let's go.'

As they walked to the car Innocent stopped Laura and pulled her to him. Her damp hands fused with the back of his satin jacket and she smelt his deodorant. As he bent to kiss her she saw the small white pimples around his mouth.

Innocent seemed unaware of Adriana's mood in the car while Laura could feel it against the back of her neck. The road passed through the huge city tip; the smell was so strong it was almost solid. As Laura rolled up her window, Innocent rolled his down. He put his head out, flaring his nostrils, drawing in the smell deeply and laughing.

'Aah, it's good to be home.'

'Stop it!' shouted Adriana. 'It's disgusting!'

Innocent ignored her, putting his shoulders out and breathing in more fiercely.

'Take it, Laura!'

He was waist out now, throwing his head back. Laura took the steering wheel in one hand and the car swayed.

'I can't,' she said.

'Stop it!' Adriana said as she rocked the back of Laura's seat.

Laura's arm jerked sideways and Innocent slipped back in and they were jolted forwards for a moment, unsure of what they had hit. An old man with matted hair lay across the car bonnet, his eyes open and staring inside the car. The car slowed and he rolled onto the road. Innocent sped up and the car bumped over him like a speed hump, twice.

'Jesus Maria, Jesus Maria, stop the car. Stop! Laura, make him stop!' Adriana screamed.

Innocent was pale and gripping the steering wheel.

'You want to go back? And do what? Mouth to mouth? Put him in the back of the car next to Adriana? You want that, Adriana?'

His eyes were very white and big as he spoke, his voice getting louder.

'Or maybe we just go to the police station and explain very nicely to them what happened? And we will be months explaining. And you will call in the embassies for some help and goodbye me. Believe me, nobody cares about him. And my dear Laura, was I driving or were you?'

Adriana leaned forward and pulled Laura's hair.

'Stop him!'

'Let go of my hair you bitch. How can I make him stop?' Laura shouted at her, pushing her hand away.

As the car slowed in front of the hotel, Laura opened the door and vomited chicken and rice and beer and her own spit and bile onto gravel.

The next afternoon Laura went to Adriana's room. She was still in bed, tearful.

'Laura, I think I get malaria. I want you to stay with me, here in this room. Please close the windows, the sea is making me sick.'

Laura brought her coffee and bread. She ate it at the dressing table.

'So alone, so alone,' she said to her face in the mirror, smiling.

'Why don't you go back to Italy, Adriana?'

'How can I go back until I find my boyfriend?'

She looked at Laura in the mirror.

'Laura, do you think Innocent would help me find him?'

In the taxi to the airport Laura sat in the back seat between gashes in the red plastic upholstery. She chewed the flaking skin from around her nails.

The taxi driver said, 'Can I come wid you?'

She spat a fleck of skin and it landed on the shoulder of his brown jacket. She thought how it would probably stay there all day.

KERI HULME

Sometimes I Dream I'm Driving

The steering-wheel is slim, with raised almost sculpted lines to assist my grip, and it always feels cold and hard beneath my fingers no matter how odd, how dangerous, the drive becomes, no matter how sweaty my palms turn. The steering-wheel is darkgrey in my dreams, although I cannot now remember what colour it really was. Maybe it was red, to match the red leather upholstery. Maybe it was black, to match the paintwork. Maybe it truly was darkgrey.

The roads unreel before me. I straddle three or four lanes with ease. Occasionally, with disconcerting naturalness and inevitability, the Snipe turns amoebic and fissions, and I am driving both vehicles happily along different and separating roads.

In this vehicle, the roads are straight and sealed, and despite the fact that road markings and signage, catseyes even, were not around during my childhood (and these dream-roads are riddled with them, are riddles from them), I know them, the straight, endlessly straight, bitumen roads that cross the Canterbury Plains heading south to Oamaru, the roads that lead to home.

Not Christchurch home, but my Nana's place, where she always has bread drying in the oven so it turns crisp and more potent than ordinary bread, and when spread with butter (which never is hard, or melted to grease, merely perfect spreadable golden butter), becomes a sacrament of welcome to the travelling child, a sign she has arrived safely again. Nana's place has a scullery, made magic because she always kept her flour and sugar in cloth sacks in tin liners in the kauri flour-bin. The scullery is redolent of homemade soap and old lino. The scullery is quite often just over the back seat of the Snipe, somehow wedged in there before the boot. More often, Uncle Bill's shed is there, with the ton of coal in the corner coalbox, Grand-dad's anvils and vices (where I once tried setting off bullets by locking them in and hitting them with a hammer—they were only .22s fortunately, and, even more fortunately, I couldn't get them to explode, resorting in my frustration to asking for adult help in the matter. Which this time, indulged eldest child of a first generation although I was, I didn't get); all the gardening tools, the long-handled ones, are stacked in another corner, and best of all, Uncle Bill's gun-cupboard, with the evil knives we weren't allowed to use, the two shotguns and the .303, .308 and 9mm beasts Bill used when hunting. A reassuring optional extra, the shed, for any vehicle, even for the Snipe which had haul-down armrests and pullout ashtrays and gasp wow a radio with buttons that would whisk you from one preset station to another *that* (snick) quick.

Whether the shed's in the back of the back, or the scullery, or just the passengers, doesn't seem to make much difference to the road-holding capacities of the Snipe. It's a big, heavy, black car, elegantly solid, and powerful in its way and time ('same engine as a Commer truck,' said the Oamaru uncles, nodding to each other, 'plenty of grunt'. Well, I never drove the relevant Commer truck, just a Commer van many many years later, and it had as much grunt as your average moped as well as all the aerodynamics of a brick. I put it in a roadside ditch once, when trying to adjust a contact lens—ditch? Nah, it was a sort of runnel, about six inches down, but the Commer van squealed and puffed and ground its gears and snorted until I had to flag down a passing car to give us a tow. The car dragged us out with ease. It was a Honda Civic. I sold the Commer shortly afterwards, still beetroot with embarrassment (me, not it), to a person who liked puttering through life. Once, driving to the hill-hut in the Tigers, my mother put the Snipe into a mud rut that came three-quarters of the way up the hubcaps. The Snipe revved a bit, was chopped down a cog (as we said to each other) and solidly, powerfully, chewed its way through a hundred yards of rut onto the solid, where it gave a kind of elegant shudder and sailed on once more.

Yes, I drive on water often, particularly in the Super Snipe. Dream-roads frequently edge into fogbound causeways over lakes. The road narrows to a charcoal wisp, the sides steam and the black water creeps onwards. I know there is a knob on the dash specifically for this kind of travel but my fingers have forgotten where it is and I keep pulling out the cigarette lighter instead. Not that it matters very much: tarseal or mud or lake, the Snipe keeps going. It is just that one of the kids in the back seat will always reach over and tap my shoulder and complain we're not going very fast. I know the errant knob on the dash increases our speed by reducing friction (the owner's manual in its leather binding is quite clear on this point, the words underlining themselves as I read them again) so, reach down and pull the knob and blast, there's the red coil of the lighter again. But look, the black water is expiring in fog, and the fog is rising over the dwarf manuka groves that alternate with the concrete balustrading of the longest bridge in the southern hemisphere, the Rakaia bridge, all nine-eighths of a mile of it.

That was a childhood mantra, a mile and an *eighth* long, not your common quarter or half but an *eighth*, the measurement to be chanted whenever we crossed the bridge in daylight, but only during daylight. I don't know why we didn't say it at night. Rakaia was close enough to Christchurch for us older kids to be awake, and we weren't expected to be quiet when we were awake. Indeed, if my parents began singing, we were encouraged to join in. It is one of my favourite memories of the endless journeys south, my mother and father harmonising together, singing because they loved to sing, John a light tenor, Mary a fine contralto, and the songs any songs that came into their heads, from 'Little Brown Jug' to 'Toora loora lai'.

I can't remember them singing in the Snipe. John bought the vehicle the year he died, 1958, and that year was a terrible one, my mother becoming deathly ill after a hysterectomy and, in consequence, us six kids being divided up round relations. We weren't used to being separated and although we frequently fought among ourselves (and violently on occasion—I can remember socking one of my brothers in the stomach so it first winded him and then made him vomit all over the red carpeted floor of the Snipe. For which *he* got told off, not having enough presence of mind (or air) to tell on me), we also loved one another dearly, and were used to being an intrinsic gang, just us, just family.

John had his Humber Super Snipe, a car he had coveted for many years, for mere months before his heart gave out, at forty-two. It made an interesting statement, next car after the hearse in his very long funeral cortège; a sleek symbol of decent wealth, the wealth of a man who began his working life as a carpenter, and painter and decorator, and wound up, by dint of his own hard work and considerable skills, President of the Working Men's Club and President of the Business Men's Association (at one and the same time), Justice of the Peace; owner of and partner in two New Brighton businesses; husband of a beautiful woman; father of many children; proud possessor of the Snipe. Well, it was roomy enough to carry all the floral tributes that couldn't fit in the hearse.

I never smell flowers on any dream drive. Frequently there *are* smells (which I am told is slightly unusual in dreams). The leather is sunwarmed, and that is a distinctive scent, as memorable as the rankness of old butts in the three ashtrays. Sometimes, it's warm sausage rolls, or the slightly sulphury reek of egg sandwiches. The Snipe transported so many picnics. Occasionally, one of the kids has puked. ('Wind the window down *first* next time!') The Snipe transported so many kids, entire wriggly basketball teams, a marching girls' troupe, my brother John's Scout pack, my sister Diane's St John's Cadets group . . . by the time my siblings were involved in those kinds of activities, I could drive them and their mates legally, and yet they aren't among the passengers that freight the long back seat. People I don't know come out of the scullery, and sit for a while on the red leather. Very few of them talk. I can see them clearly, for the rear vision mirror takes up most of the windscreen. I can hear them clearly too, because I almost never hear road noise inside the Snipe, even when I drive through the dark lakes, even when we spin in mad circles on gravel, even when the bullet hail breaks all the windows—we were in such a frightening hail-storm once, coming back from Oamaru. It chipped the windscreen and left tiny sinister dents on the bonnet.

And once, feeling an uncontrollable wobble as I took us round a shingly corner just past Templeton one night, I hit the brakes hard and sent the Snipe 180 degrees fast, facing us back to Christchurch on the wrong side of the road in a breath-robbing instant. My warrior mother let me drive another ten miles further on, in a quivering silence, my siblings having all come wideawake in the spinning second but wise enough not to even whimper.

Mary had begun to teach me to drive when I was twelve, the year after my father died, and by fourteen, I was regularly spelling her on the long drives south. I came to know, relatively early, the mesmerising power of a grey road unreeling before you, the mesmerising power of a rainy road glittering before you as far as your headlights could reach, the mesmerising power of a road you came to know intimately but which could always surprise.

A tractor pulling straight out in front from a paddock of stubble. I remember the stubble. I remember the nondescript reddybrown of the tractor. I remember the ache in my young and very strong legs as I put everything I had into pushing the brake through the floor. And the shrieking sound and the smell of brakedrum against wheel.

We never had an accident in the Snipe, and it was the family car for many years. It was the other vehicles that the crashes came in, the humble creeping little beasts like the Hillman Imp, or the Commer, or the Avenger, or the Trekka, putty-coloured cars and vans with vinyl seats and jerky floor-shift gears, things you'd never bother to hose down or lux out, let alone cut and wax.

Simonize: Turtle Wax. The Snipe's grill was heavy chrome, with a lot of slots. The bumper bars were fat. Everything could be polished to a glory of mirrors, distorting mirrors turning a delicate face into a wicked or woeful gargoyle, and my own heavy features to an unlikely Buddha-serenity.

You got the mirrors after a lot of rubbing with a rag smeared with gritty thick orangeybrown acrid gloop. (You got the gloop out from under your nails with difficulty.) There was extra pocket money as a reward for doing the car (as we said) provided you did a good job. We often pooled our energies. For instance, I preferred creating mirrors, but others liked brushing out the interior (there was a good chance of coins being found in the smooth leather cracks) or cleaning the paintwork, because that was not only easy but even fun. There was a brush with long soft bristles, and a compartment in the handle wherein you could insert a pellet of special soap. The brush screwed onto a hose fitting—run the water, and presto! instant suds. One of my sisters became besotted with the bubbles so produced and sprayed away many month's worth of pellets. She was not popular. One of my brothers made himself even less popular by attempting to prove the boot of the Snipe was waterproof.

But it never leaks in the lakes of dreams. The coal is always dry in the shed, a little dust moting the air: my Nana's flour is safe in the kauri bin, always ready to be made into bread to be made into a wayfarer's sacrament. The Snipe bowls along the long roads of the night, the wheel cool and hard and ready between my hands, and if the people on the back seat are quiet, why, sometimes they smile—

ANNA JACKSON

My life when I had a life: I wake up.

In the morning I wake up
and see in the night I have written
on a scrap of paper
to Bridget
red wine / love—is this
a recurring dream?
Hardly matters—
I have a recurring life
to go out in to—
already Lisa is ringing up
to cry about the latest
incident with Nigel
and I am late
for lunch with Stacy
who has just got back
from being away—
'nothing can have gone terribly wrong
in *Ngaruawahia*,' I say
but it *has*.
I get red wine in my hair
from laughing so hard—
we are pretty and unhappy
and loving it—
'people would *kill* for
my unhappiness'
says Stacy—
a line I use later
over wine and cigarettes
with Diana.

My life when I had a life: I actually *am* twenty.

I actually *am* twenty but they are right
to wonder whether I should be allowed
in a bar and I have no ID because
I haven't got a driver's licence yet
and when it is time to go
I haven't got any money
and have to pay for my drinks
with a poem even though
I really want to be
a short story writer—it is so *sad*
when you get bored of a story before
you have written it, almost as sad
as when you get bored with a boy
before you have slept with him
—where did you go? Greg asks
the next day. But Stacy
promised to drink herself
between us if she must—
where did *Stacy* go is what
I want to know.

My life when I had a life: 12 a.m. and don't I show Jane.

12 a.m. and don't I show Jane
and undo my watch
to throw it before
my heart—
              —I can't *read*
it says Jane and I think
that is pretty
sad but keep writing
anyway—
              —3 a.m. and now
I am sober although feeling

sick with all this coffee
in fact it is now 10 past 3
and I am astonished
it is not later since between
3 and now I have climbed
all over Tim's shelves
searching for new
coffee beans—
now Jane comes to the door
and I hear myself
scream and think
perhaps I am not sober
enough to write
after all—

My life when I had a life: it isn't unusual.

It isn't unusual to think Keith and Stacy
are there but tonight they actually
are there—it has to be the night
when my shawl keeps sliding off
and all my lines sound stupid.
I don't even get to pick up the fan
because Heather picks up
the fan, and afterwards
nobody comes backstage,
probably because they don't want to be
associated with such a bad actress—
'Last show I did, the guy had these
deep eye sockets, we had three
lights along the front
and still I couldn't get rid
of the eye sockets,' says Gordon
consoling me later, looking
like he might kiss me.

My life when I had a life: afterwards no one talks.

Afterwards no one talks.
Opposite the park I say
'I wonder what they did
with the body'—my voice
sounding high-pitched,
Australian—like
hearing it on tape.
As soon as we let off Rose
and Marcia—Marcia's
shoulders set—we talk,
me and Lisa: 'it was that
remark about the body,'
Lisa tells me, watching
the rats crawl in and out of
the bin like an extension
of the movie.

My life when I had a life: Lisa drinks her vodka neater.

Lisa drinks her vodka neater
but I drink mine faster.
Likewise, our talking.
Likewise, our getting dressed—
I spring out of bed first thing
and usually get back before
she's up, too—what does she *do*
all day in bed? I don't ask.
I talk quickly about
other things, knocking back
the vodka—this was when
we were younger.
(*She* still is—I was
always older.)

My life when I had a life: fun at twenty-four.

It was Bridget Orr who reassured
me, at twenty-two, I'd still
have fun at twenty-four.
'*Fun*,' she said, French-feminist,
with long red hair,
italics already in 1990
the new ampersand for her,
'you can have fun
in *there*'—making a gesture
towards the photocopying room—
I looked to see if *he* was there—
but it was empty—

My life when I had a life: how Stacy it was.

Stacy always said the apartment block
where Simon released the rat
looked like a ring-binder,
which I couldn't see, except
for how *Stacy* that was.
Everything about Stacy was.
Including everyone else—
that's what we were—we were
who Stacy would have found, and *did*
since she was Stacy.

ANDREW JOHNSTON

Binoculars

for Marc Nieson

I was a stranger. But you look
familiar, people would say.

Big cars, big country. You need
binoculars, here, said a man, I can sell you some.

I took them back to my room
and watched hawks over the river,

sun reddening their tail feathers,
then I looked at everything in my room

through them, the wrong way round—
tiny photographs, books, tiny lamp—

which made me feel instantly philosophical,
distant, a little taller. Infinitely stranger.

Saudade

Saudade,
'the freedom to be sad'—

the very idea can make you glad,
and *lusophone*—hello?—

this is Portuguese speaking.
Ladies and gentlemen,

life is hard. But
there are grilled sardines for lunch—

we crunch their
delicate skeletons.

LLOYD JONES

Journey Through a Painted Landscape

Some years ago an elderly man answered my newspaper advertisement to ask if I would chop his wood to kindling. I quoted three hours; it took four and a half. It was a load of soggy pine, full of knots, and the axe wouldn't bite. I was near the end when he came out of his house carrying a tray with a teapot and chocolate thins. 'Milk. Sugar?' he asked. As he poured the milk he calmly confessed to not having any money. Unfortunately, as it seemed. He thought he had, but was mistaken. However, if I wished, he had a painting by a famous artist.

He was surprised, I think, when I asked to see the painting, and a moment passed when I wondered whether he actually had it. He set down the tray and was gone inside the house. It was a few minutes before he reappeared in the doorway, struggling with a large painting of my father laying a fenceline in South Canterbury.

I took the painting and showed it to my mother. She put on her glasses, and gave the man in Theo Schoon's painting a dark look. She thought it could be Ron.

'Your father had "Kramer" tattooed on his right shoulder. Where's "Kramer"? Everything else however seems to be there.'

In the painting Ron is pile-driving a post into the hillside. The artist has ghosted in his underarms a fleshy whiteness, but the other details leave no doubt as to the season. The hillside is still green and the upended earth moist as Christmas pudding. The arms on Ron's flannel shirt have been torn away, and his shoulders are ripe with new sunburn. In the bottom right hand corner of the painting is the year, 1947. It made perfect sense. Ron is farm-labouring for money to tie him over his campaigning months, December/January, the time of the year he entered tennis tournaments about the country.

I hung on to the painting, since my mother had no use for it.

Then, six months ago, she rang me late at night to say that
Ron had been killed. The club captain of Ron's tennis club had
just been on the phone to her. It was a Sunday night and Ron,
in his trademark long white trousers, had left the club full of
gin and good times, and while fumbling with a key to open
his driver's-side door had been side-swiped by a passing car.
It was bad luck. Well, Ron had moved too far out of my life
for me to feel devastated. As for my mother, she had long since
dismissed Ron, first from the house, then from her mind, and
herself remarried. The club captain, believing he was in contact
with Ron's next-of-kin, had in fact notified strangers, and I
was sorry about this, and all the grey space Ron had placed in
between.

My mother had wondered if Ron had 'left anyone behind'
who might clean out his drawers and wardrobe. I think she
had in mind a brown paper parcel of Ron's underwear and
socks to be dropped off at St Vincent's, or the Sallies. It was
uncharacteristically sentimental of her.

As for me I had lost touch with the man. There was the odd
memory from childhood; an unexpected visit, my mother's
cool reception of a man who appeared to be full of favours, his
pockets full of sweets, and his disappearing again. The only
material connection left was this painting. One of Ron's few
reliable addresses which I now thought of investigating; instead
of taking possession of Ron's old socks, as might have been
expected, as clearly the tennis club captain had hoped, I would
feel out this old landscape.

I spent a day at the National Art Gallery archive fishing among
Theo Schoon's files and notes. A small newsclipping reports
Theo's death in Sydney's Prince of Wales Hospital three years
earlier. A decrepit end in a Sydney boarding house, opposite
the hospital, where Theo had shared a room with another old
man. Death notices always seem to deny there ever having been
a youth. But pinned to this death notice was a photograph of
the artist as a young man. It is not what you might expect of the
war years: sunburnt shoulders, large ears and a shorn neck. No.
The photograph is of Theo performing a Balinese dance. He is
barechested but for a silk scarf and a flowing robe attached by

a single shoulder strap. It is not what you might expect for an acquaintance of your father.

Theo, the son of a Dutch administrator, had been brought up in Keboemen, Central Java. His boyhood was spent wandering through abandoned temples of the ancient Hindu empire, and along with his Javanese peers Theo learnt traditional dance, mime and shadowplay. When the Japanese chased out the Dutch, in 1939, the Schoon family moved to Christchurch. Theo, now 25, had already studied art in Rotterdam and his heady rise in the local art circles is easily imagined. In the archive I had noticed a photostat copy of his painting of Rita Angus and other works exhibited at the leading galleries of the day. What my mother used to call a 'Dutchman's stroppiness' probably applied to Theo, who didn't think highly of the local art scene, or the fruits of egalitarianism if the quote is to be believed: 'I could not stand the vulgar and ridiculous, so I went out in search for the superb—in a very depressing country.'

Theo found it down the road from the Raincliffe Station in South Canterbury. Two kilometres from the farmgates, above the roadside are three caves with drawings—the end one with the 'desklid' initials of more recent visitors. Underneath this escarpment sheltered the original artists during their fair-weather trips up river valleys in search of moa, and other bird-life. Centuries later Theo followed them here with his art materials to reproduce what he called the 'frozen music' of the mytho-poetic Polynesians.

Two hours south of Christchurch this rock drawing area was the best clue I had. For now it would do. I never expected the location of Theo's painting to be a place-name on a map, to drive up to, refuel, stretch a leg, and buy an egg sandwich from a woman in a white coat.

In the tearooms at Geraldine I was given directions to Gudex Road by a man in a white apron and running shoes. The road was full of dips and dales; here's a quiet valley with yellowing haybales in the shape of covered wagons, the air busy with insects, and suddenly—the snow, the Alps. And just the way a child might have drawn it. 'Beautiful Valley' it turns out is indeed beautiful. 'Pleasant Valley' was only pleasant. Early

October and green foothills were still shouldering the winter snow. An uneasy alliance of seasons: to go with the tall man with the short wife. The thin mother with the obese son.

On the map the Opihi River runs nearby. Riverstones have been piled over paddocks either side of the road. At the bottom of Gudex Road is Raincliffe Station, a large farmhouse made from blocks of limestone. I unhitched the farmgates and drove up in the hope of being shown to the shearer's quarters with the aging weatherboards, where I might have expected to find Ron's name carved into a bedpost. But old blinds were drawn in every window, and no one came to the door. For a few minutes I stood on the verandah and it occurred to me what was wrong with the view. I should have been driving across a valley of forest. The Alps are not supposed to be wholly digested, or viewed like white cue balls across a vast green felt table. The Alps are better glimpsed through branches, and on rises over treetops. But only the names have stuck—'Totara Road' and 'Three Mile Bush Road.'

The church in Theo's 'Colonial Church Raincliffe' is just up the road, past the rockdrawings, before the bridge over the Opihi River. It is a small wooden church with a handful of graves. Amy Bartrum's headstone reads: 'Born Northampton . . . fell asleep in 1907.' There was no traffic, I could hear the wind, and nothing else. Apparently Amy Bartrum had just nodded off.

In Theo's painting the church is full of collapsed lines: it sags between peaked roofs like a wet sheet pegged to a clothesline.

Theo had a good view of the church. According to his notes, he camped in the scout reserve opposite. Each morning he would have passed it on his way to record the rock drawings back up the road.

I spent the night in a farmhouse that offered bed and breakfast. A retired farmer and his wife, June, gave me a room in the back of the house overlooking green paddocks that stretched for miles. None of this pasture was theirs. Jim had had a farm up north. He had bought at the wrong time and overnight seen half its paper value wiped. He laughed when he told of this experience. Folding back the eiderdown on my bed, June smiled quietly to herself. She had heard it all before, many times, this story which was outside grief, more like some huge natural occurrence, like Pompeii, where over the years human cost has become a footnote to the event. The Harrisons' walk off the land had become a useful anecdote. An ice-breaker. Later, after dinner, I started to tell Jim of my interest in rock drawings in the area. But at that moment his wife entered carrying a tray of bowls, ice cream and canned fruit, and Jim said, 'Ooh goodie. Pudding. *MacGyver*'s on at eight.' So I let it pass. I watched the farmer in his slippers, for a while, so I would not be thought impolite, and got to my room just as dusk was closing over the hills.

If any hour belongs to Theo it is this one: camped underneath a damp rock ledge, drawing his sleeping bag around his shoulders; damning himself, watchful of his own metamorphosis from 'city dweller, with European outlook, to a cross between a deerstalker and hermit.'

In the morning I did ask Jim if the details in Theo's painting—a copper water tank next to a clump of cabbage trees—summoned up any particular place. We were in the kitchen. June was scraping bacon fat from the pan. I was getting ready to pay for the night, and the retired farmer was eager to be helpful. His eyes squinted up over the rack of dishes.

'Could be Twigg's,' he thought. 'Or Morrison's.'

'Plenty of cabbage trees over Smythe's,' said his wife.

'No. That's Morrison's country. You are thinking of Morrison's.' Then he said to me, 'Turley's boy might have a spare water tank. Two hundred gallon. He digs wells too, of course. Depends what you're after.'

I thanked him, and was obliged to take note of his directions to Murray Turley's place on Monument Road. I was headed in that direction, anyway, and somewhere along the empty road I happened to look out the passenger-side window and catch a small cottage with an assortment of tanks out the back.

The greenness, the matrix of fences, I think it would have pleased Ron. The cows and the sheep lifting their gaze to a man playing imaginary forehands and backhands; his picking up a stone and backhanding it with a fence post. The idea

of Wimbledon—and this other reality, of a young man with
sunburnt shoulders fitting the earth with fenceposts.

If this is the subject of the painting, then it is also a
masquerade. There is the farmwork, but beneath this bread-and-
butter task the heart beats to a different tune. Theo is painting
pot-boilers to earn his keep and pay for the paint supplies. It is
just a matter of time before he will bring to the world's attention
the extraordinary 'frozen music' of this limestone country; and
before Ron will collect his trophies.

I passed the turn-off for Hanging Rock and drove on to
Pleasant Point. There, I turned for the coast to sample, briefly,
Ron's triumph, which follows on the heels of Theo's painting.

In the offices of the *Timaru Herald* I dug out the New Year's
Day edition of more than forty years ago, and found the name of
Ron's old doubles partner, Murray Tinder. Over the telephone
it took a moment for the connection to register. Close on fifty
years to comb through, then, once he had arrived at the fact
that it was Ron's son calling, he fumbled for the right order of
things. He wanted to invite me home. He gave his address in
Beverley Road. Gave meticulous directions. Then, he changed
his mind. His wife was sick. The house was untidy. So we fixed
to meet at the tennis courts at Maori Park. On the way I snuck
up Beverley Road. It was lined with solid two-storey houses,
quiet, and well-treed. I cruised past Murray's house. He must
have already made his way down to the park. In front of his
house was a nicely maintained grass court. It was unused, and
all the more luxurious because of it. I could imagine Murray
spending his weekends pampering the grass, greening it up and
on his hands and knees, the way another will lick a vintage car
with a chamois cloth.

Murray was in the green windbreaker he had described on
the phone. He was seated on a bench in front of the tennis
courts, old and frail, dependent on a walking stick, watching
the tennis.

Murray thought I had come to hear stories of Ron's glory.
Like the time he beat one of the Forde brothers—the younger
one, or was it the older one in line for Davis Cup honours two
years later—I had forgotten, but Murray said it was the younger

one, Cyril. As for making the Davis Cup he had a peep in . . .
'But an incident with a horse during muster crushed his ankle
and he hobbled around after that. Still a force at net but I mean
a man can't play and win from there.'

Before the horse injury Ron rode into town and stripped
Cyril Forde of his expected honours in the South Island
Championships.

Poor old Murray. His blue eyes glistening, he made as if he
remembered a topsy turvey battle . . . fortune swinging one way,
then the other. Ron's crisp play . . . Cyril's doggedness. The only
details I trusted were: the sweat marks in Ron's sandshoes and
the severe sunburn along the tops of his ears. The final started
early afternoon and finished at quarter to six in the evening. A
ball was planned in Caroline Bay to see in the New Year. But
Ron's feet were so badly blistered that he missed the first half
of the evening. Ron and Murray went to the pictures to see
Cowboy From Lonesome River. It gave Ron time for his feet
to heal, and when they came out of the theatre they joined a
stream of people headed for Maori Park. The main street had
been roped off, the shops were still open late at night and young
women in cotton dresses held hands with farm boys, come to
town for the night.

Bronwyn Sellars was mentioned. Beyond the tidying up
details Murray didn't offer much. Cyril Forde, the defeated
finalist, had gotten himself drunk and was lying stupored in the
sand at the Port end of Caroline Beach. Consequently Bronwyn
spent much of the evening walking around the sideshows with
her bare arms folded against the chill. It was during a huge
rendition of 'Auld Lang Syne' around the bonfire on the beach
that Bronwyn fell into Ron's arms. The next thing Murray saw
the two head off for the ferris wheel. Murray lay down on the
grass to watch the wheel spin, and listen to the women squeal.
About one-thirty in the morning a fog drove in from the sea,
and there was a light drizzle. An hour later an electrical problem
stopped the ferris wheel and stranded its riders. Murray decided
he would wait for Ron, and some hours later he awoke stiff and
cold on the ground. Other party revellers from all around were
doing the same, brushing the dew off themselves, and looking

around for the sun. Some minutes later, there was a groaning sound from the ferris wheel.

'The wheel turned and heads rose above the safety bars. People shook out their legs. Ron came down then. He jumped out and held a hand out for Bronwyn. She was wearing Ron's jacket. Her skin was shiny, and her face had kind of narrowed up. I guess at your age I can say these things to you,' Murray Tinder said. 'But it was a beautiful thing really.'

Around ten in the morning the Forde brothers threw open the doors to the rooms on the upstairs floor of the Grosvenor Hotel, but Ron was at the railway station. Murray waved his doubles partner aboard, tennis racquet in hand, writing materials, trophy, and some sandwiches he had thoughtfully pocketed the previous day, sticking out the tops of the pockets in his sports jacket.

Murray gave me directions to the railway station. I thanked him and was on my way when he startled me, asking, 'How is Ron anyway? In good health?'

'Yes,' I said. 'He's doing fine.'

At the back of the railway station near Merchants & Auctioneers I could make out the top floor of the Grosvenor. This was the old part of town, the flash part in 1947. More recently the hotel has been refurbished. Bright, new canvas awnings. The ceiling mould in the foyer newly painted. The tables with starched white tablecloths in the dining-room numbered, so that the year 1947 does not feel so distant.

Spilling down to the pavement were a series of fire escape ladders. I looked up to one of the third-floor windows and imagined Ron putting aside his packing, for the moment, content to enjoy the town, and his pulling back the curtains, raising the sash, his long arms folded along the sill, and his sleeping dog's smile beneath the cigarette smoke, at the thought of the ferris wheel, and Bronwyn Sellars.

Farewelling his doubles partner Ron moves first to Christchurch to play in the Canterbury Championships, then on to Blenheim to narrowly miss out on the Malborough title, onward to Wellington, aboard the *Tamihere*, to the Casa Fontana where he will meet my mother.

My mother is easily imagined. All hip and shank. She was often short with people she suspected of 'having education'. People who attempted to be nice with her met with a surprising tartness. A man scribbling over the backs of used envelopes might think he was the cat's pyjamas but there was the outstanding matter of payment for that third cup of coffee. Ron looked up from his writing—at this woman—all hip, shank, and lip, he later said. He reached into his coat pockets, and found a lonely coin. He flipped it. 'Heads or tails?' My mother obediently called 'Tails'. This is the story which my mother tells. In our worst moments I have seen the thought flash in her eyes that here before her, as she is tempted to say, is the result of a losing toss.

I bought a meat pie from a dairy, then headed back for the landscape of Theo's painting, back to the interior; this time travelling along Hazelburn Road to the rock drawings at Acacia Downs. On the spur, a farmhouse, with a tennis court. Beneath the farm, and a short rise from the road, a long shallow cave with raft and bird motifs.

I sat up there—as Theo must have done—with questions for the cave dwellers centuries earlier, and meanwhile wondering what went on under the iron roof of the farmhouse further along the road. A cottage locked into place by a solid steeple of limestone rock. Its frail stem of chimney smoke disappearing into an overcast day.

My father went north. Theo stayed in the caves, painting, convinced of the originality and artistic merit of these sketchy figures of dogs, moa, crayfish, reed rafts, and the stylised human figures. Searching out their 'hidden thread'.

On the roadside below the Raincliffe drawings is a brass plaque of a taniwha, with the official invitation to 'rub a picture'. Further up the bank, a steel grille protects the actual drawings from enthusiasts after a tracing of the real article. But it was here, at Acacia Downs, that Theo erred. He retouched a spiral with crayon to aid his photography, and suddenly Theo Schoon was a vandal. A forger. A faker. Funny isn't it? Ron copied as best he could Jack Kramer's backhand, and if anyone had commented on the likeness, I believe, he would have been very happy. Then there is Theo's old classmate, Van Meregen, whose brilliant copies of Vermeer took him no further than prison.

Intentions are everything, so we are told. Re-touching the spiral, argued Theo, was the best solution at the time. In 1916 a spiritualist had arrived from Kansas to chisel out the rockdrawings so as to remove them to 'safety'. His activities were stopped and export of the drawings diverted to the Otago Museum.

Leaving Acacia Downs I drove over to Hanging Rock. At the turn-off at Gay's Pass, from an AA sign hung a rock on the end of a piece of string.

'Bev and Kev' and 'Tui McIwi' belong to more recent work on the rockface near Hanging Rock. Betrothals. Humour. It makes you wonder—at least it made me wonder about the original artists. Did they have a wicked or ironic sense of humour. Did they constantly put themselves down like the Brits? Were they patriotic? What kind of jokes might be considered in bad taste? Were they good at sport? Were women allowed to do rock art? Were rock artists given time off moa-hunting? What sort of personal habits were annoying? Such as unnecessary throat-clearing.

I had to open a farmgate, and cross a paddock of sheep and lambs. Down a short ravine of burnt flax, over the soggy banks of a creek and up the other side, I found the cave with the drawings of five crescent-shaped dogs. As with the drawings at Acacia Downs and Raincliffe, the dogs are behind metal grilles, weathered and indistinct, the sharper lines rubbed away by sheltering cattle of an earlier period.

It was here I threw my penny in the well. A childish notion turned me quickly about; a flimsy hope that the landscape might suddenly reveal itself; that half-glimpsed truth. I might catch out Ron, his bare arms and Kramer working against the skyline on the hillside across the creek. It might have been there; and just here, that Theo sat down with his canvas and painted.

Theo's files and notes in the end, I think, provide Ron's unspoken explanations about life after the painting. Really, it seems to me the artist and subject merge into the same story about singlemindedness without reward, or success, finally losing its charm.

Ill-health finally prises Theo from the caves. But he has discovered gourds and, from a Maori up north, how to grow them. A gourd-grower by day; a drummer in a jazzband at an Auckland nightclub by night. Theo painted his gourds with spirals similar to those which he had gazed at for hours in the limestone caves. An exhibition of Theo's gourds in the seventies, at Rotorua, led to some being destroyed by a gallery-visitor upset at their phallic-likeness. Theo is a prolific letter-writer to *The Gourd*, the bible for American gourd-culture, where gourds from calabash trees are made into raccoon masks, Big Bird, model trains; in Florida, a retired metal-worker in a pattern shirtsleeve poses with a lampbase made from a gourd; from Queen gourds the stalks are turned into giraffes and sold to gift shops. Entering into the spirit of things, Theo once turned out a gourd for Elvis Presley to use as a musical instrument. In the early seventies there were gourd exchanges between the Soviet Union and America. But, once again, it is the same old story of floundering among the 'vulgar and ridiculous' in search of the superb. Theo's earnest letters are quick to give *Gourd* readers free advice on growing techniques pioneered by himself. In later issues the magazine features 'excerpts from letters of Mr Theo Schoon'. Soon *The Gourd* was running a regular 'Letter from Mr Schoon'.

Theo would have been in Rotorua photographing the changing patterns of mud pools when Ron travelled up there for the veterans tournament in 1965. On a pitstop Ron called in and took me down to the Epuni tennis courts. On that occasion we were rallying, back and forth, trading forehand for forehand and so forth, when a car slowed down on the street outside the court. The passenger-side window wound down, and a man yelled out at Ron, 'You stinking bastard!' Ron played on with a cheap little crosscourt slice. I pretended not to hear and rushed to scoop it back for Ron to volley away. I looked up; the car was turning up the next street; and Ron had turned back for the service line.

I was on my way back to Geraldine when I remembered that

incident. I thought it probably had to do with somebody's wife, or girlfriend. I seemed to be realising this for the first time. I had been too young to understand that Ron was slowing up, and not getting out of town fast enough. No one ever wants to think of their father in that light. He had published his book— *How To Play Winning Tennis*—where he writes, 'In percentage tennis there's less opportunity to enjoy the game than to win the match.' That's as much philosophy as I ever heard from Ron. But it seems very close to Theo's: 'I have only one certainty, that is, whatever I choose to tackle I do that intensely and well. Whether it is appreciated or not has little meaning.'

During the years I lost track of Ron I believe he was coaching kids up north, in his long white pants, still combing his hair with Brylcreem, and getting by. Theo, however, had given up on New Zealand. He had come into an inheritance and was busy in a fruitless attempt to resurrect Balinese opera.

In Geraldine I stopped back at the tea rooms from where I had got directions to Gudex Road. The man in the running shoes wasn't about. I sat near a table with two Americans. The woman was lecturing a local man, but I could only see the back of his head, nodding, his arms folded in schoolmat obeisance. Theo would have known how to deal with her. She was saying how the American political system was different from here. 'More like the Australian Federal system,' she was saying. The next time I listened in, she was saying how she and her husband knew the Governor of Florida. 'Well not know him personally, although of course I have met him. But he's a friend of a close friend of Bill's.' Bill, in a zipped-up pale blue golf-jacket, looked away out the window to the street, bored out of his mind.

A council truck drew up to the door. Three men jumped out, tightened their buckles, and found a need to scowl. And like the bare, grass-sown hills, these faces could not be trusted with a secret. Not a bold idea between them. Despite the hard-wearing cloth, their shirts trace soft, rounded bellies. Yes, I did notice. I was in a contemptuous mood. For the sake of Ron and Theo, which shows too, sentimentality can have its arms around contempt, like sickly sweets with hard centres.

In Christchurch airport I saw a woman knitting. A ball of

wool had unravelled over her lap, and at first glance—that snatched glimpse again—it offered a myriad of paths and possibilities; but gradually the scrawl grew taut and entered the one strand.

I must say I like the idea of Theo and Ron having been along the same track, for the simple reason it would appal them both. Ron, of course, would never have worn leather thongs, and Theo surely never gave a thought to Kramer.

Theo chainsmoked Camel cigarettes. As for Ron I remember once seeing orange rind stuck in behind his fingernails. Other than that, my father was a lefthander with special gifts in and around a tennis net, who married the wrong woman and became the wrong father, and whose path once crossed with a stranger's, a Dutchman, who painted his picture.

KAPKA KASSABOVA

The Field

Your mother brings the strangest plants
she gives them to you, though she knows
you have no special interest in plants
then she waters them for you.
You don't understand but you're resigned to her
knowing what's important. You're used
to her taking care of the plants.

Sometimes you wait in the big house
behind closed curtains because you're secretly afraid
(she'll never know how much you wait for her)
You touch a door-knob
                                    it comes off
You stroke a loaf of bread
                                    it feels like a broken spine
You turn on the heater
                                    a carpet burns to ashes
You water the plants
                                    they die instantly
(Your mother brings the strangest plants)

Meanwhile your mother lies in a furrow
somewhere in the white fields of light
facing a sky so dark nobody can see it

AUGUST KLEINZAHLER

Sunday, Across the Tasman

Big weather is moving over the heads.
Turrets and steeples jab up at it
and the bank towers stand rooted,
logos ablaze at the edge of the earth.

In a suburban church basement the AA faithful
are singing hymns of renewal, devotion
and praise. He struggles with his umbrella
in the lobby of the Art Deco theatre,

plaster Buddhas and kitsch arabesques
towering over the popcorn counter—
the Preservation Society's last, best stand.
Young couples walk past hand in hand

as golden oldies flood onto the sidewalk
from the sweat shirt emporium next door.
His heart bobs, a small craft
awash for a moment with nostalgia.

Bartók liked to pick out a folk melody
and set it, a jewel in the thick
of hammered discords and shifting registers:
not unlike this dippy *Mamas and Papas* tune

floating along nicely among the debris.
The rain turns heavy, and the first
of the night's wild southerlies keens through,
laying waste the camellia and toi toi.

He wonders how the islanders managed
in their outriggers; if they flipped
or rode it through, plunging
from trough to trough with their ballast

of hoki, maomao, cod. Time for a drink.
A feral little businessman shakes
the bartender's left breast in greeting,
amiably, old friends.
                    Hi, Jack—she says.

Country people, he thinks, mistakenly.
The routines of home seem a lifetime away
and the scenes of his life rather quaint:
an old genre flick, never quite distinct

enough or strange to be revived
except on TV, and then only very late,

with discount mattress and hair transplant ads.

ELIZABETH KNOX

Afraid

*They are passing the plate and I toss in my schooling; I toss in my
rank in the royal navy, my erroneous and incomplete charts, my
pious refusal to eat sled dogs, my watch, my keys and my shoes. I was
looking for bigger game, not little moral lessons; but who can argue
with conditions?*
—Annie Dillard, *Teaching a Stone to Talk*

*'But no one . . . no one in the world could ever seriously believe that I
myself did sleep—on that Thursday night in the garden.'*
—Isak Dinesen, *'Night Walk'*

1

My grandmother saved things. In a side room at right angles
to the wash house, dark but for the open door, or the holes in
its moth-eaten iron roof, Grandma kept salvaged newspapers,
flattened Weetbix packets, egg cartons and carefully washed tin
cans with their labels stripped off. We used to play with the
cans, take them and some old table spoons—EPS worn down to
raw steel—around the back of the house to the patch of gravel
by the wooden steps sheltering the gas meter. We would use
the spoons to shovel stones into the tins. My sister was baking
or feeding baby. I was three and the many measures between
empty and full were fascinating to me in themselves.

In my childhood, God was a closed and curtained house of
which my grandmother was the proprietor. A house my father
escaped by breaking a window and climbing out. The way
Dad would talk, about Grandma and the Catholic church,
encouraged us to regard her—a believer—as an exotic animal,
of a species nearing extinction. We would watch her with
reverent pity.

But I won't tell you about Dad and Grandma; I'll just show you a stone in a can in the hands of a little girl.

She walks up the steps at the top of Pitanga Crescent. She's not supposed to have been able to unlatch the gate and get out. The adults think her sister is watching her. Someone *is* watching her. The steps are long shelves of cement, each step quite an undertaking for a child whose knees are still padded with soft baby fat. She walks up the steps towards the silent forest—talking back to the one watching by rattling a stone in her tin can. The sound it makes is every word, from her first, stretching out a chubby hand and a piece of banana to her mother, saying experimentally, imitating, 'There.' Every word, first to last, and every proposition, command, question in between—a stone in a tin can, rattling as she climbs towards the silent forest.

Tinakori Hill

I took my second illicit walk twenty-seven years later. Sure, I trespassed plenty between times, but that isn't the same. Tinakori Hill was the inside surface of a breaking wave I tried to scale. Years later, one night in a strange city, I took a walk turning thirty corners to the left to find, not sleep, but sense.

Levity

The effort of leaving New Zealand set me off. We saved our money and bought our tickets. We found handholds over the horizon and hauled ourselves across the great populated distances of the Pacific and Asia and North Africa.

    The seats are narrow and everything is reassuringly dull. They show movies; a certain degree of concentration and dexterity is involved in eating your meal. Then you sleep, sometimes between strangers, in an exhausted intimacy. And even if you wake and find all the cabin lights low, everyone asleep, the cabin crew sprawled out in their reserved seats, the jet probably on automatic pilot while its crew of two (747–400) take turns, ideally, catching a bit of shut-eye—even then you know that you're quite safe, because *surely* nothing terrible can happen to an overnight *hui* of insensible people in their stocking feet.

The plane turned from north-west to north-north-west and dawn caught up with us. I leant gingerly on the emergency door and saw islands and rugged peninsulas, mist and mountains.

What fun we'd have.

All roads lead me to believe

It was early morning; the fields steamed. I'd cheated winter. From the bus I saw blossom, and the warmth of sun on ochre walls: Trattoria, Tabacchi, Farmacia, Alimentari. The traffic jammed, exhaling acid. In a garden above the road, on one of those sudden limestone hills, I heard a nightingale. Dad had a record he had played often when I was a child—Respighi, *The Pines of Rome*—a legion passes and the road is restored to silence and a sound like someone writing well about water.

All this is pathology. I am reporting on the progress of my disease: euphoria, then dread, fever, then a walk along narrow streets turning thirty left-hand corners.

I entered my first serpentine city, knowledge ripening in its every coil, at once decrepit and a blood-oiled newborn, shedding its skin with every mention of its name.

I felt smug that I'd cheated winter—but the feeling was dangerous, not worn-in, roaring-twenties-languid-Riviera-tan smug. I wasn't seasoned, spring cut me, sap flowed, some Great Art grafted in God. The graft took, it had a hybrid vigour.

On our third evening, walking back to the pensione, hand in hand, we went along the street of the Three Fountains (there are four, including the art nouveau addition). We passed the Villa Barberini, now an art gallery. The gates were open and we went in to stand on the yellow path. The lawn was covered in daisies, grass as green as it is only when it comes up through sub-zero soil. The fresh smell of the daisies was unhomely at that time of year. My body knew it was autumn—but I had spent three days not on earth. The plane landed. An angel rolled away the stone. Spring came into my nose and mouth as appetising as paradise.

From that moment on my hands, full of nothing but air, seemed to be holding something that squirmed and rustled, and the air between my tongue and palate swelled and unravelled like an itchy bud.

You see

I was happy with my husband, but not with my happiness. Being in love I learned how to carry water. I was always on the level, even in steep places. I'd been put out of my misery and longed to leap back in the window and kick the door shut on my bouncer—like the sabretooth in the closing titles of *The Flintstones*.

Dinner, dishes, an hour with our books, a bath, bed, naked or not. Yes, I can see we all need routine to endure our alloted average seventy years of free will; with indulgences—untimely infatuations, drunken binges, temper tantrums, and holidays in Europe, sampling the great painters like sweets of different flavours, blood sugar boosted, but nothing essentially changed.

The only true virility is pleasure

Our room in Rome overlooks the Piazza della Repubblica. Italy too is rationalising its health services, so every morning we wake up to the sound of traffic through the window and solid shutters and a man shouting something we can't understand. He stands on the curb by the fountain in the Piazza's centre; he waves his genitals at the traffic who hit their horns in outrage or approval or in lieu of lifting a hat to a slight acquaintance. Everything in our room is painted cream, everything but the marble dresser tops, and the cracked, self-adhesive vinyl on the dining table. The floor shakes; the beams beneath its marble tiles have dry rot. We eat panini, white butter, cherry jam, caffe latte. It is cold; I fold my cuffs down over my fingers.

The wisteria at the Forum—constricting woody vines and tassels of blossom—is like ghosts of grape bunches. Each bloom is to a grape what the cast skin of a cicada pupa is to that sound high up the side of power poles, stretching and stretching.

I have fallen ill with tonsilitis, laryngitis and bronchitis. The Italian doctor in horn-rims and a cable knit jersey consults his Collins English Dictionary and explains 'powder' to my husband. Neither of us speaks Italian, but I am prone, little, wearing a Nuclear Free Pacific T-shirt which sweat has adhered to my breasts.

The air shaves my throat. I carry a water bottle, blue label; Aqua Minerale Naturale. The Trevi fountain is under repairs, the workmen wear hard hats to spare their skulls the rain of coins. (Titian's *Danae*, her parted legs and the liquid currency. Lorenzo Lotto's *Nuptials of Venus*—Eros urinates in an arc through a floral wreath and into Venus's cleft hairless lap.)

Inadmissible extremities

The Flupim is oily. It hangs, a haze in the water—tastes very bitter. I can't sleep. I sit on the bidet and run the water till it runs warm, then I wash myself—losing my fresh lacquer of mucus, mine and his.

There. That's as private as the eye-level grime on the feet of Caravaggio's pilgrims in the *Madonna of Loreto* in the church of Sant Agostino. I know what I'm not allowed to say. Writing this I omit my arguments, my evidence: a saintly poet, a door closed for two days, crap in the wastepaper basket. I am no holy man—matted, flea-ridden, mad—nor a Kiwi sybil (there are a number of options, but her hair is carefully clean). My voice will break no by-laws, will never roar through the sleeping suburbs unmuffled by a beard.

No monarch myself, how can God be my subject? There are words that won't be heard at this pitch. I might be sentimental, but not monumental (despite George Eliot's marble pallor and slablike cheeks, despite her able seaman's knots of metaphor). I might be weightless, fly as thistledown in the face of Heaven, but not vigorously winged. I might sing Dido, Violetta, Tosca, even Turandot; but never the sacred music of the Vatican—*Miserere Mei*—the chilly boy treble scaling the cathedral's alpine peaks;

nor the bass masked devil of *Don Giovanni*. Still, here's my pitch, thin hands lifted and lips parted like Donatello's wooden Magdalene. I am she, attenuated, sexless, limbs still marked by the chisel.

When the Martyr Theodora of Thrace wouldn't recant, her enemies fixed barbs in her tongue, drew it out and fastened it to her chest. Then they coated it with seasalt.

In a tutorial on the history of film several of my students are incredulous seeing Eisenstein's citizens of Odessa filing past the body of the martyred sailor.

'He's stretching it a bit there.'

'It's morbid and overwrought.'

My sister conscientiously tells her daughter, 'Unicorns don't *really* exist. We can talk about them, but really, they're made-up.'

In this province and at this hour we are the sum of history, surely, the smooth lower stretches of the river, a safe, sane place. We who came from Europe checked our gods and fears at the door, obedient to the colony's sanitary precautions. Our society is abnormally secular—and passes it off as common sense. Religious appetite, amorousness and anger are diseases—our schools, clubs, places of work, even our places of worship, are quarantines. The morbid, fanatical, heartfelt are set against—as an aunt of mine would say—'bread and butter people', the dour soviet of the man-on-the-street.

What has this secular sun-bonnet ever sheltered me from in an overcast age? Brief illumination—you feed your two hundred lire into the coin box and the spotlights go on for a minute in which you *must notice everything*. Surely the truth is there, colours under candle soot and a troubling perspective (why does the far lintel of the manger come down as far as Saint Joseph's foot?).

God's myths are not medicine

I tell my students about Saint Victoria Martine.

One side chapel in a large Roman church is dedicated to

Victoria Martine, a girl of fifteen who died in the 1820s. Her life is described in late-nineteenth-century paintings: a fat-cheeked Victoria Martine sitting up in bed to converse with a fair-haired Virgin, who gestures with plump hands at an oozing spectral crucifix. Under the altar, in a glass reliquary with golden pillars, is the saint herself. She is the size of a ten-year-old, her narrow feet covered in embroidered satin dancing slippers. She is dressed in bleached muslin and red velvet, her hair dull, arid, matted as felt. Her head is veiled in white gauze, the veil tied at her throat like an improvised beekeeper's mask—through it you can see the deep beige papier-mâché of her mummy's face.

Prestigious, rare, dangerous, ambiguous, forbidden. Different from me. More different than the russet coatimundi with tilted snout and bent tail I gaze at in the Melbourne Zoo, wondering how such a creature came to be (on the far side of the wire, *looking at me*). A corpse is the only truly heterogeneous thing; a tree is a tree, a stone a stone, beneath my notice. A corpse won't talk back, with the coatimundi's dark convex eyes, won't look and look away.

The Flupim is oily. It hangs, a haze in the water, and I drink it down. It's a cough suppressant. I musn't keep my husband awake. But there is something in my chest that I can't shift; perhaps a tinny prayer. *Our Father* where art thou? I'm sorry, this possessive pronoun is taken. *Our father is a journalist. Our father used to climb mountains.* Am I enough of an adult to learn to say 'our' with authority, meaning humanity? Have I ever learned to see the world other than from where I stand?

Look

The Map Room at the Vatican is the length of a rugby field from the halfway line to the goal. All the maps show where the map-maker stood—not by the tourists' flashing arrow, YOU ARE HERE, but because each map has a vantage and, receding from that, the lie of the land.

In the foreground you can see a hermit in his cave, and women washing clothes in a pool beneath a cataract; then the butterfly collection of distant villages, fixed and surmounted by their steeples. Then the land flattens out, landscape becomes chart, the rivers red, the towns tiny dots. The land rises, there is no horizon, Umbria is a curling scroll. Or the inside surface of a breaking wave.

The lie of the land is this: that these Principalities (as they once were) are the same landscapes as the backgrounds of paintings whose foregrounds are occupied by nursing Virgins (the child with coral around his wrist and a finch in his fist), agonies in the garden, Lazarus coming forth, and other crucial fictions (ashy skies hanging over this same hill). I wonder, if I searched carefully enough in Umbria, Tuscany, Lombardy, finding this conical hill, or that scalloped stream-bed, will I have found the site of disputed miracles? And, maybe, evidence—the steaming spore of St Jerome's lion, or a frayed rope around the branch of a flowering tree.

My husband leaves me in the lumpy bed at the Pensione Esedra, with water and a packet of sweet lemon wafers. He leaves me too long and I go to sleep. Then it is evening and the blue in the casement, between the wings of cream painted shutters, is not home's homely terrifying gulf, the sun thrown back by the tilted mirror of southern ice. This sky is different. Even lacking clouds, this sky has a sort of geography, various perspectives of light that make it look somehow habitable—say, by angels.

My husband comes in with the the sights I haven't seen stored in my camera. He is a curly-haired shadow. He puts the camera on the bed. Only the blue isn't fading. Our bodies are indistinct in the dusk, in a fur of mould, or smeared with ash. My husband has bought bread with a thick crust; fibrous, whey-saturated mozzarella; porcini paste; tomatoes two days off the vine; olives only a few days in brine, and still crisp; blood oranges and Vino Rustico, a flagon bottle with a tin screw cap. He turns on the light—bravely manning the pumps to bail that blue back out of the room.

Andiamo.

2

Venice in spring. 10° Celsius. A place where reality has worn
thin. The crust of the earth is only thirty metres thick—and
undermined by the wells of Mestre. The city has 'a certain slant
of light' that 'depresses'. Or perhaps not a slant, but a flatness,
pallor, a glassiness. Here, it is said, someone discovered, then
lost, a pattern of tessellated mosaic capable of driving men mad.
There's a retentive lunacy in the names of its streets: 'Alley of
Curly-Haired Women', 'Filled Canal of Thoughts'—or, more
famous: 'Calle degli Assissini' or 'Ponte dei Sospiri' (The Bridge
of Sighs is also that hairy suede emptiness between a man's
anus and testicles). Venice—a wasps' nest made of spit and
shavings; or a great funeral barge, sailing down the centuries,
carrying plague and treasure, heaped around Saint Mark's
stolen corpse.

A night walk

I went out the two security doors of the hotel's annex, into the
blind alley. For once the windows above me were shut, no one
leaning out conversing on either the vertical or horizontal axis.
I passed under the black wooden beams over the entrance to
the alley and turned left. The street was crooked, broad for
Venice, about fifteen feet across. It was lined with Trattorias,
Alimentaris, shops selling film and cameras. During the day
there were stalls festooned with flags, stripped shirts, sailor's
caps, straw boaters with long black ribbons, and strings of
beads: pearls, pyrites, tiger's-eyes, lapis lazuli, coral, jasper, and
glass mosaic. The street was quiet now. I passed the church with
scarred brickwork, grass on its cornices and a tower full of flat-
toned bells, like a head full of cracked teeth. I crossed a canal,
left, over the first unadorned marble bridge.

   Each turn I took was a door closing securely, biting the air
behind me. I entered another broader street, beside a canal. The
tide was high; it gulped at submerged steps. A tenth of the solid
world was at anchor, in motion, nodding out of unison. I skirted

the edge of a piazza, past a stone well capped by a heavy iron lid. The piazza was sectioned by steel sheets suspended in frames— they looked like backstage thunder machines, but were only the city's hoardings brought out at election time for the campaign posters. The homeless of Venice, a group of cats, eyed me; dirty tortoiseshells and tabbies with kinky tails, tailbones showing like peas in a peapod. I turned into a narrow street. Here there was little light—the moon diffused through the pelt of mist that lay over the whole lagoon. The street was very narrow; I could stretch my arms across it. There were narrower streets—like the one two days before that had forced me to close my umbrella as its spokes were scraping the stonework on either side.

Another bridge, marble, arched, its steps coated in asphalt. On the corner an ornate iron lamp. Then oddly, growing and dying, muffled by buildings, the throb of a barge's engine. In the next street someone was leaning out a third-storey window lowering a cat in a basket. The basket touched down and the cat jumped out. The basket was taken up again and the shutters closed. I called the cat, 'Puss, puss . . .' but it only looked back at me warily and without comprehension.

I suspected I would find myself walking a loop if I took the next left hand turn, so I walked on a little further knowing that, doing so, I'd almost certainly get lost. I turned at a corner decorated by a shrine, a painting of the Virgin and child, topped by a plaque remembering some martyred partisans. The shrine was adorned with wilted Easter flowers and two candles, flames guttering in jars filled with red wax. It was another very narrow street. Above, the hands-breadth of sky was only slightly lighter that the eaves. Then came another canal, a gust of choleric silt, and another bridge, this one not upgraded, the edges of its stone steps worn into ripples, a depression in the middle of each as though centuries of traffic had compacted its atoms.

At the head of the next street there was a statue, a high relief sculpture of a man, battered, pitted by ice and blanched by acid—and the victim of some home-handyman restoration. Someone had covered the syphilitic hole in the centre of his face with a wedge of tin. The tin was rusted, I reached up to touch it and flakes of rust dirtied my fingertips.

This street brought me out adjacent to a wider canal. I turned my thirtieth corner, went along the embankment, passed a bridge on my right hand. I found myself before a high Gothic arch, a tunnel beneath a gatehouse, and a closed door. The door was ancient, anaemic wood, criss-crossed with narrow bands of studded iron, the studs long ago worn down to nipples. I took hold of the door's iron ring handles and pulled back, then leant forward. As I did so the door gave a little on its bolt and I put my eye to the gap that appeared. I saw the stonework of an enclosed passage, a curved wall covered in condensation, sidelit by some unsteady, artificial light—fire, candle, lamp.

Of hidden thoughts, and of heaven

Behind me someone said, 'It's locked.'

I walked out from under the arch. There was a man standing on the bridge. He wore a long pale coat and, at the moment I turned to look at him, the lit ripples of the canal were reflecting on one side of his face in tigerish stripes. How had I failed to notice him when I passed?

'How do you know to speak to me in English?' I asked.

'By your shoes.'

I looked at my shoes: ox-blood leather, high gloss, with rounded, roomy toes. 'There are Germans wearing shoes like these too.'

'But you don't look German.' He had turned to face me and was leaning the small of his back against the balustrade. Giving me his attention in invitation. I was too timid to come closer.

'So,' he said, 'There's this bridge, and the way back.' He was a native English speaker, but I couldn't place his accent. He said, 'I wonder what you are doing out on the streets in the middle of the night. Venice isn't exactly well-endowed with night-spots.'

I had begun to worry about being alone with this man, when a light went on in a window high up the wall behind me. I saw him turn his eyes up to the light, without moving his head, then look back at me with confiding good humour. It was like that electric moment in *The Third Man* when a light goes on and there is Harry Lime, an apparition, smiling at his old

friend: *Well, as you can see, you haven't been told the truth.* He
said, 'Don't be edgy, it's just a nasty side effect of a very nice
prescription—mystery, that is.'

I walked up on to the bridge beside him. The light went off
and something seemed to spring back into place around him.
Force at rest—that's what it was. I stood beside him, leaning
into this invisible volume of being. I looked up at him, he was
taller than me, and standing a step higher on the arch. 'I've been
sick,' I said. 'My fever has me on a long lead now, and is taking
me for a walk.'

He watched me and waited. The shape of his head was less
distinct; his movements had pulled some of his long hair free of
the collar of his coat.

'I'm leaving Italy in four days. My white whale is about to
sound and disappear into a deep trench.'

'Are you quite sure it *is* a white whale and not a white
elephant?'

'I'm like the horse in Caravaggio's *Conversion of St Paul* —
sluggish and envious, my eye suspiciously rolled back to watch
the man lying at my feet, spread-eagled in ecstasy in a great
noontide eclipsing light. And all I'm thinking is, "This will
never happen to me." I never *wanted* God before. How could I
want something I was sure didn't exist? God doesn't exist in the
southern hemisphere, but He does here.'

'Sure—He's in retirement in some small villa in Tuscany.'

I shook my head. 'No. He's everywhere here, looking out of
the paintings and buildings and the seven separate shades of
seven different colours in the sky above the causeway between
Mestre and Santa Lucia. He keeps retreating ahead of me,
around the next corner.' I pointed at the dark arch, the locked
door. 'I'm out walking because I can't sleep. Because I've four
more days to find God.'

'And you're afraid you won't.'

'I'm afraid I'll stop wanting to.'

He laughed and I said sulkily, 'God doesn't exist anyway. So
I won't find Him.'

'Should He exist?'

'I don't know. But this *desire* should. Anyway, I wanted to do something organised while I was thinking, something like magic, so I set out to turn thirty left hand corners.'

'*Left* hand? Are you sure it's God you're looking for?'

A clipped-nail moon had cleared the television aerials and conical chimney pots, and was shining its filtered radiance on the canal. Light caught his face in watery flashes.

Still trying to explain I told him what I saw in the Sistine Chapel. How, on the ceiling, Michelangelo had painted God separating light from darkness and casting Lucifer from heaven. And how, in that painting, God, set against the light, and Lucifer, set against darkness, were the same. 'They have the same stormy grey hair, the same beard, same clothes. But Lucifer has his back turned and his buttocks bared—like: *kiss my arse*. His body and draperies make an eye shape, the buttocks are a cataract-covered iris.'

'I see. Like a total eclipse; really nothing could be more revealing.'

I stroked the satiny marble of the balustrade. 'I have even more trouble believing in the devil than in God. But I'm looking for *something*, something I saw in the mosaic ceiling of the Baptistry in Florence. It wasn't just a *picture* of the time when people believed like I can't, it *was* that time, suspended above ours, like a shell around our world. The realm of the fixed stars they believed in, with the light of heaven shining through its many apertures.'

'Sounds as though you want God's grace. *I'd* rather have a job to do than God's grace.'

'Why are you out on the street in the middle of the night?'

He smiled, then said, 'Look, have you ever heard the unofficial biography of Christ?'

'"The son of a Roman soldier"?'

'No, not that one.'

'Tell me.'

The Hebrews had no one jealous God Yahweh, but instead a collection of gods and goddesses. Not that this made them any less ripe victims of Imperial Rome. In a time shortly after the tribes of Israel had surrendered unwillingly to the sovereignty

of Rome, a son was born to a couple in Nazareth, an elderly
carpenter and his young wife, who was descended by a decayed
line from an important Israelite king.

The child, Yeshua bar Joseph, was trained in carpentry by
his father. But he was always too restless and enquiring for
the trade and was wont to wander off and be found nosing
around the libraries of various temples. Really, he was a bit of a
disappointment to his father, but his mother doted on him.

In his late teens Yeshua left Nazareth to travel. He drifted
around the east, Babylon and Egypt, Sumeria and even as far
as India. Travelling, he made his living by acting and story-
telling. Sometimes, when hard pressed, he would court favour,
or food, or a bed for the night, by healing people. Generally
he was inhibited and secretive about this talent. Whatever his
intentions were on each occasion he resorted to it—to pacify
some unfriendly locals, or just to take away the suffering of the
person in front of him—he could always feel vistas of *future*
opening up before him like hungry, uncrossed deserts.

On his journey back home Yeshua made friends with a
number of other wandering Jews: a public letter writer called
John; a trio of siblings who sang and danced and collected
songs and dances, Mary, Martha and Lazarus; and a couple of
actors cum political agitators, Simon and Mark. When he joined
these countrymen Yeshua stopped performing his miracles
altogether, afraid of setting himself apart from them. They led
such difficult, conscribed lives, his healing made him feel too
able for their company.

On their return to their homeland the friends settled for a time
in Galilee. There they performed to tavern-keepers, fishermen,
shepherds, tax collectors, their plays—mainly political satires
about the concupiscent King and vacillating Roman Governor.
Yeshua wrote many of these satires, and often took the leading
role. He had such great personal charm that he won a large
following of admirers and hangers-on—mostly from the poor
and politically disaffected. Although he was loving and frank
with all his friends, and with strangers, all Yeshua's friendships
stayed on the far side of intimacy. He didn't want to get so close
to anyone that they could gauge the discrepancies between him

and other people. As it was, when his widowed mother joined
him in Galilee, even she—who had held his hand as he took his
first steps—could sense the potential power in him. He was like
a great rock, balanced precariously on top of a high mountain,
surveying the world, camps of friends and enemies, all beneath
him.

Yeshua and his friends, fired up by their success in the
provinces, decided to go to Jerusalem to perform their plays.
Their reception was enthusiastic, but not universal. The King
and various priests were thoroughly incensed and wanted the
Roman Governor to do something about Yeshua, if not all his
colleagues. In an audience with the King, one of the priestesses
of Astarte pointed out that Yeshua was a perfect candidate
for the yearly sacrifice. The sacrifice commemorated the death
of Astarte's lover Atis, who was torn apart by being lashed
to the branches of two bent trees. It was the main spring rite
in Jerusalem. Yeshua, the priestess observed, was a perfect
candidate: handsome, healthy, reputedly chaste, talented, and a
descendant of a royal line. In these difficult times the spilling of
royal blood was necessary to mollify the goddess.

On a blazing hot, still afternoon—a Thursday—Yeshua
received a warning to leave the city. He and his friends were
at the house of a cousin of Matthew the tax collector. Just
after the noon meal, the household and guests were sitting
about drinking watered wine and arguing politics. A messenger
arrived and asked to see Yeshua. The messenger, the servant of
a Roman official, was Hebrew, but clean-shaven, Romanised—
a young man with his red hair cut short and curling around
his brow. The messenger delivered a package and left. Yeshua
unravelled the cloth wrapping and found a bag of coins—thirty
silver talents—and a length of rope. There was a scrolled strip
of vellum with the coins and rope, on which was written: 'Leave
the city. These are now the only means by which you may
leave of your own *free will*. After tonight I cannot accept any
responsibility for your fate.' Yeshua hid the letter and gifts and
went out into the walled yard of the house. He washed his hands
in the fountain. Its water was as warm as blood. There was a fig
tree growing by the fountain, but it had no fruit and cast only a

thin shade. Yeshua looked back into the hot shadowy house at
Martha speaking while everyone else listened, their robes limp
and sweat varnishing their faces. She talked and they listened as
though her talk and their listening would change something, as
though they'd be recorded and repeated, as though their minds
were energy that would neither change nor migrate to another
part of the universe. The water dried sticky on his hands
and, impulsively, Yeshua reached out one hand and, touching
the trunk of the barren fig tree, he cursed it. The blow was
casually malicious, but lethal. It was many days till the women
of the house noticed the fig was dead (dead leaves had fouled
the fountain when a servant went out to fetch water to wash a
corpse). They said it was the heat, or the wrath of the goddess
at a tree without fruit during her fertility festival.

That night, Yeshua was arrested, taken to the temple of
Astarte, and dedicated for sacrifice. But his friends loved him
enough to defy the goddess. They talked up a storm in the city's
marketplace, raised a mob, broke into the temple, and spirited
Yeshua away. They took him to the house of Mary, Martha and
Lazarus's family. The house was in mourning, shuttered and
secluded. Lazarus had died of a sudden illness during the day of
Yeshua's imprisonment. His family had readied a tomb for him
in the valley of catacombs on the road between Jerusalem and
Bethany. The sisters of the dead man wrapped Yeshua in the
grave-clothes they had washed and scented for their brother.
While the servants of the house took Lazarus's body to a secret
burial in the Potter's field, Yeshua left Jerusalem in the midst of
mourners, on a bier and shrouded head to foot.

The Roman Governor was beset by priests and courtiers
demanding that Yeshua's friends be arrested. The Governor
was afraid that the riot would lead to more unrest, so he had
Yeshua's male friends sought out and taken prisoner. This was a
miscalculation of the part of the Governor. Contrary to his plans
these arrests precipitated an overnight rebellion in Jerusalem. It
was a bloody uprising and the legion suffered heavy losses in
putting it down. When the rebellion was quelled the Governor
publicly executed, by crucifixion, a number of its 'instigators',
including Yeshua's friends.

Martha, Mary and Yeshua's mother, knowing he would try
to return to Jerusalem as soon as he heard about the uprising,
shut him in Lazarus's tomb for three days. When they released
him they tried to persuade him that he should accept his losses
as they did, that his friends were gone and he should look to his
own safety. But grief seemed to have driven him insane—grief or
the entombment. He swore that, as a healer, he could restore his
dead friends to life. With the women he returned to Jerusalem,
and stole the corpses off the grove of crosses lining the road
to the summit of Golgotha. They hid away at the house of
Matthew's cousin, and there Yeshua tried to restore his friends'
torn, sun-blistered, disjointed, parched bodies to life. For a time
it seemed he might succeed; the welts faded, the watery blisters
melted back into their skin, their wrenched joints straightened.
One even opened his eyes. Peter, who was always so attentive,
loyal and obedient, opened his eyes and lay all night, trying
to focus, idly, like a very young baby. But, at cockcrow, Peter
closed his eyes again and stopped breathing. The three women
washed the corpses while Yeshua sat to one side (and a servant,
fetching water, found the fountain fouled by fallen leaves, as
black as rotten seaweed). Yeshua sat, silent, with a cloth over
his head. Eventually he got up and, looking at Peter's body, said,
'He's like a hail-spoiled apple; it looks perfect but is spotted
with bruises beneath its skin.' He said to Mary and Martha,
'Take care of my mother.' Then he wrapped the cloth tighter
around his head, and left the city.

Shortly afterward a plague fell on the house of the Roman
Governor, and spread to the city's garrison, killing and crippling
many. The Governor fled, taking with him only his favourite
manservant, the red-haired, clean-shaven Romanised Jew. The
Governor and his servant carried the plague back to Rome.
That summer half the population of that great city perished.
All the patrician families were decimated. The empire became
bankrupt, the legions rebelled, and Rome fell.

As for Yeshua, he walked out of his life and into a desert. A
wilderness of sand and thorns, unplanted, not with the cedar,
nor the myrtle, the oil tree, the fir tree, the pine and the box tree
together. A habitation for dragons and a court for owls. From

that wilderness he went still further, where the dunes crested above him like breaking waves, whose inside surfaces he scaled, defying gravity with his greater gravity. With so much grief, he was a super-heavy body, like a collapsed sun, a starter-kit black hole.

Yes, he walked up dunes like the gold mosaic-adorned domes of great temples, arching and burning above the world he had known. He passed from the Still There, the world of his people, into the Always There, the world of self-made men (but until he came, there were none). And when he had forsaken the Still There he lost something forever, because although it was a lesser and sadder order of existence, it was marvellous in the way that skin is more marvellous than sound.

How can I find words to describe where he found himself? And here *I* am, muscling my way into his story looking for words.

I stayed quiet, looking along the canal—around its dog-leg corner a sliver of watery distance, the lights on the Lido, and a lemon-rind dawn horizon. After a moment, sifting himself out of his story, the stranger went on.

In the place his grief and self-disgust and denial of death had taken him, Yeshua grew into the emptiness, into the low pressure, like one of those deep water fish which swell when hauled up into the air. He grew strong enough to break time and time's desires; so returned to reshape his own life, beginning thirty centuries before his birth—with a world of green meadows, white mountains, dark blue lakes fringed with frothy white lilies, and with angels. There he began to hoard souls as they left earth, so that one day he could collect the souls of his friends. He made promises to the people of the tribes of Israel, sent his voice through burning bushes and columns of smoke. They called him their God, Yahweh. He awaited his own birth, planning a life for himself in which, this time, the sacrifice would be his, in which he could offer eternal security from death to his beloved friends, in which he would be irresistibly strong and his great love would guarantee their lives.

He sent his mother an angel to tell her she had conceived God—to God. He was born, an infant honoured with gifts and enemies. He was baptised. He spoke words and many believed Him. He healed the sick and raised the dead, came to Jerusalem and quarrelled with the Rabbis; turned the money-changers out of the temple. He had a last meal with His friends before the fast of Passover, and He sweated in the garden. He was betrayed, imprisoned, lashed, questioned, mocked and taken to an appointed place of execution and nailed to a cross between two thieves (two bent trees).

Everything had been different. He had lost His own earthly treasure. His friends' lives in the land of the One Jealous God were so different that, when He met them, He would scarcely have known them. Mary, who had been lithe and joyful, was tired and sick with shame when they first met; John and Peter and Simon, all so pious and stay-at-home. They would watch Him as He spoke, their faces reverent and compliant. They were careful not to stand too close to Him unless offering protection in a crush. It was as though they were studying His life, not living theirs. Not that this Yeshua clearly remembered His former life. But He was haunted by sadness, even sitting on the shores of Galilee, watching the coals of the fire crumbling and savouring the taste of baked fish. And there were times when His loneliness terrified him—when He faced that cave with the stone four days upon it, His sense of remembered defeat was so strong it had Him in tears.

And Yahweh? Eventually they came to him—the women, the disciples—came to the one who loved them. They gazed at him, their faces wiped clean with peace. They called him 'Father'. They did not know him.

Above us, along the eaves, pigeons had begun to warble, a sound like someone rubbing a pane of glass. I stared at the stranger and he smiled back at me with high good humour, like someone who has won a bet. He said, 'So you see, the folly of over-extending your reach.'

'If I don't find what I want I'm going to feel like a failure. I'll get on a plane home but my heart will keep on faithfully flying its holding pattern, waiting for a signal from some celestial air traffic control. I'm more likely to come into money—for more air tickets—than I am to come in to land.'

The water of the canal was grey now, not black, and the sky between the eaves was cream. He had his hands tucked into his armpits and I could see the grain in his steaming breath. 'I don't think I can find my way back,' I said.

His answer was prosaic: 'If we cross this bridge and turn right, we'll find ourselves on the waterfront, I think.'

We walked down the far side of the arch together. He was right. We came out on to the wharfs where the tugs were moored. The sun was rising and the mist turned melon pink. I looked at him, expecting red hair and a smooth shaven face. Well, his face was smooth, but his hair was black and his eyes dark blue (but not fringed with frothy lilies, or with angels). We turned right again, towards San Marco, from where everyone is able to find their way. As we walked he told me: 'Before you leave the city you must go to the Cappella Cortigiani and look at the statue in its porch. It was sculpted by Angelo Santisilia, a Neapolitan, the finest pupil of Leonidas Allori. When his master died Santisilia became a drunken drifter for some time. But he kept his hand in. The statue was his only uncommissioned work. It isn't a sacred subject; but everyone loved it, that's why it's in the porch of the Cappella.'

'Is it in the guide books?'

'I don't know.'

We stopped by the Doge's palace and looked across the mouth of the Grand Canal at the sun on a golden globe atop the wedge-shaped custom-house—and at the domes and decorations of the Salute, its marble crystalline white. The wind was trying to stir the pigeons into the sky and behind us a waiter was cranking up a restaurant's aluminium awning. The man beside me took my arm and, still staring at the Salute as if trying to outface its whiteness, he said, to it: 'Loose her; let her go.'

I stand with my husband in the porch of the Cappella Cortigiani, our backs to the stretched, dusty afternoon sunlight. The statue is on a plinth. It is of a man, down on one knee, his knee and foot level with my mouth. Like the statue of St Jerome in San Zanipolo it is sculpted of white marble flawed by cysts of red. On the shoulder of St Jerome the red marble seemed like liver-coloured birthmarks; on *this* face and bared breast the flaws are blood. Judas—not a sacred subject—is down on one knee, his robe loose. He has just unfastened his rope sash and holds it before him, looped around one hand as if he has begun to make a knot. His head is turned to one side, listening. His shoulders are bent inwards in a cringe, and his muscles are *forced*—upper arms striated, marked by runnels, like the muscles of Rodin's models. He is youthful, his face shaven, his hair in ratted curls. From somewhere above him—the shade of a tree the sculptor has imagined—flowers have fallen. They are rendered, as delicate as carved ivory, one in his hair, one caught in a fold of the robe, and one on his wrist. By his foot rests a deflated bag and spilled coins. There is something about his pose, his furtive distress, his youth, that has made people want to comfort him—his foot and knee have that polished, many-times-touched look. But the coins (the talents) are still sharp and distinct—the spilled money that no one touches.

On the night train to Paris, I was rocked in my couchette, the compartment utterly black. I had taken a Halcyon tablet. In my sleep I felt the changes of gradient as we reached the pass through the Alps. I heard the hollow sound of iron bridges, and in the tunnels the voice of the train constantly referring to itself. I heard the trumpeting of cuttings and felt the fringes of giant herds of wind grazing the sides of the train. I was too groggy even to get up, go into the corridor and look at the black window, the reflected corridor lights, and my own face.

We left Italy.

EMMA LEW

Grace to the Goodsyard

I break things because I am afraid and I spend my time
    repairing
It's almost the expression of love
I found these beautiful machines abandoned here
Sometimes there is nothing to inherit

It's almost the expression of love
To hunt, to seduce, to deal with a stone
Sometimes there is nothing to inherit
Footprints on the path that leads to the house

To hunt, to seduce, to deal with a stone
I did not even know that I was naked
Footprints on the path that leads to the house
In that street, close to the sky

I did not even know that I was naked
I set out, taking my precautions
In that street, close to the sky
I must tell my story, and I must forget my story

I set out, taking my precautions
I found these beautiful machines abandoned here
I must tell my story, and I must forget my story
I break things because I am afraid and I spend my time
    repairing

J.H. MACDONALD

from On the Burning Deck

The British Empire has 40 million square kilometres . . . Germany,
600,000. It is quite clear who desires to conquer the world.
—Adolf Hitler

4 August 1986

It is just before night comes down, those few minutes when the
trees fill with irrelevant birds and the world hesitates. Front is
pixilated. He stands stock still, alert to every possibility that
might shiver in the dusk, then bolts into the dark beneath the
Moreton Bay figs at the end of the lawn. He reappears a moment
or two later, pedigree, investigative, at the foot of a clump of
giant bamboo.

These grounds belong to a former Government mansion that
has been incorporated into the University, and Alec brings his
dog across here for exercise every night. He treats the grounds
like a keyholder to a London square. He took the right as
professor emeritus.

The gardens are secluded and romantic with their flame trees
and Bird of Paradise plants that imply the real tropics; however
there are groves of leafless oak trees that contradict them, and
a venerable group of Campbell's magnolia, planted late last
century by the wife of some high colonial official. Even though
midwinter has barely passed, it is the viewing season, for these
trees are in flower. I can't decide about them. Their flowers are
a coarse, music-hall pink, but the swollen buds you might take
for small birds, sparrows, so lifelike are they, perched on those
elaborate, Chinese branches.

Tonight I have brought Olga over to take the air, since there
seemed to be a break in the almost unceasing showers of rain. She
and Alec rest on the terrace of the mansion. Alec lounges against
the balustrade, and in her wheelchair, a taffeta waterproof over

her shoulders, Olga sits like a wooden god enthroned. She talks endlessly to Alec. I am out of earshot, but I can see that he is getting restless and puts his hand into the pocket of his jacket for his cigarette case.

I whistle Front up, 'End of the game, Front,' and we go back towards the terrace.

I can hear Olga now, 'And after all that, how is it that one can never find the exact word to describe the expression on a person's face? And that is not quite what I wanted to say either. I mean the history of a face too.'

Alec stops leaning on the balustrade and stands up. 'The things you talk about, Olga, are simply not there.' He begins along the terrace.

'Alec,' Olga calls out, 'remember the pooper-scooper.' Olga can't reach down far enough to be able to pick it up. When Alec turns back she says quietly, 'The dog is yours, and you cannot expect your secretary to carry that thing.'

Alec walks ahead, and I follow pushing Olga. The chair needs a bit of manoeuvring over the single step when we go inside. Their flat is in an old block. The fanlight gives the name in ruby glass: *Valmouth*. Olga and Alec live on the top floor in an apartment made out of several of the original small flats. We have to wait in the lobby for the lift.

Alec says, 'I mean there's no logical connection between what you see and what you want to read into it, Olga.' Olga ignores him. The lift mechanism makes a noise, and through the grille I see it begin to pull the slack loop of cable up as the cage descends.

Alec bends down and speaks to Front. 'Doggy. And doggy, what if human beings all had tails like you, eh?' Front promptly sits down in expectation of something: a pat, a titbit. 'What if that were the case? Poker, diplomacy, human intercourse itself, would not be possible.'

Olga laughs. She turns her wheelchair in a complete circle so as to come to rest facing Alec. She raises a finger in admonition. 'Watch out, riverboat gambler,' she says. 'Tonight's the night the lights went out all over Europe.'

The lift arrives. There isn't enough room for a wheelchair

and another person, so Olga goes up first and sends it back for
Alec and me.

I have been Alec's nominal assistant now for almost six weeks.
There is very little to do. Alec has hardly any correspondence
anymore, and seems to prefer to spend most of the day by
himself. He stays in his studio, where he makes buildings for
an immense model city he is devising. Nevertheless he wants
me round in the flat, as we have arranged, should he need
me. Sometimes he calls me in to help adjust something in the
city, or add a new building. The model is much bigger than a
ping-pong table, and we use a boathook. Or at least I do. Alec
is not strong enough in the shoulders now to keep the thing
steady, and he could easily drop it on the model. We edge the
toy edifices out on to the streets and gently nudge them along.
When I get them within reach I can sweep them up with a
long-handled brush and shovel. Adding things is the reverse.
You just put them down in a convenient street, as close to the
eventual site as you can reach, and push them the rest of the
way with the hook.

Alec is nervous as a cat while we are making these alterations
to his city. When I do not quite follow what he has in mind, he
gets slightly impatient. 'I do believe, Nicholas, that I shall have
to reinstate the system I used with my previous assistants. I will
bring the big plan up to date again, and then I can simply give
you the drawings and the address. I will go to Olga's room and
talk to her while you put the changes into effect.' All the streets
on the model have names in Alec's mind, and all these little
blocks of wood like cigarette packets are tall houses with street
numbers and occupants. He never gets round to doing anything
about the map though. It's almost as if he would rather keep it
all in his head.

There is a trapdoor in the middle of the city where Alec has
made a park. This part seems to be finalised because Alec has
glued the miniature trees to the top of the trap so they don't
fall off when you open it up and put your head out. But maybe
you just have to do that with toy cities. Now and then to move
things Alec wants moved, I have to crawl under the table and

come out through the trapdoor in the centre of the city. I have an idea then why he has made it.

Olga's room always has flowers. People bring them to her. Really quite a lot of people come to see Olga and sit in her room and talk. Dr Lindenbaum pays more house calls than are strictly necessary, for example. Then there are callers in the late afternoon. They gush at me in the hall when I let them out, 'Isn't she wonderful? Such an appetite for life at her age.'

I have to answer the door. Alec skulks in his studio at that hour of the day.

Olga likes her flowers to be lavish. She likes branches of them in her room if she can get them. The university groundsman cut down an armful of magnolia and gave them to Alec, for Olga. 'Did you ask him for them?' Olga said when Alec brought them in.

'It took me a bit by surprise,' Alec said. He told Olga that the groundsman had called out to him and asked after her. He had seen us come across the night before. So Alec told the groundsman it was our blossom viewing party. He had thought for a moment, then said abruptly that he'd cut some down for her, and gone away and fetched his pruning shears. 'I couldn't say no,' Alec finished.

'Lean man, very bright blue eyes?' Olga asked. Alec said he thought so. Couldn't be sure.

'He's been in those grounds for almost forty years, man and boy,' Olga said. 'He used to wolf whistle at me. It was a standing joke.'

Alec allows himself three cigarettes a day: one with lunch, one after dinner, and one for emergencies. He doesn't always use the emergency one and saves them up for Wednesday and Saturday. Alec does the cooking, and he has people to dinner on those days. Sunday evening is given over to watching television since there might be something 'presentable' to watch that night. On Wednesday Alec's friend Geoff Butler generally comes to dinner. Geoff Butler was once Alec's student. Now he is fifty-five, and they share an interest in wine and food. And they talk about public life. There is a Mrs Butler. The permanent invitation to her has never been dropped, but it is never spoken of. On Saturday Miss Rose comes. Miss Rose lives in one of the flats downstairs. She met Olga when they were both mixed up in the theatre. Miss Rose was the wardrobe mistress sometimes, and sometimes the prompt.

Olga can be a snob. She will not accept that the woman who delivers books to house-bound readers for the public library simply brings the books and takes them away again. She comes once a fortnight, and they have elevenses. It is easiest for the volunteer to find a parking place at that time. The reason is not clear.

Olga says that she is such a nice, intelligent woman, who is very good at choosing books. The volunteer is rather ordinary and suburban. Olga blandly flatters her on her judgment and sensititivity in bringing exactly the books that Olga wants to read, and ignores her embarrassment. Olga's tastes are actually not that specific. She munches steadily through biographies that cover the period of her life. Granted she does have a preference for careers in arts, letters, theatre, music, but politics, the profession of arms, anything touching this century will do. She isn't interested in Frederick the Great, but she is very interested in what Cyril Connolly thinks about Frederick the Great.

A woman comes to clean the flat four mornings a week. She and Olga are thick as thieves. She is the salt of the earth. It is probably a good thing that they are cronies. Her cleaning is pretty perfunctory, but Mrs Wells does a lot of things for Olga that she can't do for herself anymore. Olga can't reach up to hang things in the wardrobe, and she leaves them out for Mrs Wells to put away. Olga wears a mandarin dressing gown all morning, and Mrs Wells helps her get dressed before she leaves at midday.

I don't have lunch with Olga and Alec. I try to get out for a couple of hours when they are having their naps, so I have a snack afterwards.

You've got to get a break, or you start to feel as old as they are.

But this job suits me. It gives me time. I get a room and board, and a small allowance: pocket money. At least since Alec's an economist, he has realistic ideas about what you need for pocket money.

And it's a nice room, up under the roof away from the main part of their flat. There's a desk and a bookcase, and I can look over the parapet, away down the harbour to the islands in the distance. They do want me in the flat a lot of the time, but that's all right. It's just wanting me there, not wanting me to be doing anything in particular, and I get plenty of time to get on with my own interests. I had heard about Alec and Olga before I came here, they're well known, and I expected there would be more to it than being simply Alec's secretary. Anyway I couldn't bear the idea of trudging to work at a set time every day with all the other sheep, and trudging home again, and not having anything useful to do in between. Just some stupid job.

I have taken to conducting long conversations with Olga in her room during the second part of the afternoon. She is happy to talk. Then the three of us take tea in there at five o'clock, and afterward Alec goes to cook dinner. 'It keeps him alive,' says Olga.

At first Alec took me with him when he went out for provisions. Now he tends to stay in, and I go out more and more on errands by myself. He still takes Front out every day. Olga goes with him in her wheelchair on the days 'when her legs feel like it'.

Dinner takes place in Alec's studio. It is a vast space that he has carved out of two floors at the top of the building. The outside wall is made of glass bricks. The base for the model city takes up most of the floorspace in the high part of the studio, and there is a sleeping gallery where Alec and Front have their lair. Below that there is an alcove lined with books that is used as a living area. There is a long sofa, covered with a piece of folk weaving, and the round table that we eat at.

Olga's room is quite different from the studio, which is a sort of modern monastery. Her room is full of what she calls her 'souvenirs'. She has a fondness for objects that are Victorian and surrealist at the same time, like small vases in the form of hands. There is an engraving in an ebony frame by the door that I look at as I go in and out. It shows red-coated Marines getting out of a rowing boat beached on a tropical strand, and advancing towards figures in grass skirts. Underneath it is entitled *Interview with the Chief of the Gambier Islands.* 'That is my souvenir of West Africa,' Olga says, 'not that I have ever been there.'

Olga doesn't use the wheelchair in the house. It folds up and goes with the overcoats and umbrellas in the hall. She has been supplied with a walking frame. She is supposed to use her legs as much as possible to keep them functioning.

I sneak into Alec's room now and then and gaze at the model. He knows I am doing it but hasn't said anything. It's like old travellers' tales that speak of the first view of foreign parts: Venice rising like a dream from the Lagoon as you approach in a silent boat; Naples seen from the Bay, before you land and discover its matrix of noise, decaying buildings, public spaces, private rooms, buying and selling, bad government, domestic life, washing out over narrow streets, noblemen, fishwives, urchins, black cats, cut-velvet hangings, broken tables and chairs; the gilded spires and domes of St Petersburg, glittering on a low horizon against the grey skies of the Gulf of Finland; Constantinople; or an Englishwoman who writes in the early nineteenth century about the first sight of the Eternal City after crossing the Campagna, when the guide stops your horses on an empty hilltop and says in grave and sonorous tones, *'Ecco— Roma.'*

I find it difficult to, imagine exactly how Olga sees her own life now. She must spend a lot of time thinking back, although she doesn't talk about it very much. I try to see myself as a boy. It's not easy to get hold of; it seems to be like fishing, you've got to wait for them to rise. There's a flicker. It's almost as if I felt a small body crouching inside me for a moment, and the recollection surfaces of Snail Racing. I save it up to tell Olga.

'I used to have a game when I was a little boy, about three or four. You found two snails and put them down on the path, then waited for them to come out of their shells again, put their eyes up, and then you saw which one would go the greatest distance. My father called it that first, I suppose, not me. He would have enjoyed the irony.'

'You like it there?' my mother asks.

'Yes, I do.' It is almost too candid, that question.

'I hope you're getting out of the house. It can become very depressing in the end, cooped up all day with old people.'

'I'm getting a bit of work done, and I try to go for a swim every day. I see my friends.'

'Well, just be careful the old bitch doesn't put a spell on you. You've been spellbound before.'

I suppose she's right. I suppose I'd better make sure I'm getting on with my own things.

3 September 1986

Alec takes me out to buy provisions. These expeditions take all morning. We have to go by bus to the other edge of the central business district, about a mile and a half away. 'It used to be possible to get everything one needed downtown,' Alec says, 'but there's no grocer, no fishmonger there now. Or if there are, I don't know where to find them.'

So we sit in the spring sunshine at the bus shelter on the other side of our little triangular park, and wait. 'I do wish that they wouldn't cover the buses with advertisements,' Alec says. 'I find it very difficult to tell whether it's a lorry or a bus coming. It was much better when they were all yellow.'

We sit for a while longer, then he says, 'I don't care much for supermarkets. They move everything all the time.'

'It's deliberate,' I say. 'It's meant to be part of the psychology. It makes you look at a whole lot of other things while you're trying to find what you want, and maybe some of the others will go into your trolley as well.'

'That's very interesting,' Alec says, 'but it's no good to me. I couldn't carry home everything I might want.'

On the bus Alec makes for the back seat, where he can sit

half screwed round and get a good look out the rear window at anything that might catch his eye. 'You get a much better view here,' he says, 'and a much longer one, looking backwards. I like to keep track of the changes on the route.'

Shopping follows a set pattern. We go to the delicatessen to get coffee and cheese, then to the butcher. Alec has telephoned beforehand, and picks up a small parcel. Alec carries these light items in a string kit. Then we go to the grocer and fill the basket. I carry this. We go on to Chan's for fruit and vegetables. 'This is the best greengrocer in the city,' Alec says. 'Well I think it's the best, and they know it's the best, and they're proud to be running it. I like that.' After Alec has bought the fruit and vegetables he requires, he sits on an upside-down orange crate at the back of the shop with old Mr Chan while young Mr Chan telephones a taxi, and I stand with the carton of vegetables and the basket at the kerb.

Alec's conversation with old Mr Chan is always the same. Old Mr Chan says that it is a nice day, or that it is not a nice day. Since he never leaves the back of the shop his opinion is erratic. Then he asks Alec how long he has been their customer. This is a rhetorical question, but Alec answers it just the same. 'Eight years.' Finally Mr Chan indicates all the choice items on supply and asks if Alec has bought any. He already knows the answer because he watches everything. 'Mr Chan, you'd have me big as a house. And beggar me at the same time,' says Alec. Old Mr Chan replies that as a beggar Alec would not remain big as a house for long, and that equilibrium would soon be restored. He probably knows.

The taxi arrives and we go home in it.

'Thank God the wine merchant will still make deliveries,' Alec says. 'And take the empty bottles away.'

I run into Ivor in a bookshop, and we go for a coffee.

'They call the dog "Front". It's short for "Popular Front", because sometimes he pleases everybody, and sometimes he pleases nobody at all.'

Ivor looks into his cup.

'I wonder how old they are,' I say.

'She would have to be at least ten years older than him, I should think,' Ivor says. 'Old enough, anyway, to make it not very secure for you. Either of them could drop off the twig, just like that, and where would you be? Out on the street. And don't expect me to take you in.'

I ignore that.

We don't say anything. Ivor looks out the window into the street. There's nothing very much going on. He turns back. 'Find out about when Bernice Bobs Her Hair. I'd like to hear about that, Nicky.'

The company that owns the building is having a meeting downtown. Alec is a director and has to go. He looks worn when he comes home.

He sits down heavily and pulls a parcel from his briefcase and puts it on the table.

'I bought us some *petits fours* on the way home to have with tea.'

'Did the meeting not go well?' Olga asks.

'It's just that I'm tired. I don't have the energy for business any longer. And the hill.'

'Do you have angina, Alec?'

'Only a little.' He fishes a bottle of pills out of his pocket and takes one. 'It will go.'

'Fetch Alexander,' Olga says when I go into her room before tea. It turns out that Olga has seen a dog turd behind her bureau. When Alec goes to pick it up with his handkerchief, Olga stops him and makes him bring the pooper-scooper and do it with that.

Olga's room is a low room at the front of the building and looks down into the street. It seems to have been made by joining two rooms in the original flats. It is painted yellow all over, even the ceiling, and when the sun comes in in the morning, it seems like a cornfield. At night when the lamps are on, it glows amber like the inside of a honeycomb.

'Initially Alec didn't approve of what I've done with this room,' Olga tells me. 'He thought it was self-indulgent. I said,

"Alec this is my last room. When I leave it will be because I'm dead. I want a burrow." He saw my point of view.'

There is a quite extraordinary collection of papier-mâché furniture that Olga has collected. It seems sinful somehow with its rococo outline and glossy black set with shards of mother of pearl. There is a day bed by the window, a high one so she can observe things outside. 'I am like Madame Colette,' she says. 'She spent the last twenty years of her life on a bed like this, looking into the courtyard of the Palais Royale. She called it her raft. This is my raft.'

25 October 1986

It's only after seeing her next to Kitty Rose that you begin to notice how stagy and slapdash Olga's clothes are. It's a hot night, the beginning of the strawberry season, but Miss Rose is sitting straight at the table in her narrow jacket with sleeves down to the wrist. She has a body like a playing card. It's as good as a seat in the front of the stalls for her, dinner.

Alec and Olga perform for Miss Rose. 'Scratch tonight, Kitty. Times are hard. Cold fish and potato. Picnic wine.' Alec's picnic wine is a Tuscan rosé. And he brings dinner in on a handsome plate. He has smothered smoked fish and sliced potato with glistening yellow *aïoli* and garnished it with black olives and slices of red pepper.

Olga shouts, 'Bravo, the German flag.'

So it is,' says Miss Rose.

People turn up their noses at this sort of thing if you describe it to them,' Alec says, 'and they can't get enough of it if you put it in front of them.

'Other people's behaviour,' says Olga.

'Is beyond comprehension,' finishes Alec.

The food is delicious. And so is the wine. Alec's right. It is an outside wine: a shirt unbuttoned, lying in the sun wine. It's just right. The other three eat and drink sparingly even so, and Alec gives me a large second helping.

'It's a joy to watch the young eat,' Alec says. 'No thought of tomorrow. Nor of liver and lights.'

'Food is the most important thing.' Olga picks up a speck of *aïoli* on her index finger. 'We think food is the most important thing.

We pay a lot of attention to our food. You should take an interest in food over and above consuming it, Nicholas.'

'I like cooking, but I don't do very much,' I say.

'Kitty Rose here,' says Alec, 'eats out of pure force of habit. What sort of food do you cook?'

'Oh, stews, that sort of thing.'

'Nothing wrong with a well thought out stew. Good food,' he goes on, 'must be simple. That was perfectly simple tonight, fish, potato, garlic mayonnaise, and perfect for a summer night, a night in late spring. But you can't be mean. You must have good ingredients.'

Now comes a green salad. Alec grows things in an old sink on the fire escape. He has put a bit of his rocket and cress in with the lettuce.

'Olga invented this salad dressing,' Alec says. 'You make it in the bottom of the bowl: cut fine a clove of garlic, and grind it up with a pinch of salt and a little bit of sugar. Then add the oil and vinegar. It's rather good. Well we think so.' 'It's the bit of sugar that does it,' says Olga. 'People always eat every last scrap of my salad. I believe in putting a bit of sugar with everything.'

Then we have dessert. Strawberries *al limone*.

'First fruit,' Alec says. 'Make a wish. Make a wish, Kitty.'

'I see, Nicky, that you don't have one of those dreadful new watches with the numbers changing all the time. Geoff Butler does,' Olga says. 'I should find it most disconcerting, like a neon sign flashing away on your wrist all the time. Wouldn't you, Kitty?'

Miss Rose says something about a pocket watch.

'A pocket watch would be worse. It would be like a time bomb on your person. Or one of those things they put into you by surgery to make your heart beat in an orderly fashion. What would happen if one fell in love?'

'A pacemaker,' Alec offers.

'A peacemaker, imagine. How do they do it?'

'It's got a lump of quartz in it,' I say. 'It oscillates, and that's what regulates the time-keeping mechanism, instead of clockwork. I don't quite understand how it does it.'

'Magic?' says Olga. 'None of our clocks work anymore. You can't find a clockmaker to fix them. Can you, Kitty? We get the time from the wireless.'

'You're a romantic, Olga,' says Alec. 'Clocks are a thing of the past. Soon one won't be able to speak of a clock ticking in an empty house. Nobody will understand.'

He goes into the kitchen to get coffee. Alec and Olga have favourite demitasse cups that vary with their mood. Tonight we have orange porcelain cups with black saucers, very fifties.

Alec lights himself a cigarette and offers one to Miss Rose. She has her own, menthol. I have one of Alec's. Olga never smokes. My attention wanders. I like running my eye along the bookcase and reading the titles. There are a lot of interesting books to be read on these shelves. Alec would let me use the library as I please, but it would take years to make a dent in it.

'Olga is truly cosmopolitan,' Alec is saying. 'Everyone jumps to the conclusion that she is Russian because of her name. She's nothing of the kind. Look. I'll show you.'

He takes his empty wineglass and sets it out in the centre of the table. Then he picks up the cream jug and pours half an inch of cream into the bottom of the glass. Next he adds an equal quantity of coffee out of the pot. After that a measure of wine, and finally water. 'There, that's Olga,' Alec crows. 'It was one grandfather that was Russian.'

Olga has watched this performance in silence.

'I should like a *digestivo*,' she says. 'Nicky, there's a bottle of *Laphroaig* in the sideboard.'

I fetch it to the table with four glass thimbles. Olga picks up the bottle and gives it to me. I should have thought to unscrew the top. I do it for her now and hand it back. Without saying a word Olga pours a breakfast cup of whisky into the mess that Alec has already concocted.

'That was good malt whisky, Olga,' says Alec.

'One must pay for one's pleasures. Nationalism is an indulgence.'

'We all detest the recruiting sergeant beating the drum.'

Miss Rose takes a little round case out of her purse. She looks at her mouth. Just at the moment it looks as if it was made as a place to put pins while you're dressmaking. She does her lipstick again, dark red, using the mirror inside the lid of the case. My grandmother did that too.

'I must go,' says Miss Rose. She takes her bag and puts on one kid glove. Holding the other in her gloved hand, she descends two flights of stairs home.

When she has gone Olga asks, 'Alec, did I remember to take my pills?'

Olga must take cortisone four times daily with food. She suffers from osteo-arthritis.

Olga fell on the lavatory floor. She slid down like a rag doll and now sits on her bottom with her legs stuck straight out in front of her. She is bleeding from her scalp. Alec and I are frightened to move her. I sense in Alec's voice that he is beginning to panic. 'Telephone Dr Lindenbaum and get him to come quickly.'

Olga puts her hand in his. 'I do not think that I am hurt, Alec,' she says.

Dr Lindenbaum comes. Olga has nothing broken fortunately, but she is badly bruised. Dr Lindenbaum and I manage to get her into bed, and he cleans her scalp up. We give Olga a small glass of brandy.

'Thank God,' says Alec after we have closed the door on Dr Lindenbaum. 'We had a long talk with him about eighteen months ago. Olga couldn't manage without someone here. If anything happens to me, Dr Lindenbaum has a place for her to go to. And if Olga goes first I don't know what I do.'

Olga has a hospital bed: the kind you can tilt up. It is in the inner part of the room and is usually screened off from the part of the room where Olga sits. Brandy is good medicine, and Olga seems to want to talk. So I listen. It's a rambling stream of reminiscence:

'I remember the first time I saw an aeroplane. There was a military review, and the aeroplane was to be part of it. I was still a young girl, I must have been eight or ten, and my father took me to see it. I was my father's favourite. I suppose I was spoilt, but exactly what for I don't know; it didn't turn me sour like milk. He doted on me.

'We waited all afternoon in a great crowd on the embankment near the Winter Palace. Then toward supper the aeroplane came. First all one saw was a small speck over the island. It must have been summertime. I remember the sky was very pale green—luminous—and as the speck of the aeroplane came closer it became a red dot.

'My father was a physicist. I suppose he would now be called an electrical engineer. He was employed by the Marconi company and worked on the installation of wireless telegraphy in the Imperial Navy. He was very excited and pushed us to the front of the crowd. We were close to the Palace Bridge. It was one of those bridges that are made on boats, you know?'

'A pontoon bridge?'

'A pontoon bridge,' Olga confirms the expression. 'All the time the water was slapping against the hulls of the boats. It is very cold, the Neva, even in summer. You know how cold water can look cold, sound cold?

'The aeroplane came on very slowly like a dragonfly. It flew quite near to the Palace Bridge, where it turned. It . . . banked, and its wings were turned against the green sky. It was beautiful. It was like looking at the light shining through the petal of a flower. But a geometric petal, perhaps a wine red peony. It was so curious, the silent crowd, the drone of the aeroplane like a big bee, and the water slapping on the hulls of the boats. My father was almost laughing. His eyes were twinkling with happiness. "Olga," he said, "never forget this. You have just seen the twentieth century." Those were his exact words. They seem silly now, but he saw something different from what I saw.'

Olga stops. 'I am very tired now, and I think I should rest.'

There is a letter in Alec's mail from the company that owns the building. I open it with the ivory paper knife as usual and give it to Alec to read.

When he hands the letter back to me he says, 'I shall have to tell Olga now. I tried to avoid it since it will worry her. It'll worry her a lot, but there's no other choice.'

I read the letter. It's not clear exactly what's going on. It's something to do with the redevelopment of the building, and I don't know whether to make any comment or not.

'Just file the letter,' Alec says. 'The situation's quite fluid, however it affects Olga, and I shall have to tell her about it.'

Alec takes out his emergency cigarette, but he doesn't light it.

A squall of barking breaks out in the silent flat: Olga is playing with Front. They have discovered a ritual game that Olga can still play despite her immobility. They observe its rules without referring to proper, livelier games in the past. Olga sits bolt upright in a stiff little armchair with her feet placed square on the floor. Front waits. Quiet. She taps one foot sharply. Front jumps at it, barking and making the play bow of dogs. Olga taps the other foot. Front springs to attend to that. Olga taps the first foot again.

I watch them for a while. Finally Olga stops the game. 'Enough, Front. Sit, sit. That's a good dog.'

I think the greater part of the fascination of the toy city for Alec has come to lie simply in model-making. He is certainly very skilful. He has several buildings of one sort and another in various stages of completion. At present he is painting an elaborate baroque toy. I suppose it's a palace, but I can't see where it fits in the city. He is painting it dusky pink like superior home-made fudge. One is allowed to admire the work silently, but comments seem to annoy him. The palace is more than accurate. When you crouch down to peer at it, you can almost hear Monteverdi.

'When this is finished, it can be fixed in place,' Alec says.

'Oh.'

'It goes here.' Alec points to a place on the boundary of the central park that's the trapdoor. I now see that there's a much more rudimentary model there with the same plan: a building that is a hollow square with a central quadrangle.

'I take the interim version away, and we install this with adhesive once the paint dries.'

The palace will stand on the perimeter of a huddle of winding streets whose hub is another one of the basic models, which might be a large church or cathedral. There is a piazza shaped like half an octagon in front of the palace, between it and this mediaeval tangle. A dog-leg street, wide in parts, narrow in others, runs like a river from palace to cathedral.

I look on the bench at the other replacement models Alec is making. There is a large church, two railway termini, and another palace. The eventual location of the stations is easy enough to identify by the ragged open spaces that end with them, but the other palace is a puzzle.

'It's not unlike counting the rings on a tree,' Alec says. 'You see the old city grows inside its wall. Gunpowder makes the wall useless, so the citadel becomes a palace, and a new ring of fortifications that can withstand artillery fire are . . .' He hesitates. 'Is built some distance away. Suburbs in the exact sense continue to grow outside the fortifications, and when railways are constructed, they are taken to the edge of the town where there is still open space. The town grows like Topsy after the railway age begins. The fortifications are now quite useless, since the city has outgrown them. When the inner fortification is demolished, the open space is converted into boulevards. This is a type of fortification as well, because the danger is beginning to come more and more from within. The boulevards prevent the town from fortifying itself against the sovereign.'

I cannot tell from the way Alec is talking whether the model represents a real city or not. It is pointless to ask him; he will let me know if he wants me to know. I have observed that both Olga and he just disregard remarks and questions that they don't care to acknowledge. They have the ability to behave as if the words hadn't been uttered. The self-possession of it amazes me. I couldn't do it. I wonder if it is a trick of the mind that you acquire with age.

SAMARA McDOWELL

As soon as another human being permits you to write about him, he is opening his life to you and you must be constantly aware that you have a responsibility in regard to that person. Even if that person encourages you to be careless about how you use your intimate knowledge of him or if he is indiscreet about himself or actually eager to invade his own privacy, it is up to you to use your own judgement in deciding what to write. Just because someone 'said it' is no reason for you to use it in your own writing. Your obligation to the people you write about does not end once your piece is in print. Anyone who trusts you enough to talk about himself to you is giving you a form of friendship. You are not 'doing him a favour' by writing about him, even if he happens to be in a profession or business in which publicity of any kind is valued. If you spend weeks or months with someone, not only taking his time and energy but entering into his life . . .
— Lillian Ross, Reporting

Off the Record

(Long pause. Exhales.) —The thing—the thing was, I didn't actually realise music was sort of anything that unusual for, for most people. It, it—I thought it grew. Like trees. I knew people wrote pop songs and stuff, like songs on the radio, bands on the radio, on TV and stuff, that—and they had an act, and they would, like, they'd get a song together, and—But—a lot of, a lot of the more involved music, like Mozart or, or Charlie Parker, or—just the music that seemed to go into every crevice—I, I assumed that grew. It seemed to be too perfect to—Too naturally right to have been made up. And—I still believe that. That, that notion hasn't left me.

Jonathan

What's interesting is what happens to the musicians' faces when they play. They look and lock into each other's eyes with the sustained intensity usually reserved for lovers. Jonathan, who off-stage ambles around loose-limbed and amiable to the point of goofy, who maintains the loose-limbed amiable imperturbability of your classic stoner, on-stage becomes someone absolutely different. His feet twitch and flex at the pedals, curl away, strain back; his face also twitches, flexes, and strains. He can bend almost double over the keyboard, so that his left cheekbone—his eyes closed, his teeth grinding; he's hissing through his lips—is almost touching the keys. It can be so intimate or so revealing that you are obliged to look away. It would be embarrassing—it *is* embarrassing, actually; this is, after all, New Zealand; our present is like another country; we do things differently here—if it weren't so clearly unforced. Ask him about it later and he will look back at you blankly, halfway between puzzled and indignant. 'If the music's really happening,' Jonathan will say, flatly, 'I don't know what it looks like from the outside.'

He does a good flat, Jonathan. A good blank, too—he can blank you like he was born for it. He is, one suspects, easily bored. Also: easily impatient, and quick to anger. Indulged, in fact, and therefore oddly vulnerable, overly defended, in the way of all those who have been indulged: well, he got found young. He got mentored and protégéd young; and his mentors, the ones to whom he played protégé, were amongst the best across several businesses. Bruno Lawrence. Geoff Murphy. Gaylene Preston.

—Patrick Bleakley, perhaps. Certainly if you ask Jonathan Crayford—half in a kind of faux innocence, half in genuine curiosity—why it isn't called The Patrick Bleakley Trio, his reaction is out of all proportion: he will do everything but stop the Volvo and throw you out. In the middle of Khandallah, yet (he's dropping Alda home; it's four o'clock in the morning, again).

His face looks like God set out working to a classical mould—cheekbones, brow, jawline—and then accidentally sat on it. The hair, which is longish, a rich dark brown and curly, is often contained beneath a battered beanie: he is unkempt to the point of studied. The eyes are green, darkly shadowed, unusually large, and set unusually far apart: he maintains a kind of permanent I-don't-give-a-fuck stubble. At the break—when he is approached and embraced, rapturously, by half a dozen punters—he smells, strongly but not unpleasantly, of sweat. Well: it's hot work, this jazz thing.

Opinions about Jonathan vary. 'He's an arsehole,' is certainly one you'll hear without going looking for it, although it's always coupled with a grudging admission of the kind and degree of his talent. He has this unlikely alpha male thing going on, not necessarily pitched to endear him to other men. It makes you wonder. Are hippies allowed to be alpha males? —Aren't they meant to have bought out of all that structure, patriarchy, capitalist competitive war-y sort of shit? —But then hippies aren't meant to be control freaks, either. Welcome to the difficult, idiosyncratic, infuriating and invigorating world of Jonathan Crayford. Either you accept the rules here—which will contradict themselves, gratuitously, at random and without warning—or you just don't bother, 'cos he ain't coming into anyone else's. Too lazy? Too scared? Too weary? Just over it? —Who knows (and if anyone does, it almost certainly isn't Jonathan).

It is his intention or fantasy to abandon the IAP; to seed it, to establish it, and then let it go, to flourish without him. It is hard to imagine this happening any time in the foreseeable future. Jonathan combines a distaste for the telephone, a resistance to schedule, and a marked wariness of encroachment on his private time to think, with an apparently complete inability to delegate. This manifests not purely musically: for Alda's farewell, he will spend an entire day, from nine in the morning till seven at night, shopping for food and then cooking for upwards of thirty people; and this is toward the end of the first IAP wave, when he has not slept for more than a few hours at a time for weeks, when he has become silently frantic with exhaustion and suppressed resentment, when all his resources are close to depleted. By the time people start arriving he is white-faced and subdued; but all offers of help have been refused (and the food, the tables, the set-up, are perfect).

Or: packing up. Watch him, wearily, patiently looping cables and extension cords, shifting boxes, moving gear, loading the van. When one of the doco crew asks him if he needs help he will shake his head. 'Nah thanks man,' he will say, friendly but uninflected. No one else can do it right, it seems. Just easier to do it on your own, it seems, no matter how tired you are. Just to do it.

I've been an ugly duckling all my life   wondering why I   when all my friends were
and becoming well-known and I
I
I'm actually not all that much into recording   I
I want to
I want to be a part o
I want to be a part of something that makes things change

The Project

The Inspiring Artists Project (IAP) is the brainchild of musician Jonathan Crayford, whose seven years playing jazz in New York convinced him of the value of connecting international talent with emerging artists here. Its intention is to act as a conduit: to build a talent bridge to and from Aotearoa, promoting a global artistic community through the interexchange of musical ideas, cultures and talents.

—IAP Brochure

Alda

I think I have a very particular voice ... and I had many teachers who tried to change it. To, to put it more ... tried to put it more, more into the patterns, you know? And my voice is very out of, of the patterns, I think.

Even after repeated hearings, the voice remains a surprise. The first time, it is a revelation: astonishingly deep, unfurling like smoke-infused honey across the floor to curl about your ankles as directed and seductive as a black cat intending to be fed.

This chic smiling woman, in high-necked sequins or in a full-length evening dress curiously scalloped around the hem, in a marvellous brown mid-length leather coat, belted at the waist, or a rich heavy paua choker given to her by her parents-in-law and a halterneck revealing most of her breasts, is the keeper of the Voice: she smiles at you over the top of it, signalling amusement, or irony: something wry.

. . . It took me such a long time to really find my voice. . . . It took me ages to, to realise that my voice is my instrument, and unique because it's mine.

Her lashes are so long and so thick that when the light throws her shadow against the wall, you can see them in silhouette.

In Wellington Alda has only been singing for four months, and she's already developing a cult following. You become aware of her arrival at Blondini's in particular when a discernible *rustle* passes through the crowd, punctuated by her name. It's the rustle *Shortland Street* regulars get, but this is a very different audience, and she's done it without half-hourly nationwide exposure five nights a week: it's quite something, the Alda buzz.

'Apples,' Alda tells a luscious young woman, who listens so intently it's almost painful to watch, who repeats 'Apples?' like Moses repeated the ten commandments. Yeah, honey: eat enough apples, and you'll have a voice like this one.

Or drink the Blondini martini—usually two, one before the performance, one after. Alda can be persuaded to three, but it's a special night. She is not and has never been a truly late-night girl, she was never a barfly: at home she performs mostly in theatres, which she prefers.

In Brazil she also fronts a TV show, a film showcase: 'I think it will still be there for me when I get back,' she says, in her heavy, charming accent.

And then she smiles.

Patrick

Patrick does ironic. Ironic is Patrick's stock-in-trade, his default mode: he wears his irony proudly, the way ageing hippies wear their wilder pasts. Patrick is, in fact, the oldest of the Trio, and the one least interested in the audience: all this, Patrick would have you know, he's seen before. He plays, doesn't talk much to the others: all those searing and seering glances, that intensity that passes between, Patrick rides without much returning. His hands are extraordinary, like large knobbled spiders. They way they gallop and prance on the strings is completely absorbing, once you begin to watch it. He frowns downward, looking neither at the double bass nor at the floor: some imagined space in between. He does not smile, although he's a big-time (ironic) smiler off-stage. At two in the morning, when Jonathan and Alda are recording, Alda singing intently into the peak of a black microphone the size and shape of a sombrero, her beautiful little half-tomboy, half-*femme fatale* face half-swallowed by it, Patrick will start shoving and horse-biting and pretend-slapping at Jonathan's sixteen-year-old niece, who previously has been watching and listening in irreproachable silence; she will dissolve into helpless giggles. (Jonathan will look up from the keyboard and frown; and then, seeing it's Bonnie and Patrick, look down again and smile.)

Riki

I kind of feel like [the drums] chose me . . . They were on my frequency, and I resonated with them. You find your instrument, and it's kind of like finding your soulmate . . . Until you learn to master it; and then it's like—you meet all its cousins, and its friends. (Laughs.)

Yeah man—everybody loves Riki.

Riki—medium height, medium build, street-handsome, baggy clothes, heavy brows—wears a white cloche hat pulled down to his eyes like a teacosy, almost all of the time. He seems very shy until you get to know him. In fact he is warm, serious, cheerful, principled, and engaging. He has a kind of inspired silliness masking a great depth of knowledge: his studio contains rare vinyls in vintage condition from twenty, thirty, forty years ago. He still DJs, though he's mostly known through Trinity Roots now.

Riki does Dumb Maori Boy. You know the one. As deflections go, this is brilliant. No one can object to it (his skin's the wrong colour for anyone to have a right to object to it). It's charming, and funny, and disarming. It's also bullshit. But then Riki doesn't fight with anyone, won't: if this is true, and at the same time you're proud, figuring out how to disarm is important.

The Dumb Maori Boy thing becomes the more interesting when he tells you he was brought up Pakeha, essentially. 'Yeah man,' he says, poker-faced, 'I grew up in Dunedin.'

There's a very Maori or at least Pacific way of teasing, that involves outrageous claims made deadpan. Riki is a past master at this. When you ask him about the huge drum in his studio, he will turn to look at it. 'That's my pet cow, man,' he will say.

'No it isn't,' you will say.

Riki will look at you indignantly, his eyes enormous. 'It *is*,' he will say. 'She died when I was six.' He's so piteous with this you actually buy it.

Riki also does a superb imitation of Jonathan, although, it has to be said, not, as far as you are aware, in front of him.

Once, parting at three in the morning after a gig at the Matterhorn, Riki and Jonathan stand in the centre of the floor with their heads bent so their foreheads are touching, not exactly embracing, with one arm around each other's shoulders. They stand in this position for at least a minute, breathing in each other's breath. Yeah and they're straight men: standing, stilled, this close to one another for this long: breathing the same breath.

The straight women on either side of them watch in silence: fascinated, moved, amused, and not catching each other's eyes.

*I look at him like a brother. And a, and a father as well, in a lot
of ways. But more like a bro.*

Lucien

Lucien—slouching, lounging, woollen-hat-wearing, carefully
expressionless, nearly twenty-two—is on the point of leaving.
Lucien's on his way to Paris.

When he plays he bends and sways, backwards mostly. He's
very tall, and is, when you look closely (you need to look closely),
beautiful, along surprisingly conventional lines. A classically
handsome boy who's gone, successfully, for geek.

Off-stage, not playing, Lucien sits hidden from view at the back
wall, half watching the crowd, half gazing blankly into space.
On-stage, not playing, he will stand half watching the others,
half gazing blankly into space, completely unselfconsciously
cradling the sax in his arms, as you hold a child: it's about the
same size as a small child, too.

At the first of the IAP gigs at Blondini's—Miguel Fuentes is
playing; the band is being both filmed and recorded—Lucien
arrives late and tired; he has been at a rehearsal of his own
band for some hours. Jonathan lends him the Volvo to go
home and change. Fifteen minutes later Lucien reappears in the
cathedral-like foyer of the Embassy wearing the most dreadful
grandfather-esque woollen vest over a checked shirt; even
Jonathan has dressed for this one, in a pretty grey suit, a white
shirt open at the neck, and a pair of heavy black Clark Kent
glasses that do not seem, actually, to frame any lenses (*we make
no real concessions here; we are Artists even if we do know how
to look elegant* is the message received, if it isn't the one being
consciously sent). Jonathan, standing chatting with a mix of the
doco crew and the groupies, leans over the balcony to check it
out and groans aloud. 'I'm charging you for petrol, man,' he
yells down the stairwell. Lucien looks up and grins, unfazed.
—Maybe Lucien's the true Artist here. Maybe, on the other
hand, he either absolutely lacks personal vanity, or absolutely
lacks personal taste. —And maybe it's simply that he's not quite
twenty-two. One can delight in deliberately dressing badly, at

twenty-two. *Fuck you* is the message received here, if it is not the one being consciously sent.

For Lucien, who hates the unblinking attention of the lens, who will scowl and blank his face and hunch his shoulder away, is a riveting subject, an unwilling natural. The one time he does dress—this is at the Matterhorn; no one else has bothered—he moves from looking like someone out of Dr Seuss, only taller, to looking like Frank Sinatra, only more handsome: he plays leaning against a pillar in his Rat Pack suit with his feet crossed at the ankle, by the angle of his head against the pillar manages to tilt his slouch hat slowly down over his eyes, and catching the gaze of one of his pretty girls will give his rare transforming smile. 'God he's cool,' the key camera will say, amused and admiring, watching the footage of Lucien's interview (we unfortunately must deal with the Dr Seuss woollen hat here, but we do get a pair of avaiator-esque yellowy transparent sunglasses).

At the last break of the Embassy gig, the band will retreat to what passes for backstage. It's a little room, windowless and airless, off the lefthand entrance to the cinema: there's a small red plastic toy car, out of a Kinder maybe, and apart from a battered two-seater sofa and a couple of chairs, almost nothing else. They smoke a joint in here—this is jazz, remember. Lucien slouches on the sofa, with his mouth half-open and his blue woollen hat over his eyes, watching people dryly. It is impossible to know whether he's actually taking anything in.

The Documentary

There's no money.

There's about a dozen people, working for free, working on good equipment which has been begged or charmed or, at any rate, borrowed, working on weekends, late nights, around paid jobs and the mild resentment of their partners.

There are people who have been doing camera, or sound, or editing, or in some cases all three, for twenty years.

There are people who are doing this because they have not, and they want to learn.

There are four months, during which time pretty much no one sleeps.

After a while the crew drops off to about four or five, rotating gigs when they can.

There's no money.

Band Rotunda

The room under the band rotunda on Oriental Parade is airless, stifling. It's the tail-end of summer. The two groups meet in here uneasily: there's something odd in the very idea of documenting, something disconcerting. There needs to be intimacy, and there needs to be not-intimacy. Very quickly the two groups come to reflect each other: there are mirror people playing mirror roles, facing each other, and not always smiling.

Emma and Tara are the two representatives of the IAP. Emma has a perpetual cold. She sits huddled in cream fur, pretty and frowning and anxious and firm, all at once—sort of like the nicer of the sixth form prefects. She is, strikingly, pretty—she has long fair hair usually drawn back in a ponytail, and very large, very pale brown eyes; her voice is to die for in its sweetness, in the carefulness of its modulation. Women who get a certain amount of mileage out of being small, and pretty, and probably blonde, tend to have an issue with Emma: she's better at this than anyone else. She's good at what she does, too. She can be tough. Once she's reached or conferred toward a decision, she's pretty much immovable. She will let you know this, whilst creasing her twenty-six-year-old brow in anxious horizontal lines, to indicate how much she hopes you will understand her position.

Tara has hair as long and thick and black as Pocohontas. She wears it tied back. When you ask her why she never lets it down, she tells you she got sick of people coming up to her and touching it. Tara has eyes of a clear green. She grew up in a vegetarian household in a small town, and as soon as she left home became an avid advocate of red meat and fast living. She's innately distrustful of the doco crew: she wants to keep a distance between them and the musicians: she wants to be the conduit. It can be exasperating, it can waste time, it has created conflict; but rather than being about control, maybe it's her need to remain as close as she can to *the music*. Tara stopped playing, at all, when she came to believe she was never going to be as good as she wanted to be. This invests her involvement with the group, and her intimacy with each of the musicians, with painful urgency. *Music's my life.*

One of the soundies is demonstrating levels on a DAT machine.

'So if you get the levels right, you can pretty much leave it alone?' one of us asks hopefully.

The soundie looks startled. 'Well, no,' he says. 'For one thing the level of the music is going to be changing all the time, and for another, you need to be able to respond fast to random dynamic changes.'

That's a cough, to laypeople.

Take Notes

—*What about Angeleyes?*
—*In B flat?*
—*In C minor?*
—*In C minor?* —*OK*—

You don't even know what they're saying to each other. You just know enough to stay close enough to hear it, or to watch closely enough from some distance to read their lips; you know just enough to know you must write it down. You don't know anything else. B flat? C minor? —*Yeah man* (as they would say). Whatever. —You, you don't know anything. You watch and listen and conceal your panic, at all the things you don't know. You watch, and you listen, and you write it down.

Late Night at the Embassy

They keep playing longer than you think they're going to, and then after that they play quite a lot more. It's one o'clock. It's two o'clock. What's interesting about the crowd is who sticks around.

There's a man in glasses that should be half-moon and he's wearing a bow-tie, and he's balding and every reasonable expectation you have is somehow confounded by how intently he's listening, how absolute is his attention. Even when his friend, the friend with the beard, takes his leave he sits on.

One of the three girls in the corner calls out, giggling sadly, 'No! Don't go!'

'Not the end! Not the end!'

'One more! One more! One more!' cries the red-headed girl. Honestly, this is the kind of girl you'd sleep with a member of the band in front of, just so that she knew you could.

'Grant us our last wish!' she cries, then subsides and collapses again, giggling and wriggling.

But now it is clear even to the red-head that, really, they need to stop. There it is: the crash and scramble across the bar of coins being emptied from the till. Jonathan stands. There are a half-dozen people still seated. He ambles forward and mumbles into the microphone, 'We're the Jonathan Crayford Trio.'

'And,' says Patrick, moving off the stage and into the scattered tables, 'we can't understand why you're still here.'

Composing (one's face): Zen and the Art of Documentary

Later they will discover the beauty and space of the men's room, which unlike the women's is tiled and startlingly spacious; it's here they will end up smoking joints, telling jokes, playing percussion on the hand-dryers and the urinals; right out in the open, in full view, you're watching them, and yet still somehow secretly, keeping your face pleasant, composed, neutral, concealing how, in brief flashing moments gone too fast in the scramble between schedule and equipment and unanswered messages, this job is making your heart twist or jolt in your chest with loneliness and furious envy: of their musicality, of their ease with and pleasure in each other, of their very maleness, actually. Men seem to you sometimes to move so easily, so comfortably through the world: if they think someone is looking at them, what they are allowed to do is turn and look directly back. Sometimes on this job you find being female tiring, alienating, disheartening, and

lonely. —It's because, very quickly, after the first few weeks or
so, you are the only one: none of the musicians are women on
most of the gigs, and on most of the gigs none of the film crew
are either. —Being the object of even fleeting sexual curiosity or
speculation when you're working is disconcerting to the point
of unpleasant, and yet what else have you? When what you
do well does not interest them, and what they do wonderfully
well, you cannot do at all? What else makes you interesting
enough for them to turn toward you enough to tell you what
it is you need to know, and to trust you enough to tell you,
at least some of the time, on camera? —Every interview is the
secret, compressed, infused product of the hours, and hours,
and hours you have spent listening, watching, listening again,
keeping your face open, neutral, composed, making notes and
drawing diagrams in your head, weaving links, connections, and
theories; right there, in full view, and yet still somehow secretly;
your eyes recording, your mind whirling, never in neutral, your
face composed, while before you they play, rehearse, occupy
without question or hesitation that central space that waits in
every collection of people, together; there is in every interview a
deep and secret pleasure in asking the one question you know—
you suspect, but also, you simply know—is going to make the
subject draw in their breath sharply, look at you like they only
just saw you, stumble or flow on their answer.

In Taupo, the very first morning, you get up early, hours
before anyone else, go to the phone booth on the lake, and
ring Charles. Charles, by virtue of the kind of coincidence
that given a quarter of a chance the world most likes to
operate in, is both Alda's husband and a friend of yours
since you and he were both eight. You don't know you are
going to do this—you were merely calling to ask when he was
arriving—but as soon as he answers the phone you burst into
tears. It's horrible, because you can't talk and the minutes on
the phone card are running out. Charles makes startled but
soothing noises from his pillow. 'I can't do it, it's too hard, I
didn't know it was going to be this hard,' you say, in between
these awful ratcheting breaths. Hiccupping, with the light
flattening itself across the lake. You can't explain it, this thing

like grief that has overwhelmed you, the very first morning on tour. You are so lonely you feel like you could die of it: and you would, you feel you would die rather than let any of the (all male) musicians, any of the (all male) doco crew, see you cry, or have the slightest indication why you might. —This thing, this thing that woke you so early, is both absurd, and serious: you can feel the two working together, and you pincered between them, sleeping or not sleeping in the tiny room you and the two camera boys are sharing, three bunk beds stacked like Weetbix against three walls, listening or not listening to each other breathe, the smell of men's bodies, how the three of you marooned in this tiny room seek *together,* the secret frightening ways in which you fear you will fail. —Charles—who has, remember, known you since you were a child, who has worked for years in film, whose partner has worked for years in music—picks his way through the gasping half-sentences and works it out. 'Boys and equipment, huh,' he says, with so much kindness he could be Steven and Rio when you got too cold and had to be wrapped in a blanket, as briskly and carefully as one of the instruments, and put in the van with the motor running—'boys and equipment.' The accuracy of this assessment in itself startles and soothes you. The phone card runs out as Charles is saying, urgently, 'Go for a walk by the lake. Take deep breaths. You're okay.' You go for a walk by the lake, you take deep breaths. You think, dryly, in Charles' voice, *boys and equipment,* and you think about that, you think about boys and equipment, you think about film sets you have known and hated ('It's a fucking boys' club,' you tell your friends in the public service, which has actual and enforceable laws governing this issue; they are incredulous at some of your stories, and so are you), you think about boys and tools, you think about boys and instruments, you probably think about boys and pissing standing up. You come up with some fairly creaking theories about all this—and yet it is, genuinely, really very odd, how women overwhelmingly *don't play instruments.* Why *not?* —For the same reason they overwhelmingly don't play (with) cameras, sound equipment? —Film boys. Music boys. Boys and tools; equipment; and instruments.

Jonathan and Riki, in particular, won't be the ones to lead you away from this alarming, simplistic and, anyway, well-worn train of thought. Jonathan and Riki make penis jokes with vocational fervour. The first time they do it in front of you you are so startled you don't know where to look, or what to do with your face; you keep your eyes on your plate, and chew on grimly. Alda, on your right, is the only other woman present, but Alda's English isn't quick enough this time for the innuendo; you glance at her and see she didn't understand. God, you bastards, you think crossly, don't say that in front of me, and keep your face smooth and neutral, your elbows tucked well in; you'd like to punch Jonathan in the ribs with the left one, and simultaneously kick Riki, who is across from you, as hard as you can under the table with your right foot.

Jonathan and Riki make wanking jokes endlessly too—there's a particular, frenetic, unfriendly *slapping* sound they recreate with their palms that it takes you a couple of unwitting audiences, puzzled by why it's funny, to identify. —Oh ick, you think to yourself primly, getting it.

And keep your eyes wide and innocent of thought, your face neutral and composed.

—For there is another time. There is a time at dawn, when everything is still, and the light comes up behind the mountains and floods the sea, that heart-catching blue, when they forget you are in the van at all; you have been with them for hours and hours and hours, setting up, performing, drinking, recording, smoking dope, eating at Kenny's, smoking cigarettes, drinking more, playing *with* the instruments in the huge freezing Post Office Building after the gig, out of too much energy and joy to stop; Jonathan and Alda have been recording, Alda exhausted, on the point of leaving for Brazil, lying flat on the dirty carpet listening to the playback with her head pillowed on her coat, most of the light coming from the little wooden organ or the computer; you have been so still, or moving so smoothly into the interstices and between the notes, you have made yourself variously useful or silent, you have been listening and watching so intently for so long that you have rendered yourself invisible. The van drives past your apartment, and keeps on going. You glance across. No one looks at you. You don't know what to do; you can't break this rich encoded silence. After about a mile you reach over and wind down the window; and then you are there again, and people laugh, and on the little winding coast road the van stops and turns around and takes you home.

Maybe this shouldn't feel like a personal victory. Maybe this shouldn't feel like an accolade. Maybe you shouldn't go to bed, finally, wearily, with your blood singing with pride, that you have, finally, made yourself disappear. Maybe *being there, and not being there* shouldn't feel to you like such an accomplishment; being ignored like, finally, the best kind of acknowledgement.

But it does.

Meet Brian de Grane

Brian de Grane sells used cars. *Brian de Grane, Quality Used Vehicles at an affordable price.* Brian de Grane has a thin pencil moustache. *Bring your sons down to the yard; we'll have them selling within a week.* Brian de Grane speaks in an invidious, insidious, sleazy-caressing boom. *Bring your daughters down to the yard; we'll get them working in the office, and doing a bit of modelling on the side.* It is difficult to convey on the page quite how successfully repulsive Brian de Grane is.

He emerges when Jonathan is bored, or happy, or suffering from an excess of energy; he was born, fully formed, like Venus, at a birthday of Terry Crayford's, Jonathan's father. Jonathan went into the bathroom with a full beard, and came out moustachioed, transformed. Someone else. *Brian de Grane, Quality Used Vehicles.*

Sons, and their Fathers

Terry Crayford also plays at Blondini's. You meet him this one time. You sit at the same table, and exchange some quite surprising confidences, and giggle. That stays with you, though at other gigs you don't really meet again; and also the two questions you asked him, one thirty seconds after you met, one

three hours; and the identical naïve astonishment with which he
answered both.

Jonathan is in one of his hysterically active moods. He is
moving in that manic robotic way that reminds you of a duck,
though you can't quite place why: in the end you decide it's the
jerk in the way he moves his head when in this state, in the quirky
splay in the way he places his feet. He waves one arm between
the two of you distractedly, half-making introductions, as Terry
idles before the ivory keys of the grand piano, as you hesitate
before the dead microphone. Jonathan turns to keep winding
cables, and Terry politely stands, accepting your proffered right
hand.

—*He must have been a nightmare as a toddler,* you volunteer.
Although perhaps it would have been less risky simply to say
Hello.

Terry looks at you in astonishment. *Oh no,* he says, with
absolute sweetness, with complete sincerity, still shaking your
hand. —*Oh no, he was wonderful.* His pupils widen.

—Or: three hours later, both of you half-cut. You've been
nice to his friends, he's been nice to yours, you've bought each
other drinks. And now the music has claimed him. This man's
involvement in the music is so deep you can watch him, closely,
from inches away, from point blank range, not in your peripheral
vision, not bothering to blink, not bothering to glance down,
not bothering to smile. He watches his son play, fascinated.

The piece ends. The pianist's father turns, jerking his neck,
ducking his head, placing his feet a little quirky, blinking shyly
over the rim of his European beer, and turns to you. You say, so
curious you've decided you're just going to risk it, *Is he better
than you?*

Oh yes, Terry Crayford says, smiling vague and uninvolved
around the room, like you've asked if he wonders if the sun
comes up in the morning.

Do you mind? you say. And this time he does look at you,
kind but unavoidably a little shocked, like you've asked if he
enjoys seeing kittens chopped into smallish pieces, or picking
his nose.

Oh, he says, sweet but embarrassed for you, for how much
you just haven't got this. *Oh no,* he says. *Oh no, of course not.*

Brian de Grane, Quality Used Vehicles.

*Bring your sons down to the yard: we'll get them selling within
a week.*

Etcetera.

Come Over Dere

You know how when they're training call centre staff, some of
the incomings get taped?

Someone sent Riki this crazy conversation, it got onto the
internet somehow, this Samoan whose mother's luggage has
been lost, and he's going off completely, he's completely lost
it, he's yelling at this poor woman, and she's trying to explain,
staying desperately polite: she's saying to him, *But, sir, this is
not the airport, sir, we can't trace your luggage from here, this
is a call centre, sir, what you need to do is—*

And this guy's just yelling, getting more and more violent,
screaming, *I'm gonna come over dere, you know what I'm
gonna do, I'm gonna come over dere and slap you round, you
want me to come over dere and sort you out, I'm gonna—*

All of them do spirited and noisy imitations of this man
(all of them have the cruelly accurate musician's ear for voices,
accent, inflection, intonation). What's curious is what gradually
happens to the phrase *Come over dere*, as in its repetition the
anecdote is whittled down, reduced to its pith. What it comes
to mean is the very opposite of threatening. *Come over dere*,
they'll say, meaning: Come here to us, come play, come join
in. *Come over dere*. Meaning: we understand each other, we
operate the same way, we speak the same language, do we not?

Hiatus

Jonathan's daughter has cut his hair brutally short. Something
about this, and the cap he wears over it, makes him look like the
Disney Pinocchio. Momentarily red wine and weariness have
you confused. What was it that Pinocchio wanted—was it to be
a *real* boy, or was it never to grow up?

There's a moment's hiatus between songs. Riki slumps forward over the drumset as if in despair. Jonathan takes a draught of the nasty milk-and-rum cocktail on the top of the organ. Rio's bent to his right over the congas, as if looking for something.

They begin playing again.

Naming

It's mid-afternoon, and already mostly dark in the Bodega, where the musicians are packing in for the night's concert: there will be at one point fourteen musicians and two vocalists on stage at the same time. Everyone seems tired, listless; they mooch around, not really talking.

Outside on the street there is a sudden screech of brakes. Someone looks up, and names it—names the note. The others nod, not making much of this.

In the loony half-dark Lucien is about to grumpily pace, where Miguel's sharp profile gleams as he drowses with his head tilted back against a pillar, in the afternoon bargloom mostly lit by the white glint of your laptop, with the named note shimmering and disappearing in the air, you are silenced, astonished and ashamed.

What it reminds you of is the twins in Oliver Sacks, in *The Man Who Mistook His Wife For a Hat*. The twins who were autistic, whose only communication was with each other, whose only conversation was to sit passing prime numbers between them, back and forth, savouring each tiny explosion of flavour against the palate. The good doctor decoded the conversation, he briefly joined them, he named the right numbers; and the twins briefly turned to him, in pleasure and surprise. *Come over dere*, the twins might have said. —Oh it could make you weep, mathematics, music, the way the rest of us stay, wondering, outside, listening, struggling for the right note.

Indigo

The vibraphone sticks have, actually, broken: they're splaying outward, the left one particularly. It looks like a dandelion clock, spraying seeds, or wishes. Jonathan examines it, holds it up for the delectation or amusement of the double bass player.

Rhythm

Chris, who used to play drums for the Trio before he went to Dublin, on his last night.

He is sitting before the drum-set on a pumpkin-coloured suitcase, turned vertically. It is a very narrow space to balance on, and in fact at one point he tumbles off. But plays valiantly on, to cheers.

Or:

Two o'clock in the morning, again. In the Men's Room in the Embassy, again. A joint being passed around, jokes being passed around. Riki's got a rhythm going in his head; he's tapping with his feet, clicking with his tongue. No one pays any attention.

Riki starts playing percussion on the urinals; then on the hand-dryer; then back to the urinals.

There, unremarked, in the greenish light, this beautiful thing.

Like—I could take a sample—sample some footsteps, or the cars—and then find the, the sort of consistent rhythm through that by looping it, finding a rhythm out of just a sound from around the city . . .

Consequences

There is that thing, of course. About how when you look into the abyss, the abyss also looks into you.

This happens:

Cadences pulse, break, murmur harshly in your ear: you wake up blinking, reaching out for dream shards. You've fallen asleep on the floor, again, in front of the monitor. Up there the musicians are playing, the sound low; or, one of them is talking; and in every sentence there seems buried or twisting a rich arcane knowledge, a key you must reach for, something urgent you must learn to understand.

Poetry comes back to you, abruptly, forcefully: its skeletal difficult form stalking the page, its aural imprint beat-beat-beating in your inner ear. The words are like notes, the words are music, the rhythms sing in your head. You can't believe you're so stupid you never noticed before, the rhythms, what they mean, what they're beating, breathing, hissing, insisting. *Listen.*

You stalk the city, muttering lines under your breath. Your booted feet tap. Rhythm.

This happens:

There's a track playing and it's one of your favourites, you've listened to it a thousand times. As you stand idly staring out the window, half-worrying about logistics, mostly not thinking, the piece of music falls apart in front of your very ears.

You turn and look at the speakers. What just happened? — It's true that sometimes you have to talk real nice to your stereo to make the CD spin, but this is rather different, it's the sound itself. It's the weirdest effect, like an optical illusion, only it's happening inside your cranium: like you're hearing two versions of the piece at once: the one you already know, contained, wrapped, pre-delivered in one unbroken impenetrable surface, and this other thing, ribbons of sound, uncoiling, how the different instruments and the different recordings of the same voice are laid over each other, braided, winding around each other, commenting on each other, lightening and deepening each other as complementary colours do, making up the pattern. Is there something wrong with the machine?

After a while you go over and kneel down and start fiddling ineptly with levels.

There isn't a ghost in the machine; you can still hear what you're hearing. You sit back on your haunches and stare at the matt black case of the stereo. *Ha*, you say to yourself, experimentally. You're absolutely beaming, though you know this is stupid and you're trying not to. But you can't help it. You feel like you just split the atom.

This happens:

You fall in love with an instrument.

Not any old double bass, not *the* double bass, just this very specific and particular one. It even has a name, it's called Marie'sbass, all in one word. ('*This* bass? . . . Oh, this is *Marie's*bass.' For example.) It reminds you, vividly, of your blackly perfect, perfectly black cat: in its beauty, its gentleness, in how completely female its energy. The way they both look up and chirrup in happy recognition when you come into the room: the cat audibly, the double bass, not. *Oh, you again. I see you.*

Standing watching the cameraman and the musicians beyond him in the big empty space of Herd Street, you can feel a warmth beating toward the back of your knees from where Marie'sbass lies behind you indolently on its side. You edge backward, not taking your eyes from the others, until you can reach down and stroke it. Feel the instrument itself, beating up through the grain of the hundred-and-fifty-year-old wood. Loving you back. Arching under your touch, with sensual pleasure in your sensual pleasure in it: the way the cat does.

You think, a lot, out of the corner of your eyes or mind, as it were: you wonder, in your internal peripheral vision, if this is suggesting to you you are meant to start learning the double bass.

But it probably doesn't. You don't even think the instrument itself wants you to play it (anyway, it's Marie's). It just likes you to love it: when you're in the same room you are half-consciously aware of Marie'sbass as one is half-consciously aware of a subtle source of warmth, as invisibly and without moving Marie'sbass stretches, preens, glows toward you.

You don't tell anyone this, of course. It's not that words fail you.

Sometimes an instrument . . . it's just—yours.

Jimi

The Matterhorn—which gets referred to as The Matterho', or, The Horn—has the legend PEOPLE engraved into their funky doorhandles. You have to turn your head sideways to read it.

It's three in the morning, and cold. They all stand in the long corridor/alley leading to Cuba Mall, not talking much. There's a kind of specialty cult comic store next door: Jonathan stands looking blankly through the window at life-size cardboard images of befanged, befurred, beclawed superheroes. Then he starts talking, starts doing one of the characters or voices; this one is not familiar; maybe it's new, invented just for the occasion.

—*Yeah, man, I was in my pyjamas on the sofa, man, and it was three in the morning, and I was eating icecream, I was on the sofa, and suddenly there's this thunderbolt, man, and it's Jimi Hendrix—*

This bizarre monologue goes on for some time. Riki and Rio ignore it, continue staring toward the Mall, giving no indication of hearing. It reminds you of breakfast, touring, when while his host stood waiting for the kettle to boil, Brian de Grane unexpectedly was taken to court for speeding. *No, Your Honour, Brian de Grane. Quality Used Vehicles, Your Honour, at an affordable price. In fact perhaps I could interest you in—?*

It went on for ages, over the smell of burnt toast, and the birds twittering. No one paid any attention whatsoever.

Groupies

Now, classical and/or jazz and/or Latin groupies are not in the same order as rock groupies, but even they will leave you with a new, mildly nauseated disrespect for your fellow woman. And they *are* dispropor-tionately women, groupies: partly because the musicians are so disproportionately men, and a longing for what you do not have, and imagining you may get some of it by sleeping with it, is a misconception as old as art itself.

—So no, they aren't ripping all their clothes off when they catch your eye across the room, or throwing their skimpy musky panties on stage—onto the organ, perhaps; into the rhythm section; into the horn section (you know: the one with the instruments that get blown). —Okay, so they're not doing that. Okay. —They just look, with their pupils as round and dark and dilated as mouths; with their eyes and lips as glossy and glistening as labia. Oh and they giggle. The most spirited of them will venture opinions—even dissenting opinions, which they will then defend, spiritedly but never for too long—and then they all toss their hair around. I mean, you know. I mean, really.

Secretly I think I'd prefer the rock groupies, the naked girls with the coke and (appropriately enough) the Brazilians; the girls with *real* attitude, who are at least very, very honest about what they're doing. Classical and jazz groupies? —God only knows what they hope to get out of what they do, as even a rigorous fuck doesn't seem to be all or simply the answer. Merely a titillating, perhaps literal, brush up against the talent? For all the nice middle-class young women? —Maybe it's that. —And, to be fair, for all of us there is some confusion over how one tells the dancer from the dance.

Except for the musicians themselves, interestingly enough. They know, clearly, they're not it, they're not the music. Which is maybe how else they differ from rock musicians, even leaving aside the cocaine and the Brazilian waxes.

Capitalism

Jonathan extracts a note from the small plastic self-sealing baggie with the bank logo on it, squints at the notes—blue and green in colour, and not so very many of them—and then throws the bag over his shoulder, into the utilitarian and unfriendly back space of the white van.

'Savings plan,' he says, disconcertingly, and to no one in particular.

Alchemy

There is a mysterious alchemy that occurs between the watcher and the watched. To watch someone, closely, to direct toward them your full attention, is a powerful act: transformative. It seems, first, to transform the process of watching. It is not simply that this kind of observation yields dividends—it is not simply that *you notice more*, although that is of course true. The alchemy lies in what occurs with the watched: as if close observation has a galvanising effect, as if someone being observed is redefined even to themselves, as if their behaviour subtly rearranges itself into sharper focus.

Then there is the alchemy between the musician and the instrument. You ask all of them, one by one, if particular personality types are drawn to particular instruments. *No*, they will answer, immediately and flatly; something about this question renders musicians indignant. Then they will proceed to tell you, with no awareness of contradiction, *Drummers are all crazy. Sax players are egocentric, real show-ponies. Bass players tend to be quieter, you know, their energy's kinda more still, like they're holding you all together—*

Rio the Rock

And so when Rio plays bass, he stands with his feet planted as firmly in the ground as a tree plants its roots. He pumps from the torso, his shoulders jumping rhythmically: it's an idiosyncratic bodily gesture, instantly identifiable when imitated. His face remains tranquil, his eyes cautious. He's a big man, broad-shouldered, with waist-length dreads that he pulls back in a ponytail; he seems far more guarded than the others, less immediately warm, much less of an extrovert.

This seems to be Rio's musical persona. It is not: it is only one of them. Seeing him play with Trinity Roots is startling. Riki is always the same, no matter where, no matter what, no matter with whom he's playing. Rio with Trinity Roots is *someone else*. He is a far more powerful presence on stage, far more vital: he expands, solidifies, reaches outward; he throws his gaze toward the audience, which he never does when he's playing jazz, pulling them in. Rio with Trinity Roots plays with passion.

'Well it's our music, you see,' Rio says when you ask him about this. He segues into Sweet Dumb Maori Boy, the way Riki can (both of them graduated from Jazz School; nothing at all dumb here, though certainly some sweet). 'That jazz stuff, man. It's intimidating.'

Toward the end of the shooting, Rio starts fooling around with percussion. It delights him; and here's a *third* persona. Again, here is someone else. Someone loose-limbed and grinning, shifting his feet, his whole body moving. This is light-years away from Rio the Rock playing bass, playing the same music with the same people.

The only conclusion you can come to around personality types and instruments is that the man (to speak advisedly) does not play the instrument; the instrument plays the man.

Abstraction

You say aloud, watching the musicians' faces, something you've thought every time you've seen them play, and have always been too well brought-up to mention. To these other two women, watching the (all male) musicians at one remove, on the Avid, you say, 'Isn't it amazing, how they all look like they're fucking?'

The youngest of you says dryly, 'Like they're masturbating,' and the other two shriek with delight. '*Yes*,' you all say. '*Yes, exactly.*' That look of intense, pained concentration, that utter self-absorption.

And then, of course, they're all doing something both frenetic and highly skilled. With their hands.

Milieu

There are the spaces: rehearsal spaces, performance spaces, the tiny boxroom off the left-hand entrance to the Embassy cinema, the Blondini's Men's Room, the small edit suite half-lit through the shutters, the bars after-hours, the spaces between the notes.

Kenny's

The carpet is grey, the tables formica, the walls yellow, the place iconic. White-bread sandwiches curl under glass.

When one comes in here, traditionally, is three, four, five o'clock in the morning. What one orders, traditionally, is a pot of tea, a burger and chips; maybe egg and chips with white bread and butter on the side. 'Is it okay to smoke here?' one of the hangers-on asks. 'Hey man, this is *Kenny's. Everything's* okay here,' is the correct answer.

You can't fall asleep, though—that's the only thing that's not okay. The tranny at the next table, sitting alone, beautiful, fragile, with a black eye and bruises down the length of bare back exposed by her dress, is woken by the soft-spoken waitress. 'You can't sleep here, dear,' she says, not unkindly.

'I'm offending people,' the tranny whispers, dreadfully, to her- self.

Riki's trying to tell a joke. He and Jonathan are so tired they can't stop laughing. 'Man, you fucked that up so bad,' Jonathan says, wiping tears from his eyes.

Outside the taxis and the drunks slide along Courtenay Place, looking for destinations.

Herd Street

The old Post Office Building stands on the waterfront, mostly empty. The IAP has been gifted the use of the fourth floor for rehearsal space. This can't last long: the building is going to be sold off, developed, millionaire apartments put in. The light washes in grey from the harbour. Even before the musicians arrive instruments stand around against walls: drums, percussion, the Hammond organ, a vibraphone. A painting done on separate boards, which are then hung together, is on one wall: numbers from one to ten.

'McCahon for children,' one of the cameramen says unkindly.

Havana Nirvana

Poti runs the Havana Bar. It was wrought, semi-legally, from a tiny cottage, the last on Wigan Street: it was scooped out from the inside like a papaya, by Tim and Geoff—the partners in Havana Coffee. After hours, with indefatigable energy: till two, three, four in the morning. Tara tells you—she happened to be living on Wigan Street at the time, long before she met Jonathan and Riki, and often unable to sleep because of the noise—that she would knock on the door, two, three, four in the morning, and they'd sit her in the corner and feed her creamy cocktails until she fell asleep.

Jonathan and Riki play here Thursday nights, and anyone else who turns up. It's hard to know. Patrick might. Rio often does. Lucien won't, because they can't afford to pay him and Lucien has a clear idea of his own worth, but he could wander in for a drink just the same. Mabeth has. The very idea of the IAP was born from the Cuban-born Kiko, brought in by a friend, sitting down and playing, unannounced, in this tiny space.

You've seen this place packed to the rafters, almost literally. The night both Fima and Miguel played, looking in from the balcony from where the crew was shooting, people were banked like in an amphitheatre; they must have been standing on tables.

Other Thursdays almost no one is there. No one else comes to play; Riki and Jonathan lock into each other, deep in a private conversation, played in public, which could go anywhere, watching each other the way they do, like lovers. They might swap instruments. (Emma, coming in from the bathroom, laughs and says, 'I *thought* something funny was going on. Even in there I couldn't believe how loud the drums were.')

It's warm and intimate, with only the candles burning, and the stills photographer gone. Being here on one of the quiet Thursdays gives you all the comfortable, pleased-with-yourself feeling of being in a club so exclusive no one else knows it exists.

Flattery

'A,' Jonathan mouths to Riki and Rio. 'E.' They play. 'E flat.'

Havana again, and enough of a crowd to have Jonathan in an expansive mood.

'Sponsored by Rex Wheels and Castors, Limited, Petone,' he will announce, apropos of nothing at all, from behind the organ; and take a swig of his drink.

'That tune was called "The Long and Winding Road".' Which it most certainly was not. A long pause. 'Sponsored by Transit New Zealand.'

'That was a very famous tune called "Black Market".' Pause. 'Sponsored by Social Welfare.'

Yes; and from the punters, knowing, insiders' laughter. This kind of messing around between numbers, *at* the audience, is a subtle and effective form of flattery: it draws you in.

The Cult of Personality

It was a period of my life when I wasn't actually feeling music that much—I wasn't, wasn't actually—I wasn't sure if I wanted to keep doing it . . . [It felt] pretty cold, especially when that's all you—I mean, to me, that's kind of like losing—like turning the lights out and turning the heater off. Jonathan was the guy who came and turned the lights and the heater back on.

It is impossible to overstate the centrality of Jonathan to the group. He organises all the gigs, he runs all the rehearsals, he composes the original music, he works the hardest, he sets the standard; the idea of the IAP was his, he got the funding, he set everything in motion. But it's more than that. He sets the mood, too. There's no challenge for leadership here. He can be hard to cope with, but he is also, often, warm, kind, and very, very funny. Charisma can't be learned, or earned; the bequeathing of it is as unfair as that of any other talent.

Jonathan believes, apparently sincerely, that he is open to all comers, open to all lines of inquiry: it's something—one is given to understand, subtly, through a series of changing, downward-sent facial expressions, through a series of subtle, pointed shifts through the body and voice—that he struggled after, at some cost to himself, and found. This particular self-concept is easily challenged, though. Just take a line he doesn't wish followed and then pursue it against the early storm warnings, and watch what happens. He will, literally, tense and swell with barely-suppressed fury; his movements will speed up, and his diction slow down. Yes. Scratch the funny, charming, loose-limbed surface here and then get the fuck out of the way, before he shoves you there.

Now, Jonathan has a number of effective ways of doing this: he can stare at you arctically, which takes a little getting used to—this is the coldest bluegreen stare since the Third Reich—or he can cut you out of the group (and remember, they unconsciously follow his every lead, this particular hub of beautiful, talented, idealistic young people; in order to do your job effectively you need to be somewhere only just outside of the loop), or . . . he can turn vicious.

Vicious is certainly in the repertoire, don't imagine it isn't—personal and direct, with a series of well-chosen well-drawn unkind versions of the truth, delivered at cutting pitch. There are a lot of people who'll validate this particular impression, although none of them will consent to be identified doing so. Apparently he is intimidating, Jonathan Crayford: the number of people who have been offended by him seem reluctant to tell him so to his face. One cannot avoid wondering if this is, perhaps, a shame: if this inadvertent side-effect of the inadvertent force of his personality is unfortunate, for someone who—without question: truly, no question—genuinely struggles after fair, who genuinely believes he is doing a great right, who has been prepared to sacrifice a great deal (financial stability; recording contracts; an easyish, or at least earned and fought for, name; New York, in fact) to do what he believes he is here to do, to do what he believes he is, through an accident of birth, and God-given talent, and received or sought-after vision, uniquely qualified to do. Maybe what he deserves from the people around him is something better. The expectation that he is and will be accountable, for instance: that he can and will be called to account. A silent, or else clearly enunciated, demand that he learn to better manage the veering and tidal fluctuations of his mood.

I had this horrible dream when I was a kid. I've never forgotten it. I dreamt I was in the sea, and I was swimming to the surface, and I didn't have enough breath to reach it, and I swam and swam, and I wasn't going to make it . . . and just as I reached out to touch the surface, I realised it was the bottom. I'd been swimming in the wrong direction.

—But let us too struggle to be fair, let us go after balance here. Certainly he is a wonderful, astonishing interview subject: this is, you are forced to acknowledge—and Jonathan can be so rude and so ungracious that you *do* grudge acknowledging it, in spite of your own best intentions—a brilliant and a generous mind. He is articulate to a fault: after a fluid seven and a half minutes (most of which it would be absolutely possible to use), you take advantage of him drawing a breath to push him slightly toward clarifying one of the many intricacies he has already thrown at the camera and hovering boom: during the fifteen seconds it will take to pose the redirection, Jonathan will look down, scowl, study his fingernails, inaudibly sigh, and scowl again before looking up reluctantly, under his brows: this is not a man who enjoys being interrupted.

Touring

The Varied and Complex Joys of Travelling with Musicians:

They lie about time. 'We're leaving at seven-twenty' (as opposed to seven-thirty, or eight-thirty, or ten o'clock, or even seven-twenty-one) means, we may mosey out of Wellington at elevenish, if we feel like it, though we're going to play a few games of soccer in the carpark behind Herd Street first. This means, since it's Good Friday and we'll be caught in traffic between Waikanae and Paraparaumu alone for a good hour and a half, that they'll miss, by hours, the first Workshop they were going to lead, throwing the organisers of the Jambalaya Festival into a blind panic.

Related conversation between Riki and Lucien:

'We had to be in the studio by *nine-thirty*, man.'

'What's the point of that? . . . What're you gonna get done before midday anyway? . . . I don't get *out* of bed before eleven.'

'I know, man.'

They cook real nice, though. Jonathan reveals an unexpected Camp Mother persona, lurking in there with Brian de Grane and the *Come over dere* lunatic. Rather sweetly, he *fusses*. He will, in fact, interrupt his own monologue in the living room to come and boss you around the table, as you move from dish to dish: No, first you make the bed of rice, and *then* you arrange the beans, and *then* the meat, and the greens go like this, and the baked banana you're meant to eat with *that*—

You're doing dinner all wrong.

Breakfast

'For Christmas one year,' Jonathan says, 'I bought six Tintin books and a box of Sante bars, and for three days all I did was eat chocolate and read and swim in the sea. —God I enjoyed it,' he adds, after a moment's thought, and returns with gusto to his breakfast.

He is in constant movement; he is eating, talking animatedly, waving his fork around, all at the same time. His skin is clear and brown; the shadows that have been gathering around his eyes and mouth over the last few weeks have vanished. There is egg yolk in his hair. He seems completely happy.

Women's Work

Riki is vacuuming the living room with less enthusiasm than anyone you have ever seen. He stands dispiritedly in one place, near the door to the balcony, and makes half-hearted sweeps around him with the nozzle. Jonathan, on the other hand, is bounding around in one of his excesses of energy, organising people, carrying armloads of boxes, records, blankets, equipment down to the van. He picks up something you can't see, from where you're sitting on the ledge of the balcony chatting to Fima, and yells to Riki, 'Hey whose is this penis enlarger, man?'

Riki doesn't even look up from his limp Wilma the Happy Housewife impression. 'Lucien's,' he says, without missing a beat.

Nectar

'You haven't been having much of that cider recently,' Jonathan tells Riki across the table, chewing, grinning, shifting, his eyes alight with that manic gleam.

Riki looks back at him. 'Nah man,' he says mildly. Riki exudes a kind of stillness, where Jonathan is constantly moving. Riki plays straight man much of the time: this is the game they play together, to their mutual advantage.

'You used to like that cider in the morning, didn't you?' Jonathan says.

'Yeah,' Riki says.

'What was that cider called again, man?' Jonathan presses. Riki looks away.

'Dickon, man,' he says.

'Yeah,' Jonathan says, laughing, returning to his sausages.

According to Jonathan and Riki, there really *is* a beverage somewhere in the world labouring under the brand of Dickon cider. All you can think is, even in the unlikely event that this is true, trust those two to have found it.

Behaving Badly in Rotorua

Jonathan and Riki manage to get themselves thrown out of a bar in Rotorua, which one would imagine was nearly impossible. Riki's slightly garbled version of this turns around one of Jonathan's elaborate metaphors. *Imagine there's this island, and there's four people on it, and all of them are deaf . . .*

The proprietor, according to him—the proprietor's loser son, according to them—listens to the tale of the island and the four deaf people in bemused silence. Finally he says, 'That's the biggest load of New Age shit I've ever heard.'

'You've really offended me, man,' Jonathan says, with dignity.

And then—surely there's a step missing somewhere here?—Riki and Jonathan get thrown out.

Or: the radio interview in Rotorua, when, exasperated beyond bearing by being asked yet again what it is they do when they are not making music—being infuriated by the repeated unspoken question, *Yes, but what do you* really *do?*—Jonathan drawls, on air, 'Well, I masturbate a lot.'

Or: driving around Rotorua in the van, drumming up business for the gig that night out the loudhailer on the roof, when Brian de Grane makes an unscheduled appearance. *Bring your daughters down to the yard; we'll have them working in the office, and doing a bit of part-time modelling on the side.* How this brings potential audience members to a show is unclear; it just has everyone in the van helpless with laughter.

Falling

In Leigh, at the end of the tour, they all take an afternoon and go horse-riding. Except that no one had explained to Jonathan about tightening girths, so the saddle simply . . . revolved, to end up suspended under the horse's stomach, taking Jonathan with it. Emma, gurgling, manages to give the impression of a Catherine wheel: all four limbs extended, and whirling.

Lucien, in the front seat of the Volvo, is wriggling with irritation that he missed this. 'Bet he didn't stop talking the whole time, either,' he mutters, changing gear.

Master Percussionist

[Miguel's] got that Master stature about him . . . he's a beautiful cat.

Miguel's father was from Cuba; he met Miguel's mother in Puerto Rico; he left that small family when Miguel was two, and Miguel has no memories of him, no photographs; they never met again. Miguel went to New York as a young man. For months all he could order, travelling with his band, was a hamburger, fries, and orange juice, because that's all he knew how to say. When he first auditioned he did recognise his own name; he came up to the stage, played, smiled nice, and left to catch the train back from Philadelphia to New York, where he was met by his cousin at the station, frantic. 'What you doing, man—why you here, man—you got the gig, man—they want you to start playing *tonight*—'

He met his ex-wife in New York. She was a New Zealander. When they split up and she came home, Miguel followed, leaving behind him the very successful career he had carved out over twenty years. No son of Miguel's was going to have only intermittent memories of his father, let alone none.

Miguel's early training was in classical music. He played with all the big Motown names. He played with all the big jazz names. Miguel can play anything. 'I watch,' he tells his students, fiercely, at a Master class. 'First I listen, but mostly, with the greats, I *watch*. I watch to see how they do it.' He demonstrates on the instrument, his big hands hard as teak. It's like the top half-inch of skin is all callus.

Miguel's suitcase reminds you of Mary Plain's, in *Mary Plain Goes to the USA*. It's covered, plastered, with stickers, cities visited, cities lived in, venues played at: they overlap, they peel and fade, the colours are often in stark contrast but do not shout at each other. You want to sit down with the suitcase in your lap and study it, like a mosaic. Miguel receives your pleasure in it with mild pleasure of his own. It's a portable version of the corkboard people have in their kitchens: tattered photographs, curling at the corners, of babies, lovers, holidaymakers with their arms around each other, beaming out at the viewer, exotic locations in the background. What you never know, of course, is who, exactly, is in the foreground: taking the picture.

'Miguel's full on, man,' Jonathan says to the others, after one of the Monday meetings in Havana. He stands behind the wooden bar, making coffee, and does an impersonation of Miguel panicking about reaching his plane in time; Miguel meeting Fima at the airport; Miguel refusing to understand that there is a difference between the drummer Rik, and the drummer Nick.

And it's true, Miguel is intense. He speaks hoarsely, insistently. His profile is sharp, his eyes hooded. Words, stories, anecdotes, opinions come from him in a flood; until the camera starts rolling, where most disconcertingly he transforms into Yum-Yum, batting his eyes and looking up shyly from under his lashes. You must be careful what questions you ask; none that could possibly lead to a one-word answer. 'Yes', or 'No', for example.

Sometimes, playing, when things are going well, Miguel will break out into a huge, generous smile, ear to ear. In pure joy.

Those Fiery Latins

'This Alda, I can't bear it, she never come in on the beat. Brazilians, they are hopeless, they have *no* sense of rhythm,' Miguel grumbles, to Mabeth, who grew up in the Netherlands but whose father was Spanish: the Spanish, presumably, are acknowledged to have a sense of rhythm.

Mabeth thinks this is nationalism gone crazy, and will have no truck with it. Some of it may also be that Alda hasn't always been able to rehearse new material enough with the band; on stage she will glance backward at Jonathan, looking for her cue. 'In Brazil we call it chicken eyes,' Alda says, and demonstrates, darting her head from side to side in sharp, scratching movements.

At the festival in Taupo, there is a photographer from California, little and black and cute, with shoulder-length dreads and an American-sized attitude. His way of introducing himself to you is to throw his arms around you, tucking himself confidingly into your sternum (that's where the top of his head comes to). New Zealanders tend to be so bemused by this kind of behaviour they're charmed by it. Miguel is not. The photographer comes to one of Miguel's Master classes, and succeeds both literally and figuratively in getting in Miguel's face. Miguel orders him out; so the next time the photographer sees Miguel in one of the subterranean, neon-lit corridors behind the stage, the photographer says, 'Hey how's that ego going man?'

Miguel slaps his face. Think of it: those hands, those slabs of teak. The shouting, on both sides, echoes around the whole ground floor.

Mary and Sappho

Mabeth's this small dark fireball, this cropped-haired sweetheart of wide-eyed voluble enthusiasm. She wants to know the names of everyone on the doco crew; she nods her head vigorously, repeating them, until she gets them right. She is the most recent addition to the core band, and is always the only woman musician. 'Singers, they are not women,' she says. 'Singers are *divas*.'

Singers do not pack in, or out. Singers merely swan onto stage at the beginning of their first set, looking beautiful.

Mabeth is proud that she lugs and carries with the best of them. She remarks indignantly on the fact that when on tour Tara does the laundry for all the boys; it does not occur to Tara to do Mabeth's.

At an early rehearsal at Herd Street, you're sitting watching, listening, and you don't think anything is showing on your face; but Mabeth comes by on the way to the loo and slaps you on the knee—it's the first time you've spoken to each other—and says conspiratorially, 'Real guys' stuff, huh?'

She and her partner Simone also perform, just the two of them, Mabeth on percussion and Simone on guitar. At Easter, in Taupo, by beautiful accident, they are set up on the corner of the stage right before a six-foot statue of the Virgin Mary, all blue cloak, white gown, downcast eyes, golden halo, hands piously folded. A gloriously unholy trinity.

Patent It

The making of coffee, in the kitchen of the house that has been put at their disposal in Taupo, is a drawn-out, ceremonial process. The water is put into a coffee jug first; then the grounds are lowered in, gently and slowly.

'It's the Gravitational Method, man,' Jonathan says. 'We're going to patent it.'

Riki watches in silence. After a while he says, very quietly, '*I* thought of that.'

Bad Dream

Everyone's sleeping in a couple of bunk rooms. At four or five in the morning, Riki stirs and cries out.

'I'm so thirsty,' he moans, mostly asleep. Emma, mostly asleep herself, gets up and brings him what she believes, in the shadows of the kitchen, to be a cup of orange juice. 'Errghh,' says Riki, and splutters: it is, in fact, cold tea. Emma, repeating this story, laughs and laughs and laughs: she sees it as a story against herself, and seems to miss what's really telling about it.

If in the dead of the night one of the group is thirsty, Emma will rouse herself and go and find him something to drink.

Fima

Bass players are really warm, mellow, nothing's really a problem—That's what a good bass player will sound like— warm, mellow, just right there, just keeping everything steady . . . Fima can whip up a major storm.

Fima seems the antithesis of the stereotypical Jewish New Yorker: he's mild-mannered, unassuming, soft-spoken when he speaks at all. He blinks myopic blue eyes behind glasses. He's the antithesis of the preconception of a very successful musician, too: he travels with his wife and two children, the youngest a baby of only a few months. When he and Jonathan greet each other at the airport (*'Hey, man. You made it'*) they clasp their right hands at chest height, and then put their left arms around each other: this means Jonathan also ends up with his arm around the bass guitar. He pats the case affectionately, in lieu of Fima's back: and indeed the instrument does seem part of Fima's body, an unusually melodic detachable limb.

His calm is reflected in the way the other musicians speak of him: their faces smooth out as their eyes slide up and to the right, imagining Fima playing; their voices drop. When he plays, he seems barely to move, the way a very, very talented rider seems barely to move while the horse beneath them performs flawlessly.

Fima sits before Lake Taupo and speaks softly of music, musicians, composing, his career. Does he have war stories? Fima thinks about this for a moment. 'Well,' he answers mildly, 'I have done yoga with Sting.'

Whoopsydaisy

A, a good, good musician in general will know what space is—generally—knows when to shut up, knows when to come in, knows when they're giving too much or they're not giving enough—

Riki's got another gig. There's another drummer playing, instead. And he's really fucking up. He's playing kind of big-time—you don't know the word for it—oh; ugly drums. Big-time show-offy not-melodic not-listening kind of dumb stadium drums. Yawn, only much louder. It makes you feel embarrassed, you don't want to catch his eye, it's awful, how badly he's fucking it up and he doesn't even know, he's beaming, he thinks he's doing it right.

But the drums are, simply, horrible. Before Riki you wouldn't have known you knew this, you would just have lost interest, touched your girlfriend or flatmate on the arm, either fallen into a more absorbing conversation than the one they're having up

there, or left. Now you know. You watch, half-scared for the
guest musician, half-angry for the music, wholly fascinated:
what will they do now? —He can be so rude, Jonathan; and
here, playing, with someone much less powerful than he is
fucking it up in the way he most detests—the one that involves
your ego, and the music secondarily—here, surely, is where
he will be *most* rude. It's only here, after all, that it's kind of
deserved, kind of okay.

—No. (It's amazing, really.) He does the opposite. He waits,
courteously; at one point he bites his lip, but his face is wiped
utterly clean of contempt. Here, he is courteous in a way that
seems astounding. Admirable, too. —It's because it's not toward
another person: he is being courteous toward *the music*.

He's drunk, actually. At the last break you saw this clearly:
the way he stumbled first over his words as he introduced the
other musicians, then over his own feet as he squished between
the vibraphone and the punters toward the bar, or toward the
alley outside. He doesn't seem drunk playing, though. He's
waiting, his face sober, in all senses, his gaze serious, careful.
It's beginning to make you highly nervous for the guest player,
how Jonathan's face is being slowly wiped of all expression.
He is, most unexpectedly (you didn't know he had it in him),
doing *neutral and composed*. At one point—you're sitting so
close in this tiny bar you can see him do it—he draws a breath
and then jumps in, the way a subtle, highly skilled dinner party
conversationalist will leap into the monologue of a boor. The
vibraphone sticks whir, blur, fly.

The drummer pounds on. There's no room for any other
sound. After a while the two other musicians stand back and
watch, their faces blank.

And then Jonathan's eyes slide stage-left (his right), to the
double bass player: they look at each other for a moment and
then—fatally—they smile.

Well, he won't be playing for them again, you guess—that
particular guy on drums—

Bon Voyage

His last night in New Zealand, two in the morning, the Sawmill in Leigh, Lucien dances.

He dances expressionlessly, still wearing the ridiculous Dr Seuss hat, still wearing the homeless person's overcoat and the granddaddy's hideous woollen vest. He pirouettes, raises (expressionlessly) his long arms over his head like a ballerina, twirls; his legs kick out like compasses, and fold back into themselves with exactly a compass's skeletal complexity. Lucien can take the piss out of himself with grace, it would seem. Feet away, rolling cigarettes, drinking water, leaning against a wooden bench and against each other, Emma and Tara are helpless with laughter. 'Oh, Lucien—' they say, to the air, to one another. This will be Lucien's leaving-New-Zealand epitaph, the thing that signifies this period of his life: that (falling, or dying) cry: 'Oh, Lucien—'

His last morning in New Zealand, nine o'clock in the morning, Lucien discovers road rage.

Part of this is that it takes him at least half an hour of the hour and a half drive from Leigh to the Auckland airport to figure out that the Volvo's speedometer is in miles, not kilometres; hence doing sixty along smallish curvedish countryish roads is going quite fast, really. (And here it is again, from the three women in the car, from the forty-year-old lesbian riding shotgun, from the twenty-five- and the thirty-five-year-old straight women in the back: that falling or wailing laughter: 'Oh, Lucien—')

For Lucien, now *just* twenty-two—with all that talent, all that technique; the technique that does something technique isn't meant to do, that is, it came (one senses) to him instinctively; with the trained and, anyway, excellent mind he prefers to veil beneath the uninflected mumbling of boys mooching, together, along Cuba Street Saturday afternoons; with all his chops, as the musicians say to each other, and not to anyone else—is still enough of a child to want, desperately, to win at the impromptu, stoned and absurd quiz game that starts up between him and Alda's husband, one o'clock in the morning, the Sawmill. He wants to win so much that when Charles is distracted by another conversation and turns and then wanders away, Lucien insists the quiz continues, up to ten points, as was originally agreed. He bends forward, fiercely scowling. When you run out of questions, Lucien will give you the question. 'Ask me—' he'll say, and then will speak of Greek texts, of ancient battles three or five thousand years past, of the golden stable built for Caligula's horse, with some learnedness of twentieth century poetry. Nothing could be more surprising, from this beautiful, sarcastic, flat-voiced boy; the understanding that these esoteric and non-musical minutiae are things he knows about, and must once have cared about passionately.

'I used to read them,' Lucien will tell you, fiercely scowling. 'When I was eight, I read—' —Everyone, it seems. Maybe (it occurs to you) Lucien is, or at any rate was, lonely. Gifted children usually are. Yes. Loneliness, and the fierce angry awareness of your own gift, and the surly angry knowledge that your peers don't get it, and being very tall, and then finding out you're very handsome, and being sardonic. Yes.

Lucien was a prick in Jazz School—he will volunteer this, it's not something you need to extract from him. He will fold his crazy compass legs over the balcony at Havana, in unusually expansive mood, and announce it. 'I was really young,' he will remind you, flatly (he was sixteen when he started; he had two degrees by twenty). Being very young, in the group you move in: and it's still years and years before he's going to be released from that one. What can you do, really; except keep being as very very good as you are, and wearing Dr Seuss hats, and liking girls, and being sarcastic, before the world can be sarcastic at you. What can you say, really: except, on that dying, laughing, faintly anxious fall: . . . Oh, Lucien.

Music Is the Universal Language

For a time, when another one of the musicians informs you of this yet one more time, you nod respectfully. *Say it, brother.* You feel rebuked and inadequate on behalf of language, for all that it fails to accomplish, for all the chasms it fails to bridge.

After a while how glibly this is spoken—spoken, mind you;

language can even describe its own shortcomings—and its carelessness are beginning to make you wriggle a little in your seat. Music isn't composed of a cobweb of *different* languages? Music doesn't have dialects? Music works like a Babel fish? Someone whose ear was trained in classical music, or drums and bass, would hear the other for the first time, and the translation would be instantaneous?

Finally you venture, 'But you could just as easily say, *Language is the universal music.*'

They consider this. 'Yeah,' they say slowly, thoughtfully, 'yeah, you probably could.'

How Do You Write about Music?

Even if you had an insider's knowledge of what a piece of music is doing (to you), and how it's doing it, being able to describe what's going on is not the same as describing what's happening. The map is not the territory.

Music doesn't exist on the page. It doesn't live in the notation.

When a piece of art is played or recorded, it's already dead.

When it's going right, when the stars are in the right place, when the still dance between the people playing and the people listening is alive and the channel is open, music is an exchange, for want of a less laden phrase, of a kind of love.

One—one is exposed in that—(long pause) you, you, you do put a sail up, to catch the wind. And, um, people can—that sail is exposed. That's, if you like—(long pause)—it's something, something that you—You need to be open, in order to—(long pause)—Well, open is about the word; you just need to be open. To receive anything, or, or—to put anything out, or—You don't get it for free, you've got—You don't get to play nice music without giving something to get it. So you have to actually expose yourself, in quite an inner way. Most—probably most people don't realise this. I know—You're really aware when an audience does realise that, because they actually give you, or give the music, um, an incredible amount of energy, which, which—is—just silently transferred, but, but—when some— when someone's consciousness is beyond, where, where the room and the—where you are, when some—you feel it; and so when someone is listening to your music with the hope that it will bring them some kind of thing that—uplifting thing, or—you know—It will; you'll feel that, and it will help you to actually get it. From somewhere else.

Guy Fawkes

The sea is glassy, black, bitterly cold. It's a lake canoe, actually, that Jonathan and Riki have pushed out from the Havana yacht into the middle of the Wellington harbour. They swing over fathoms of water; above their heads the fireworks flare, break, multi-coloured points of light pushing outward against the dark, falling in again toward themselves. Jonathan and Riki watch, rocking with the waves. Then, Jonathan, becoming momentarily too comfortable in the medium, stands up; and the canoe capsizes.

Both of them falling, the warm wrapped fug of their bodies alight with shock, the sea searingly cold and dark, and endless, the way the world feels when you're not playing.

'We were a long way out,' Riki says laconically. 'I think Jonathan thought I was going to drown.'

You can get lost out there. You can mistake the bottom of the sea for the surface. You can swim in the wrong direction.

Good Night

The bar staff are bemused but friendly. Yes, one of the band hangers-on can make a cellphone call from the office downstairs; yes, Jonathan can steal an icecream from behind the candy bar; yes, it's time to go now.

Jonathan, standing on the Embassy stairs before the soaring silver of the mirrors, offers the butt-end of his icecream to the girl who's lost her friends, the one who needed to make the cellphone call. 'I would have got you one, but they're not mine,' he explains kindly.

Out there is Courtenay Place, what the beleaguered City Council and the recently hobbled-together *Dominion Post* is trying to rename Wellington's Golden Mile; out there the adventurers of Lower Hutt are tying a load on, experimenting with city cool and the intricate glass pipes of P, getting beaten up by bouncers and vomiting colourfully onto the sidewalk before Kenny's. In here, though, there's just the twenty-foot striped silk curtains, and the grand piano blackly gleaming, and the jazz fading into the walls, and the lights shedding small pools of gold before the bartender leans over and turns them off.

February–June 2003

DENNIS MCELDOWNEY

Some Folk-singers and a Theologian

In 1960 Peter Cape, in his mid-thirties, was supervisor of religious programmes for the New Zealand Broadcasting Service. On Sunday he was assistant priest at the Trentham Anglican Church. During the week, in whatever nightspots were available in Wellington at the time, he sang to a guitar 'folk songs' he had written himself, 'Down the Hall on Saturday Night', 'Taumaranui', 'The Okaihau Express', and the rest. He was sometimes joined by Les Cleveland, a collector of genuine folk songs, especially from World War II, and by a young solicitor named Ken Bryan. An occasional, somewhat incongruous guest performer was an Aucklander, Willow Macky, who had, like her friend Gloria Rawlinson, survived a reputation as a child poet and now wrote and performed her own rather willowy songs.

My entrée to the fringe of this group came through Ken's wife Josette, a beautiful young woman with a slightly bluish tinge to her complexion. We had both been patients at Greenlane Hospital (not at the same time) and had written books about our experiences, though in my case the Greenlane episode was only part of the book and in hers the whole of it. My operation at Greenlane was successful but her condition was judged inoperable; my book was published and hers was not: two facts which made me feel guilty and Josette possibly resentful. In spite of it we remained friends of a sort, and it was at the Bryans' flat in Upper Hutt that I met the folk-singers. I never heard them perform in public—I was still, at that time, less mobile than Josette. My aquaintance with them led to my hearing Peter Cape discuss theology over dinner with a friendly but baffled minister of the Netherlands Reformed Church, to whom he afterwards sang and played his guitar; and to the only time I was ever driven at night, at speed, over winding and hilly roads by a seriously drunk driver.

*

To start with the theologian: Pieter de Bres was brought to
New Zealand by the Presbyterian Church (which in Europe
would have been called 'Reformed'), to work among the Dutch
immigrants then arriving in large numbers. It is confusing that
a 'Reformed Church of New Zealand' had been established by
people who had belonged in the Netherlands to a fundamentalist
breakaway called (the Dutch equivalent of) the Re-reformed
Church. This also appealed, for mainly ethnic reasons, to some
Dutch people who were not particularly conservative in their
theology. But many were also linked, by Pieter and three or four
colleagues, with the Presbyterian Church.

After he had been here for a year or two, Pieter concluded
that he could work most effectively from an established parish,
made his availability known, and in due course was 'called'
by the Upper Hutt Presbyterian Church. On an early pastoral
visit to one of his elders, my father, he got his eye on me, as
someone who had an ability with words. Thereafter, every
Saturday morning for five years, he brought along his sermon
for me to vet. Our conversations soon ranged far beyond
the English of his sermon, into history, sociology, theology,
politics; and occasionally became arguments. Pieter was later
a liberal theologian in the Geering mould. He was not so at
this time. He was a neo-orthodox Barthian. One of the tenets
of this tradition, to summarise ruthlessly the many volumes of
Karl Barth's *Church Dogmatics* (which I have not read), was
to concede what biblical scholars said about the human and
flawed authorship of the books of Scripture, and to carry on as
if nothing had changed. What had mostly not changed was the
high Calvinist conception of an absolute gulf between God and
man, a gulf that could be bridged only from God's side.

Yet Barth had admitted the enemy through the back door,
and eventually, for many, the absolutist theology collapsed under
the weight of the biblical scholarship. While it held, however,
Barthians were noted for being uncompromisingly principled
about things that mattered. Most of the German Protestants
who resisted Hitler were Barthians, including the most famous
of them, Dietrich Bonhoeffer. Pieter himself, his family and his
in-laws, joined the Dutch resistance, specialising in hiding Jews.

Pieter's principles sometimes led him into strife in Upper Hutt. He was invited to address the Anzac Day service, and delivered an anti-war, specifically anti-Cold War, message. RSA members muttered that he ought to be shot. Barth appeared at second-hand in most of his sermons—hence some of the arguments. In 1960 he was forty-five.

Pieter and Leni and their many children (eight eventually) took to life in New Zealand like ducks to water, but many things puzzled Pieter, as often of Anglo-Saxon origin as specifically New Zealand. How could a person claim to be both a Christian and a Freemason? What was the logic of English prepositions? Why do we live *in* the world but *on* earth? One of his greatest puzzles was the Anglican Church. The Presbyterian Church, for all its ethnic differences, he could feel at home in. He could understand if not approve of Roman Catholics. After all they and the Protestants shared the Netherlands, uneasily but peacefully, in about equal numbers. He could even appreciate Methodists. His father-in-law had been a missionary in South America for the Moravian Church, which had similar eighteenth-century evangelical origins. But the Anglican Church he couldn't place at all. What was the point of it? What *on earth* was the use of it?

So when I invited him to dinner with Peter Cape it was rather in the spirit in which James Boswell invited the high-tory Samuel Johnson to dine with the arch-radical John Wilkes, to see what would happen, not least for the benefit of his diary.

The 'Victorian' villa (built about 1910), in which I lived with my parents, was the best they could afford when my father retired. Previous owners had made a number of alterations, but had never got around to trying to remove the villa look, as others had done, by boxing in the verandah and flattening the gable. Perhaps they had run out of money; perhaps they had even liked the villa look—an eccentric thought which occurred to me only because I was secretly beginning to share it, despite the strictures of Ernst Plischke in his book *Design and Living* (1947), which had hitherto been my architectural Bible. In any case, the finials and the verandah fretwork had been removed, so perhaps it

was lack of money that prevented further improvements. My
bedsitter, where Pieter and Peter and I ate our dinner on our
knees, still had a twelve-foot stud.

The food was provided by my mother, but she and my father
discreetly retired to eat and read and listen to the wireless in
the added-on sunporch at the back. At first the conversation
was halting—as it was with Johnson and Wilkes. I did most of
the talking. Eventually Pieter mentioned one thing Anglican he
did approve of, a column of mildly radical opinion in *Church
and People*, signed 'Clavis'. Peter looked modestly self-effacing,
which confirmed the suspicion I had already formed that Peter
was Clavis. I had indeed been relishing the fact that his vicar,
a conservative Canon called Smallfield, had been sounding off
about this dreadful column to my father. Pieter's commendation
of the column sparked the conversation, though by making it
Pieter felt he had been polite enough. From then on he asked
sharpish questions which Peter good-naturedly parried. After
they had skirmished on a number of topics, Pieter settled on
the archaic language of the prayer book, and the barrier this
placed on evangelism. Ah, yes, Peter said, but the service is the
beginning of a setting apart of the people of God, for which
a special language conveying a sense of the numinous was
appropriate. Pieter could see his point but thought it selfish. At
a later date he would have said elitist. Neither foresaw that in a
short time the Anglican Church would be agreeing with Pieter
rather than Peter.

Why had Peter wanted to be a priest? Pieter wanted to know.
Peter told his story, of a childhood which had nothing to do
with the church, until at the age of fourteen or fifteen he became
a Scout and went to a church parade. The service was Anglican,
and the general confession blew him away. ('We have erred,
and strayed from thy ways like lost sheep. We have followed
too much the devices and desires of our own hearts. We have
offended against thy holy laws. We have left undone those
things which we ought to have done; and we have done those
things which we ought not to have done; and there is no health
in us.' I wondered about that adolescent.) He continued going to
services, tasting a variety of churches but always coming back

to the Anglicans; and from that point had his heart fixed on the priesthood, although it was some time before he was even confirmed because he dreaded being asked why he had not been baptised.

But why, if a priest, not a parish priest? Pieter asked. I had my private suspicion that Peter had perhaps been too unorthodox, not in belief but in behaviour, to be a success as a parish priest; but Peter responded with a spirited defense of the place for a priest in secular life. Not that his current job was all that secular anyway.

Then, when we had finished our salmon pie and fruit and ice-cream and had exhausted divinity, Peter went out to his car and brought back his shining new guitar, bought from the last royalty cheque on the sale of his records, and soon had Pieter thoroughly bushed among the sheilas and bints and jokers and boozers. I wondered whether Pieter had been able to make anything of Peter at all; but when he brought along his sermon the following Saturday he said he had enjoyed the evening, 'though he is perhaps a little conscious that he is Peter Cape'.

It was a less staid gathering, though not all that less staid, to which the Bryans took me a couple of months later, on a wet, cold Saturday in July. Josette rang after lunch, proposing that I should go with them to a party at Noel Hoggard's in Pukerua Bay. 'The party will go on all day and all night,' she said, 'but we aren't intending to stay long.' I was tempted, and they arrived for me shortly afterwards. The Bryans always had interesting cars. Their previous one had been a pre-war Rover or Riley, I can't remember which, with pre-selector gears. In this precursor of automatic transmission, you selected with your gear-change, but Ken in traffic seemed to be relying on second sight. Now they had an aged but spectacular red Fiat, in which Ken sped us down the valley, over Haywards Hill, and around the Paremata Harbour, while I was already regretting my decision to come. Parties weren't really my scene.

Noel Hoggard was a public servant, a widower or deserted husband according to the person you spoke to, who had at least one daughter. A shed in his back yard housed a treadle-operated printing press, which he called the Handcraft Press. On it he printed, one opening at a time, hand-set pamphlets of verse. More importantly he edited and printed a long-running little magazine, also set by hand, which changed its name from time to time. By 1960 it had settled into its last and best-know name, *Arena*. Hoggard had the distinction of publishing the early work of many writers who later became recognised names, a few of whom, notably Louis Johnson and Kendrick Smithyman, remained faithful to him. His authors that year included Marilyn Duckworth (who had however already published a novel), Peter Hooper, Jack Lasenby, Renée Taylor. Yet ungratefully I concluded that his ability to pick future winners was not due to acute discernment so much as to lack of it. If everything went in something was bound to be of interest. Ungratefully? Well, I was one of the young writers whose work he printed. (I wrote short stories in those days.) Normally, a writer discovers an editor's limits of taste and tolerance from the submissions accepted and those rejected. I never had a rejection slip from Noel Hoggard, even for the most callow work. I never had a letter of acceptance, either, but in due course everything was printed—without payment, it goes without saying. I began to wonder whether anyone received rejection slips from him. Presumably some did, since he only published the magazine two or three times a year, and each number had only twenty-eight pages. But on what grounds I could not judge. I had never met him.

Hoggard put so much time and work into his magazine that one could hardly object to his enjoyment of a few perks which came with it. He took pride in the number of overseas little magazines for which he exchanged *Arena*. Piles of them in every corner of the house were the first thing I noticed when we arrived. And he enjoyed giving parties. He lived in a small house, probably originally a weekend bach, high on the hill above the sea.

Several people were already there, but if I had looked forward to meeting some of my fellow contributors I was disappointed. There were none. His mother and daughter bustled around with food. I talked to the Coles, John and Christine, but they soon went. I talked to a woman I had not met before and discovered we were both writing children's books with the same plot (neither ever published). This added to the gloom I was already feeling, seeping in from the dark afternoon. Les Cleveland strummed a guitar as if he was bored with strumming a guitar. We trooped out through dripping bushes to examine Noel's press in its shed by the light of a torch.

Ken and a friend decided to liven things up by going off to fetch Denis Glover. They were away for a long time, partly because Denis insisted on his wife coming too, and she had to be coaxed from a bed of sickness. Denis was in his usual state, as I sometimes thought he knew he was expected to be, and carrying it off with his usual panache. This worried me not a little, but Josette had made one glass of sherry last the afternoon, and I hoped she would drive home. I had to go with them, anyway. There was no way I could get myself from Pukerua Bay to Upper Hutt late on a Saturday afternoon, or at any other time. The trouble was that I was not drinking at all, except lemonade, because I was taking medication which alcohol did not agree with. As I watched other guests rocking on their feet, including the woman who was writing my children's story, I reflected that it was a mistake to stay sober when everyone around was getting drunk. Our host so far was not affected. He kept unobtrusively in the shadows. In the shadows he remains in my memory: I have little impression of what he looked like.

After early darkness had fallen, Josette managed with difficulty to prise Ken from Glover and we set off, Josette driving. Ken sang, he laughed, he fiddled with the controls of the car, he said how wonderful it was that Glover believed it was the duty of a writer to *communicate*. He induced Josette to take the narrower, less frequented secondary road around the northern side of Paremata Harbour. Josette had not been that way before, and did not know what was beyond the range of her headlights. Ken begged to be allowed to drive: sitting there was so *boring*. Josette drove doggedly on, but when Ken urged her to go *faster, faster* she did her best to oblige. Finally, after nearly driving us into the sea at a bend she had not anticipated, she let Ken take over. He roared us over Haywards Hill at a

speed I could only guess at, because the speedometer was not
working; yet fairly steadily except for the corners he cut. He
was marginally safer in the driving seat than nagging from the
passenger seat. At Silverstream he stopped to be sick over the
fence into the playing fields of St Patrick's College, and Josette
resumed the wheel. It was only about eight when I arrived
home.

The Bryans' marriage did not last, though I doubt whether
the party at Hoggard's much influenced that outcome. Josette
moved to Auckland. Denied a high-tech cure, she took like
Katherine Mansfield to alternative medicine and alternative
religion, and indeed lived longer than she was expected to,
although she was still in her forties when she died. Ken had
his brief moment of fame when he drove away from Raetihi, or
some such place, where he was practising law, and disappeared;
neither he nor his car was ever seen again. Peter Cape, after
a fling at directing films, became a freelance writer, published
a series of books about arts and crafts, and died in his early
fifties. After Pieter de Bres retired from the ministry at the age
of sixty-five he studied for a law degree, and spent the rest of
his life as a voluntary solicitor for a community law office in
Christchurch, until he dropped dead in the street just short of
eighty.

Not Telling

I've been wondering for sixty-odd years why, when Arnold Humphrey and his friends beat me up, I never told anyone. By that I mean never. Perhaps it is understandable that I didn't tell anyone at the time, though I'm not even sure about that; but why never since?

It was not typical of my childhood. Most of my childhood memories are happy: even if in odd disconnected pictures. Like the soft glow of a gas-lamp on a brass bracket in the sitting room. The house was lit by electricity (it wasn't that long ago); the gas-lamp was a standby in case of a power cut, but was sometimes lit for effect when my parents entertained. But after a few uses the mantle would crumble at a touch. The wind-up gramophone and the old records—old meaning they belonged to the twenties. I realised later, but not then, that during the depression my parents could not afford records. Caruso, Gigli, Galli-Curci, Melba, the J.H. Squire Celeste Octet. Marches and excerpts from the *Mikado* were more to my taste, but on rainy days (it seemed to suit rainy, sad and drippy days) my favourite record was the Intermezzo from *Cavalleria Rusticana*. Which would sometimes be blotted out by the screech and rumble of a tram.

That sounds too poetic, though. We didn't always passively overhear the passing trams. We played games with them. Gravel laid on the rail crushed into dust; halfpennies, if we could afford them, flattened into discs three times their original size. Boxes of wax matches, filched from the kitchen, went off with a satisfying explosion, at least to us, crouched against the fence round the corner in Hardwicke Street. The motorman never noticed. And the pebbles were far from a derailing size. We were good children. When David Shirley wrote 'Have a fuck' in pencil on the outside wall of the surf pavilion I knew he ought not to, although I didn't know what it meant, any more than he did.

I had an older brother and sister. Fred was very much older, five years, so didn't often acknowledge us; though I'm pretty sure the matchbox trick came from him. My sister, two years older, also had her friends. They coalesced with mine from time to time. In summer our focus was on the beach. Ours was the last generation to fully enjoy that beach, and the sandhills, held together with marram grass and lupins. I heard my parents discussing the borough council's plan to remove the sandhills, and replace them with a flat promenade, protected by a stone wall. I gathered the council didn't like what went on among the lupins. The word immorality was used. When I heard it I blushed, remembering the cigarette David Shirley pinched from his mother and shared with me. After we moved away the promenade was built, and the sea removed the rest of the sand from the beach. It was still there for us. For the castles we built and canals that filled with water, and the pipis we dug up (but didn't eat). We waded through the white foam on the edge of the tide and jumped through the breakers. Not many of us learnt to swim.

At the end of a hot day we walked home in the concrete gutter because it was cooler than the melting tar on bare feet. Bad weather promised more excitement. A yacht might overturn or be stranded on the bar. The siren pulsed through the bay to summon the volunteer crew of *Rescue II* and we waited for news of the drowned. Usually there weren't any.

I was not a solitary child. I liked being with people, and assumed they liked being with me. My mother worked on the principle that she would prefer us to have our friends at home where she could keep an eye on us. The beach often defeated her there, but not all the time. Fred and his friends were beginning to talk about philately instead of stamp-collecting, they made elaborate Meccano models, a steam roller, a clock that almost worked, they wrote and edited a magazine, besides playing cricket on the back lawn. We didn't have a radio of our own and Fred partly chose friends at whose houses he could listen to *The Japanese Houseboy*. That excluded Arnold Humphrey next door, but there were other reasons as well. They were the same age, and both caught the second trailer behind the 7.30 tram every morning (to go to different schools), but Fred didn't like Arnold, for some reason. He referred to him as a little squirt. I think he might have called him that to his face. It is true that Arnold was smaller than Fred.

My sister Beth's full name was Elizabeth, after our grandmother, but she was Beth by the time she was born, after the angelic sister in *Little Women*. She turned out to be more a mixture of Jo and Amy; but this didn't prevent Beth from identifying with Beth in the book. She read the deathbed scene over and over, weeping buckets. (So did I, surreptitiously.) She thought now and then it would serve our mother right if she caught a fever and died. Meantime she and her friends had tea-parties for dolls with fabric bodies and porcelain faces, and celluloid kewpie dolls (one, two or four for a penny according to size from Woolworths in town), and cut out and dressed paper dolls.

We were well-brought-up children, but we weren't as well-brought-up as the Humphreys. We were less disciplined with our Easter eggs. Our cheap chocolate eggs were gone by the time we went back to school on Wednesday. The Humphreys' grandmother gave them large, expensive, hollow eggs made of hard sugar icing with piped, coloured decorations. They lasted until Christmas. They were kept in their original boxes in Mrs Humphrey's wardrobe and a square inch was broken off now and then for a special occasion. Ann and Tom once turned up at the pictures with their little squares of Easter egg, and though they sat next to Beth and me they didn't share. That rankled later, though at the time eyes and mind were focused on the screen. At the end of the weekly serial the luxurious airship on which all the characters were travelling broke in half over mid-Atlantic (we didn't go to the pictures often enough to see how any of the cliffhangers were resolved); Shirley Temple, the poor little orphan, danced on a dining table singing 'Animal crackers in my soup'. The only animal biscuits we knew had coloured icing. In *soup*?

I think even then I could sense though not explain some

kind of constraint between the Humphrey parents and ours. Now and then I would see my father at the Humphreys' front door, handing over an envelope and talking seriously for a few minutes. I knew that our house had formerly belonged to Mrs Humphrey's father. There had been a gate in the corrugated-iron fence between the two backyards, nailed up before we arrived. It wasn't until much later I learnt that when the house was sold the Humphreys left money on mortgage, and that my father had got behind in the payments.

Mrs Humphrey never came even near forbidding her children to associate with us, and was affectionate and generous when we played at their house, but she kept an anxious eye on what went on in our backyard. She could just see over the fence if she stood on tip-toe at the edge of the window in Arnold's bedroom. I sometimes saw her eye, her cheek, and her fair wavy hair, if I looked up from the sandpit. The sandpit was the source of her anxiety. We had grown out of it, as a sandpit; but in the middle of it, on a base of loose bricks, was an old bench-top gas cooker. It was not of course connected with the gas, but we made fires of paper and twigs in the little oven and roasted potatoes on top. They were burnt black before they were cooked, but we got a thrill out of eating half-raw potatoes with charcoal skins. The cooking was Beth's department, and she often invented dishes from weeds in the garden, especially dock leaves and roots of which there were plenty, and gave them to us not to eat but to pretend to eat. We spooned them daintily to our mouths and exclaimed with pleasure. One afternoon, however, she made a soup, in a saucepan from the kitchen, of parsley in large quantities, turnip leaves, nasturtium leaves, and sow thistle; and this was real. At her insistence we each took one or two spoonfuls *into* our mouths, before even Beth conceded the recipe needed a few changes. Next day Ann Humphrey came over after school, looking pleased with herself, and told us her mother said they were never to eat anything cooked on our gas stove again. 'Were you sick?' I said. 'No,' she said, 'but it put Tom and me off our tea.'

To me, the attractions of the Humphreys' place were greater than our own. The Hornby train was the greatest of them, but

it was added to by the size of the house and garden. The trees in
their backyard (fruit trees mainly: apples, peaches, greengages,
quinces) were great for stalking and guerrilla wars. Hanging
up in the big shed, which had half-doors because it had once
been a stable, were a back pack and a gas-mask from Mr
Humphrey's service in Flanders during the Great War. I envied
these (my father had been confined to home service because of
a 'spot on the lung'); we were not allowed to touch them, but
they made our play more real. The trees also made the ideal
landscape for the train. Tom had three clockwork locomotives
and several boxes of rolling stock (they were Arnold's really,
and occasionally he turned up to direct operations loftily), but
the set's main distinction was the incredible number of rails,
which could weave through almost every room in the house if
we had to play indoors, or about the trees, crossing one another
with special pieces, parting at junctions and rejoining further
on. Having put together a passenger train, with compartmented
coaches (the model trains page of the *Boy's Own Paper*
insisted on 'coaches', not 'carriages') labelled LNER and GWR
and SR (not, Tom said, that they would all have been on the
same train at Home), and a goods train with flats and sheep
wagons and petrol tankers, and a mixed train, and wound up
the locomotives, the great thing was to set them going all at
once but make sure, by deftly switching the points, that they
never collided. Tom, who at our place was sometimes a bit lost
among Beth's wilder imaginings and mine, was here in charge.
He knew all the technical words and techniques, and I followed
him respectfully. There was a lot of following, at speed, because
if we had miscalculated, the only way to stop the trains before
they collided was to grab hold of the engine and press the lever in
the cab. Sometimes we were not in time, and the trains sprawled
beside the line, engine wheels spinning. We fell about laughing
and competed with one another to estimate the death toll. 'I bet
it's at least fifty.' 'I bet it's two hundred.'

One day, instead of setting up the lines in the yard we stretched
them along the side of the house to the front. The reason was
that we wanted to see whether the engines could make it up a
gradient in the path. There were enough rails to continue along

the path under the front veranda. On the front lawn, down a short flight of steps, Arnold and a couple of his friends from College were kicking a football. It always impressed me that they went to College, not to school. Mr Humphrey taught at College. He was sitting on the steps smoking his pipe. Arnold did something tricky with the ball which I couldn't follow. 'You need a kick on the backside,' one of the friends said. 'You need a knee up your arse,' Arnold replied. It was not the first time I'd heard such language at the Humphreys' but I found it very shocking. It also astonished me, knowing that the senior Humphreys were strict parents who rationed Easter eggs, that Mr Humphrey took no notice. Perhaps there was something about College that allowed arses. 'Come *on*,' said Tom, and we went back to find the trains and test them on the gradient. The largest of the engines made it up the slope on its own but couldn't manage to take even a guard's van with it, and all the other combinations slipped and slid.

Ann Humphrey was my age and in my class at school, but I saw less of her than of Tom, who was a year younger. She did play with the Hornby train from time to time, though, and we all played together on the beach, not to mention our sandpit. The beach was where I came across her one day when I'd gone down alone in a huff. I had just quarrelled with Beth, or rather she had quarrelled with me because I had cut out all the clothes from a newly acquired sheet of paper dolls, and was attaching a frock to one of the dolls with the little tabs when she found me, and put on a display of the temper that was said to go with her red hair. She didn't even listen when I told her I was doing it as a surprise for her, which seemed to me a perfectly reasonable explanation although it was a lie. She continued to storm and say she'd tell on me. It was an odd argument because in spite of its passion it was conducted *sotto voce*. Our mother was having one of her migraines and, although I doubt whether compassion came into it, there was something electric in the air on a migraine day that counselled restraint. Finally I couldn't cope with Beth's anger and fled. I ran to the beach, my mind seething with indignation, and with anxiety in case she did tell.

On the beach I found Ann, just beginning to make a sandcastle with vicious jabs into the wet beach with a stick she had picked up. She had quarrelled with Tom, I couldn't quite work out what about except that it had something to do with the greengage tree and who was allowed to climb it. We didn't like our families just then, we agreed, and joined forces on the sandcastle. She built up the turrets and decorated them with shells; I dug a moat with another stick, a board as wide as my hand which had floated in on the tide; then I branched off from the moat, dug a river, bridged it with another piece of board, built a road along the bank. 'I can see you're going to be an engineer,' said a lady walking along the beach wearing tweeds and brown brogues. Shortly afterwards four standard six boys came along and kicked down the castle and shuffled across my engineering works. 'I'll tell on you, George Edwards,' Ann said. 'See if I care,' said George, whose shorts were held up by braces, and they walked on.

We weren't as upset as we might have been: the tide was about to demolish our work anyway. But what with our shared work and shared grievances I was feeling friendly towards Ann and invited her to come home to tea. By the time we were halfway along the single block between the beach and home I was regretting the impulse. I had forgotten the migraine. Ann was so eager I didn't like to back down, and hoped for the best. The fear was a better guide than the hope. When we went into the kitchen and I asked my mother if Ann could stay to tea she did her best to be kind, but suggested another day would be better. Ann flushed, and ran off.

In ten minutes she was back, knocking at the door, coming in without being asked (as we all did), and asked my mother if I could come home with her for a few minutes for a treat. I was in my room by then, reading, but I heard what she said and came out. 'What kind of a treat?' I asked. 'That would be telling,' she said. She was jiggling about and her eyes were shining with excitement. 'Don't be late for tea,' said my mother. 'Round the back,' Ann said at their gate. We went round the back. Arnold and two of his College friends were there. Arnold was holding a cricket bat. 'You've been asking for a swipe across the arse, you

lying little squirt,' he said and did just that. His friends each had
a cricket stump, and joined in. 'That's enough,' Arnold said,
and let me escape. I ran, crying, round the house. Just before
I reached the gate Mr Humphrey came through it. 'Hello, old
chap,' he said, 'what's up?' 'I fell over,' I said.

Once home I burrowed into our macrocarpa hedge, my
favourite hiding-place, and spent half an hour calming myself
down and feeling my injuries. They weren't very bad, I had
not been hit very hard. But I thought they were very bad, and
limped inside. My mother came out of her migraine cloud to
show her concern and ask what had happened. 'I fell down the
Humphreys' steps.' I said. 'Let's have a look,' she said and I
pulled down my pants. There were no underpants to pull down:
we didn't wear any. 'You did land on your seat,' she said; 'no
skin broken, but you may be uncomfortable for a while. Why
not go to bed for tea?' And then, 'What was the treat?' I was
ready for that. 'Ice-cream from Mrs Smither's fridge,' I said.
The widow who lived in the house beyond the Humphreys had
the only fridge in our neighbourhood.

So why didn't I tell? Fear? Possibly, though I would have had the
adults on my side, not to mention Fred. The code of silence? You
didn't tell, except on siblings. That's nearer the mark, but still
doesn't explain why I *never* told. Shame is nearer the mark still
but is too simple. I think it just didn't square with my sense of
reality. Happy, good, popular, loved and loving children didn't
get beaten up.

Not telling did me no harm. I was wary of the Humphreys for
a week or two, but they proved as good at pretending it hadn't
happened as I was. It only slowly dawned on me that Arnold and
Ann were scared. Their father had been within a few seconds
of coming upon a scene he wouldn't have approved of. Arnold
was no friendlier afterwards than he had been before, but he
was not less friendly, either. I didn't build sandcastles with Ann
again: I left her to Beth and the paper dolls. Tom never gave
any sign that he knew what had happened, and that may be
true: he was out with his mother at the time. We played with
his trains as ever, though *played* never seems the right word for

a dedicated pursuit. I continued to be in and out of their house. It was on their radio, a few weeks after they got it, and a week or two before we got ours, that one morning I heard through shortwave crackles and surges the man who had been king until the day before explaining he couldn't continue on the throne without the woman he loved. What this meant to me I can't say; it has been so overlaid with later hearings.

Early the following year we moved to another suburb. My father had a new job with a house attached. After tea one Saturday in the late winter he and my mother went back to our old house, which they hadn't been able to sell, to visit their tenant. I went along for the ride in our first car (1929 Ford Model A), and they suggested I visit the Humphreys. Arnold was the only one home, along with some of his College friends. 'They'll be back soon,' he said. 'You can come in and wait if you like.' I sat on the edge of a chair and listened to them discussing the test match they'd watched that afternoon at Lancaster Park, Springboks versus the All Blacks (from which I can date this visit precisely to 4 September 1937). They were sore at the result and believed the All Blacks ought to have won after leading at half time. I gathered this much, but didn't know enough about rugby to be interested. They ignored me. There was no sign of the rest of the family, and soon I went back to our old house. I never saw the Humphreys again.

STUART McKENZIE

Convert to You

Miranda and I went on
the *Raw Energy Diet*.
That is what the book is called,
anyway, by Lesley Kenton

and her daughter whose name I
forget. It's some idea dreamed
up in California,
big in the 80s amongst

film stars, before surgery
made fasting as obsolete
as typewriters. The first few
days you're only allowed one

sort of fruit. As much water
as you want. I had splitting
headaches while all the toxins
leached out. Miranda kept on

nodding off. By the middle
of next week, I was a new
man. My head was clear, like a
line of hyper-text. I could

see for miles. I saw right back
to the day after the day
you were born. You open your
mouth to holler, but grab my

glasses instead and won't let
go. I hand you back to your
mother and she passes you
to her husband to hold. I

remember the first time I
met your mother. It was at
a smart university
party. Her dress is the same

blue as the girl who falls off
the tower in a Tarot
pack. She talks passionately
about Keats' negative

capability. Leonard
Cohen is singing. We went
outside and three years later
you were born. When I look at

you, my heart skips a beat. I
think I inherited my
features from you! I've got your
eyes, your lips, your sharp jaw. I've

got your skin. It's like you showed
up before me. Maybe that's
because I'm looking back. But
even when I turn to the

future I see you in the
distance somewhere. Do you eat
Indian food? Miranda
and I went to The Curry

Club to break our fruit diet.
She leaned across the table
and her hair caught fire. I can
hear her hair crackling. There was

a quick whoosh of flame and then
a fine coat of ash settled
on our saag gosht. She looked as
though she had just become a

Hare Krsna. What would I
think if I bumped into you
handing out religious
paperbacks at overseas

terminals? But you know I'm
already a convert to
you. I'd yell out, 'Hey, listen
up, this kid really makes sense!'

FRANKIE McMILLAN

Marshmallow

Every now and again Cliff Hinkley appears in the most unexpected places. Just yesterday he was at the slide lecture on 'How you can travel and work in the UK'. I recognised his skinny shoulder blades from the back row. I just up and left without even waiting for the free supper.

Tonight he's behind the counter at the Bamboo Takeaway.

'What'll it be love?' he says, wiping his thin hands down his front. I look glumly at the bow-tie that's lurched off-centre, the apron two sizes too big for him. 'She's a cold night out there,' he continues and makes a show of shivering as if we've got something in common after all.

Back in the car with my hot chop suey I find he's left the plastic fork out. It's going to be difficult to eat, but no way am I going back in for a fork. I wouldn't give him the satisfaction.

'Forget the fork did we love?' he'd say tilting his dark head and rolling his eyes to the customers. So I use the tips of my fingers to snatch the steaming broccoli and flip the pork pieces to the side. After a while the windows fog up and all I can see is the occasional blur of colour as another customer walks past.

I wonder if they see *me*, waving my burning fingers in the air.

The woman next door bites her red nails and asks how is it possible for Cliff to be in so many places at once. All I can say is don't underestimate Cliff. That's the mistake I made.

The first time I saw Cliff Hinkley I had to laugh. He came bolting into the Enterprise Course for the Unemployed wearing a black pinstripe suit and a greasy tie.

'Sorry I'm late,' he gasped, waving a brown paper bag. The class had already gone through the introductions and nobody wanted to go through them again, so he was on the back foot for a while.

I sat with him at lunchtime.

'We're doing a Start Your Own Business tomorrow,' I offered. 'I saw it on the board.' Cliff smiled and took the biro from behind his ear. He wrote the topic in his red notebook.

The next lunchtime Cliff told me he had a lot of confidence in himself. He was going places, and in between mouthfuls of pie he wondered whether I might be going places too? I wasn't quite sure where all this was leading. But then Cliff explained that he urgently wanted to go into business with someone.

Someone older, like myself, who wasn't a fly-by-night. 'It's marshmallows,' he said looking over his shoulder.

It was all a bit sudden, but I was sick of hearing about inflation and cashflow forecasts so I said why not, everyone loves sweets. Besides I needed a change.

Setting up the sinks in the spare room wasn't too difficult. Cliff's dad was a plumber so he knew where the drainpipes went. But it took a while to get the hang of the marshmallows. You had to remember to put the sugar and glucose in one pot and the gelatine in the other. Otherwise the mixture didn't cream up and thicken. And the dishes had to be wet before you poured the steaming mixture into it. That way it would cut clean with a sharp knife when it set.

Cliff said if I was 'Sweets' then he was 'Sales' and at first it worked out well. I really threw myself into the marshmallows. Up at seven in the morning—frost on the windows still—and so cold I seemed to shrink under my candlewick dressing-gown. I told myself, 'Forget the cold you moaning cow, you're going to be thirty-eight next birthday and you've got to make a go of something in your life. And who knows where marshmallows might take you?' So I'd turn the Atlas on and go through my routine. Weigh the sugar and wet the moulds. Toast the coconut and carefully mix the colours drop by drop. And while the mixture was creaming and Cliff lay asleep in the loft with his gob open and his pale arm flung out on the pillow—I'd experiment.

I tried lime green cut into triangles, pink dusted lightly with roasted coconut, and some I mounted on a little scalloped biscuit, but they fell off after half an hour so I gave them a miss. My biggest success was with the pink flamingoes. They had a fluffy top with a raspberry stripe piped down the centre. It took a steady hand to do the stripe. I was so excited with the way they turned out I flung open the back door and roared to next-door's cats, 'I'm the Marshmallow Queen so stick that . . . !'

'We'll do the offices, go round the lot of them at lunchtime, that's the way to build up your clientele,' said Cliff. Cliff was a great believer in the power of positive thinking. 'Every day and in every way money is flowing into my life,' he'd snarl into the bathroom mirror. I watched Cliff slick his dark hair back and imagined the two of us featured in the *Woman's Weekly*. 'Local couple go from rags to riches. Sweet success comes from Marshmallows', ran the headlines. I'd wear my white smock I'd pinched from the Hospitality course and Cliff would wear his black suit with the shiny lapels. That would make the woman next-door sit up and think.

As it turned out the offices weren't such a good idea. The marshmallows got a bit battered in their cane baskets from all the travelling. We were in and out of the car umpteen dozen times, so it's no wonder the secretaries shook their heads and politely declined—'Perhaps another day, thank you.' Cliff took it bad. He drove home in a sulk and spent the rest of the day under the tartan rug with his suit on and his pointy-toe boots flicking back and forth.

I had a sinking feeling that was the end of the marshmallows and what was I going to do with all the sugar and the unpaid bills? The next day we got the call.

'Is that Memorable Marshmallows? Can you do a tray of lime greens for tomorrow?'

Cliff's back was trembling as he scribbled the details into his special order book.

'This is just the beginning,' he said kissing my neck and for a moment I forgot about where the money was coming from to buy more sugar and I forgot about all the disappointments I'd had in my life and I was happy, really happy.

*

Within a week we were rushed off our feet. The school shop on Bowenvale corner rang to say they were amazed we could produce the marshmallows so cheaply and could we supply them with a weekly order of pink flamingoes. K-Mart followed with a regular order of marshmallows in the cane baskets. The kitchen soon got into a hell of a mess. The floor developed a nasty tackiness from all the spilt sugar, and there was nowhere to store the big boxes of gelatine so we kept on tripping over ourselves in the morning rush. But then we'd have a break at eleven . . . and time to spin our own sort of sugar. Upstairs in the loft behind the delivery boxes. 'My dream come true,' Cliff would murmur—but I was never sure whether he meant the marshmallows or my fat thighs. I was putting on weight, that was for sure. I just stuffed myself with marshmallows to keep myself going.

The woman next-door reckoned that's when the trouble started. I wasn't my old self any more she said.

I don't know about that. It's true I put on weight and when you put on weight your electrolytes get out of balance. And that can lead to mood disorders. Like waking up at four in the morning to weigh the bags of sugar over and over, just in case you got the wrong amount the first time. Laughing your head off when you clean the benches and crying when you drop the cloth. And seeing things you shouldn't.

But I wasn't the only one with problems. Cliff began having trouble with his teeth. His front tooth snapped off after the dentist did a bad job on it. He managed to superglue the piece back on and it stuck really well for a few weeks. But now it was loose and he was having to superglue the piece back on every day.

'Keep the bloody mirror still,' he'd yell at me while he opened his mouth and tried to glue.

'We'll pull through,' I told Cliff, stroking his thin neck. 'I'll lose two stone and things will come right.' And I really believe we would have come right. Cliff and I had a lot of affection for each other.

It was the mice that beat us.

'Look at this will you?' roared Cliff, pointing his long finger at the bench. At first I couldn't work out why there were black seeds scattered on the bench. When I realised what it was I went straight to the hardware shop and brought six mouse traps.

'There's no excuse for this,' said Cliff, pulling back the metal spring. 'It's slovenliness that's what it is . . .'

He wanted to blame me so I told him to go jump, and Cliff said he might just do that and he was sick of my mood disorders anyway, they were getting him down, and I could see where this was leading, so I said let's forget it and how about we go to the loft.

'Where there's one, there's twenty,' said Cliff gloomily as he put his hand up my shirt. 'They'll just take over. I've seen it before.'

'Oh sshh,' I said, directing his hand.

It wasn't long after that I heard the trap go off. Cliff noticed I wasn't responding so he propped himself up on his elbows and went back to French-kissing me.

'I can't go on,' I whispered. 'There's a dying mouse down-stairs.' I could hear its body go thump, thump and then a loud clack as the trap catapulted off the bench.

Cliff was furious, his mouth slack with disappointment. I had to laugh. And when I didn't stop laughing Cliff climbed down the ladder, grabbed his suit and slammed the door.

Just like that.

I waited all night and the next. On Wednesday I knew he wasn't coming back. I walked out of the kitchen and left everything on the benches. I don't blame Cliff as much as I blame the mice. Mice are terrible things. They dig in, shred all your clothes to make nests, and then the lot of them take over. That's what caused the Black Plague.

So this whole experience has changed me. I've told the woman next door it was the balance sheets that were at fault. But in my heart I'm a changed woman.

I see things differently now.

CILLA McQUEEN

Map

Here is the map used by Charles Brasch in his hiking days, a Lands and Survey Department map of the Otago Peninsula published in 1942. Its folds divide it into 24 tattered squares, held together by a fragile muslin backing. The paper is creamy and brittle.

The city and the coastal area take up the left hand side of the map, the right hand side being mostly sea of a southern blue. A fine purple grid is superimposed on the landscape, which you may reach by slipping through the one-dimensional map as if it were the surface of a mirror.

Charles and Rodney are standing on the spine of the peninsula, facing north. Rodney is puffing and his eyes are bright. In one hand he has a stout stick and in the other the map of Charles Brasch. Charles is tall and thin. He has bushy eyebrows. He is dressed in khaki shorts and shirt. In his rucksack he carries a compass, a pair of binoculars, a water bottle, a green pullover, a battered Auden, two notebooks and several pencils.

Running due south, the centre fold line passes through the graceful font of the word 'Dunedin' at the top of the paper, through Aramoana township and across the narrow harbour heads, through the marae at Otakou, the church and the graveyard and the cockle beds, across the peninsula and the tidal flats at Papanui inlet, through Mount Charles and out over the cliffs of Allan's Beach, towards Antarctica.

Rodney wishes he had a gin. He mops his face with a silk handkerchief. Charles is sitting on a rock, writing in his notebook. His handsome face is stern. From up here they can see the whole panorama. The length of the peninsula lies before them, the harbour on their left and the ocean on their right.

'Purple!' chortles Rodney suddenly, as he unpacks his rucksack.

Charles looks up, frowning.

'What?'

'Purple passage, let's have a purple passage,' carols Rodney. He spreads out the groundsheet. 'A purple passage before lunch.'

MARGARET MAHY

A Dissolving Ghost

Possible Operations of Truth in Children's Books & the Lives of Children

The Lovers and the Shark

Two years ago it happened that I found myself in a hotel swimming pool in New Mexico. I like swimming. I swim quite purposefully and I had the swimming pool almost to myself. Not quite, however. At the shallow end of the pool stood a young man and woman, passionately, indeed it sometimes seemed permanently, embracing. I didn't mind this while I was swimming away from them but, as I swam towards them, I found myself filled with the embarrassment of someone who is intruding into a private space—a space which they have no right to violate.

My shyness, my wish not to intrude upon this couple, alternated with something less charitable—self-righteous indignation. After all, this was not a private space; it was a public swimming pool and I was swimming backwards and forwards, which everyone knows is the proper thing to do in a swimming pool. Why should I be the one to feel intrusive and guilty? I felt like this swimming away from them. Then swimming towards them I began to think—ah but am I jealous of their youth and passion and so on (kicking regularly, surging to the other end of the pool)? Yet who wants to be bothered with self-analysis when you are trying to shoot through the water like a silver arrow?

As I swam backwards and forwards I began to dream of dressing up as a shark, and gliding up the pool towards them. I could see myself: soundless, menacing and ruthless, my skin set with sharp, close-set denticles, my silent crescent snarl filled with rows and rows of teeth. The lovers would suddenly see my dorsal fin approaching. They would leap out of the water screaming. I would have the whole pool to myself, free to be a silver arrow to my heart's content. It would all be my space, and deservedly so.

After I left the pool, I found myself haunted, not by the lovers themselves, but by the one who had wanted all the space in the swimming pool, this person usurping the primitive power of the shark, the fin cutting through the water, the huge mouthful of teeth rising up over the back of the boat—this temporary villain I had contemplated becoming, in order to have all the swimming pool to myself. It had in some ways been a tempting and empowering persona, and one I recognised, although I had never met it in that shape before. My temporary shark began to make other sharkish connections. Sharks have been part of my life for a long time. Though shark attacks are almost unknown in New Zealand, we all know the sharks are there. Parents sometimes warn their children, 'Don't go out deep! There might be sharks!' Of course the children already know. Sharks!
Once, dramatically, I saw a shark caught on a hand line, pulled up and left to die on the sand. It was only a small one, but it was a genuine shark. I stood over it, watching it drown in the sunny air of a remote North Island beach. When it began to rot away, someone threw it back into the deep water where smaller fish flickered around it for a while eating what was left, but even then its bones still glimmered mysteriously through the water, if you knew where to look.

It was the year I turned five. It was also the year I learned to swim. I couldn't write much in those days, but was already a slave to fiction. I talked aloud, waving sticks in the air, conducting unseen orchestras of stories, stories remembered, recreated and invented, stories which I inhabited by temporarily becoming what I was inventing. That shark and the mystery and menace of the glimmering bones and what might have happened (that it might have been *my* bones glimmering there, I suppose) were part of those stories in those days.

They were certainly part of the first nightmare I can ever remember having—that my little sister vanished under the water and after a second or two her sunbonnet came floating to the top. We were living in a caravan in those days. I woke up in the top bunk, crying, and bewildered to find that something which, only a moment before, had seemed utterly real had dissolved into nothing.

I think it was that same shark, flesh on its bones once more, that came out of the past to inhabit me and swim up and down the motel swimming pool. It's just as well I didn't have my shark suit with me.

I like to swim in deep water. I like to be where I can't feel the bottom, and I have always liked that from the time I was very small, but there is always the fear of the shark sneaking up from down below, grabbing your foot. After you've been frightened of it for a while you begin to tell stories about it, to take it over—and in odd moments of life, when you have a little go at being the shark yourself, you recognise something true in what you are doing.

A Marvellous Code

I am going to propose that there is a code in our lives, something we automatically recognise when we encounter it in the outside world, something personal, but possibly primeval too, something which gives form to our political responses, to our art, our religious feelings, sometimes to our science and, recently in New Zealand at least, to the way the television weather forecast is presented as a sort of little serial drama. It is something eagerly recognised by young children, so perhaps there is no first encounter. Perhaps it is already in them.

My own knowledge of this code has been that, by giving experience a recognisable structure, it has also made this experience easier to recall and use. It makes use of cause and effect, though sometimes it precedes and transcends it. It can be suspected or duplicated, but I don't think it can be really dismantled. Broken to bits, it starts to reassemble itself, like the Iron Man described by Ted Hughes, and creeps back into our lives, patient but inexorable. I'm talking about *story*, of course, and I am planning to speculate about its relationships with truth and desire.

A Misleading Question

Many years ago now, I read for the first time a novel by Noel Streatfeild called *Ballet Shoes*, possibly the book for which she is best known. Most of you will know that it is the story of three children: Pauline, Petrova and Posy Fossil, who took this surname because they were all adopted by a kindly fossil hunter, Great Uncle Matthew or G.U.M. It tells of their lives at home and on the stage, and is a career and a family story in one book.

Some years later, in the act of being a librarian, I found in a library stack an adult novel by Noel Streatfeild, written in 1931, five years before *Ballet Shoes* was published. It was called *The Whicharts* and was about a family of three girls and their lives at home and on the stage, and it tells the same story as *Ballet Shoes*, but tells it for adults.

The three girls are now revealed as half-sisters, all illegitimate daughters of a charming but irresponsible, well-born Englishman. They are cared for by a woman (the Sylvia of *Ballet Shoes*) who loved him deeply in spite of his facile character and who grew to love his daughters as if they were her own. He dies leaving them in difficult circumstances, and in an effort to make a reasonable middle-class living the girls become involved in life on the wicked stage. The story pursues them through adolescence, tells us how the girl who corresponds to Pauline in *Ballet Shoes* is seduced, I think by a theatrical director, and how the one who corresponds to Petrova actually locates her mother after their loving guardian dies, and finds herself shyly welcomed by a woman as odd and adventurous as she is herself. The family in this book is not called the Fossils but the Whicharts (a name which also involves a play on words, however, coming as it does from their mishearing of the Lord's Prayer, *Our Father, Which art in heaven*—something eloquent to children who had been told, on debatable evidence I must say, that that's where their father was).

I was fascinated by all this new information, which suggested that Noel Streatfeild certainly knew more about the family than she had revealed in *Ballet Shoes*, and I gave the book to a friend of mine who had enjoyed *Ballet Shoes*. She read it and, feeling betrayed in some intangible way, became very angry. 'It just made me wonder—how much truth do we tell children?' she said. 'How much should we tell?' She was asking leading questions, which were also *misleading*.

Well, it is an old debate with many answers. For instance, I don't think Noel Streatfeild would have been allowed to tell everything she knew about the Fossils in a children's book back in 1936, though she certainly would be permitted to tell more today, since our interpretation of childhood has altered since then. As an adult reading *Ballet Shoes*, I am now always aware of that ghostly *other* story, that extra truth, and something about the nature of my adult experience makes me think that *The Whicharts* is the truer story, partly because that was the way it was told first, but also because as an adult I see a stronger rationale in the adult story. I think *Ballet Shoes* is a better book for what it is than *The Whicharts* for what *it* is, and yet for all that I feel I have unfair knowledge, for I can't help including what I know of the adult story as part of the truth of *Ballet Shoes*. I say to myself, 'This is what was really happening, but we couldn't tell the kids.' Unlike my friend, I don't think Noel Streatfeild should have either insisted on telling the full truth or not told any of it. No one tells the full truth anyway, and children's literature would have been the poorer for not having *Ballet Shoes*. Nevertheless, I have never forgotten my friend's question, and there is a dislocation of my feelings about it all, a sort of puzzlement which I am perhaps unfairly trying to get rid of by passing it on to others.

How much truth do we tell children? We certainly encourage them to tell all the truth themselves. I impressed on my children what my mother had impressed on me, that we should always tell the truth. (Funnily enough, now they're grown up I quite often find that I wish they wouldn't, and I know my mother often wished I would shut up.) How much truth we choose to tell children is an important question, but not a fair one. How much truth should we tell grown-ups for that matter? After all, children often want to know about things, and adults often don't. A lot of people want to protect the innocence of childhood, but isn't it also a pity to disturb security and innocence in adulthood? Sometimes we don't like to see people living happy lives for what we perceive as wrong reasons. This poor single word 'truth' has to bear a heavy burden. It's not fair to ask one word to do so much and, unlike Humpty Dumpty, we exploit our labour force. We don't pay words extra when we ask them to do a lot of work for us. Pursuing truth in literature is like pursuing a chimera, a dissolving ghost . . . Yet there is something there we feel is worth hunting, and the pursuit is not altogether useless since the dissolving ghost leaves a trail of curious clues behind it—clues which we gather up and, in odd moments, try to assemble into an equally curious collage. I suppose my stories are attempts to reveal the collage I am assembling, parts of which are assembled blindly. This is equally true for a simple book like the one in the Jellybean series called *The Cake* as it is for a book like *Memory*.

Fact and Fiction

I was born in 1936, the year *Ballet Shoes* was published, and from the time I was very small I was encouraged to listen to stories. I began as a listener, and then, since I wanted to join in that particular dance, I put together stories of my own, as I have already mentioned, telling them aloud to walls and trees. Because I couldn't write back then, I learned them by heart as a way of containing them, but I went on to become a reader. Very shortly after that, I learned to write and began to contain stories by putting them down in notebooks. I began as a listener, became a teller, then a reader and then a writer, in that order. Later still I became a librarian, which in some ways is the ultimate result of this evolutionary process, since a lot of library work is concerned with orderly containment. (But I must advise you to beware a little of my description of myself which is automatically starting to gather the elements of a romantic story around it.)

Being a librarian forces you to think a lot about truth and to pretend you have got over any confusions you might ever have had about it. You have a book and it has to go in some particular physical place on the library shelves. It can't really be both here and there. Even if you have a big enough book grant, and can afford to buy two copies of the same book and put it in two different places, a book like *The Endless Steppe*, say, is not quite the same story in the non-fiction shelves as it is in the fiction (where it was rather more likely to be read, in our library at least). If you are a librarian (allowing for the general advice we get about putting a book where it is going to be looked for and best used), you have fiction on one side of the library and non-fiction on the other. Ask a child the difference between fiction and non-fiction and the child will often answer that non-fiction is true and fiction is not true. 'That's right,' we say. 'Fiction is not true and non-fiction is.' But writers and readers often dispute this simple division, and I'm sure there must be many librarians like me—librarians who suddenly find themselves staring around wildly at their library walls (all that *knowledge*, all that *emotion*, all that *astonishment*! What am I doing here at the focus of all these great fields? I am trying to *shelve* it!), their own sense of reality terminally eroded by this service for others. Making books available in the most sensible way makes us aware that in serving one function we are distorting others. We are standing astride the line of a great dislocation.

I'm used to dislocations, as I'm sure we are all mixed children of earthquakes, and I feel they can be useful at times. In a Polynesian country I was brought up exclusively on European ways. In a practical and pragmatic land I was encouraged to look at the world of wonders, to have an appetite for marvels.

Dislocations in a True Landscape

I have more than one dislocation running right through me. Dislocation is in some ways an image of the country I grew up in (and it also has to be one image of the USA, I think), even if we agree to call it diversity. If dislocation wasn't the *source* of my sense of things not matching up, of them rushing together and immediately beginning to fall apart, it is to some extent the mirror of it.

New Zealand, the country which is in every meaningful way

my home, is a country in the Pacific Ocean, but my family were European, not Polynesian, and consciously and unconsciously regarded the European, and more specifically British, culture as the highest form of civilisation in the world. The result was a big imaginative displacement, for though there were a few children's books written in and about New Zealand when I was a child, the majority of stories, including those that inexorably fixed me, came largely from Britain with a few, a very few, from the USA. Coming in from swimming on Christmas Day, I would sit with my sun hat on, reading stories of snow and robins and holly, and though I have never once spent a Christmas in the Northern Hemisphere, those things are now part of my Christmas nostalgia. Nor was I alone in this; the Christmas paradox is one quoted by many antipodean writers. The imaginative truth and the factual truth are at odds with one another but, personally, I still need those opposites to make Christmas come alive for me—the sunny sea and the awareness of dark firs on snowy hillsides.

But containing and synthesising such contradictions is easy for an imagination nourished on stories in which so much becomes possible. I did indeed grow up with a fault line running through me, but that is a very New Zealandish feature when you consider that it is a country of earthquakes and volcanoes. A fault line ran right through the town I was born in so perhaps my disjunction is part of what makes an essential New Zealander of me after all. Perhaps the country has imposed its own unstable geography on my power to perceive. I don't mind. I regret it only in the sense that one always regrets not being able to be everything all at once. Dislocations can expose the secret nature of the land. They can make for an intensely interesting landscape, provided one doesn't come to feel that a landscape full of fault lines is the only legitimate kind. Dislocations made me a world reader rather than a local one, and they made me contingent rather than categorical.

New Zealand at present is celebrating in a small way the development of a more indigenous children's fiction than at any time previously. Having at last got a foothold in the imagination of its writers, New Zealand is now an innate part of most of

its indigenous children's books, which are increasingly free
of unnaturally deliberate reference, of the self-consciousness
that marked the first attempts to have *I am a New Zealander
writing about New Zealand* as a sort of subtext. There is a
certain relieved mood of congratulation within the writing
community, and a lot of talk, some of it meretricious, I think,
about 'relevance'.

I think it is most important that a local literature should
exist, so that the imaginations of children are colonised in the
first instance by images from their immediate world—that
their immediate world should be acknowledged and so verified
(certified, Walker Percy would say)[1] somewhere in their informed
inner worlds. Ideally there should be a sympathetic resonance
between these inner and outer worlds. I am not in favour of
dislocation for the sake of dislocation. But I am curious, too,
about why I should have become such an enthusiastic reader
myself when so little of what was immediately relevant was
offered to me, and why later, on the rare occasions that I did
encounter books presenting my own street and my own idiom,
I tended to pass them over in favour of exotic alternatives. Why
was it that what seemed truest to me had nothing to do with the
facts and images of my everyday life, which, mistakenly enough,
I came to regard as inadequate stuff for a story?

Truth and Desire

In his celebrated essay *Tree and Leaf*, Tolkien speculates about
why Andrew Lang turned his adult study of myth and folklore
into a series of stories for children. *I suspect*, Lang apparently
says, *that belief and appetite for marvels are regarded as identical
or closely related. They are radically different, though the
appetite for marvels is not at once or at first differentiated by a
growing human mind from its general appetite.* Lang, according
to Tolkien, may be implying that the teller of marvellous tales
for children trades on the credulity that makes it less easy for
children to distinguish fact from fiction, *though* (Tolkien says,
correctly, I think) *the distinction is fundamental to the human
mind, and to fairy stories.* Tolkien disapproves of this attitude,

and if Lang means this, so do I. All the same, I think that the appetite for marvels may reinforce some aspects of truth that the fact-or-fiction dichotomy seems to obscure.

Talking further about the appetite for marvels, and his own appetite for reading, Tolkien then says of himself:

> I had no special wish to believe . . . At no time can I remember that the enjoyment of a story was dependent on belief that such things could happen or had happened in real life. Fairy stories were plainly not concerned with possibility but with desirability. If they awakened desire, satisfying it while whetting it unbearably, they succeeded.

I think that, like Tolkien and many readers before and since, I was filled with an appetite for marvels, and desire alone seemed to me to be a sufficient justification for a story, even though longing for what is not true has been seen as a wicked thing to do, particularly by those readers who also strenuously maintain that we should not disturb the innocence of children by telling them all the truth. I tend to think, since the appetite for marvels appears to be so much a part of humanity, that it exists in us for a reason, and that in an odd way it may be connected with truth. That's not to say it isn't dangerous. My enjoyment of a story certainly did not depend on belief while I was *reading* the story, for the story generated its own belief, but afterwards I would often try to adjust the world so that the story could be fitted into it. To find something that was marvellous was wonderful; to find something that was wonderful and true was ecstasy for it meant wonderful things might be possible for me too.

The function of the story teller is to relate the truth in a manner that is simple, to integrate without reduction, for it is barely possible to declare the truth as it is because the universe presents itself as a mystery, says Alan Garner, in an essay in *Children's Literature in Education*, after saying that the true story is religious and adding that he is using the word *religious* to indicate concern for the way we are in the cosmos. Since all the important processes of our lives (like eating and reproducing) are reinforced with powerful pleasure principles, perhaps we are constructed to look for pleasure in stories—to *desire* them, because we need to know about them and to be able to use them. Stories enable us first to give form to, and then take possession of, a variety of truths, both literal and figurative. Once we have part of the truth caught up in a story we can name it and get some sort of power over it. But of course we have to be careful about the way we believe stories. They can make us not only into temporary heroes and wizards but temporary villains too . . . even into sharks.

Poor Judgements

When I was a small child and read H. Rider Haggard's *King Solomon's Mines*, a book inherited from my father, I knew it was an invention. And when I read in another of my father's childhood books (volume one of an Edwardian edition of *Arthur Mee's Encyclopaedia*) that the earth had once been a fiery ball and that it had dropped off the sun, I knew it was true. The encyclopaedia was true and *King Solomon's Mines* wasn't. Nevertheless, at one stage I tried to tell a cousin of mine that the events in *King Solomon's Mines* were historical facts even though I knew they weren't; trying by powerful assertion, by faith alone, to drag the story through to sit alongside the fiery ball which had fallen off the sun. Well, it wouldn't go. I needed an identical act of faith from other people to give it even the semblance of this other truth, and no one else would agree to play that game with me. I was alone with the story and my desire for it to be true.

It wasn't the only attempt I made to bring a marvellous fiction through into the real world, to force a general agreement that I was in charge of truth and not the other way round. From the time I was seven until I was about ten, I spasmodically maintained that I could talk the language of the animals. The immediate source of this assertion was *The Jungle Book*—not the book but a film of the book, the one starring Sabu and a variety of real animals. It absolutely overwhelmed me. My mother must have enjoyed it too, because for the only time in my childhood that I can remember, I was taken to see a film twice. I couldn't bear that that particular story should remain in what I then perceived as the half life of fiction. Coleridge has described works of fiction as acts of secondary creation, and I wanted to make *The Jungle Book* primary. I wanted to make it as if it had been created by God and not by man, Kipling.

In order to achieve this, I claimed that I had the powers of Mowgli. Challenged, I would talk an invented gibberish that fooled nobody, least of all any passing dogs or birds, and not one of the lively, knowing children around me. So I became more and more extreme in my attempts to demonstrate my oneness with animal creation. I ate leaves in public—all sorts of leaves—children came up to me in the playground and offered me leaves which I ate instantaneously and indiscriminately— leaves, grass, little twigs, berries, even I'm told caterpillars. I drank from roadside puddles as dogs do.

Of course I was subjected to derision, which I deserved for poor judgement if nothing else. I knew all the time I couldn't really speak the language of the animals in the world of primary creation, but I imagine now that I wanted people to agree to create the secondary world with me, a world in which I had already given myself a starring role.

I also believe there were elements of the story existing in me already, that it was not that Kipling's imagination, filtered through the medium of the film, imposed itself on me, but that something already in me leaped out to make a powerful connection—perhaps a primitive dreamtime belief in the oneness of nature. Certainly at some level I was powerless to resist whatever it was that came crashing in or perhaps out. Nor am I suggesting that this susceptibility is a thing to be encouraged uncritically. I do think, however, it is far from unique and in order for it to be understood it needs to be described. It certainly can be dangerous (after all, I could have poisoned myself eating so much vegetation that unqualified way), but the same thing can be said of a lot of human reactions, including patriotism and love and even truth itself—they're all very risky. We can imbue them with morality, but after a certain point they just stop working and are quite likely to be exploited to less admirable ends. In any case, having received that story, I think I had to incorporate it; having incorporated it I had to discharge it and, as I was young and simple, the discharging took a wrong turn—an inappropriately literal one.

Now, oddly enough, at the same time as I was being teased about my claim to talk the language of the animals, I was subject to an equal derision, which once resulted in my being chased home by indignant children (some of them cousins of mine, which seemed to add insult to injury). I publically asserted that the earth had once dropped off the sun, that I had a picture at home that proved it, and I added on the same authority (that of *Arthur Mee's Encyclopaedia*) that the world would some day, a million years from now, come to an end. I can remember running home with other outraged children after me, turning in at a strange gate, knocking on the door and saying to an astonished woman who answered it that children were waiting outside to beat me up because I said the world had once fallen off the sun and that it would come to an end one day. I was confident that an adult would recognise and confirm the truth I was telling and rally to support it. Well, whether she believed it or not, there was nothing she could do to help me. She turned down the chance to become involved in this great debate.

Of course, if you present certain facts too confidently it sounds as if you are taking personal credit for them, and perhaps I sounded as if I thought I was the one who had caused the world to fall off the sun in the first place, and would one day will its end. And I certainly don't want to sound as if I'm standing here tonight whinging because I didn't have the respect I should have had at school. I think I deserved all I got for eating leaves and drinking from puddles, which is not a sign of superior sensibility, only of poor judgement, tragically coupled with the will to be marvellous. I totally agree with the person who said that a difficult time at school doesn't necessarily entitle you to write a novel. And there isn't time to tell you of the time I joined a gang to torment somebody else which nevertheless seems an important part of this particular story.

But what I do want to record is that non-fiction could provoke as much derision, disbelief and resentment as fiction—and, just to make the situation a little more complicated, nowadays no astronomer seems to believe that the earth ever fell off the sun.

The other children were right to suspect it, even if they suspected it for the wrong reasons. What I learned as truth back then was another mistake.

Variations on a Divine Gift

Because of the way science has developed over the last three hundred years, we do live in a time when we expect truth to be objectively provable. Measurement is a vital part of our lives today. We live, our children along with us, in a very mathematised society. In the past, before astronomer Tycho Brahe, if a minor detail did not fit into a major hypothesis it was easy to shrug it away. The idea that anyone might be accountable to that sort of truth was a foreign one. But fellow astronomer Johannes Kepler, in computing the orbit of Mars, acknowledged as significant an error of eight minutes of arc which Copernicus had been able to ignore. Kepler wrote, 'But for us, who by divine kindness, were given an accurate observer such as Tycho Brahe, for us it is fitting we should acknowledge this divine gift and put it to use,' and what mathematician and philosopher Alfred North Whitehead describes as 'stubborn and irreducible fact' became increasingly important.

Like Kepler, I believe intricate and accurate measurement is a fight we are given by divine kindness, and that the inventive mind, coming up against stubborn and irreducible facts, is forced to surrender. Today, 'stubborn and irreducible fact' seems paramount because of the kind of power that attention to such details confers, including the power to make money, which often involves the power to get one's own way, very seductive powers indeed. So stubborn and irreducible facts are frequently seen as coinciding with truth, or truth is seen as being the same sort of thing as the facts are and nothing more.

It often seems to me that deterministic accounts of existence never quite face up to the fact that they don't eliminate mystery but merely shift it into areas where it can be acceptably labelled, and then by sleight of hand pretend it isn't there. And history shows all sorts of aberrations, built even into part of the truth we librarians shelved in the 500s. For example, in the beginning of chapter sixteen of his book *New Astronomy*, Kepler, who thought of accurate observation as a divine gift, absentmindedly put three erroneous figures for three vital longitudes of Mars, and then towards the end of the chapter committed several mistakes in simple arithmetic which virtually cancelled his first mistakes out so that he got more or less the right answer. At the most crucial point in the process of discovering his Second Law, Kepler again made a series of mathematical errors that cancelled themselves out, allowing him to arrive at a correct result. What sort of truth was operating there? Perhaps something was so *determined* to be discovered that even mathematical error was forced to yield a true result? Somewhere recently I read that Gregor Mendel cheated in recording the results of his experiments in genetic inheritance in peas and produced a nice pattern that illuminated what currently passes for truth, and is taught in Sixth Form Biology in New Zealand schools. Perhaps something *wants* to be found.

Nowadays we are told that even chaos has a structure. I got a book about it in New York, of which I haven't read much except the first chapter, which says that chaos is the shorthand name for a movement that is reshaping the fabric of the scientific establishment. Government programme managers, the CIA and the Department of Energy are all putting money into chaos research. At university research centres everywhere, theorists are allying themselves first with chaos, and only secondly with their nominal studies. This hasn't much to do with my talk, though you might like to know about it. I was thrilled. Chaos conferences.

Earlier this century, 1903 to be precise, at a time when there was much thrilling new information on radiation coming to hand, René Blondlot, an experienced physicist, discovered a new ray which he called the N-Ray. One of its characteristics was that it treated substances opaque to visible light, including wood, iron, silver etc, as if they were transparent. Many notable scientists, particularly French ones, subsequently detected the same ray. But the American physicist R.W. Wood found he was absolutely unable to reproduce Blondlot's striking results. Blondlot and his colleagues later declared that it was the sensitivity of the observer not the validity of the phenomenon that was in question, but by 1905 only French scientists, and by no means all of them, believed in the N-Ray (though some of them still maintained that only the Latin races had sufficient sensitivity to detect the N-Ray, that fog had ruined the perception of Anglo-Saxon observers and beer the perception of the German ones). Nowadays, no one believes the N-Ray ever existed. The *Scientific American* May 1980, from which I got much of this good information, says that the times had psychologically prepared Blondlot to discover a new sort of radiation. I suggest that one might say, with equal truth, that he was imaginatively prepared to eat leaves and drink from puddles, but the way in which he did this matched up so closely with accepted reality or desire that he did what I was not able to do—he actually altered perception for a while and won people to his side. Scientific truths, which should be pure and objective, can stagger and sway on their way to becoming recognised as scientific truths, can be as bizarre as the plots of the stories they partly resemble, or the stories that are told about them afterwards.

Yet, though the scientists who advised the editors of *Arthur Mee's Encyclopaedia* about the beginning of the world had made what I now take to be a genuine mistake, it was a mistake that fixed my attention in childhood, and (it is even tempting to think) enabled me to see something true which stayed true, even when the information turned out to be false. If so, the true thing was wonder—wonder which dissolves into Tolkien's desire. And so I have come to think that wonder must be a part of truth—not completely coinciding with it of course, a part of truth which our physical systems are anxious to conceal.

A perpetual state of wonder and desire (which seems to me the truest state with which to confront the universe) is certainly not the most practical state to try and live in. We are biologically engineered to have the wonder filtered out of our lives, to learn to take astonishing things for granted, so that we don't waste too much energy on being surprised but get on with the eating and mating, gardening, feeding cats, complaining about taxes or being pleased about economic recovery and so on. We have the power to entertain visions, but operate best when most things are humdrum. When I first flew in an aeroplane it was an experience of amazement. Now I think of the flying time (a time when gravity is confounded, when a metal machine filled with people rises more or less safely into the air) as time when I am going to get a chance to read without any guilty feeling that I should be doing something else. Our systems are anxious to hide the truth from us in case we become alarmed to go on.

To encounter the amazements, partly compounded by fear and beauty, which I recognised so eagerly when I was a child, I now give myself the space to achieve a rare and difficult mood, or to search through the various disclosures of science and history or, more frequently, to read a story.

I've certainly never had any trouble abandoning the falling-off-the-sun theory in favour of the Big Bang and slow condensation out of the stuff of the primordial universe. I know by now that facts, even marvellous ones, slide around, and that people get things wrong, and always will get things wrong, and the truest thing in science is wonder, just as it is in story. And I never forget that the story is as important to human beings as science; more powerful at times because it is more subversive. It was the wonder of facts not the accuracy of them (though at any given time one has to have a measure of belief in their accuracy) that tied me into an area of knowledge for which I have no talent. It's the wonder that makes me read Stephen Hawking and physicist Paul Davies as opposed to *Arthur Mee's Encyclopaedia*. (That is, I read the words, of course, and wonder at the concepts.) I talk about anthropic principles, renormalisation and Aclerotic String Theory as if by naming them I understand them.

A Fairy Tale Disguised

If any story I have told has the mark of social realism on it, it is certainly *Memory*. In it I have told young readers a lot of my personal truth about the metamorphosis of a rational human being, replete with knowledge, memory and the power to make a cup of tea several times a day, into a demented old woman, losing command of all the things in which self-respect is traditionally established, and driven to wear a tea cosy instead of a hat.

For a number of years I was in charge of my aunt, and though my aunt and Sophie are not the same person, they are similar in many ways. A lot of the happenings, a lot of the conversations in *Memory*, are directly transposed from my life with my aunt, and if the story lacks the nastiness, the sheer fatigue of response involved in looking after a demented person, it is partly because, though those elements were present, they were not a commanding part of my life with my aunt. Because I had a background of story to draw on, she never lost her imaginative function in my life.

An English review criticised the book because, somehow, at the end, Sophie was tidied up rather too quickly, but there are two odd things about that. One is that, in the real world, once I indicated I needed help I actually got a certain amount. The support services were good, partly because I was sufficiently well educated to know where to go and what sort of things to say, and also because I had been prepared to cope with quite a lot before I asked for some support. A district nurse and a housekeeper appeared once a week, and things were tidied up quite quickly. In between times things went downhill rapidly, but neither my aunt nor I bothered too much about a certain amount of squalor.

The other odd thing is that, because *Memory* is full of factual experiences which are readily recognisable, and because it deals with a condition that, in New Zealand at least, enjoys a reasonably high public profile at present, it may be seen to be intended as a book of social realism. However, for me it is a fairy tale of a sort (the fantasy of earlier books of mine is still present, but in the imaginative subtext, rather than explicit in any happenings in the story), because that fantasy is part of the truth of my own life, and I cannot truthfully omit it. I didn't set out to write a fairy tale but, in an effort to convey truthfully the quality of the experiences I had had, I found myself telling the story of a young man who, having quarrelled with his father, sets out into the world with no blessing and no money to make his fortune. He meets a strange old woman needing help—a strange old woman who asks him a question and, through giving her the help she needs, he answers the question and is strengthened by the answer. His response to her need determines the way he learns, just as the kind responses of third sons or younger princes to the old people and animals they meet on their journeys results in them finding their fortunes. These elements are recognisable fairy-tale elements, I think.

Yet something like this fairy tale really happened in Christchurch once. A gang of rather derelict young people took over a house in which a demented old woman was living. Neighbours who were vaguely aware of her were naturally alarmed to see this, and probably anxious not to have a gang as their neighbours, and they called in the social workers, who found she was actually being looked after, though admittedly in a rough and ready fashion. She was being fed regularly and bathed, talked to and cared for. Her unlikely companions had grown fond of her, and after all there was no one else to look after her (the neighbours who complained weren't prepared to do so—and I'm not being self-righteous and suggesting they should) and nowhere for her to go, as all the appropriate homes had waiting lists. I was told this story when I was already writing *Memory* by a social worker to whom I mentioned the book. And the first idea for the story came to me, as so many ideas do, not from my own direct experience but as a haunting image seen from the window of a car in the early hours of the morning. Driving home through an empty city at about 2 a.m. I saw an old man coming out of a supermarket car park pushing an empty trolley. The image connected with everyday experiences of my own life, but also with the odd branching structure established by the metaphors of fairy tales. It came from outside to connect with the inside world as well.

Now, I am not trying to suggest my story is true because it contains its share of irreducible facts, or even that it's particularly good because of them. I mention the facts and associated anecdotes because they are eloquent in their own way, but just as much of the truth of this story, always supposing it has any, lies in its form. This seems to me to come from folktale, which has combined with many other things to give me a code by which to decipher experience. I used it in part to interpret my experiences with my aunt. I found story and folktale as useful in their way as the visits of the district nurse. It was contained in me and always available. 'Are you the one?' So when I came to tell the truth, as it were, about those experiences, I could not do so without the conscious and unconscious references to folktale. The part of the book from the second chapter, when the hero, Jonny, wakes, like Crusoe on his island—a traffic island—to the second-to-last one, when he wakes under Sophie's balcony, seems to me like a story within a story—Jonny moves into his own Narnia as it were, but it is almost indistinguishable from real life. *Memory* has been described as tackling the subject of Alzheimer's disease, but it seems to me that it doesn't so much tackle it as recognise it, for the story is not in essence about Alzheimer's disease, but about a magical encounter between two unlikely people, both of whom are possessed in different ways by a dissolving rationality. It is intended to be a serious story composed of many different sorts of truth, yet if I was asked to give a quick answer to the question, 'Is it true?', I would have to say, 'No. It isn't true.' All the same, I have tried to make it tell the truth or part of the truth at least.

And so at last by fading paths I come back to a different sort of story: to the shark who wanted all the swimming space to himself.

The Great White Man-Eating Shark

As I have already indicated, the initial incident, true in the most literal sense of the word, began to hook itself into many others: some past, some present, some fantastic, some commonplace, but all part of a personal reality. The imaginative process involved is not so much an instantaneous flash of inspiration as an act—a series of acts—of synthesis, the ideas and associations forming a network, rather than a linear account; a network in which the spaces between the cords are as important as the irreducible knots that hold the whole thing together.

Fantasy writers are not noted for their adherence to truth. In fact, often their books are seen as being ways of deliberately escaping from what is true into what is not true. However, to quote Angela Carter, imagination severed from reality festers, and writers of fantasy are often anxious to demonstrate that they are tied into real life in some way, and to assert that they have a part to play there too. We may claim to deal with abstract truths rather than mere facts, or perhaps that we deal in metaphor. But behind the printed page crouches the story, looking out at us between the lines that have temporarily caged it, making it stand still so that it can be considered. First stories were approximations to history and science, though nowadays science and story are seen as separate and maybe even antagonistic; science being an outer adventure, while story is an inner one, if I may anticipate something Walter de la Mare said about story which I will quote later.

As I thought about my temporary sharkness, it suggested a simple story which I would find entertaining to write. There are a lot of different sorts of sharks, many of them quite harmless, but I wanted to evoke the most sinister of all—the great white man-eating shark. I wanted there to be no misunderstanding about just what sort of shark this was. This reminded me of a piece in Russell Hoban's novel *Turtle Diary*, which I promptly began to search for.

One of the narrators, Neara, herself a writer for children, has read of an attempt by a rich man to photograph a great white shark. *Eventually they found a great white shark which they attracted with whale oil, blood and horse meat. It was a truly terrifying creature and they very wisely stayed in their cage while the shark took the bars in his teeth and shook them about.* She then goes on to say—Hoban makes her say—that socially the rich man was out of his class . . . *the shark would not have swum from ocean to ocean seeking them. It would have gone on its mute and deadly way, mindlessly being its awful self, innocent and murderous. It was the people who lusted for the attention of the shark.*

Well, perhaps by reading and writing stories I too am guilty of trying to attract the attention of wonderful sharks. Locked in the cage of words, I have stared out entranced while wonderful sharks took the bars of my cage in their teeth and shook it. As

I have already indicated, I am capable to some extent at least of being a shark and worrying at the bars. Thinking of my own temporary sharkness I wrote a short story entitled *The Great White Man-Eating Shark*.

Like most stories I write, I intended it primarily to be told aloud, but it has been produced as a picture book, and tells the story of the villain, a plain boy who happens to be a very good actor and who dresses up as a great white man-eating shark, frightening other swimmers out of the sea so that he could have it all to himself. He acted the part so well that a female shark fell in love with him and proposed something approximating to marriage. He fled from her in terror and scrambled onto the beach, his false dorsal fin still tied to his back. His duplicity was revealed, and he was too scared to go swimming for a long time after—and serve him right.

This is obviously didactic (but, I hope, ironically didactic), and seems far from true, since we all know that, in real life, people do not dress up as sharks, and that the figurative sharks often go undetected because they don't allow people to see their dorsal fins. But in another way I have told the children all the truth I know from personal experience. Kurt Vonnegut says in the introduction to *Mother Night*, *We are what we pretend to be, so we must be careful of what we pretend to be*. That turned out to be the hidden truth of my New Mexico swimming pool experience. But it would have been a hidden truth if I hadn't already read books like *Mother Night*, or if I didn't already know in a personal way that we become what we pretend to be. I did not learn to speak the language of animals through eating leaves and drinking out of puddles, but I was chased and herded and treated rather like an animal, for all that.

But the story of the shark is a joke and that is how I expect it to be enjoyed, as a joke and only as a joke. It is only in the context of this occasion that I am bothering to tell about the experience compacted in it, offering it as a joke at the expense of my temporary villainy, and also as part of a network, to a child who may one day read *Mother Night* or other books whose titles I can't guess at, and appreciate the truths in those books because they already know them. My own experience was real, funny, momentarily sinister and salutary, all at once, but someone else in that swimming pool on that day might have seen a different, more anguished truth, might have realised that the lovers were saying goodbye, or that they were meeting after a long separation, or that they were honeymooners, or that the thought of being together without touching was unbearable to them. A thousand other stories were potentially there in the swimming pool with me, but my story was about the person who chose to become a shark.

Oddly enough, as I sat with *Turtle Diary* open in front of me, seeing tenuous connections between my own childhood memories of sharks and my New Mexico fantasy, and Tolkien's speculations about desire, and the rich man lusting for the attention of the shark, I glanced at the opposite page where I absentmindedly read these lines:

> People write books for children and other people write books about the books written for children, but I don't think it's for the children at all. I think that all the people who worry so much about the children are really worrying about themselves, about keeping their world together and getting the children to help them do it, getting the children to agree that it is a world. Each new generation of children has been told 'this is a world, that is what one does, one lives like this'. Maybe our constant fear is that a generation of children will come along and say: 'this is not a world, this is nothing, there is no way to live at all'.

I can believe this, but I think Hoban has only told half the story. After all, we don't simply tell children what is and is not true. They demand to be told, and we try to tell them what we know to the best of our ability. When a child writes and asks me, 'Do you believe in supernatural things?' they may be asking me to confirm that a story like *The Haunting* is literally true. But mostly they are asking, 'Just where am I to fit this story into my view of the world?' They want to be told what sort of world it is, and part of giving them the truest answers we can give also involves telling stories of desire . . . once there was a man who rode on a winged horse, once there was a boy who spoke to the animals, and the animals talked back to him, once there was a girl who grew so powerful that she was able not only to overcome her enemy but to overcome the base part of herself. Beware or the wolf will eat you and then you will become part of the wolf until something eats the wolf and so on. It is a gamble because we cannot tell just what is going to happen in the individual head when the story gets there and starts working. We can only predict the effect of telling our children about hobbits or about atomic fission, or that the earth fell off the sun, or about photosynthesis or that there was a lovable old archaeologist called G.U.M. who once adopted three little girls. Perhaps that is why I was so fascinated, long before I began to think on these subjects, by a line in Borges' story 'Tlon Uqbar Orbis Tertius'. He writes about a land brought into existence by a sort of assertion: *the metaphysicians of Tlon are not looking for truth, nor even an approximation of it; they are after a kind of amazement.*

I also believe that what I am looking for is truth, which by now I confidently expect to be more amazing than anything else. One of the ways in which I try to pin down the dissolving ghosts is by writing a story, sharing a joke, hoping a reader will see some true thing in it out of the corner of their reading eye.

These days it seems to me that when I look at the world I see many people, including politicians, television newsreaders, real-estate agents and free-market financiers, librarians too at times, dressing as sharks, eating leaves and drinking out of puddles, casually taking over the powerful and dangerous images that the imagination presents, eager to exploit the fictional forms that haunt us all, and sometimes becoming what, in the beginning, they only pretended to be. I once read that sub-atomic particles shouldn't be seen as tiny bits of matter but as mathematical singularities haunting space. I believe that inner space is haunted by other singularities, by stories, lines of power along which our lives align themselves, like iron filings around a magnet, defining the magnetic field by the patterns they form around it, and that we yearn for the structure stories confer, that we inhabit their patterns and often, but not always, know instinctively how to use them well.

World Without, World Within

The mere cadence of six syllables 'a tale of adventure' instantly conjures up in the mind a jumble and motley host of memories. Memories not only personal but we may well suspect racial; and not only racial but primeval. Ages before history had learned its letters, there being no letters to learn, ages before the children of men built the city and the tower called Babel, and their language was confounded, the rudiments of this kind of oral narrative must have begun to flourish. Indeed the greater part of even the largest of dictionaries, with every page in the most comprehensive of atlases, consists of relics and records in the concisest shorthand from bygone chapters of the tale whereof we know neither the beginning nor the end—that of Man's supreme venture into the world without and into the world within.[2]

1   In his novel *The Moviegoer*, Percy's narrator and a woman friend go to a film and see their own landscape as a background to the action. The woman turns to the narrator and says, 'Yes, it is certified now.'
2   Quotation from Walter de la Mare.

BILL MANHIRE

The Poet's Wife

The poet looks at the poet's wife and says: You are my best poem. Did I ever tell you that?

The poet's wife looks at the poet. And you are my best poet, she says.

Giving a little laugh. Thinking a little thought.

The point is this, he says.

*

Years ago, before the poet's wife was, strictly speaking, the poet's wife, she wrote a little poem. She was so sick of holding open refrigerator doors. She was so sick of it all.

> dedum dedum dedum dedum
> out where Kapiti lies
> like a dark mummy on the horizon
> forever unwrapping its bandages
> into the future . . .

She took it to the poet, who read it aloud in that special voice of his.

When I put in the bandages, she said, I was thinking of clouds.

The poet said: Would you like to move in with me and we could talk about books and stuff?

*

She is sick of his talk of Douglas Bader's legs. She thinks: Probably some people might be impressed. But I know better.

*

Would their life together be significantly better if the poet's book royalties were put towards an annual holiday? A holiday for them both.

No it would not be better.

Last year, the poet's royalties were $43.75.

＊

In fact, holidays aside, the poet has a job that brings in plenty of money. She has no idea what kind of job it is. It takes him out of the house each day, the way jobs do, and sometimes he wears walk-shorts.

＊

The poet is working on his opera libretto, CARNAGE ON THE ROADS.

Don't hover! he says to his wife.

Am I hovering? says the poet's wife.

Yes, you are. Hovering.

Sorry, says the poet's wife.

It's just that it's extremely difficult with you hovering like that. I had something really good coming and I lost it.

＊

He is actually a geography teacher and assistant careers adviser in a large North Auckland school. All he can do is warn.

＊

The poet's wife reads a magazine at the hairdresser's. An article catches her eye: DANGEROUS LOVERS.

You could be looking for love in all the wrong faces. You could be ignoring the warning signs that you're romancing Mr Wrong.

I wonder, wonders the poet's wife, if he is a Don Juan or a

Mother's Boy, an Obsessive Possessive or a Danger to Shipping? Or are poets different, like they say?

*

She watches a television documentary about lighthouse keepers. The loneliness. The isolation. The children taking correspondence courses. She tries to feel God in her muscles, but there is no sign of him.

*

The poet judges a poetry competition. He awards the $150.00 first prize to a poem about refrigerators written by an entrant with the pen name, Rumpelstiltskin. The poet receives a $500.00 judging fee. It is good the way everything is getting on to a proper professional basis he thinks. He spends his fee on personalised number plates. Now the number plates on his car say: POET 7.

Six other poets have had the number plate idea before him. They all live in Dunedin. The Dunedin school.

The poet does not live in Dunedin. He lives in his imagination.

*

The poet's wife watches a television programme about two brave elderly stroke victims. One has lost the use of her left arm, one her right. They play the piano together, each using her one good arm. They are helping each other to turn adversity into harmony.

*

Reach for the Sky. Still one of the great titles. This is only the poet's opinion, but he thinks it is a good one.

*

In the newspaper she reads about a two-headed baby which has been born in Tehran. The baby's body is outwardly almost normal, except for a third short arm. Internally, it has two hearts and four lungs, a main stomach and a sub-stomach. Each head has its own neuro system. The baby's movements are not harmonious. While one head cries, the other may be sound asleep.

*

Well, wonders the poet's wife, AM I romancing Mr Wrong?

*

The poet's wife once had a job as a woman opening refrigerator doors. It was on television advertisements mostly, in the early days of television, though also some magazines, and sometimes there were trade displays, up on a stage, it was quite hard work actually, though it did take you round the country. This is how the poet first saw her—on television, opening a refrigerator door, in the days before colour.

*

The poet's wife hums and puts on the kettle. The poet is at a literary festival in Hamilton—reading his poems, and presenting the winning cheque to 'Rumpelstiltskin'. Soon he will be home again.

A small cloud on her horizon. What if 'Rumpelstiltskin' turns out to be a woman and not a grotesque little man? What if 'Rumpelstiltskin' is . . . beautiful?

*

The telephone rings. It is a journalist who is writing an article on poets' wives—from the angle of the wife, of course. He has come to feel a lot of sympathy for poets' wives in the course of his researches. He wonders if they can set up an interview?

How do you mean, says the poet's wife.

Just talk and that, says the journalist. He has a soft Irish brogue.

Will I or won't I? thinks the poet's wife.

*

He writes: 'There's a tree, one of many, of many one . . .' Then scores out the line with a practised scoring movement.

*

He reads Osip Mandelstam. In his sleep he cries: Nadezda!

*

She looks out of the window. Grey day. The grey before rain, the grey after rain.

The whole garden seems to sag, like a hammock sunk in the earth, slung between two stumpy lemon trees. Neither of them exactly covered with fruit.

A simile, thinks the poet's wife.

She claps her hands in excitement. A simile!

*

He tells the pretty girl that he likes to rescue words—take them by the arm and lead them to some unlikely place, where they tend to look more interesting.

How do you mean? says 'Rumpelstiltskin'.

Like putting a boy from Dunedin on the streets of New York, says the poet, in a voice which indicates this is his final word on the matter.

*

Riff-raff: he cannot get the word out of his head. Dunedin riff-raff. He looks it up in the OED. Persons of a disreputable character or belonging to the lowest class of a community. Persons of no importance or social position. Unlearned rifraffe, nobodie. There were a good many riff-raff in the upper gallery. The riffe-raffe of the scribbling rascality. The Rabble or Scum of the People, Tagrag and Long-tail. A collection of worthless persons. Odds and ends. Trumpery; trash; rubbish. A hurly-burly, a racket, a rude piece of verse.

Ah, thinks the poet, there is the title of my next book.

*

He has become interested in Douglas Bader's legs because Douglas Bader's widow wants to sell one of them. It says so in the newspaper.

*

One day the poet's wife writes a poem:

> Out where Soames Island
>   like a dark tape recorder
>   endlessly unwinds its reels
>   into the unrecorded storm

Stepping the lines down like that. Covering several pages.

*

The poet reads one of his recent poems in the foyer of the Founders Theatre in Hamilton:

> Out where Rangitoto lies
> like a dark breast
> forever bearing its nipple
> to the insatiable city . . .

The applause, he guesses, is somewhere between perfunctory and reluctant. He catches Rumpelstiltskin's eye. Ah! Would it he fair to call that an adoring gaze?

*

I hope he is not a TRAVELLING MAN, thinks the poet's wife.

Away from home a married man becomes a travelling man. He can take off his wedding ring. A salesman can become a company president, a company president can become a poet, a poet can become an All Black. The warning signal is seen through fog. By falling for this fellow, you are seduced by a phantom: he is no longer visible when he leaves town.

The Travelling Man can be a particularly Dangerous Lover.

*

Toynbee. The poet is on fire for her. Toynbee is Rumpelstiltskin's real name. The poet's lines flame with her being. She is the match which sets imagination alight.

He starts a little poem:

> Here she comes, with her
> Douglas Bader eyes,
> scanning the clouds
> & wild enemy skies.

But he will probably throw it away. Something tiresome about the rhyme.

*

Why only one, anyway? What has happened to the other leg? Is it lost? Is she hanging on to it for some reason? These are the sort of questions which pass through the poet's head.

*

The poet leaves his wife and goes to live with Toynbee. A big decision, but he makes it. He writes romantic passages about clouds and a few somewhat bitter lines about his wife. None of it much good. All I can do is warn, he thinks. All I can do is warn.

*

The poet's wife joins a support group for poet's wives. There are hundreds of members in the larger organisation, with branch offices all over the country.

*

She meets a woman who is now married to a stockbroker. And then there is another woman who goes around with a man who owns a whole chain of boutiques in the South Island. Her mind drifts off on the cloudy winds of envy . . .
    Begorrah! (She has just remembered the Irish journalist.)

*

The poet receives an invitation to a writers' festival in Dunedin. All expenses paid. Just after the August holidays.

*

'Throw your heart over the bar, and your body will follow.'
    The poet's wife reads this in a book. Because she is the kind of person who fumes and frets a lot, she keeps turning to a chapter called 'Stop Fuming and Fretting'. It tells her that she needs the peace of God in her muscles, in her joints. Then she will stop fuming and fretting.
    The book says: Speak to your muscles every day and to your joints and to your nerves, saying: 'Fret not thyself' (Psalm xxxviii. i.) Think of each important muscle from head to feet, and say to each: 'The peace of God is touching you.'

*

The point is this, the poet says to her on the telephone.

But then he says nothing.

*

That wasn't you in those refrigerator ads, was it? says the journalist. Back in the 60s when television was just starting up? I was straight off the boat. By God, you were the first good thing I saw.

*

The journalist moves in with the poet's wife. The first good thing I saw. His word processor comes with him. Several nights a week they go to the pub. One day the journalist writes a poem:

> Dedum dedum dedum dedum
> Out where Stewart Island lies
> like an old refrigerator
> opening and opening its door
> upon the vastness of Antarctica . . .

He looks her straight in the eye. So there you are then, he says. You are still a poet's wife.

*

The poet travels to Dunedin. He steps up to the podium—his eye in a fine frenzy rolling. I am the prince of clouds, he thinks, I ride out the tempest and laugh at the archer. He thinks: The Burns Fellowship. He thinks: Riff-raff. He thinks: All I can do is warn.

*

They make love, a strenuous bout.

Afterwards, the poet's wife draws a rectangle; in it she draws

two lines which intersect to form a cross. Guess what it is, she
says.

A window? says the journalist.

No.

A parcel?

No.

What, then?

A short story, she says. With a trick ending.

*

The poet's wife sits at the word processor. Her fingers fly over
the keys. Now what is that? A simile? Of course not. Perhaps a
cliché? Or—an image of transcendence?

*

The poet explains how he used to be fascinated by the idea of
a poop deck—the phrase itself seemed naughty. He imagined
a deck covered in . . . well, not to put too fine a point on it . . .
poop. But looking back . . . looking back, he can see the first
stirrings of the poet there. That interest in language—the young
boy sniggering in the playground—in love with the sea, in love
with his native tongue . . .

Stop me, he says, if this is boring you. Or if it isn't the sort of
thing you want.

No, says the *Landfall* interviewer. No not at all. She smiles
behind her hand.

*

The journalist stands on the roof of the house. For a while he
stares down at the garden: one rhododendron, two lemon trees.
Other houses in the distance. Is he going to jump? Of course
not. He is going to fall. My beautiful one! he cries. My icebox
girl! My mistress of the lonely voice . . .

My Sunshine

He sings you are my sunshine
and the skies are grey, she tries
to make him happy, things
just turn out that way.

She'll never know
how much he loves her
and yet he loves her so much
he might lay down his old guitar
and walk her home, musician
singing with the voice alone.

Oh love is sweet and love is all, it's
evening and the purple shadows fall
about the baby and the toddler
on the bed. It's true he loves her
but he should have told her,
he should have, should have said.

Foolish evening, boy with a foolish head.
He sighs like a flower above his instrument
and his sticky fingers stick. He fumbles
a simple chord progression,
then stares at the neck.
He never seems to learn his lesson.

Here comes the rain. Oh if she were only
sweet sixteen and running from the room again,
and if he were a blackbird
he would whistle and sing
and he'd something
something something something.

Moonlight

Kate Gray (1975–1991)

I start up a conversation
with occasional Kate. Too late,
too late, but with a big sigh
she appears in the sky.

I tell her the home doesn't forget—
her mother's lullaby step
still reaches the chair
where her father sits deep in the forest.

I hear myself saying
please and please and please;
I want to go back
to the start of the nineties.

Sleepless night, big almond eyes,
and a hand rocks a pram in the passage;
from somewhere a long way
outside of our houses

the moon sends its light to this page.

OWEN MARSHALL

Tunes for Bears to Dance to

It's a truism that we structure our past by processes of deliberate or unwitting selection, and the brief we have begins the distortion. To talk of my beginnings as a writer brings one aspect of myself to the fore. I'm a writer by temperament and inclination rather than reputation or occupation. The bulk of my time and energy has been spent of necessity on other things, and the writer in me has until quite recently known his place.

Even now, at forty-seven, I'm uneasy with what I feel a compulsion to do: like the sensible alcoholic I play down the enduring link with an incurable disease. It's not shame, or modesty. Increasingly I speak on authorship, or read my work; I belong to local writers' organisations and to PEN. Yet living my life in provincial towns I am always aware that in these communities there is no accepted or accustomed role for the writer of fiction. 'How's the writing going?' uncertainly asks the amiable countenance of society, and accepts my brief glibness thankfully.

Reading is different. I have felt secure within a wide fraternity of readers. As a boy and young man I was a great reader, though more recently my reading has been sacrificed to writing. Books were a feature of my home. My father, a Methodist minister, is largely self-educated and has a reverence for scholarship and literature which is often the mark of those who have come late to learning, and despite obstacles. My father is a man of reason; a calm, self-sufficient man who doesn't express emotion easily. Our means of making contact was usually a mutual appreciation of books.

For my father the great writers were the natural nobility of the world, and in our house the value of books was so unquestioned that it shook me to realise things were different in the households and minds of other people. My father's study held many hundreds of books, almost all bought second-hand, which was perhaps one reason for his tastes being somewhat old fashioned even then. As well as theology his library included much fiction and poetry, and more history. He cared more for Gladstone and Disraeli than he cared for the politics of New Zealand in the 1950s. He loved the Lake Poets, and the work of Hardy, Dickens, Scott, Galsworthy and Kipling. As my stepmother hurried about the house to get her work done, he would follow, mellifluously reciting from Lamb's essays, or a quip from Boswell's life of Johnson.

There was a lighter side to his reading. He enjoyed stories of colonial adventure—the Boer War seemed to figure strongly—and especially loved Sherlock Holmes. He would read Conan Doyle to us as a family. I have mentioned elsewhere that the personal context of books can powerfully influence our response to them whatever their intrinsic merit. Just a title, 'The Speckled Band' or 'The Dancing Men', will bring his voice back to me; bring back also the very shape and feel of the furniture in the kitchen of the Blenheim parsonage, and a host of less tangible associations. He had a tone of particular delight whenever the redoubtable brother Mycroft featured in the story.

I was twelve when we shifted to Timaru, and I recall walking down in the evenings from the parsonage in North Street to the old library by the Post Office. Towards the end of my time at Timaru Boys' High I had the habit of reading everything on the shelves by an author who took my fancy, before starting another. Most I have forgotten, but not Aldous Huxley and J.B. Priestley, whom I read in this way and enjoyed despite the risk of literary indigestion. I also read rubbish of course. At school we used to swap paperbacks called Carter Browns; the Ian Flemings of the time perhaps. Few books made me laugh, but Kingsley Amis's *Lucky Jim* was one that did. At that slapstick age I loved it, but was disappointed in everything else he wrote.

M.A. Bull was the Rector of Timaru Boys' High in my time there. He was a man of formidable presence. During my seventh form year he thought me under-employed and generously decided that he would personally teach me Greek and in the process learn it himself. It was not to be the beginning of a startling career in classics for me. Bull was so busy that he had no time to complete the exercises: I had more time, but less inclination.

Our tutorials were agreeable, but largely unproductive and gradually tailed off. Until recently I could at least recite the Greek alphabet. Bull was a mathematician and once told me he had calculated how much of his life was wasted in shaving his face, and that the figure astounded him. In later life I too came to resent that chore.

Only one English teacher at the school struck me as being a true book man. He was Alan Miles, a very able, unhappy man who allowed me glimpses of his literary enthusiasm, but also read in class interminable passages from Masefield's *Sard Harker*. Even with the limited critical faculty I had then I was convinced that Masefield was no novelist.

I have no tales of precocious authorship, no aunts to wheel on who fortold great things for me. My juvenilia were scant and worthless. My university friends were not writers; they didn't admit to any such ambition, or even talk much about writing. I was the same. I led a simple, predictable, pleasant life as a student at Canterbury in the early 60s, flatting with the same close friends for several years. I was a conventional student, although naively I imagined otherwise. My flatmates and I purchased a hookah, and we scandalised the neighbours by smoking it together in full view, though its large, white bowl held nothing more exotic than cheap tobacco. I spent a good deal of time playing sport, going to the movies and meeting girls. I had several writhen pipes and talked of death.

Yet my other life went on; my life with books, and I was sometimes taken aback by the extent to which I was moved by what I read, and disconcerted by an awareness that there was another world beneath the directly observable one. A world of emotional configuration. I became aware of the fallibility of the real: aware that the splendidly detailed objective world of sound and colours, shapes and textures, was essentially opaque and that beneath it could be glimpsed the shimmer of things of great horror and ineffable joy. I began to see that fiction at its best was a way of communicating truths that are often too difficult to talk about face to face. I saw it most clearly at this time in the works of T.F. Powys and H.E. Bates; some years later Janet Frame was to affect me in the same way.

Powys was unduly neglected; Bates has received the acclaim and popularity he deserved. Both are especially successful in their different treatment of the countryside and rural people. Powys's work is suffused with mysticism and delineated allegorically, but there is a hard edge of violence and almost pagan fatalism. How I marvelled at his novel *Mr Weston's Good Wine*, and stories as fine as 'Lie Thee Down, Oddity'. In Powys I was aware also of an almost majestic contempt for any attempt by an author to ingratiate himself with a readership, or follow literary fads. His characters never completely fade, but stand as ironic spectators in the wings of consciousness. Lord Bullman and clergyman Hayhoe; Mrs Moggs walking to the beautiful sea. Wold Jar the tinker, in all his guises.

In Bates I always felt warmth, sympathy, a determination to enjoy the hour at hand despite his knowledge of the fragility of things. My Bates was not so much the Bates of the Larkin tales, but more the author of *Fair Stood the Wind for France*, *The Purple Plain* and the stories, some written during the war as Flying Officer X, which displayed unsurpassed powers of natural description, such compassionate humour, such original characterisation.

I sat reading in long evenings, with a kerosene heater which I had to keep the Christchurch winter at bay. The mist curled from the nearby Avon, and my duffel coat was perpetually damp on its hook behind the door.

I enjoyed my years at university, yet was mildly disappointed. Disappointed because as usual my expectation based on reading did not agree with experience. I anticipated toasted muffins with a tutor perhaps, intellectual euphoria, wit lightly tossed like salads, crises of conscience. Our universities were different it seemed. The staff ratios hampered close acquaintance with lecturers, as did the reserve and stolidness of the New Zealand character I suspect. Certainly I had those qualities. I appreciated the physical environment of the old Cantebury campus; its towers and cloisters accorded in some miniature way with my impression of what a university should look like, and I coped with the work without trauma, although I took a unit of Geology one year hoping to learn of Jurassic monsters and spent the time instead noting the arcane shell markings of brachiopods and trilobites.

For the first time in many years I have thought carefully about the English lectures which I attended. In honesty the only author in whom I can remember becoming interested through formal studies is Virginia Woolf. I chose History to carry on with, not because of any disillusion with English, but because there was I think some language prerequisite for the English honours course. In the labyrinthine recesses of the History wing I enjoyed listening to Mr Saunders. He had a detached, sonorous voice like vast waves breaking at a distance, and his sweeping images reduced the centuries with ease. Professor Pocock impressed me as an intellect. His lectures were spun out like spiders' silk in the sun, but later without his presence they were sadly collapsed jottings on my pad. Mr Gardner was the kindest of them. He drew me aside before the exams of my final year to tell me it was unlikely anyone would be awarded first class honours in the subject. Most of the lecturers were ordinary enough. They seemed to have perpetual colds; all those stone staircases and antiquated heaters perhaps.

My time at Canterbury was complicated by National Service as a twenty-year-old, and together with other students who drew short straws in that peculiar birthday lottery, I had two stints at Waiouru. I certainly did no writing there, but it was a juxtaposition of lifestyle and values that gave me food for thought. Army life could hardly have been further from my habits as a student, yet each brought the other into relief and sometimes into question. Not for the only time I was confronted with the antithesis of individual integrity and the values of group loyalty and support. I have never reconciled them completely. What was new during my months in camp was to be mixing with an appreciable number of Maoris. Many North Islanders don't realise how little the Polynesian dimension of national life affects many communities in the south. I also became really fit for the first time, experiencing occasionally because of it a strange sense which approached exhilaration.

I have passed through several phases during my life in respect to the priorities of my admiration. I first held physical skill and beauty as the most important things (as most adolescents do), then there was a period of intellectualism during which I thought that the worst thing in all the world was to be stupid. In middle age I have moved on to regard character as more important in the assessment of my fellows. What will be next I wonder— spirituality as an indication of worth perhaps, or a neat return to the physical?

During my four years at university I was on a secondary teaching studentship; a luxury long since abandoned by the authorities. Thus after finishing my degree I had a year at Teachers' College, and during it I felt the first real urge to write. In my Ranfurly Street flat overlooking the Blind Foundation, an ironic situation perhaps, I wrote the opening few pages for a novel, having no idea how it was to go on. 'Hell is no furnace and prongs agony, he thought. It's a railway system; an aimless complex of shuntings, sidings, dilapidated water towers, small forgotten stations bulging with unwanted bags of barley, and disillusioned demons in decaying black waistcoats, forcing lone travellers to alight before the passive gaze of erstwhile fellow travellers to find no one awaiting them.' It has the world weary languor of youth. It has besides a complexity of syntax which I have never dared attempt again.

After a few pages of it I grew discouraged with my inability to express myself adequately, and because of an intuitive realisation that I hadn't the experience of people and events to sustain it. I placed it aside and went on with my life, and my reading which was a life too. I have always been horrified by the banality of my own work.

In 1965 I went to teach at Waitaki Boys' High School in Oamaru: Janet Frame's Kingdom by the Sea. I stayed there for over twenty years. Waitaki was in gradual, autumnal decline from the great days of Frank Milner, but it was still a special place. In Frame's work the town of Oamaru is the strong childhood presence; as an adult I found the wider North Otago landscape equally influential. The dry downs, with grey limestone outcrops and ridged caves; the pink country roads of crushed Ngapara gravel, and the single cabbage trees on the slopes. The heavy, Oamaru stone gateposts marked many of the older farms, and the broad Waitaki river marked the way to the lake high country. It was a quiet land, often drowsy under a heavy sun: Peebles, Kakanui, Papakaio, Livingstone, Hampden, Kurow, Kia Ora, Otekaieke, Tokarahi, Herbert, Duntroon, Moeraki. I went duck-shooting over that land, mushrooming, visiting, strolling, picnicking with my family in the small streams such as the Waianakarua past the old mill.

My reading continued as much as time allowed, as haphazard yet satisfying as always, enlivened by many discussions with my colleagues. And the urge to write wouldn't die. Sometimes in the evenings on duty as I walked across the quad to the prep rooms, or arced out into the back field to nab a smoker or two, I would turn over ideas in my mind. I liked to walk the foreshore too; the same clay cliffed foreshore with its stunted pines and gorse giving way before the sea that Charles Brasch wrote of in his poems as a schoolboy.

In my experience however, teaching is not a fortunate choice of occupation for someone who wishes to write. Not only does it draw from the same intellectual and emotional springs as one's writing, but it is an exceedingly busy job. In nearly twenty-five years of teaching I have never found the chance to spend any school time on my writing. In the memoirs of other writers I'm struck by the many comments concerning their opportunity in a variety of employment to sit for hours, even days, at a time and write; the time available either because they had nothing to do, or because what they had to do could be so easily avoided. School teaching is not that sort of occupation. Why should it be, indeed! At least there were the vacations.

Youth has at least one thing which need not be learned, and that is energy. I made time outside my teaching, my family, my sport, my friends, my idleness, to practice writing. Some evenings, some Sunday afternoons, increasingly the long vacation; the struggle to write went on. I began a comic novel. On the closely typed original which I still have the title page is missing, and I had forgotten the name—at one time I would have thought that impossible—but find in a 1969 rejection from Reeds that I called it *Higher Education*. The rejection was in the form of a kind and lengthy letter from Arnold Wall, suggesting improvements, encouraging strengths he claimed to see, inviting me to visit him in Wellington. I never did; just kept on trying. In my limited experience people in publishing are caring in the main. I know other writers have found differently.

Sometime in the early 70s there was a competition for unpublished novels. It was connected with the Auckland Centenary I think, and I used the contest as a spur to write a second novel; longer, more serious, and better than the first. I can remember getting up at six o'clock some mornings to work on it before going to school. I can also remember deciding on many occasions not to get up at six o'clock to work on it. In that novel for the first time I began to explore the moral duality of rural life in New Zealand, and to approach some mastery of essential techniques. Interest has been shown recently in the novel, but I have decided it will never be published. I had high hopes of it at the time of course, but it didn't win. From one publisher I sent it to afterwards it came back by return post. I was working in my garden when my wife brought the package out to me. The spade continued to cut through the chickweed and the good earth, but an internal voice ridiculed me for ever imagining that I could write something people might wish to read.

In the bleak clarity of that disappointment I reassessed my writing. I was in my early thirties, and had still published nothing. I was aware of an episodic quality in my work; aware that what vision I possessed suited the compression of the tableau rather than narrative drive and plot. I was conscious that my most intense reading experiences were largely from the short story genre, that its poetic affinities attracted me, and I was not prepared to risk again the investment of time that a novel means for a part-time writer. I decided to write short stories, and to follow my own inclination and judgement in their language and theme. Through the mid 70s I stuck to my last, sending pieces to such publications as *Landfall*, the *Listener* and *Argosy*. I bolstered myself by setting a limit of so many years in which to succeed, or then quit, but I knew in my heart that there would always be an extension. In the end writing becomes part of you, and can't be cut away without causing a sort of death. And there is also the daunting feeling that you are too heavily committed to turn back.

It was a dour struggle at times: I couldn't succeed, and I couldn't give up. The greatest difference I notice between my own extended apprenticeship and that of most other writers is the isolation. I had no one to share the intensity of my interest. My wife was supportive, creative in her own right as a stoneware potter, but not of a literary disposition. In part this isolation was an aspect of living in Oamaru, a rural town. I imagine a provincial writer such as Ronald Morrieson had much the same experience. Another cause however I suspect to be my own nature. I found it difficult to announce myself a writer, and so perhaps discover others like myself. When I did begin publishing, I used my christian names to maintain anonymity. I have always valued the fulfilment of being a writer, rather than that of being seen a writer.

Others talk of close literary friendships at the time they were developing as writers: of mentors, rivals, convivial pub sessions in the cities, regional cliques, salons even. I had none of those, but a writer's isolation though sharply felt is thankfully incomplete for the books themselves are there. The finest writers are with us—not distance, temperament, not death itself can stand in the way of that. One of the few returns from writing at this stage of my life was the way in which it enhanced my appreciation of those who could do it superbly well. The disappointment with my own efforts was partly assuaged by the joy I had from reading Coppard, Salinger, Chekhov, Saroyan, Pritchett, Faulkner, O'Connor, Maupassant, Babel, Austen, Cheever, Hemingway, Woolf, Bowen, Powys and Bates. I was reading our own writers too, poets as well. Davin, Mansfield, Duggan, Middleton, Shadbolt, Cowley, Ihimaera among prose writers, though Sargeson and Frame made the most impact on me. Sargeson by his compassion, and astute creation of a configuration for New Zealand character and environment: Frame by her unerring personal sensitivity and symbolic view of the world which constitute the closest thing to genius that we have experienced in this country's writing.

This was all the personal life still; not hidden, but by its nature and my situation, little shared. Other things went on, generally far more successfully than in my writing. I was more likely to be on the tennis court in my own time in the 70s than at my desk. Hundreds of hours I spent, mainly on the lovely grass courts in the Oamaru gardens, and I went happily with the team to play Southland, South Canterbury or the like. I don't consider the time wasted. I have gained from all the sports to which I've given time; gained knowledge of myself and others, gained friendships from a wider cross-section of adults than just my occupation offered.

The first story of mine published was called 'Descent From The Flugelhorn': a story set firmly in North Otago and in the New Zealand vernacular. It was accepted in 1977 by Tony Reid at the *Listener*. It was the beginning of continued support and encouragement from the *Listener*, particularly by Andrew Mason after he was appointed Literary Editor. First success has its own fierce joy. I destroy the manuscripts of my stories as a rule, but I've kept 'Descent From The Flugelhorn', written in green biro as it chanced. Soon after that I had work accepted in *Islands*, then *Landfall* and other magazines. *Morepork* and *Pilgrims* accepted work, although I'm not sure if it appeared before these publications succumbed.

The individual publication of stories was progress and a source of satisfaction, but I thought it a long road before I would be able to interest a publisher in a collection, for short stories are not popular in the market place. So I approached Pegasus Press of Christchurch and paid for the publication in 1979 of a collection called *Supper Waltz Wilson*. To take that course I needed a trust in my own work and an understanding wife, for I knew the money would not be recouped. It was the only work I paid to have published but I haven't regretted the decision. My relationship with Pegasus was straightforward; the book was well produced and drew good reviews.

In 1981 I had the good fortune to be the Literary Fellow at the University of Canterbury, at Ilam though, not my old haunts. For the first time in my life I had a substantial block of time to devote to my writing. It marked a turning point: a decision to work harder at my writing, even if it meant in the end drawing back from further advancement in my teaching career. Some weeks went well at Canterbury; there were other long periods when the empty page mocked me. I was learning the lesson that writing is not only a matter of having time available for its completion. There was always stimulus and good company though; Michael Harlow, Patrick Evans, Peter Simpson. I remember having lunch with M.K. Joseph not so long before his sudden death.

During 1981 I contacted several publishers in the hope of a second collection. One leading firm told me that they were no longer publishing stories, another said that short stories were at the 'difficult marketing end of New Zealand fiction'. Sadly true. Brian Turner, Editor at John McIndoe Ltd, wrote saying he liked my work, and invited me to send a group of stories down. Towards the end of the year he rang, and in his typically diffident voice, which disguises perception and puckish sensitivity, told me that McIndoe would like to publish my collection.

This is the place to finish an account of my progress to authorship I suppose. More than any other external factor the support of Brian Turner, and Barbara Larson his successor as Editor, has allowed me to be a writer, and I welcome the opportunity to acknowledge my debt. My second collection, *The Master Of Big Jingles*, was published in 1982; *The Day Hemingway Died*, *The Lynx Hunter* and *The Divided World* have followed.

I try to be realistic in my view of the part writing plays in my life. The demands and compromises could be seen as having been greater than the rewards, certainly observable success has all been in recent years, but how does one calculate the value of intangibles; and how express them. The only authentic scrutiny of a writer is through the work. The nature of the short story genre, and the very small New Zealand market, make it unlikely that I can be a full-time writer, and there is no burgeoning overseas interest. But I'm not discontented in allegiance to the short story form. I delight in its challenges and constraints, its traditions and possibilities, in its accomplished practitioners amongst my fellow writers.

The struggle now is not so much to write, as to write well.

The work tends to twist in the hand, always less in the end than the hopes for it. 'Human language is like a cracked kettle on which we beat out tunes for bears to dance to, when all the time we are longing to move the stars to pity.' (Flaubert.) My Kiwi fear of any pretension won't allow me to express myself so romantically—more's the pity perhaps.

Mad Hatter Days

As a student I read biographical pieces in which old men addressed their youthful selves as if complete strangers, and claimed to be baffled by the motivations and attitudes they once possessed. My reaction was that the stance was an irritating and pompous affectation. Now however, in my fifties, I'm beginning to change my mind.

I turned 21 in August 1962; my final BA year at the University of Canterbury. I remember little of the year apart from a smattering of my own trivial, selfish pursuits. World events, national issues, even regional happenings, have no place in my recollections, presumably because they played no part in my life.

I was a varsity wallah, as I had found myself termed when balloted into National Military Service as a 20-year-old the year before—something of a shock, but that's another story. I had a duffel coat, corduroys and desert boots: for 'sharp' wear I had an ivy league shirt—just like the Kingston Trio—and a small-brimmed green hat with a feather. I owned several pipes, the most prized being a Tanganyikan block meerschaum, the most severely intellectual, a curved Peterson. Wearing coat, hat, and Peterson, I must have resembled someone in search of a Conan Doyle theme party.

A green Series E Morris gave grand mobility and kept me poor despite my secondary studentship. It had an iron key I remember which unlocked the bonnet. Rather than sell that lovable old Morris cheaply a few years later, I should have shut it away and waited for the steep increase in value that the model was about to undergo. But then I have always lacked any entrepreneurial nous.

I read a great deal, almost exclusively 'high' literature, though sometimes my intellectualism slipped and I would play tennis for days at a time, before guilt overwhelmed me. I had several trite responses in conversation which I thought worldly wise—'But it's all relative isn't it,' or, 'The question is one of pure semantics.' I had an inclination to write, but most of my time was spent in reading and talk. God, how we talked: at the university, at the café, at parties, the pub, the flat, while walking from one to another of these places. All of us jawing on with preposterous nonsense which was largely a way of showing off. What bullshit-artists students are, and what sound preparation for life that often proves to be.

I pursued women, but was clumsy in those arts necessary to captivate them. Either I pitted myself against them verbally in vigorous intellectual competition, or observed them in brooding silence and wondered how they would look without their clothes. The personal solicitude, easy flattery and banter, the brotherly ease, which disarmed them, I was slow to learn. One young woman with whom I had a vigorous dispute over British Fascism of the thirties, did move from a passion for the right-wing position to become more liberal and accommodating during an evening. I thought I had discovered something essential concerning the female psyche, but the trick never worked again. I have retained, however, as a consequence, a fondness for the historical lessons of the thirties. Her shoulders and upper arms were particularly beautiful.

Of my 21st itself I recall little. My own family made no fuss over it, and the modest party I did have was put on by parents of a friend. These people were very generous to me, treating me in much the same way as they did their own son, and allowing me to stay with them while I was working at vacation jobs. I paid only a small amount for board, and the recollection of my imposition and their generosity now embarrasses me. I hope that I thanked them more often than I remember doing so.

My girlfriend gave me a Parker pen which I've lost. I still have the cuff-link set which is the only other 21st gift I can identify. It was given to me by one of my oldest friends and his partner. They later married, and now live in the same town as myself, where he is a prosperous accountant. I see my friend rarely, and on these occasions we retell school and university anecdotes with enjoyment, and have virtually nothing else to talk about, so much have our lives diverged.

During that year of 1962 I flatted with three friends in an old house in Tuam Street. The grass gradually grew until it obscured much of the window area. We had placed the lawnmower on the roof to hold down some flapping sheets of corrugated iron. Even had the mower been at ground level, we wouldn't have used it. We spent a good deal of most evenings playing a game of our own devising, wherein we took turns standing with our back to the door and tried to pot a pink fishing net float into the waste basket at the other end of the hall. The losers went miserably to their rooms castigating themselves as total academic failures who couldn't even win at throwing a float into a waste paper basket. The winner went to his room castigating himself as an academic failure good only for throwing a pink float into a trash can.

My recollection is that I had become a competent cook, but recently my flatmates vehemently insisted that each of my rostered meals was exactly the same—fried sausages, with carrots and potatoes done in the pressure cooker. I remember that large pressure cooker. We were all afraid of it. The screaming valve, which occasionally blew up, drove us from the kitchen. Even that became a sort of bizarre ritual. Almost anything could be made to serve as a refuge from academic study, but only romance left no regrets.

One of the greatest benefits of university is that the poverty experienced by many students brings them into contact for the first and last time in their lives with those at the bottom of the economic heap. A wonderful array of characters, some of whom have been defeated by life, and others who have splendidly refused to pay it conventional homage. The student's Bohemia was only one of the subcultures I experienced in the world of seedy flats, eccentric landladies, drifters and misfits, casual and menial employment, minor opportunistic criminality, pubs and takeaway food, bludgers, wrecks, emotional crises, defiantly unrecognised artists, and true friends. At that age I delighted in it all, because youth itself gave immunity to every outcome.

I'm surprised at how little I remember of being 21, and I do indeed find my young self largely a stranger. I see myself through the looking glass, and the Mad Hatter seems to be in charge. One thing I can remember faithfully—the unassailable conviction that all of life's opportunities stretched endlessly before me.

LES MURRAY

Glaze

Tiles are mostly abstract:
tiles come from Islam:
tiles have been through fire:
tiles are a sacred charm:

After the unbearable parallel
trajectories of lit blank tile,
figure-tiles restore the plural,
figuring resumes its true vein.

Harm fades from the spirit as tiles
repeat time beyond time their riddle,
neat stanzas that rhyme from the middle
styles with florets with tendrils of balm.

Henna and mulberry mos-
aics controvert space:
lattice on lattice recedes
through itself into Paradise

or parrot starbursts framing themes
of stars bursting, until they salaam
the Holy Name in sprigged consonants
crosslaced as Welsh metrical schemes.

Conjunct, the infinite doorways
of the mansions of mansions amaze
underfoot in a cool court, with sun-blaze
afloat on the hard water of glaze.

Ur shapes under old liquor
ziggurats of endless incline;
cruciform on maiolica
flourishes the true vine.

Tulip tiles on the grate of Humoresque
Villa join, by a great arabesque
cream boudoirs of Vienna, then by left-
handed rhyme, the blue pubs of Delft

and prominence stands in a circle
falling to the centre of climb:
O miming is defeated by mime:
circles circle the PR of ominence.

Cool Mesach in fused Rorschach,
old from beyond Islam,
tiles have been to Paradise,
clinkers of ghostly calm.

GREGORY O'BRIEN

The Run-Off

(a letter to Laurie Duggan, July 1996)

The landscape, Laurie, where does it start and where does it
stop,
      how far does it go and what lengths will it got to
to reach us? Aged thirteen at Sacred Heart College,
   Glen Innes—

a school famous for its rugby; fifty acres devoted largely to
    that end—
each morning I would stare across the fields
to the mouth of the Tamaki Estuary—the lush trees

and wavering grasses almost Poussinesque, awaiting
the arrival of the groundsman—Dave Dobbyn's father—
who would traverse the property on a high-speed

tractor-mower. This was our idyll, our pastorale: air
and water and light floating above the scene, like a landscape
   out of Lorrain
from which the muses had only recently fled,
                 pursued by flying rugby balls

and grunting, heaving scrum machines.
The kind of landscape you could hardly scratch the surface
of—like Jean Dubuffet's 1956 canvas *Run Grass, Jump Pebbles*,

or his *Paysage metapsychique*. Nor could you slide
down it,
      like the sloping Taranaki province where, as children,
we would holiday, considering ourselves somehow 'native'

to that place, our expansive adventures later diminishing,
themselves victim of a kind of instability we observed
in the province as a whole.
                              What details remain

of that time: a beached whale with its jaw and teeth
      chainsawed out,
            the de-horning of cattle. Someone—a cousin?—
was always setting fire to Opunake High School.

A sloping province—as if everyone might, any moment now,
      be swept
down into the Tasman Sea.
            The unpeopled landscape, Barbara tells me,
fulfils some state of mind. But landscapes are never

without their figures, even if it is only the imagined figure of
      the viewer—
the painter—standing before it. The Frenchman Pierre Tal-
      Coat
said 'landscape is the great metaphor'. I ran into his paintings

in New York, 1985, at the New Museum. Small, luminous
      expanses.
I am still walking around that exhibition—
one day I could imagine myself
                              buried in it. Tal-Coat wrote, 'One paints

as one takes a step . . . The earth moves. It is necessary to
      adjust each step . . .'
realising the world wasn't made of permanent materials
except perhaps
            this subsiding, fading, calming. . . What else is there—

a tentative industry around the edges
or instead of these things? The pursuit of sadness
or its more seductive allies? Which makes

me think of Erik Satie, whose memory 'registered everything
he read, including his apparently useless studies
at the Bibliotheque Nationale into the liturgy or Gothic

art. In this way, he acquired a curious, fragmentary erudition
which had a considerable influence on his mind,'
quoting Pierre-Daniel Templier, 'and his style'.

                              The earth moves, but it doesn't
move. I'm writing to you on June 17, 1996. The Waitangi
     Tribunal
has ruled in favour of land claims by Taranaki Maori.

I recall Lloyd Rees saying he kept returning to paint the
     Tasmanian
landscape because it obsessed and troubled him.
He said the land contained a tremor or human cry—

something emanating from the extermination
                              of the Aboriginal population
by the first settlers. You could say we felt something
similarly dark in the Taranaki landscape; also in

the Ireland our forebears left behind, themselves victims
of a botched, violent colonialism (did you know that
     Catholicism
                    was outlawed in Great Britain until

the Catholic Emancipation Act of 1829?), although they were
     accepting
of the maltreatment of the native population in turn,
                              the only way
forward for them, or so it seemed, a single-minded
     agriculture—
                              needing an amnesia

to deal with their own past, they adopted a similar
amnesia concerning the dispossession of the local population.
(That said, my mother recalls an elderly aunt's recollections of

the Parihaka siege—her description of a line of women
    singing,
surrounding the settlement as the troops approached.) What
    escapes us
the land, kumara pitted, remembers: adze heads recovered

from among boulders, the faded shadows that were trenches
around Te Namu pa. The site of the first fighting
between British infantry—the 50th Regiment,
                        'the Dirty Half Hundred'—

and Maori. A subsiding landscape . . . just as the family's
    culture subsided,
their Irishness eroded, assimilated into the run-off. A province
intent on burying its past—which included theirs—replacing it

with a pragmatism and adaptability—these the most
applicable virtues. How, then, do we inhabit this place?
                        I still see myself
on a trampoline, going up and down . . . lifting off,

never touching the ground, moving between canvas
                and the air above.
No one ever claimed for a moment money had been paid

for the old farm—it was 'confiscated' land: that which we
    inherited,
what we woke up to. So it was
the entire family was handed down an anxiety—

                leaning over aerial photographs,
with furrowed brows, as if we had to always explain
our claim on the land. And the Maori, of course, were 'bad'

farmers, because they didn't buy into a culture of productivity
and profitability—that lessened their claim.
Mostly, the farmers were hard on the land—effective, if not
   brilliant

in the rotating of crops and grazing, it would have to be said,
but also given to the alteration of land for practical purposes.
Their county council would locate rubbish dumps

on the coastline or adjoining the Otahi Stream.
They were known to create artificial lakes in anticipation of
duck-shooting season; dead tractors, farm bikes and

surreal farm implements littered the sides
of tanker tracks, as did shanty towns of dog kennels,
and the odd Ford Prefect, still operational but marooned

in an adjoining paddock, its roof cut off, rain and chickens
pouring in. One summer, confined to a non-dairy diet
on account of asthma, I arrived at Opunake to find

such constraints on nature's bounty met with
complete disbelief, then disdain. (The fact
I was allergic to dairy products, eggs, horses, cows, dogs, bees,

pollen, dust and cats underlined my emerging foreignness
                              from the place—
I was no longer the 'native' I once thought I was.)
Decades later, the morning after my grandmother's funeral, we

are driving down the rolling
         sealed road past Parihaka, past the new sewerage ponds
overlooking the Tasman Sea and the fortified gang
   headquarters,
the car rising and
              falling on its suspension, floating, drifting

as far back as the trampoline, the mountain
                              going up and down.
Whatever else the land yields: a rising and falling. Which
ever way you look at it, as my young cousin was forever

saying, you have to 'get it on the good foot
          and take it to the river'. Whatever that meant.
How much life
                              gets in, I ask myself,
                                    how we went about
where we lived. And how we wrote ourselves, darkly, into

that place—a cousin crushed under a tractor the day after
my mother's wedding. Another cousin, younger than me, who
     had
her arm all but ripped off by a hay-bailing machine.
                              All of these pasts,

none of which can be walked away from. Today, in Auckland,
I visit Rodney Kirk Smith in his gallery, staring into the black
     canvases
of his predicament. Cancer. The end of a gallery.

The way he would linger on the 'o' in
          Hotere whenever he read the painter's surname on
     the back
of these full, empty expanses. Then he would sleep,
sitting there, where he sat, at his desk with
the 'Requiem' drawings around him. I ask you,

he asked me and closed his eyes, dimly—
for the moment; the moment being
all there ever is. We dragged the stretchers

across the floor. Black and blackened windows, a pebble
dropped in a dark pond, light
                    circling outwards. How much life gets

away . . . The picture, half-painted, awaits its surface, as we
    await
a particular relationship to time—a permanence—be it an
    abundance or
        a lack, 'content' or
an expressive gloom. When the public galleries should have
    been

buying from him, they wouldn't set foot in Rodney's gallery—
preoccupied, it could be said, by less permanent materials.
The picture, an article of faith, will eventually find its
    surface—
            something to set its 'curious,

fragmentary erudition' to. Returning to Taranaki,
        what am I left with
except, at the funerals of both my grandparents, the heartfelt
    singing
of the Te Namu Maori for those of us who had gone,

in spite of everything, before—that we could
somehow have remained
            in their affection as well as
remaining on their land. What else, then, are we left

        to contemplate? The mountain as seen
from a trampoline. Everything we have held on to,
            everything we might wish for.

CHRIS ORSMAN

Tin Can Island

*(Niuafoou, where letters are sealed in
baking powder tins and cast on the water)*

Between jute mills
and the *Queen Mary*'s bowels
in the *Book of Wonder*,

a yellowed inlet
in photogravure:
boats bobbing,

a scoop net at work,
and cans on the water
all over the Pacific:

a philatelic novelty
and the world merely
a first-day-cover;

a tramp steamer
lies at anchor
and silverfish

nudge the image
of an island's image
where letters arrive

rusted and salt
with the tang
of baking-powder.

VINCENT O'SULLIVAN

The Child in the Gardens: Winter

How sudden, this entering the fallen
gardens for the first time, to feel the blisters
of the world's father, as his own hand
does. It is everything dying at once,
the slimed pond and the riffling of leaves,
shoes drenched across sapless stalks.
It is what you will read a thousand times.
You will come to think, who has not stood
there, holding that large hand, not said
Can't we go back? I don't like this place.
Your voice sounds like someone else's. You
rub a sleeve against your cheek, you want
him to laugh, to say, 'The early stars can't hurt
us, they are further than trains we hear
on the clearest of nights.' We are in a story
called Father, We Must Get Out.
Leaves scritch at the red walls,
a stone lady lies near the pond, eating
dirty grass. It is too sudden, this
walking into time for its first lesson,
its brown wind, its scummed nasty
paths. You know how lovely yellow
is your favourite colour, the kitchen at home.
You touch the big gates as you leave,
the trees stand on their bones, the shoulders
on the vandaled statue are huge cold
eggs. Nothing there wants to move.
You touch the gates and tell them, We
are not coming back to this place. Are we, Dad?

Why Biographers Fudge It

In one of those games when you're asked
'What would you be if you weren't human?',
my sister says a silverfish. I'm certain
she thinks it a kind of metallic creature
with scales slanting reflection in moonlight
thick as paste. My brother would be a dashboard
on a car with dials in the satinwood that porthole
horizons of posh. I say a plate of nectarines
left out on a table in the yard beneath the willows,
and when it was morning they'd feel wet
as touching the sea. The grown-ups said
that's the nicest, that is, not knowing
my lack of invention, my desperate need to say
something, so that's what I said, although
silverfish and *dashboard* were excellent I thought
as stars, and all I could think of were those dumb
nectarines, the last thing I'd seen when called
to come in, and I thought whoever
it was left them out like that, will they cop it,
whatever their story is to cover up.

BILL PEARSON

Beginnings and Endings

I would stand on the bar of the front gate and watch the main road. Up at the cutting there was a glimpse of passing trains or perhaps, like a revelation needing to be explained, four railwaymen propelling themselves urgently on a push-pull jigger. There were horses pulling drays, the infrequent car, and once even a traction engine chuffing and clanking like a train down the road. There might be someone going up to the hospital or to the grocer's shop and there might be old men from the Old People's Home. My brother told me how to make one of them wild. You had to call out, 'Do you think it will rain today, Mr Moseley?' I couldn't see why that would make anyone wild but one day he came slowly on the other side of the road, wearing a cap, and when I called out he bent slowly and picked up a stone and threw it at me. I didn't understand why my mother was angry with me or what was wrong about it. It wasn't like swearing. I once heard my father come out with a shocking flow of profanity. My mother said I shouldn't listen but how could I help listening? Only my father wouldn't go to heaven. Later, when I was going to school, a teacher punished me for playing up when she was out of the room. She was a Catholic (in Greymouth you always knew who was Catholic and who wasn't) and a girl and I ran out into the middle of the circle of tables and kissed. Miss Moore had a way when she punished the boys of putting them across her knees and pushing up the legs of their pants until she was slapping bare buttocks. I smarted at the injustice all afternoon and when I got home I carefully printed out my private hoard of swear words and one I made up. My feeling of boldness at the time (I was six) seemed to be connected with the new pants I was wearing that Mum had run up on the sewing machine with flour-bag lining. They had no pockets, so when I sat up on the form for tea I had to sit on my list and my sister as she got down from the table snitched it from under me and said, 'You awful boy!' I was expecting another thunderclap of punishment but my sister, who understood rebellion, simply put it in the stove. I always wanted to be a good boy but in ways that only I knew I had persistent intimations that I wasn't.

My mother was a patient woman, gentle and persevering, who hated violence and cruelty. She said she didn't want any of us to be getting into fights with other boys, she said you should turn the other cheek and always do as you would be done by. She said there wouldn't be wars if people would only remember to act like that. One afternoon she made us miss school and took us to the pictures at the Opera House. It was a silent version of *Uncle Tom's Cabin*; she said it ought to be part of everybody's education.

The first book I cherished was an atlas of the world. It was brand new, bought at a bookshop, not at back doors second-hand from mothers of kids who had been in the class the year before. The colours and shapes fascinated me; there was surprise and permanence in the ragged shape of Scotland where three of my grandparents had come from, and the more-or-less symmetry of Australia which I wanted to copy. I was already familiar with the shape of New Zealand from the A.M.P. calendar on the kitchen wall, with Greymouth near the tip of the nose of the profile of a human face that was made by the railway-line between Inangahua Junction and Rolleston. In the patches of red that made stepping-stones across the world, the Empire on which the sun would never set, New Zealand was so far from England but reassuringly red. One Saturday I did do an enlargement of Australia on a sheet of thick brown paper saved from a parcel and took it to my teacher. I expected some commendation but all I remember was a quizzical look and I never heard of it again. Months later I saw my map on the wall of another teacher's classroom with bits of wool and wheat stuck on it. We had a history book called *Our Nation's Story* that alternated between England and New Zealand: the ancient Britons and then the ancient Maoris; the Angles, Saxons and Jutes and then the navigators Abel Tasman and Captain Cook, a kind man who had been killed by ungrateful Polynesians. It did not occur to us that we could have been anything but benefactors to the

Maoris, but a more pressing puzzle often came to my mind. As I looked out of the school window to the bush on the hills behind Greymouth, if they could be seen under rain, I would wonder at the fact that of all parts of the English-speaking world my home was this particular place on the west coast of the South Island of New Zealand, six weeks by sea from England where the King lived and so much of our history had happened.

At first it wasn't easy to imagine a time when I hadn't existed, but from the talk of my parents that time of dreaming took on a pattern of mysterious events and places. There was a time when the Prince of Wales had come to the town. There was Dunedin where my father came from and Scotland which he had left as a baby in arms. His mother still lived in Dunedin and wrote me those letters saved up for me to read when I was older and then made me wriggle: 'My very own dearest wee Willie . . .' telling me always to obey the Lord Jesus who loved little children like me. There had been the Black Flu, always spoken of in ominous tones, and there had been the War. My uncle Tom in Canterbury went to that, but my father didn't, and Mr Chettle who was always giving hidings to his kids. Mum said he was bad-tempered because he had a plate in his head, a mystery I gave up trying to understand. Mr Lorking the headmaster had been to the War, he was a swarthy man with a firm loud voice and a strong arm with the strap; we didn't dare be slow to obey him. He told us boys that when we grew up if there was another war we were to do everything we could to prevent it but that if we couldn't we were to join up and fight for our country. And part of the dream-time were Rakaia and Dorie the place my grandfather had given the name to and the land for the school, where my mother had won those red and gold cards in the chiffonier drawer, from old A. & P. shows, first prize for scones, first prize for sponge-cake, second for gooseberry jam, highly commended . . . Her grandfather (I was to learn much later) was an agricultural labourer and fisherman drowned in the seas west of Rossshire, a tenant in an impoverished community of tenants living on a lip of land under the forbidding brow of Liathach at the head of an arm of the Atlantic called Loch Torridon. Her father came out in 1862 with not much more than his chest and

his Gaelic bible and worked sixteen years as a shepherd for a
Scottish land company on land that only a few years before was
the territory of the Ngai-Tahu; he bought enough land to enable
him to marry (at 39) raise a family and live comfortably as a
small farmer. He married a sister of a large family of brothers
from County Wexford who set up as farming contractors and
became farmers themselves. They said he could do the sword
dance at eighty. The only grandparent I ever saw, he was remote
and forbidding to a boy of six; almost ninety, his full beard still
a dark grey, and staring fiercely through me: 'Now come over
here and don't annoy your grandfather.'

I remember sitting on the floor listening to my mother
singing expressively at the piano ('Oh mah babby, mah curly-
headed babby . . .') and on our walls there were her paintings of
romantic seascapes and landscapes, maybe in moonlight, done
before she was married. She was 26 when she married, my father
(like hers) 39. In his album there were pages of photographs of
an earlier fiancee but (so my mother told me) she broke it off
when he failed to call one weekend when he was in town. As
one who was sure of his priorities he was aggrieved because he
had been helping his parents move house. But my mother (who
by then had been put upon by his) said she admired the girl's
spirit. He started work at twelve, working for the railways, was
in sole charge of his first rural station at sixteen, and when he
married was a clerk at Greymouth station. Somewhere in his
career he had made some technical blunder for which he got a
blister and a long-term blockage to promotion. He made two
resolutions for the sake of his children: he wouldn't let them join
the public service, and since his own school education had been
disrupted by his mother's restless shifting from house to house,
he would stay in one place once his children started school. He
played the flute, practising uncertainly for concerts of the local
Orchestral Society and he liked to listen to light classics on the
wireless when we got one. In his long bachelorhood his hobby
was photography; we used as a stool a leatherclad cube which
rattled with the broken glass negatives inside it. He was an elder
of the Presbyterian Church and a Mason (riding the goat, my
mother called it) secretary to his lodge and to one or two other

organisations. My brothers and sister had music lessons, the cornet, the piano, the violin. I was looking forward to learning the piano and was certain that unlike them I wouldn't have to be driven to practise. But his forty years service were up and he had to retire and couldn't afford it. In fact during my life he spent more years in retirement than working. For the next few years it was to be a text frequently invoked: We can't afford it.

I recognised Dunedin on the blackboard the moment the teacher had finished printing it. In the primers I used to ask for a Standard One journal to take home to read after tea. One day the teacher, in exasperation at trying to find an issue that I hadn't read, gave me a Standard Six journal with big words about the landing at Anzac Cove and a picture of the ships at Suvla Bay. It was too difficult for me and my mother was angry with the teacher.

I wrote my first book when I was eight, a miscellany of essays, verse and fiction, in a penny notebook of 32 ruled pages, with its own brand name, the Forward Note Book. The title I gave it was A Little Book of Spiders, changed later to A Little Book of Things. We had a lively teacher that year, a tall vigorous woman whose name changed during the year because she married. She must have given a lesson memorable enough to inspire my first piece in the book, an account of the varieties of spiders, of which the one that excited me most was the one that didn't bother making webs but just ran to the tops of trees to catch birds and devour them on the spot. It lived in Australia or America or Africa or Canada. I don't think I made it up. But the next story was my own invention, 'The Spiders' Party', a black morality about a spider that won the confidence of two others by inviting them to a series of parties and then captured them and also their mother when she came to look for them, but was forestalled by their father who nipped him and threw him into the river where, not being a water spider, he drowned. Later in my book there is a chapter on the Maori discovery of New Zealand and others on Tasman and Cook, with careful maps of New Zealand, of England and Holland, and of the Pacific islands, the home countries of the discoverers.

My brother knocked up a desk for me out of apple-cases and I can see myself using the backs of my father's notices of lodge meetings to write sermons. At this time (I was ten) I was religious and went to morning church as well as afternoon Sunday school because the minister put on a sermon for children and invited us to answer questions. I can remember too using my father's second-hand Remington to two-finger a sanctimonious story suggested by a notorious kidnapping of the time, of the baby of the aviator Charles Lindbergh. In my story, which never got beyond an opening, Mrs Lindbergh piously expresses faith that the Lord will see that her baby is returned. We didn't yet know that the baby would be killed but I suspect that my fascination with the affair had something to do with the fact that my young brother's arrival without warning when I was five had disturbed me more than I was prepared to acknowledge.

My father took out a subscription to the Christchurch evening paper the *Star-Sun*. It came over to Greymouth on the night goods train and was delivered in the morning in competition with the *Argus*, which although its news might be fresher, was Labour and in my parents' view, only a rag. About the same time, with the new prosperity, my mother started buying the *Australian Woman's Mirror*. Not concerned that I was impersonating an adult and a woman as well, I used an anecdote of my mother's for a par in the *Mirror* which appeared on the page headed 'Between Ourselves'. From about thirteen I was writing for Aunt Hilda's page in the *Star-Sun*. I was a solitary boy and never cared for team sports or male competitiveness and of course team captains didn't want someone who had as little confidence in his physical prowess as I had, so I never had difficulty getting through school without playing sport, and it didn't cause me much worry whether I met the canons of masculine distinction that prevailed at the time. I am not sure how or why I began a long interest in native plants and birds, with the help of a commercial teacher who was a source of knowledge of local history and an advocate of forest conservation. I got into the habit of spending my Saturday afternoons wandering in the bush, observing the birds that could be seen at lower levels, taking home seedlings for a native garden I was cultivating. I was able to identify all the trees and shrubs I came across in the bush at the back of Cottle's Hill at Karoro, with the further help of two books I had won in story competitions, Laing and Blackwell's *Plants of New Zealand* and an illustrated book of birds of the forest published by the Forest and Bird Protection Society of which I became a member. A consequence of my interest was a haughty disdain for exotics. Although I knew a few English trees, it wasn't till years later when I went to England that I could recognise an elm or birch or beech, though I was very familiar with the trees called birch and beech in the Westland bush.

The bush at Karoro had already made way for Rugby Park and the lower slopes of the hill were destined to be cleared and subdivided. The first of my stories for the *Star-Sun* was a conservationist fable about a kindly man who bought as a refuge for the birds an area of bush that was under threat of the axe. The second, published when I was fourteen, involved a discontented young kowhai, impatient to get out of the bush, who persuaded a kind man to transplant him but after seasons of frosts and winds was glad to get back home again. I gave this story a title I had seen in a photograph of the Miners' Hall at Runanga, 'Unity is Strength'.

When I was fourteen I found a weekend job selling chocolate and icecreams at the Regent Theatre. We saw the films free and over two years I must have seen a hundred or more films, nearly all from Hollywood. They were films that I was to learn to see within a few years as escapist and falsely heroic or sentimental, but I think I absorbed from them a sense of narrative, of a story that has a beginning, a middle and end and can be comprehended as a whole, that I was to think of as unimportant for a while but later to rediscover and give emphasis to in the only novel I wrote. I used to take a short cut to town by way of the railway line that crossed Sawyers Creek and ran past an extensive kowhai grove and a smaller scrap of bush that had not quite escaped the axe but was regenerating. I was sure by this time that I was going to be a writer of fiction and the problem was to find in my own experience material that would match what I read in Dickens. On a rainy day I would imagine the mud beach where the tidal creek slid into Karoro Lagoon as the marshes from

which Magwitch emerged, scaring Pip in *Great Expectations*;
I would try to visualise the prison hulks on the water. But I
despaired of finding characters to equal Miss Havisham or Mrs
Gamp. I played with the idea of caricatures of my father who
was making me, at that age, irritated or ashamed of him. He
was becoming isolated in his own family. If his recourse to the
bamboo stick in the bathroom wasn't that frequent he didn't
know how else to respond if his authority was defied and we
had all been estranged by subdual. Partly it was that we caught
on to our mother's mood of disappointment in her marriage but
mostly because we held him to blame, as Mum's women friends
did, for being as helpless as we all were in the misfortune that
beset her. She developed what they then called disseminated
sclerosis, became partly paralysed on one side and could only get
around by using a stick or leaning against the wall. We did some
of the housework, a woman came in weekly to clean, the coal
stove was replaced by gas. But she continued with the cooking.
The theory was that she was to call for help when she wanted a
saucepan lifted or carried but in practice she did it herself and
she had several falls. Once she scalded herself making jam. I
took on the family wash and some of the cooking. Later she
broke her leg and went into hospital.

There was one story that Aunt Hilda didn't print, it wasn't
even acknowledged. It was called 'The Scrap' and referred
to that little piece of regenerating bush I used to pass on my
way along the railway line. In my story there was a war and
Mussolini's planes bombed the town (as they had recently
bombed Abyssinia). The town was evacuated and left to sink
to the ground and quietly revert to bush, so that the scrap came
into its own again. A conservationist triumph, but I doubt if I
recognised myself how defeatist it was, not at all the wholesome
children's story that Aunt Hilda said my first story was.

In the sixth form we had a textbook that analysed the
novel into six aspects: plot, character, setting, craftsmanship,
movement and philosophy. I was able to illustrate them all to
the teacher's satisfaction from *Martin Chuzzlewit*. But I still
needed a key to the craft of writing from my own experience
and thoughts. If I looked for it in modern writers, Priestley's

The Good Companions was alien, and though I recognised the authoritative tone of Lawrence's *The Prussian Officer* when I discovered it in an anthology of stories, it was too far removed from experience I had known. I intended to read Galsworthy.

Over the space of two days three things happened that were important to me: I was dux of the school, my mother died, and I learned that I hadn't been accepted for training college. After Mum was buried, the problem was what to do. My father took me to see the Labour M.P., James O'Brien, though I doubt if he had ever voted for him. I remember his parting piece of advice. He said that if I ever got into a scrap I was first of all to do everything I could to stop it but if I found I couldn't I was to get stuck in and fight like hell. But I couldn't see that that would get me into training college. My father thought university was beyond his means, but the Anglican vicar's wife who had a son at university could show that it cost little more than books and board. In Christchurch I found a part-time job (doing housework for a couple of teachers' wives) but for that year of dependence lived in fear of failure in the exams. Nevertheless it was the expansive atmosphere of those years of Labour's second term of office that brought university within my reach. Even in 1938, when I was in the sixth form, a neighbour stopped me on the street, a working man, and asked me wasn't it time I had a job. That year I turned down an offer from the local evening paper but I couldn't have afforded to in the climate of three years earlier. At the end of the year at university I was accepted for training college.

Besides being dux I had won a prize donated by the two local newspapers for knowledge of current topics and someone intelligent had chosen Yeats's *Oxford Book of Modern Verse* and Mikhail Sholokhov's *And Quiet Flows the Don*. I suspect it was the excellent geography master who livened our sixth form year with a reading of Shaw's *Intelligent Woman's Guide to Socialism* and a new book on the economic geography of the Soviet Union. When Mum died some friends invited me to stay with them in Blackball, the locale of my novel. It wasn't my first stay in a coal-miner's household, but what was new was being with people who spoke with admiration for the Soviet Union.

Throughout these years I developed from my reading a revulsion against the horror and futility of the First World War, and there was the pressing sense that another war of worse horror was coming. I looked on nationalism as a dangerous passion. During that last year before the outbreak of war I had a dream of Chamberlain and Roosevelt with truncheons and dressed as policemen beating up Hitler. I had discovered James Joyce: 'brutish to the breakbone' my dream said, which I thought clever and gave me confidence because it came unsought. But I polished it: 'brutish to the crackdome' . . . I was yet to learn that one of the women we used to call penguins that I could have passed on the footpaths of Greymouth on any day, the Sisters of Mercy whose clothes had once alarmed us, was James Joyce's sister.

At the end of that last year of dependence I wrote a 25,000 word piece of fiction, a hardly disguised autobiography of my first sixteen years. I didn't even change my name. There were three sections: Home, Heart, and School; it is clumsily written and quite often I use the wrong word. But there isn't any self-pity, not too much apologia, no posturing; it was an attempt at honesty and a farewell to childhood. I didn't read it again till recently and found it surprisingly painful to be reminded of the shames and hurts that memory had tidied away. I followed this with a shorter, more accomplished treatment of the same material, beginning with a section in baby talk, modelled on *A Portrait of the Artist as a Young Man*, but after a few episodes I ran out of interest, and reading it recently left me quite cold.

So in the summer when young men were whistling *Stardust* and *Deep Purple* and the war hadn't got really serious, I presented myself at Dunedin Training College, late and panting because I hadn't moved quickly enough when the bus pulled up at the Octagon. In those two years I changed my views more rapidly than at any other time. I arrived a conventional church-going small-town conformist, I left an agnostic left-wing pacifist. My literary aims also changed radically.

The seeds had been sown the year before at Canterbury University. The students' paper *Canta* was iconoclastic, Winston

Rhodes was repeatedly dislodging preconceptions. One day in a lecture he casually referred to Virginia Woolf as the greatest living English novelist. I had never heard of her. Archie Stockwell recommended Queenie Leavis's *Fiction and the Reading Public*, and I discovered five novelists whose work I didn't know and conscientiously set out to make up for my ignorance: Woolf, D.H. Lawrence, James Joyce, T.F. Powys and E.M. Forster. Mrs Leavis persuaded me I needn't read Galsworthy or Arnold Bennett. I read her select five with reverence and with an eye to what I might pick up for my own writing. In Archie Dunningham's Dunedin Public Library I haunted the shelf of new fiction. I took home *Finnegans Wake*, intrigued by its strangeness but unable to understand for more than a short stretch or two. I decided to adopt as my style the new 'stream of consciousness' as they called it, and saw it as the long-sought key to writing from my own experience. Virginia Woolf had shown that one could use the thoughts and impressions of one's own mind and make from them rhythmical, sprightly sentences, without having to stand over experience, comment, obtrude, moralise, as Dickens did. I went through a phase (already out of fashion in England if I had known) of dismissing Dickens as a sentimental caricaturist. Some day I would walk into the Caxton Press in Christchurch and surprise them with a novel in solemn stream of consciousness. I was encouraged by the discovery that a young Australian had just published a novel in that mode. I often looked into that novel at the shelf, but if I did take it home I must have found that I didn't understand it, because when I read *Happy Valley* many years later I didn't recognise more than I had learned from the dust jacket in 1940. For me interior monologue removed the demand on the writer to be too knowledgeable, it located experience in one person's mind set in a flux of time. Virginia Woolf's style seemed so usable for commonplace experience here and now in New Zealand. The sea off St Kilda, for example, quietly sparkling on a summer morning, or the progression of shadows in the folds of the foothills, the cropped and scruffy turf and the pocks and ledges of the hillside I was climbing at the end of exams, the shuddering of reflections on a West Coast lake recomposing after a launch had passed. For shadows and reflections, skies and sea, time and change. It didn't have to be all rural experience. For the training college annual magazine, at the end of the reports of the sports clubs, I wrote a Woolfish piece set in a city dancehall.

So from these modernist novelists, and from Forster's *Aspects of the Novel*, I developed a credo of fiction that would manage without more than the lightest sketch of a plot, that would concern itself with momentary impressions and moods, conveyed sensitively by a writer who kept in the background. Anything that drew attention to the writer's presence or threatened the illusion of immediacy was forbidden. So were coincidence and happy endings. The ultimate appeal was to Life. I hadn't yet tried to write a novel.

But I conscientiously sought experience. Over the next seven or eight years I worked for short spells as a railway surfaceman, tram conductor, night porter at a city hotel, hand on a gold dredge, trucker in a coal-mine, tar-sealer, rough painter for the public works, and seaman. Once in the middle of the night at Arthurs Pass or Otira I surprised the man who goes along the train tapping wheels (I was thinking of the brakeman who appears on the freight trains that Fainey McCreary rode in *The 42nd Parallel*) when I resolutely engaged him in a conversation about his work. I think I believed that sort of experience, in which I felt myself to be particularly lacking, to be of more value to me than other kinds.

I had two iconoclastic friends in my second year at college, whose worldliness would puncture my idealism. One of them, a graduate, had been editor of *Canta* when I was at Canterbury; he had the courage to go to gaol for his pacifist objection to military service. The other was married. He thought Virginia Woolf pretentious. 'Thomas Wolfe's your man!' But when I caught up with *Look Homeward, Angel* and *The Web and the Rock*, they weren't for me. My friend was also keen on Damon Runyon and I affected to see virtue there. But the American writer for whom I developed a passion no less keen than for Virginia Woolf was John Dos Passos, who seemed to me to have his eye calmly on the object, to describe (as Joyce said) what they said and what they did. I was very much aware, in those days of Leavis and Denys Thompson, of the misuse of language in advertising and propaganda, especially the war propaganda we were daily assailed with. I was very much aware of my own weakness for sentimentality and wish-fulfilment fantasy, the throbbing pulse that used to come at moments of recognition or reunion or reconciliation in those pretentious Warner Brothers films at the Regent Theatre in Greymouth, with maybe the Celestial Choir uplifting me against my will. Or the weakness I had, until I was introduced to Duke Ellington and hot jazz, for the popular songs of the day. Fantasy and self-indulgence were to be rejected and to discover reality was not only a duty but a challenge.

We had a lecturer in English, Elsie Barrowclough, who could talk about Eliot and Joyce even if she didn't care for them, and I was overjoyed once when I questioned our art lecturer, Gordon Tovey, in his use of 'literary' to mean 'fussy, with too much detail'. I said the literary could bring out the essence of things and his reply showed that he was familiar with Dos Passos. But the English II course at Otago University left me cold. After the Canterbury teachers the Otago staff seemed remote and unadventurous. The professor told us in his Scots accent that the course was confined to literature that had been tried and trued by the test of time. But I couldn't see that seventeenth century poetry or the Voyages of Ohthere had any bearing on my current problems.

In my undifferentiated embrace of the iconoclasm of the English twenties and thirties, I accepted the new liberalism in child education and was a ready convert to the ideas of A.S. Neill who seemed a champion of the oppressed, children who had been driven to rebellion by myopic adults. I was enthusiastic about my 'sections', spells of teaching experience in schools, but didn't know how to cope with a truculent class in North East Valley who had a teacher they didn't like. One of my sections I took at the Children's Library under the guidance of Dorothy Neal White and developed an enthusiasm for the new wave of children's books like *Ferdinand the Bull* (the bull who would rather smell flowers than fight) or *Babar the Elephant* and *Emil and the Detectives*. In our cyclostyled literary magazine *Venture*

I wrote an appreciation of a children's book by Gertrude Stein, *The World is Round*.

My immediate and pressing problem was to bring myself to publicly acknowledge my objection to killing for my country. At Arthur's Pass, crossing to the Coast one May holiday, I recognised my problem when I heard a Canterbury university student speaking to her companion about a brother or friend: 'He's going to *go*, and write about it afterwards—oppose war that way.' But that struck me as an evasion. I knew I would go to gaol if I refused to go into the army, but reading Koestler had prepared me for that. Yet I didn't have the courage to face the complete ostracism that I assumed would follow an outright refusal of service. My objections were not religious and listening to a session of the board that heard objectors' appeals had convinced me of their intolerance of objections based on humanitarian grounds. And I wasn't convinced that for me complete objection was right. Accusing myself of cowardice for compromising I decided to object only to combatant service. Even so I was aware of inconsistency in my position. Wouldn't serving in the Medical Corps make it easier for others to do the killing? And now that Russia was in the war didn't I want to see the Nazis defeated?

Blackball was more tolerant of a conchie teacher than a sheep-farmers' town would have been. I won my point: an army notice arrived directing me to report to the Medical Corps at Rakaia Military Camp. But it had been sent to a Dunedin address and reached me too late. I went immediately to the army office in Greymouth. The headmaster, who didn't like me, thought he had got rid of me and wired the Education Board for a replacement. The sergeant in the army office was brother of an old schoolmate and sent me back to Blackball with assurances that he would sort it out. He eventually phoned me and cleared it with me first that I would go into the Dental Corps as a dental orderly, an unexpectedly unglorious outcome of my objection. The Dental Corps operated in all three services and for the next two or three years I was at army camps and air force stations, for sixteen months at a flying-boat base in Fiji. When I got the chance I liked talking to Americans, I saw them through the eyes of their writers, and I was angry at the xenophobic hostility so many Kiwi servicemen felt for them.

In the army I re-thought my position and concluded I could no longer logically object to combatant service. So I made no objection when I was unexpectedly transferred to the infantry, and was a member of the last reinforcement to go to Egypt and Italy, and of the first party to go to Japan as part of the occupation force. At Ma'adi I saw a sergeant practicing with a flame-thrower and I asked myself, Would I be capable of using a weapon like that? For a cause that I believed in? But having thrown away the principle I couldn't come up with any answer that made me easy.

My five months in Blackball made a lasting impression and in the army I often thought of writing about it, perhaps one of those studies that see all the parts in relation to the whole, taking in geography, history, economic and social relations, in the style that I had admired in Lewis Mumford's books on technology and cities. Some years later I was to teach in the Canterbury sheepfarming town of Oxford, the model of H.C.D. Somerset's *Littledene*, but when I read *Littledene* it wasn't the sort of study of a small town that I had in mind.

Occasionally I would be moved to shut myself in the dental surgery on a Sunday and try a story. There was a satirical piece about a campaign by the government to persuade the troops to pay back their wages to win the war with. A cynical piece about a world-weary young idealist turned nihilist who throws himself over Highcliff, down into the heaving bullkelp, but has to get drunk first and in fact slips anyway. And a long travel diary of a journey around the main island of Fiji, part of which Ian Gordon used in *New Zealand New Writing*. I found I trusted myself better at sensitive observation than at sheer invention.

At some time in those years I came across the second piece of writing by a fellow New Zealander that I remember wanting to think about: the serial version of *That Summer* in *Penguin New Writing*. (The first was *Man Alone*.) I recognised the authoritative tone of a writer who can be trusted, but that colloquial style was not one I wanted to imitate. I at last found one or two novels by Faulkner, so often mentioned in literary discussion but so difficult to find in army libraries. The tragic novels of Thomas Hardy claimed me for a while. But the most exciting discovery, another literary passion as intense as for Woolf and Dos Passos, was Graham Greene, for his disenchanted knowledge of the world, his compassion, his faith and hope, and particularly for the narrative impetus, the desire to get on with the story. I would search the shelves of army libraries in the hope of finding a Greene that I hadn't read and was overjoyed if I did. I came to admire structure in a novel, for the first time since reading Dickens. I was later to see that plot could be more than a necessary frame: in works that moved me like *Wuthering Heights* or *King Lear* or Chaucer's *Troilus and Criseyde* the structure was part of the meaning.

It was in an army hospital in Japan that I had an unmistakable visitation from the muse. The war was finished and the New Zealand medical team moved out, and we patients were left to the culture shock of being immediately taken over by Australians. One night some Australian soldiers were casually reminiscing; one of them recalled an incident of rough justice at a camp at Flemington racecourse, when a soldier caught stealing from his mates was escorted to the top of a grandstand and told to jump. The cruelty nagged me, as if I were the victim. I felt I had to make my protest in a story. But of course I had never set foot on Australia, so instead I worked it out in a setting I knew, among kiwi soldiers in Italy. I lay awake chain-smoking most of the night, the staccato phrases came with rightness and clarity, and in the morning I only had to pull up my bed-tray and write the story from memory as if it was a letter home. Charles Brasch printed the story in an early *Landfall*. Not long later, out of hospital now, the first germ of *Coal Flat* came to me in the night, with far less certainty. It was to be about a sensitive young teacher, a follower of A.S. Neill faced with a problem child in an unsympathetic mining town, a man who has hardly admitted to himself that he is homosexual. He is falsely accused of a sexual offence against the boy and goes to gaol. Later I changed the outcome: he is cleared of the charge but in the course of his defence he has revealed enough about himself to make his return to the community more difficult than before. It was to be a very subjective novel full of anxiety and guilt. There were to be devices taken from Dos Passos: Camera's Eye sections in interior monologue and maybe, if that wouldn't be too pretentious, Newsreel sections made up of headlines and news-clips. I made a beginning in third person narrative in a style like Graham Greene. Over the next two or three years, back in New Zealand, teaching at a North Canterbury school or finishing a degree at Canterbury University, I kept planning this novel, arranging characters and plot. I accused myself of self-indulgence setting a novel in a mining town and leaving out the union. The conception changed and developed with my own changes in outlook through the fifties.

My long-term aim was to be a country teacher, but only as a base from which to write fiction. I didn't even think of full-time writing and I looked on newspaper journalism as death to original invention. The real New Zealand, it seemed, was in the country and more than once I felt remiss when I went in from Oxford to Christchurch for the weekend rather than to Rangiora for the A. & P. show or up to Lees Valley for all-day dog trials. Experience it might be, but I knew I would be bored. When the opportunity came to study in England I was in two minds because an academic career seemed no less a sentence of death to creative ability. Friends told me I belonged here and I decided to take up the scholarship but come back and take up country teaching again. I remember talking about this with Maurice Duggan in London, who argued that New Zealand was becoming more urbanised and urban settings would become more common. And after two springs in London with such pleasures as open-air Shakespeare in the long summer evenings, Margot Fonteyn in *Swan Lake*, French films at the Everyman, the *New Statesman* at any bookstall on the day of publication, the distinct procession of seasons and flowers, the generally expansive mood of those post-war years and the freedom from all the kiwi obsessions, I began to have doubts about wanting to return home at all. The problem drove me to look into myself and analyse what was different in my personal experience of New Zealanders and the English and in my own outlook and

habits of thought from those of the English, and so I wrote
'Fretful Sleepers', at the end of which I knew that I would go
back to New Zealand. That essay cleared the way for my novel,
which I dutifully put off until such time as I would have finished
my doctoral thesis. But I did relax one summer and write two
sections in which I felt the lightness of spirit breathing from old
readings of those writers who had fired me years before. But it
was my own style, or styles.

When I handed in the thesis there were three chapters of the
novel already written. I stayed home and wrote full-time until
my savings ran out. I covered ground quickly. In two months
I had written half the novel or more but I had to earn, and
found work as a supply teacher for the London County Council
relieving for absent teachers in inner-city schools. I was now
planning an optimistic ending. The undeclared deviant hero was
to be won to honest normality, but during a severe revision, one
summer vacation, I dropped the homosexual theme entirely. It
was something I couldn't handle without trying to write a kind
of novel I didn't want to write.

I read *Darkness at Noon* in 1941; after that I couldn't idealise
communism or imagine that human nature might improve in
a communist society. But I still looked for simple answers and
even seriously thought about, before turning against it, a book
called *The Machiavellians* by James Burnham who put forward
arguments, with which the world would soon become all too
familiar, that in the cause of anti-communism no tactic was to
be considered morally objectionable. Greene started me on a
sentimental and fashionable interest in Catholicism. For me it
was nostalgia for certainties no longer available, and I had to
recognise that in fact I didn't believe the doctrine. I was reading
St Teresa for my thesis (on nineteenth century English Catholic
poets) and her experiences of rapture seemed remarkable but of
little relevance to our time (though in one draft of my novel I
tried to give them to Miss Dane who went into a convent). But
the event that brought me back to the mid-twentieth century
was the outbreak of the Korean War which shook my faith in
the United States government's concern for peace and made me

fear that we would have to choose between two evils. I had no doubt that American foreign policy was a greater danger to the world than that of the communist countries who needed peace and whose internal policies carried the possibility of revision, especially now that China had become communist. But I was saved the impossible choice by the birth of the peace movement which raised the hope that people all over the world might put pressure on their governments to agree to live together. I began to read the *Daily Worker* as well as the *Times*. I lost contact with contemporary new fiction, especially American. It is common to see the fifties through the eyes of the Beats as a decade of suburban complacency but for me they were a time of constant political involvement. For the whole time that I was engaged in writing and revising my novel I was also signing petitions, attending meetings, sitting on committees, marching or demonstrating against the Korean War and the atrocities with napalm and flame-throwers that Wilfred Burchett was reporting from North Korea, against the cold war and violent children's comics, against apartheid and McCarthyism and the execution of the Rosenbergs; and for peaceful coexistence and nuclear disarmament. I addressed envelopes for the Authors' World Peace Appeal, of which a number of prominent writers were signatories, I belonged to and edited the house organ for a group of Australians and New Zealanders concerned for civil liberties in their own countries, I wrote the London notes for Bob Lowry's *Here and Now*, I agreed to go to North Korea with a students' delegation that was in the end cancelled. I was a member of Teachers for Peace, the Hampstead Peace Council, and I went as New Zealand delegate to a congress of the World Peace Council at Budapest in June 1953. At the end of the decade I was involved in the Auckland equivalent of C.N.D., collected signatures against an All Black visit to South Africa and was an internal rapporteur at a conference of Maori leaders.

The conference at Budapest gave me insights that could not be more than hinted at or implied in a novel that I had long decided to anchor in 1947, but more than one revision was needed before it conformed with those new impressions of the way the world was developing or the way my reception of those

impressions would change before I was satisfied with what I
was to write. There were so many Latin American delegates, so
many monks in saffron robes from South-east Asia. We learned
that Indo-China was three countries with unfamiliar names and
separate delegations. A delegate from Vietnam read a poem of
Ho Chi Minh. Zhou Enlai addressed us. We sat under Picasso's
dove and we had, or I think we had, the blessing if not the
presence of Sartre. There were several writers from communist
countries, only names to me—Seghers, Surkov, Ehrenburg,
and many others whose reputation was confined to their own
country, like the benign Hungarian peasant writer in leather
leggings who, at a function for writers, asked a Mexican what
he thought of a novel about Mexico he had once read by the
Englishman Lawrence. There was an atmosphere of civilised
exchange about the gathering.

At least at times . . . An Egyptian speaker refused to shake
hands with an Israeli delegate who had come up to congratulate
her. The committee decided that this was one of those minor
enmities that had to be tolerated in the interest of wider
agreement . . . A white South African clergyman said he couldn't
in conscience vote for a motion that spoke of 'the people of our
countries' rather than 'the majority of the people' because there
were many white people in his country who would not agree
with it, but a Guyanese delegate said that those people were
not the people . . . The freckle-faced woman from California,
tall and slim, brought the house down when she enunciated, as
neatly as a syllogism, the sentiments we wanted to hear but knew
to be not quite true: 'the Korean people don't want them there,
the American people don't want them to be there, *they* don't
want to *be* there!' . . . On the wide balcony, on the afternoon of
amplifiers and the huge public rally in the square, the decorated
Stakhanovite steel worker, big and bald, laid a finger along his
nose when he met the other American delegate, a matron with
her hair in immaculate waves. She asked him angrily what that
was for, he said it was for Eisenhower . . . There was a conceited
apparatchik, a Londoner called David Gould say, picking up
the phone in his best French, abstractedly plucking cherries
from a bowl (compliments of the People's Government) without

noticing those who had appointments with him (an Indian delegate just got up and helped himself) who told me they would have to cut my speech to three minutes. I supposed that because they reached decisions by consensus they wanted everybody to say the same thing, especially someone from a little country like mine. It seemed odd that the leading men of the British delegation were anxious when I was invited by the Hungarian Peace Council to stay another week, and they tried very hard to persuade me not to accept.

I was sometimes paired with a Burmese delegate, a shy and staid married woman, but I spent time socially with the Australians. The man I spoke to most freely was an Irish writer Peadar O'Donnell, a very humane man. I didn't know he had been going since the Troubles of 1922 or that he had been to Spain in the late thirties, but he told me he had wandered about the city for long enough to notice that working women coming from the food shops weren't happy with their ration of bread. He was sitting on a bench when a half-paralysed elderly man engaged him in conversation, a dismissed history professor who told him he looked forward to the day the Americans would liberate them. We were both shocked that he could welcome a war against his own people. We didn't know that the shiny copper statue of a fatherly Stalin on the other side of the Danube would be pulled down in three years. But when we went strolling on the Sunday morning we at least satisfied ourselves that nobody was following us and that at the cathedral the people were freely going to mass. The composition of the crowd at an eleven o'clock service, my companion said, was the same as you would see in Dublin at the same time . . . It was meant as a compliment two or three weeks later, back teaching in a London school, when a woman teacher who took the *Daily Worker* and looked on me as an ally told me I was the spitting image of David Gould.

Home again, I distrusted the country that had re-elected the Prime Minister who had ruled with his own variant of fascism during the waterfront dispute of 1951, and I associated with left-wingers and communists. For a couple of years I edited the Peace Council's monthly *Peace*, advocating recognition of

communist China and getting out of SEATO. I was invited to
sit in on one session of a national conference of the Communist
Party and one of the hierarchy wanted me to join. But the more
I saw of the incessant heresy-hunting they practised in the name
of self-criticism and was made party to the knowledge of who
was in, who was out, and as I found myself conniving in their
mental dishonesties, the more I was determined to avoid their
own fate. Events saved me a showdown. When Russian troops
entered Hungary in 1956 I was one of those on the committee
of the New Zealand Peace Council responsible for a telegram
of protest to the Soviet Peace Council. In their party my several
communist acquaintances took their places on one side or other
of a series of expulsions and schisms that was to go on for years.
When it started up I moved into the less political CND, and in
a mood of wonder discovered I could learn a lot from Maori
students and the rural communities they took me to.

I turned again to the long put aside further revision of my
novel, finished and typed before I had left England. I had
been unhappy with it for a long time. I discarded some facile
optimism, rewrote some political episodes and re-thought the
closing chapters. It was twelve years since I first conceived that
story of a young idealist crushed by a materialist community.
As time went on I had found the young man less interesting
than the community. I had put him at an increasing distance
from myself, taken away from him those problems for which I
couldn't find a convincing resolution and given him hopes and
beliefs in common with the community. At the end I wanted
to leave him the possibility of self-fulfilment. It was a Koestler
novel *Arrival and Departure* that gave me the idea of ending
on an echo of the opening. For me the novel ends in faith and
hope. I have been told that the last sentence is bleak and laconic,
where a local resident looks forward to as good a summer as
the Coast has ever had, but those who think so don't know that
the West Coast has had some really good summers. The novel
opens with one.

EMILY PERKINS

Not Her Real Name

Mud in your pretty eye

Nine years later, you're leaving a bar with a friend and you see him across the wet road, getting on to a bus. From then, from the restaurant.

Francis

You always thought, Francis, rhymes with answers. Which it doesn't, really. But you'd change the s of answers to be soft like his name. Francis, Francis, there's no answers. It was a walking rhyme. A home from the bus-stop rhyme. The rhyme of a fifteen-year-old girl who could feel sad every time she thought of that soft s.

Hands in gloves in the hot water in the sink, you'd turn around and be surprised again, every time, when you saw his face. His eyes crinkled up and were almost lost when he laughed. His laugh was nearly silent and you tried to match it. You and your friend Thea had developed the habit of snorting whenever you laughed. You tried desperately to curb this around him. At the restaurant. You never thought of it as going to work, you thought of it as going to see Francis. You barely remembered that you were a dishwasher.

Brideshead Revisited was on television at the time.

You were not your usual self around Francis. None of the cackle, the shrieking, the tough-girl acts that you and Thea lurched around school and town with. You shrank, you backed off, you revealed nothing. If you smiled it was anxiously, if you spoke it was so softly that people said What? Eh? Speak louder. You were in love with this feeling of self-consciousness. You wanted so much that the constant holding of breath could bring tears to your eyes. The only freedom you allowed yourself was imaginary. Elaborate fantasies you dared yourself to get lost in while Francis banged in and out of the kitchen, carrying plates, scraping them, arguing with the chef. You thought maybe your

431

daydreams would be strong enough that he could read your mind, would look at you, know, love you. Or maybe your body would reach out, involuntarily, necessarily, and save itself on his thin arms. This never happened, of course. You were fifteen. Nothing ever did.

Very thin, with wispy kind of no-colour hair, not tall, pale, dark circled eyes, cheekbones. Cheekbones. Every angle you yourself did not possess was there in his cheekbones. You can't even remember the colour of his eyes. Probably blue, some cold colour. He dressed like he knew nothing about fashion and cared even less. You loved this gap in his knowledge, this laziness, this flaw. You thought nobody else could see how beautiful he was.

What happened was entirely predictable, though you never predicted it. After you'd been at the restaurant for four months, Francis left. He had exams at university and he quit his waitering job. You didn't even know it was going to happen until he said Last fucking time I have to serve up this shit. What? you asked but nobody heard you. Why? and you felt your eyes get hot and you felt dizzy and you felt like running out, now, or saying You're wrong, making a mistake, it's me I'm here, you can't, no. But the same thing happened, nothing. Nothing at all. And he left, he smiled your way and left, and you stayed on through the summer until March when your family moved to Auckland.

*

Art class

Hey Cody

How are you? I miss you. How's Auckland? Things here are OK. I want to leave school but not allowed. Mum's spazzing out because I told her I quit smoking—stupid—then she found a packet in my room. I miss you. Julie's OK but she never wants to wag school to watch *Prisoner*. There was a drug raid last week and Robert Stone got caught with an ounce in his locker. His dad is really pissed off because he's a cop and he caught Robert once before. Sucked. I can't wait for the August holidays. When are you coming to stay? Are there any OK guys at your school? GROSS the art teacher Mr O'Donnell just came over to see what I was doing, we call him Stiff O'Donnell because he gawks at the girls all the time he is so disgusting, plus he says Far Out all the time like he thinks he's really cool or something What A Dick. Anyway, the mid-year dance is on next week, I'm gonna go. I asked Celia Fox if she wants to go with me. I really like her. Is that weird? I mean, I don't think it is, well I do a bit, but—does it weird you out? I don't really want to be a Lesbian or anything, god I hate that word, but I never felt anything the whole time I went out with Paul, I mean he was a useless kisser but I think even if he wasn't I still would have felt nothing. I guess I like girls more than boys. Well that's OK, I'm not gonna get too freaked out, write back soon and tell me what you think. I've got this great dress to wear, it's purple kind of plasticky stuff, quite short, Mum'll spew. Yuck Stiff O'Donnell is perving I better go. Tell me what you think.

love Thea

PS she said yes

*

It took Cody two weeks to answer Thea's letter. She started about four before she made it sound all right. What really worried her, though, was something she couldn't say in a letter. In the August holidays, she went down to stay with Thea, who was going out with Celia Fox by now, and looking forward to term three starting so they could be the scandal of the school. Cody and Thea got Celia, a seventh former, to buy them some wine one night and they went and drank it in the park. Celia went home for dinner and Cody and Thea sat on the swings, talking. Thea told Cody that just because she liked girls, it didn't mean she was attracted to her. Cody was hugely relieved. Then Thea said not to assume that she wasn't, either, and started laughing so hard she nearly fell off her swing, which did big loopy curves out over the grass. Cody laughed too and swung her swing higher and they spent the rest of the evening there winding each other up and enjoying it more than they ever had before.

This is years ago now. Cody remembers it when Thea rings her up to tell her she's met a new woman. Her name is Thea too. Cody thinks this is very bizarre and one of the hazards of having same-sex relationships. She doesn't want to say this though in case Thea thinks she's been uptight about the whole thing all along.

—Imagine a couple both called Thea, says Thea. —Isn't it awful? One of the hazards of same-sex relationships, I suppose.

—Do you and Thea want to come for dinner this week? asks Cody.

*

Thea & Cody on August holidays

It was the boat sheds
in winter
& we ran out of
that terrible play

the invitation read
danger
no climbing
on roof

we'd have slept there
we said, passing
a joint
between us

before the rain started
dreaming California

*

What happens next

The Saturday after Cody sees Francis at the bus-stop, she goes to a party with Thea and Thea. It's a long time since Cody's been to a party. This one is in a warehouse off Cuba Street. There is a DJ playing reggae music and a lot of white people dancing to it. Cody is glad she brought her whisky.

—Something something KITCHEN something, shouts Thea at Cody.

—WHAT, shouts Cody, —WHERE?

She follows Thea into a small, brightly lit converted office. There is a bench, a sink and a stove-top element thing over which knives are heating. Thea helps herself to a bottle of wine left by somebody. Three people leave, shutting the door. It is much quieter.

—Thank fuck, says Thea, —I've got to talk to you. I think Thea's having an affair with a cycle courier.

—Oh no, says Cody. She lights a cigarette. —Male or female?

—Female, says Thea. —Which is worse, I think.

—Are you sure it's happening? asks Cody.

—No, well I am, I haven't asked her, but you know she'll only lie anyway, I'm pretty sure oh shit Code I'll really miss her if we break up.

—Now hang on, hang on, says Cody. She passes Thea a paper napkin to wipe her face. She goes round the corner of the table to hug Thea and as she does the door opens and Francis walks into the room.

—Sorry, says Francis. —Bad timing. Hi.

It's a question really, he's not sure that he knows her, or if he does, from where. A lot of people are looking familiar to him these days. But he's interrupted something so he's just going to grab a plastic cup and leave.

—Wasn't that —starts Thea, wiping her nose on the lining of her suede jacket.

—Mm? says Cody. —Who? Do you want to go now?

—No, says Thea. —I don't want to leave Thea here. That cycle bitch might show. Can I have some lipstick? They spend

a minute putting Thea back together again and then walk out
to the party. Thea finds Thea and they dance while Cody walks
over to the window not looking for Francis.

He finds her anyway, and this is what he says.

—Leo Tolstoy and his brother believed anything they wished
would come true if they could stand in a corner and not think
of a white bear.

Cody feels her rib cage expand, contract, expand, contract.
She lights another cigarette off the butt of the one she's just
smoked. She has a mouthful of whisky, making sure not to spill
any down her chin. Her hands shake. She tightens her grip on
the windowsill.

—I know you from somewhere, he says.

—Um, says Cody, —I think we might have worked in the
same restaurant once, ages ago now, about ten years ago or
something, is your name Francis?

—Yeah. He smiles. —What's yours again?

—Cody, says Cody.

—What? says Francis.

—Cody, she says again, hating this. —C–O–D–Y.

—Cody? he says.

—Yeah. She's feeling sick now even without the whisky,
wondering where her personality's gone. She could have sworn
she had it on her when she left the house.

—Visions of Cody, he smiles.

—Yeah, says Cody. —I never read it yet.

For a while they stand there at the window next to each other
not saying anything. Cody looks around the room at the other
women there. They all look completely gorgeous. She glances
carefully over at Francis. He's looking straight ahead, sucking
the rim of his plastic cup with red wine in it. Cody realises with
relief that she is bored, and walks away.

But here she is now at the end of the party and there's only a
handful of people left. Thea and Thea have gone home. The
cycle courier never showed up. Cody is talking to a red-haired
woman about Virginia Woolf and trying to sound informed but
not pretentious while keeping Francis in her peripheral vision.

She got Thea to make some enquiries for her earlier on and found out he's not with anyone, he just got back from overseas. Which potentially places him in a high-risk category but at least he's available. Cody can't get over how he looks exactly the same. She's not sure whether this is good or bad.

—Ugh, said Thea, —He looks like he crawled out from under a rock. I thought you'd gotten over that Brideshead cheekbone thing.

—I did, said Cody. —I did get over it.

Cody sees him going for his coat and manages to look as if she got up to leave first. There is an art to this manoeuvre and she has to concentrate hard, which is not easy after three and a half hours of whisky and forty-five minutes of leftover beer.

She hears him behind her on the stairs. Once she's outside she stops and looks up at the stars. The night is clear and very cold. She is wide awake. She looks at him, surprised. She smiles.

—Hi, he says.

—Hi.

They walk together down the street, hands in pockets, ears ringing from the music. Everything else is still. They reach the taxi stand.

In the taxi he asks her if she wants to go back to his place. She can't believe it's been this easy. She says OK, still looking surprised, smiling a small smile.

Actually it's not his place, it's his brother's who's away for the weekend. This is a further stroke of luck. Cody does not like to encounter strange flatmates in the morning. The mornings are awkward enough as it is. Francis pours them each a glass of wine and puts a record on. He touches Cody's face. He says, —I remember you.

They go to bed.

—Well, says Thea the next day, —how was it?

—Good, says Cody. —I think. I can't remember much.

—So, says Thea, —what happens next?

*

Swimming back upstream

but here's a
new mark

on my
white flesh

fingers
or mouth

have
bruised it fresh

and I want
to laugh

and I want
to run

and I want to
show you

what you
have done

                              *

In case INTERVIEW ever wants to know

Because there are at least eight other things she should be doing,
Cody spends the afternoon compiling the guest list for her Ideal
Dinner Party. She has a strong sense that, although she's only a
waitress right now, some day magazines will want to know this
kind of information from her. Her Desert Island Discs; Night-
Table Reading; Who Is The Sexiest Man In Politics, etc.

   She decides to limit herself to six guests, three of each
sex. She starts with Susan Sarandon. Susan is one of Cody's

favourite actresses and it's apparent that not only is she talented and beautiful, she's also a smart political thinker. Plus she's played a lot of waitresses. Cody feels Susan will be an excellent contributor to dinner party conversation.

> Susan Sarandon
> Al Gore

Al Gore? He *is* the Sexiest Man In Politics, but maybe a little earnest. Cody's unsure how his environmental stance will suit the style of evening she wants—sharp, funny, an element of risk. Leave him in for the time being. But no Tipper.

That couple the film *Lorenzo's Oil* was about. Real people who changed the world through love and determination. Whoa, then Susan will be at dinner with the woman she played in a movie. Does it matter? Are there too many Americans so far?

Mother Teresa?—maybe not.

It disturbs Cody how hard she's having to think about this. You'd imagine it would be easy enough to rattle off six heroes from the top of your head. But it involves more than that. It involves balance, precision, a successful dynamic. Cody's disappointed she can't think of more famous people in Science, or Classical Music. What about Anita Hill? She's another American, true, but she'd definitely get on well with Susan. Maybe Al could do something nasty to Clarence Thomas on her behalf. Does Al have anything to do with the Supreme Court? Surely he's got some influence.

> Susan Sarandon
> Al Gore
> *Lorenzo's Oil* couple
> ~~Mother Teresa~~
> Anita Hill

The couple from *Lorenzo's Oil* are standing on shaky ground. What Cody needs now is a man. Someone older perhaps, erudite, charming, powerful. Someone witty and wise who can offer the benefit of experience. Someone Al could learn from, and the others could be grateful to have had the opportunity to meet. In literature? Politics? Prince Rainier? Gore Vidal? Gielgud?

On the other hand, Cody does need someone to help with the dishes. And there's always the possibility of one last drink, a walk by the sea, an undeniable electric attraction that demands to be fulfilled—

> Susan Sarandon
> Al Gore
> ~~Lorenzo's Oil couple~~
> ~~Mother Teresa~~
> Anita Hill
> Daniel Day-Lewis
> Brad Pitt
> Johnny Depp

*

The weekend after Francis, Cody and Thea go to breakfast. They try and figure out which of the couples surrounding them just met the night before. Cody needs to talk about Francis.

—I can't stop thinking about him, she says.

—That's bad, says Thea.

—I know.

—You need to fuck someone else.

—Who? says Cody, looking around the room.

—Anyone, Thea says. —There are other guys. Anyone. Just don't obsess about thingy.

—Francis.

—Francis. What kind of a name is that for a guy?

—I am obsessing, aren't I? Cody slops her coffee into the saucer.

—Yes, says Thea.

—I'm enjoying it. I can't help it. I'm out of control.

—Crap, says Thea.

Their food arrives. Cody wonders if the waiter is attractive enough to sleep with. She decides that he isn't.

—And, she says, —I keep remembering things.

Thea sighs. —Spare me the details.

—No, but, like the mascara.

—What?

—Well, says Cody, There was this mascara on his bedside table. Do you think he's a cross-dresser?

—Were there any feather boas lying around?

—No. Um, I don't think so.

—Cody you moron. He's not a cross-dresser, he's got a fucking girlfriend.

—But you said he was single, Cody says, feeling a tantrum coming on.

—Well I don't know for sure. But make-up is a sure sign of a girlfriend.

—Oh.

—Either that or he's a New Romantic.

—I'd rather he had a girlfriend.

—What are you going to do tonight.

—Get drunk.

—And?

—And fuck someone else.

—Good girl.

*

Regarding Francis

I sit in my room
thinking & smoking
thinking & smoking &
whisky all day

I want to write a story
about a man I met
met & went to bed with
went to bed with & left

But it's raining & cold
& the sky is all grey

the words are too hard
the memories not old

there's something there's something
it's too hard to say

*

How do I love thee?

It's coming up to Thea and Thea's four year anniversary.
Cody goes shopping on Saturday morning for a present. She
looks at matching bath robes, matching latte bowls, matching
photograph frames. All these are too expensive. She settles for
bath oil. As she watches the shop assistant wrapping it, she feels
a fist of envy clench in her stomach. She snatches the parcel
from across the counter and shoves it deep into her bag. She
forgets about it until Thea comes around that night. There's
been a fight.

It goes like this.

Thea and Thea are having breakfast. Thea wants to go for a
walk to Cody's place. She rings and gets the answerphone but
decides to go anyway. She needs to get out of the house.

—I'm going for a walk, she tells Thea.

Thea looks up from her toast. —Do you love me?

—I love you darling, says Thea, putting on her sunglasses.

—Good.

—*Were* you seeing that cycle courier? asks Thea, smiling.

—Thea. Please.

—Were you? she asks, standing in the kitchen doorway now,
leaning against the doorframe, casual.

—No. Of course not. God.

—OK, says Thea, —I'm going for a walk now.

She doesn't move from the doorway.

Thea gets up and starts clearing the table. —I love you, Thee,
she says.

—Thee, thou, thine, says Thea from the doorway.

Thea giggles. —With all my worldly goods I Thee endow.

—Were you? asks Thea again.

—What? says Thea, scrubbing bacon grease off the grill.

—You did, didn't you, says Thea, clinging to the doorframe now, her fingernails picking at the paint. —You did fuck her. I'm not stupid.

—Thea, says Thea, warning.

—She's a bimbo, you know that?

—Leave it alone, says Thea, pushing past Thea to the living-room.

—I'm going for a walk now, Thea calls after her.

She and Cody go to a movie that night. Thea cries loudly through most of it. When the lights go on at the end her face is red and puffy.

—Can I stay at your place tonight? she asks Cody.

—No, says Cody, —go and make up with Thea. Here, she remembers, fishing in her bag, —give her this. I bought it for both of you.

—Are you sure? says Thea. She might not want to talk to me.

—One way to find out, says Cody.

She leaves Thea at a taxi stand and walks home alone as the rain starts to spit under the streetlights.

*

Cody makes sure

There's nothing more boring than people telling you their dreams. God, no. Anyone'll tell you that. And everyone thinks their dreams must be the most interesting, the most symbolic, the best evidence of their inner complexity. Jesus, the number of people who would never tell you about their sex lives but go on about their dreams all day long. It's daytime, for Christ's sake! Wake up! Nobody cares! Besides, there's only about seven dreams really, that just slip from head to head in the night. Tramps.

I'm having a baby
My teeth are crumbling

Wow, I can fly
I'm having sex with
   a) person you find repulsive
   b) person you're related to
   c) person you thought you'd gotten over by now
I'm having sex with
   a) man of your dreams
   b) woman of your dreams
   c) animal of your dreams (surely not)
I'm driving a car and it's out of control
I'm on stage naked, late, and I don't know my lines.

So, dreams are something I've vowed never to talk about. I'm not going to bore you stupid with my extended nightly soap opera. There's just one thing I want to be clear about, though: I have never, *ever* dreamed about Francis. Ever.

*

The ditch

It's been a rocky week. On Tuesday, Thea announced to Cody that she and Thea are splitting up. She's worried that they're becoming co-dependent—whatever *that* means.

—It's that four year thing, said Thea.

—Um, said Cody, who can't remember having a relationship that's lasted more than four weeks.

And then Thea said she was going to Sydney in a month.

—To live?

—Yup.

—You're fucking joking.

—Nup.

Thea will stay with her cousin until she can get a job and a place of her own. She's serious about leaving. Cody does not welcome this piece of news.

—How fantastic. I'm so jealous, you'll have such a great time.

—Yeah, I'm a bit nervous.

—Oh you'll be fine. I better start saving so I can visit.

Cody spends that evening going over her bank statements and crying. She has fifty-four dollars and the rent's due this week. She doesn't understand why she's a waitress. She doesn't understand anything anymore. She goes to the bottle store and buys a twenty-eight dollar bottle of vodka.

Wednesday, Thursday and Friday Cody says she's busy whenever Thea calls. On Saturday morning Thea turns up with a bunch of grapes.

—I'm not sick, says Cody.

—Why are you avoiding me? asks Thea.

—I'm not.

—Cody.

—What? What? There's nothing going on.

—You're mad at me.

—I'm not.

The kettle whistles and overflows.

—Fucking screaming noise, says Cody.

Thea turns the kettle off and makes tea.

—OK, says Cody, —I hate you. You're leaving.

—I'll miss you, says Thea. —Just don't ruin this last bit.

—Christ Thea. Why is it so hard for me to let people go?

—I don't know, darling. But you'd better get over it.

That night Cody dreams she is a little girl again.

*

Tender callus

talked all night
drank till four
taxi to somewhere
clothes hit the floor

sighing & laughing
ten years isn't much
again & again &
touch touch touch

so tender he says
like sirloin she smiles
sun too bright to sleep
is callousness guile

yes Francis Francis
there's no words to say
just take me to somewhere
I'd better not stay

*

Cody shows Gene, the cook where she works, the ad she's put
in the paper.

Flatmate wanted
7b Hunter St
Sat-Sun
$50pw No pets

—You're mad, says Gene. —You're going to have to stay home
all weekend and you could get any kind of freak coming round.
You should've just put your phone number.
—Been cut off, says Cody. —Where's the pepper grinder?
—Are you looking for a male or female? asks Gene.
—Don't care really, says Cody. —I just need the money. It'll
probably be a disaster whatever sex they are.
—That's the spirit, says Gene. —Take that soup now and the
fish'll be ready when you come back.

Cody knows she shouldn't be so negative about sharing her
flat. She's taken her desk and an armchair out of the sunroom.
There's just enough room for a double bed and a small chest of

drawers. She vacuumed for the first time in about a month and scrubbed the bath. The *Woman's Weekly*s are hidden under her bed and a couple of Kundera books are lying casually on the kitchen table. She wonders what she's trying to prove. She feels her misplaced pride dragging her around the house trying to create an image of a fabulous self-sufficient working woman. She buys fresh flowers. This is exhausting.

—See you Monday, she says to Gene at the end of the night.
    —Good luck, says Gene. —Hope you don't get any psychos.

*

The gentleman caller

All Saturday Cody waits at home for prospective flatmates to call around. It rains, and she plays patience and looks at the dead telephone. No one comes.
    On Sunday she wakes up in the afternoon with a hangover. She thinks, fuck this. She leaves a note on the door and goes to the market. Coming back up her path as dark is falling, she sees someone standing in her doorway trying to read the note. She calls out, —Hi. She runs up the steps to the door. It's Francis.
    She feels her tongue dry in her mouth. She can't swallow. She doesn't trust herself to speak. He looks terrified. He speaks.
    —I'm sorry I didn't call you.
    —I didn't give you my phone number.
    —Um.
    —Uh—
    Cody can't find her key. She considers running back down the path, leaving Francis on the doorstep in the dark.
    —Should I come in?
    —Uh. Sure, I'll just—here it is—uh —
    She follows him inside, turning on the lights. They stand stuck in the narrow hallway. Cody doesn't want to squeeze past Francis and he's not going anywhere on his own.
    —Have you had many people through? he asks, and she

realises he is here for the flat, there's no mistake, he hasn't tracked her down, sought her out, found her. He's looking for somewhere to live.

—No, she says. —None, I mean, so far. You're the first.

—Oh. Really?

—Yeah, well, it's been raining, so—

—Right. Um, it seems really nice. Is this, um, the room here?

He gestures to the sunroom door on his right.

—Yeah that's it, Cody says, not opening the door. —I've been here on my own, you know, I much prefer it. But um, I need the money, I'm trying to save.

—Oh yeah? How much is the room again?

—Fifty a week.

—That's really good for so central. I mean, I haven't got a lot of money, fifty's really good.

—Do you work? asks Cody.

—Yeah, at a second-hand bookshop in town.

—Oh.

—You're a waitress, right?

—Yeah. Uh, so this is the bathroom—

Cody shows Francis around her flat, surreptitiously checking herself in every reflective surface. How can this be happening? A second-hand bookshop? Jesus Christ almighty. Jesus Christ alfuckingmighty.

—Oh and that's my room, she says, flicking her hand in the direction of her closed bedroom door. —And this is the kitchen.

—Gas oven, great. Oh, Kundera. You like him?

—Mm.

—Can I see the room that's going?

—Oh sure, sorry, here—

They stand in the empty sunroom, looking out at the night. Cody is struggling to find an etiquette for this situation. Why is he still here? Why hasn't she just said, Look I'm sorry what a silly mistake, I don't need a flatmate anymore, I'm moving in with my boyfriend, we're in love you know, he's asked me to marry him . . . Shit. Shit fuck.

—Well look, says Francis, —I really like this place. So, um—

—Right.

—Do you need someone in a hurry.

—Yeah I do really, the phone's been cut off, and—

—Oh.

Well that was clever, Cody tells herself. Bang goes your escape route. And now you look like an idiot who can't manage money. You *are* an idiot who can't manage money. Gross financial mismanagement, that's what got you into this mess.

—Um, well I need somewhere straight away, Francis is saying. —My brother's fed up with me sleeping on his couch.

—So that wasn't your —Cody immediately regrets the reference to that night.

—Um no, it was my brother's um room.

—Oh right.

The image Cody has been carrying around with her of Francis's girlfriend putting on mascara while Francis watches from the bed vanishes.

—Look, she says, —Do you think—

—I guess it does look like a fairly foolish idea.

—Foolish. Mm.

—Well, says Francis, —you're desperate for a flatmate—

I'm not desperate for anything thanks very much, thinks Cody.

—And, he continues, —I really need somewhere cheap and central—

That's me, thinks Cody, cheap and central.

—Also, he says, —I am the only person who's come to look.

—Well, says Cody, —I'm working nights at the moment.

—And I work days, so we wouldn't even need to see each other.

—Yeah . . . says Cody.

—Oh, says Francis, —do you smoke?

—I've just given up, says Cody. —I can't really afford it.

—Well I'm asthmatic.

—Oh right, says Cody, trying not to smirk.

—Well I'm willing to forget what happened between us, says Francis. —I think we could be mature about this, don't you?

—Oh of course, says Cody. —Absolutely. No, it wouldn't be an issue.

—So what do you think?

Cody hates being asked this question.

—Um, she says, —sure. I mean, if you like the room—sure.

—I could move my stuff in tomorrow while you're at work.

—OK, fine.

—Could you leave a key in the letterbox?

—OK, sure.

—Great, says Francis, heading for the door. —Great, I'll see you tomorrow then, probably.

—OK, says Cody, —uh, see you.

She closes the door behind him, feeling dazed and a bit giddy. She waits to make sure he's got down the road and gets her coat and some money and goes to a phone box to call Thea.

—Code, says Thea, —are you sure you know what you're doing? You sound dangerously excited. Are you smiling?

—No, says Cody, —I'm not, I'm quite rational about this, it'll be fine.

—You *are* smiling, says Thea. —I can hear it. And you're smoking. I thought you gave up.

—Just one, says Cody. —I bludged it off the guy at the bottle store. Do you think I'm crazy?

—Yes, says Thea, —I think you're an idiot.

—I am, aren't I? says Cody. —But I don't care.

—Just don't have sex with him again, says Thea.

—Of course not, says Cody. —Of course not. I'm not that stupid.

—Oh Jesus, says Thea, —would you just stop smiling?

*

Cutting Francis's hair. We sat on the steps out the front of the house. It was the first sunny weekend in a couple of weeks. I had a comb, a bowl of water, and the kitchen snips. Francis had a towel around his neck. There was music playing and the front door was open and I thought, This is it. This is it. Francis's skull was warm under my hands. He was telling some funny story about the bookshop and I was laughing and I snorted and I didn't care. He leant back against my knees and I must have lost concentration because I cut his ear. He kind of yelped and there was a lot of blood, more than seemed natural, and I couldn't stop laughing. This was the wrong thing to do. He jumped up and knocked over the bowl of water and it ran down the steps looking dark and red in the sun. He ran into the house to get a sticking plaster and tripped over because the dark inside was such a contrast to the winter brightness and he couldn't see. I stayed on the steps, squinting, feeling guilty for not feeling guilty. Francis came blinking back outside and I apologised. He wouldn't let me near him again with the scissors. I didn't point out that I'd only finished cutting one side.

*

Flood

In the third week after Francis moved in, there is a terrible rainstorm. It starts on Wednesday night and keeps coming all day Thursday. When Francis gets home from work on Thursday evening he discovers that the sunroom roof is leaking and his bedroom's flooded.

—Bloody hell, he says, standing in the middle of his damp rug.

—Bloody hell. His voice gets louder. —Bloody bloody *bloody.*

—You sound like my father, Cody says, coming into Francis's room.

—It's bloody soaked, says Francis, his voice under control again. —It's leaking all over the bloody place. Look.

—Oh shit, says Cody. —Whoops.

—What do you mean? says Francis. —Did you know about this?

—No, says Cody, —Of course not. I just mean, you know, bummer.

—Bummer, says Francis. —Bummer? Look at this. Bummer? It's fucked. It's soaked. My bed —He goes to his bed and wrings out a corner of the sheet, —my bed is fucking soaking. Where am I going to sleep?

As soon as the question is out there they both avoid looking at each other. Cody backs out of Francis's room and down the hall.

—Well, she calls from the kitchen, opening and closing cupboard doors, not looking for anything, just needing the covering noise, —You could always stay in my room. I won't be home till late.

—Uh, calls Francis from his room, pulling his bed out from the wet wall, —yeah. Well I might have to.

—That's fine, calls Cody. —I'm going to work now—um, see you later.

—Bye, Francis mutters. —Bloody, *bloody* hell.

Francis drags his mattress onto its side and turns the heater towards it. He checks it every fifteen minutes. It's getting drier, but not dry enough.

Cody stays after work for a special coffee with Gene.
    —Go easy on the brandy, says Gene. —Cigarette?
    —Love one, says Cody. —Thanks.

When Cody gets home the lights are all out. She opens her bedroom door quietly. Francis is in the bed, on his side, asleep. She gets her T-shirt and goes to change in the bathroom.

Francis opens his eyes. He hears Cody brushing her teeth. He moves further towards the edge of the bed. Cody gets into bed very carefully. She lies on her back as far to the other side of the bed as she can go, her hands crossed over her chest. She tries to regulate her breathing.

Neither of them moves a muscle all night. Neither of them gets much sleep. Francis gets out of bed at 7 am. Cody stretches out at last. She swaps her pillow for his. The rain stops.

*

Look, Francis

she wants it &
she wants it now
she wants it
& she'll tell you how

she wants it in
the afternoon
she wants it slow
& quick & soon

she wants it soft
she wants it rough
she wants it
till she's had enough

she wants it loud
& silenced too
but more than it
she must have you

*

Three weekends after the flood, Francis and Cody spend the evening at home together. It is very windy outside and every now and then the house shudders. There is a bottle of wine nearly empty on the floor between them. Francis is berating Cody for having enjoyed a recently fashionable book which is not only sentimental, falsely optimistic and clumsily written—
    —But face it, it's also fundamentally morally flawed.
    —*You're* morally flawed.
    —Don't be so facile.
    —Don't be so anal.
    —Jargon-monger.
    —Pedant.
    —Fashion victim.
    —Bore.

They glare at each other across the room. Francis clears his throat.

—Look, he says, —We could sit here hurling insults at each other all night but I'd much rather go to bed with you.

—I'd much rather eat my own vomit.

—I find *that* hard to believe.

—I find *you* hard to believe.

—Stop it.

Cody pours herself some more wine, finishing the bottle. She is desperate for a cigarette. She sighs. The sigh goes on longer than she expected and she is suddenly afraid she might cry. She stands up. Francis stands up. He looks out the window.

—I'm sorry.

—For what, says Cody.

—That was a particularly charmless proposal. I didn't mean to assume—

Cody goes to the window and stands behind Francis. She strokes the back of his head, down to his neck. She sees Francis's reflection in the window. He has closed his eyes.

—Don't assume anything, she tells him. —And don't talk.

She leads him carefully to his bedroom. He opens his eyes.

*

An aerial photograph of a city at night-time.

Dear Cody

How are you darling? I miss you. I miss Thea too, more than I expected. I might have a job!—details later if it works out. When are you coming over? I *miss* you
    Thea
    PS I love Sydney
    PPS Are you being careful?

*

Bonfire

In the dream there is a field. Francis is in the field. She gets closer and she can see the food, the fruit and leaves and meats spilling out of the horn. The Horn of Plenty from her childhood books. A large cream shell lying on the dark grass. *Viands*, she thinks, *nectar*. Francis is back, crouching by the horn, eating everything that comes out. He's wearing his yellow raincoat. He's eating and eating and he's not getting any bigger.

> I got plenty of nothing
> Nothing's plenty for me

Cody sings these lines all day after she remembers the dream.

She doesn't imagine Francis to be the kind of guy who feels sexual frustration. He doesn't seem to be driven by anything like that. She wishes that he was.

I'm the guy here, she decides. It makes sense the more she thinks about it. The two times they've had sex, she's fallen straight to sleep after while Francis has lain awake. She can tell by the darker than usual circles under his eyes in the mornings. Also, she can drink more than him. Which is not to say she can hold it better, but she can keep going long after he's had enough. She knows this is not her most attractive feature.

She's not the guy. She knows that too. She doesn't even know what a guy is, other than Guy Fawkes. She wishes she was more politically active.

She goes to bed at night determined not to dream about Francis. She doesn't. She doesn't. She does.

*

And had nothing to do with the sea

Francis comes home from the bookshop. From the path he can hear that Cody is playing her Kurt Weill record. Again. Christ, he thinks, if I have to listen to 'Surabaya Johnny' one more time I'll smash something.

—Hi, Cody calls from her room. She's getting ready to go to work.

Francis goes into his room and shuts the door. He feels like slamming it but restrains himself. Control, he thinks, calm.

—I was young, God I'd just turned sixteen—

He can hear Cody singing along, loudly and not very well. He gets the shoe polish from under his bed and starts working on his shoes. He is rubbing furiously when Cody sticks her lipsticked face around the door. He starts, flushes, tries for some reason to cover the shoes with the rag. He feels as if he's been caught masturbating.

—I'm off, Cody says. —Have a good night.

—Yeah, he says. —See you.

He sees her out his window walking down the path, still singing. She's waving her arms in time.

—You said a lot, Johnny
All one big lie, Johnny
You cheated me blind, Johnny
From the minute we . . .

Her voice trails after her as she disappears around the corner. He should never have slept with her. He should never have moved in. What a stupid mistake. He doesn't even know her. He hates this messy complication of his life. Bloody mess. At least she's clean.

He goes to her room and stands outside the door. It would be easy to open it, walk in, look in drawers, the wardrobe, the desk. Under the bed. Get to know her that way. Cheat. This is ridiculous, he thinks, looking at himself in the hall mirror on his way back to his room. He looks tired. Older? Probably.

He falls onto his bed. The tin of shoe polish gets him directly between the shoulder blades. Twisting around, he knocks it upside down. There is a thick black streak on his blanket. He throws the shoe polish on the floor. It wheels around leaving fainter black traces before it settles. Francis gets under the blankets with his clothes still on. He counts to a hundred. His breathing slows.

When he wakes up it is dark and the room is cold. He feels a moment of lurching panic. He thinks about going into town. He could have a coffee at Cody's cafe. Sit, talk, walk home together.

He has a bath.

He reads a book.

*

A painting of a bowl of fruit.

Dearest Code

Thea says she saw you in a jeweller's shop with some weedy looking guy. *Tell me she's joking.* I'm working for one of Sydney's top production companies!—as a script editor. Scares me shitless. I love it. I miss you, write.

love Thea

*

The crowded empty bar

inside Cody
small & still
sits & waits
an act of will

outwardly, she
runs the race
spins around
for each new face

mantra chants
the inside child

hums her hymn
is meek & mild

the hurricane
outside the eye
shows no sign
does not know why

Francis is a thumb
I want to suck

*

Cody gets home from work to find Francis and a friend drinking
coffee in the living-room. The friend's name is Marc. Marc with
a c. Cody's seen it written down by the telephone. Not for the
first time, she wonders if Francis might be gay.

—How was work? asks Francis.

—Fine, says Cody. She doesn't really hear him. She can't
take her eyes off the back of Marc's head. Marc, Marc. There's
something disturbing about the name. Like Jon without an h.
Or Shayne with a y. Marc. Spelt backwards, it makes cram.
A real word. This makes it seem like code. Code for what?
Cram, cram. Trying to break the Code. OK, so her own name is
enough of a liability. She shouldn't laugh at other people's. But
Marc—it's like biting tinfoil.

—Um, I'm going to have a bath, says Cody.

—Fine, says Francis.

From the bath she can hear them talking. About what? She
has no idea what guys talk about when they're alone. Sport?
Sex? Not those two. Dungeons and dragons maybe. Or the
relative merits of MMP and STV. Her? Doubt it.

—Night, she calls on her way to bed.

—Night, Francis and Marc call after her.

It is three o'clock before she hears the front door close.

*

—I'm pregnant, says Gene at work on Monday night.

—Oh boy, says Cody. —Is that a good thing or a bad thing?

—Both I guess, says Gene, slapping a steak down on the grill.

Cody looks at her closely to see if she's changed. She's read that during pregnancy your hair is at its glossy best and your skin is glowing. But Gene's ponytail is as limp as ever and she always glows at work anyway, from the heat in the kitchen.

—Are you throwing up yet, asks Cody.

—Nah, says Gene. —Soon maybe. Hey—she looks at Cody, worried, —does it show?

She stands side-on to Cody. She's wearing her T-shirt that says *do i look as if i care* on the front, and leggings.

—No, says Cody. —Don't worry about it.

—Good, says Gene. —That means I don't have to tell him yet. He'll do a runner as soon as he finds out.

—So what are you going to do? asks Cody.

—Go ahead with it and pretend he might change, says Gene. —I want to have the baby. Even if I'm on my own.

—You're brave, says Cody.

—And stupid, says Gene.

—Yeah, says Cody, —and stupid.

Cody spends the next day at the library reading international magazines. She mostly skims through the articles, but reads the short stories in *Buzz* magazine and *The New Yorker*. She is relieved to discover that many of these deal with the same sort of man trouble problems as she has got. There's a whole bunch of American women out there writing about stuff she can relate to. The No-Good-Men Genre. Cody feels reassured, part of a global sorority of single women. Things can't be so bad if they have the same situations in San Fransico and Chicago as they do in Wellington. At least they're all in it together.

No. Wait a minute. Cody stops cold. It is not in fact a good thing if man trouble is an international phenomenon. It is in fact a disaster. The one thing she's been relying on is the fantasy of a different breed of man overseas. Every Antipodean girl's

dream—Mr Europe!—Mr Africa!—Mr Mediterranean!—take
your places please. Now Cody knows that this will never be a
reality. Even if she could ever save enough money to go to New
York, she'd still be scouring the streets for a halfway decent
man. Shit. Looks like she's going to have to ditch romance and
hold out for the fast-track, power-dressing career.

She leaves the magazines on the floor and scuffs her feet all
the way down the street to the cafe.

*

Which face

thirteen at a table
Francis the last
no-one to kiss
left with the glass

port passed round
not immune
towards the star
right through moon

here Francis
have this mask
heart sees face
this your task

have an answer
have some air
from this distance
you're so fair

*

Francis has woken up too early. He pulls a jersey on over his
pyjamas and shivers. The sky is milky blue. He traces a line
curving up and around in the condensation on the window. He

worries that the shape he's drawn is too phallic. He worries that he worries too much.

In the kitchen he tries to make coffee without disturbing Cody. She'd probably sleep through a siren anyway, he thinks as the percolator hisses over onto the gas flame. He searches the bench for a teaspoon. Old teabags, dirty knives, crumbs. Standards are slipping. On the table he finds a teaspoon under a piece of paper with writing on it.

> Mark called twice
> sorry forgot to tell you
> We need soap!
> C.

He wonders how long the note's been there. He thinks about what he has to do at work today. He's trying to make some changes to the bookshop. Get rid of some of the trash and concentrate on the upmarket, cerebral and quirky. He has a sudden vision of himself as a turn-of-the-century shop clerk, tight collar and pinched brow, pushing pieces of paper around on a desk. He wishes he were back overseas. Maybe he'll get drunk tonight.

He stops outside Cody's door. Without thinking, he opens it and slowly steps into her room. She's almost hidden underneath her blankets, face buried in a pillow. He can't see her breathing. He imagines going to shake her, giving her a fright, seeing her uncomposed morning face open in alarm. He doesn't do it. He doesn't do that sort of thing. But he thinks it, which makes him feel guilty enough.

He sits gently on the end of Cody's bed and watches her sleep. She moves her feet a little bit. Nothing much happens. He leaves her room, forgetting on purpose to close the door. On his way to work, he smiles when he imagines her waking up.

*

A black and white photograph of two schoolgirls on a road.

Cody

Anyone would think you'd disappeared off the face of the
earth. I called your machine, your voice is still on the tape.
Is that guy hiding you under the floorboards? or boiling
you up on the stove? 99% of women are murdered in their
own homes. Or something like that.

Thea.

*

I'm giving you a longing look

Cody wakes from a late morning dream. The room is hot. She's
still heavy and slow from sleep, but her mind is clear. She knows
there's something she has to do. Francis, she thinks, which is
nothing new. There is something different now though. She feels
a pulse somewhere which tells her she's going to do something.
She doesn't want to think what it is. She just wants to get there.
   She has a bath and gets dressed to music she and Thea used
to listen to at school.

   Here's some mud in your pretty eye
   But please drop in if you're passing by
   I'll tell you how much I hate you girl
   Perhaps it isn't true, perhaps it isn't true

She brushes her hair, humming, smiling at herself in the mirror.
Tears come into her eyes. She misses Thea. She'll write to her,
after she's done this.
   Walking into town she wonders if she's been kidnapped by
the FBI and brainwashed as a sleeper. I must kill John Lennon,
I must kill John Lennon, she mutters, then laughs out loud. She
feels hysteria welling up and breathes down to control it. She
realises she's heading straight for Francis's bookshop. What's

she doing? This is stupid—she's about to turn back but she gets rid of the thought, she doesn't think anything, the song runs through her head.

> To those who look snide
> And those who connive
> I say love cannot be contrived
> Love cannot be denied

She's scaring herself now, and walking still, getting closer and closer. It's a mistake, it's wrong. No. Just get there.

> And if you ask me to explain
> The rules of the game
> I'll say you missed the point again

She walks into the bookshop and up to the desk where Francis is sitting. There's no one else there.

—Hi Cody, he says.

—Hi Francis, she says. She squeezes in past the desk and stands behind his chair. For seven seconds she doesn't touch him. Then her hands reach over his shoulders and down his chest. Her mouth is very close to his right ear. One hand finds its way up inside his jersey. The other feels the worn leather of his belt. She kisses his throat. He turns and stands and the chair falls over and her back is against the wall and they are kissing each other. She twists him around and she holds him to the wall, holds his hands to the wall, kisses him and hears someone behind her. She lets him go. He is confused.

—Sorry, he says to the customer.

She isn't sorry. She laughs and says goodbye and leaves the shop.

Francis reaches in his desk drawer and pulls out his inhaler. He gulps mouthfuls of Ventolin. The customer asks him if he's got anything by Julian Barnes and he says Never heard of him, when of course he has, he's read everything he's written, but the only one he can remember right now is *Talking It Over*, and he decides that's what they've got to do.

*

When Cody gets home from work that night Francis is in the living-room smoking a cigarette.

—What about your asthma, says Cody.

—I don't care, says Francis.

—OK, says Cody.

—I'm going to move out, says Francis.

—OK, says Cody.

—It's not healthy, says Francis.

—OK, says Cody.

They look at each other. Cody lights a cigarette off the end of Francis's and steps away again.

—I want you, says Francis.

—Do you, says Cody.

—Yes, says Francis.

—Really, says Cody.

—Yes, says Francis.

—I suppose you want to consume me, says Cody.

—Yes, says Francis.

—Well, says Cody, —you can try.

Later, you can't sleep. You don't care. You reach over Cody for a cigarette. You light it and cough. You lie on your back blowing smoke into the dark above you. Cody wakes up. You pass her the cigarette. You smile at her.

—Cody, you say.

She smiles back. —What? she says.

—Cody, you say. —C–O–D–Y.

—Visions of Cody, she says, handing you back the cigarette.

—Yeah, you say, still smiling, —Every day I write the book.

CHRIS PIGOTT

Fire

I wasn't even in bed when the baby started up. It was two a.m. and I hadn't even changed into my pyjamas. I was taking a drink. Maybe it would help me get some sleep. I took a sip and the baby started up. That was the way lately. In fact, that had been the way for quite a while.

Let Carrie sleep. Why worry about it? So she hadn't been up to feed her for a week. I hadn't been to sleep in a week. Not before it was getting light. That's what I hate. The only time my body gets the picture is when I'm standing out on the balcony and the sun's coming up over the hills. It's the only part of the day I'm in love with, when the sky is blue and pink and yellow all at once and you can feel like you're the only man alive and the only one who matters. I'm damn sure I'm the only one sipping on good stuff right then anyway. That's the way it is. As soon as the sun starts coming up and I start feeling spiritual my body falls asleep right there on the balcony and then my mind goes heavy and I may as well not be out there, so I go and lie down and I'm asleep before any rooster starts up crowing.

I took another drink and then I went and put a pot on the stove. After that I put the milk in the bottle and the bottle in the pot and after that I went upstairs to get the baby. All this I can do in the dark. I can hot up a bottle in the dark and I can mix a double and I can carry my girl around too. Carrie doesn't like it. I told her one night at the start of all this, when the weather went hot. I lay in bed with her and I was going crazy just lying there looking at the light swinging on its cord. It does, all day long and all night, swing, like we're always in the middle of a quake. Nobody believes me. Down at work they used to think I was crazy, but that doesn't matter any longer. But it does swing forever, and I was at the end of my rope just watching it, so I woke Carrie up and told her how the night before I'd done it all in the dark. Boiling the water and mixing the drink and feeding the baby and all the rest. But Carrie doesn't like it. She said I

465

could burn down the house or worse. By worse she means drop the baby down the stairs. I know that. I know how Carrie's been thinking lately, and that's what she meant. So the next night I let the lights burn all night long, but that costs, so I quit. Now I do it all in the dark and I don't tell Carrie.

The first thing I saw when I was up the stairs were the fires. Our neighbour is an old man, like 90, and he's as crazy as they come. When we shifted up here everyone from the postman down told us to look out for him. So the first thing we did was invite him for dinner. We were like that before the baby. Just so we could have a good time at his expense. And he was crazy, believe me. For a start he would have said ten words all night, five about his old wife, and five about his god-damned donkey. Which, it turns out, was the oldest donkey in the land. What a donkey. It must have been around 96 according to the old man and that was about all he told us. A real talker. The next thing was that he had less teeth than my baby has now, five at the most. And Carrie serves corn. Good old Carrie, back at her best. It was the funniest thing to watch and it was only the tip of the ice. What a night. A riot.

When I made it to the top of the stairs I could see the fires burning. They were all out on his land, burning good enough to light the sky as pretty as could be. He was burning all his waste, like any farmer does in any given summer. All their thistles and old hedges and whatever the hell else they want to get rid of I guess. But the old fruit was burning his at night. Who knows why. Maybe it was to do with the air temperature. That might be it. But you can be sure that he had a reason and that it wasn't on any whim, even if it was just to have some fun with the rest of us. I looked for him out there among the fires. I knew he'd be there somewhere stoking the flames at two a.m. but I couldn't see him. The fields were lit like day and I couldn't see him. It was pretty enough to watch though. That's what I'll give him. He could stoke a good fire and if I ever want a bonfire lit I'll give him a call, which will probably be never. So I watched them burn awhile, good high strong flames, but then I got back to the baby because she was starting a riot of her own.

*

Between us we'd found a routine. The baby would cry and I'd feed her. She'd drink some, and then she'd start up again. Then I'd tell her a story and by the end of the story she'd be feeding again. We'd do it all over and at the end of this second time she'd be ready to sleep again. This took a lot of trial and error, but I'm good at both of these and she's showing signs. Anyway, it works for the two of us. And what could take an hour takes twenty minutes.

She was crying good and loud the little queen, so I was in a hurry to get her down the stairs so Carrie wouldn't come out of that slumber of hers. That's how I missed the step. I was jigging the baby on my shoulder and two-stepping and I missed a stair. My foot went right by the edge of one and I didn't feel a thing except that I was falling. I knew that. My whole body, baby and all, took a lean forward and I started thinking about a hundred things. Like my butt being on the line again. That would be it, I knew it. So I ran. It was all I could think to do, to run like it was a god-damned avalanche. Every time I've been up the mountain, that's all Carrie had said to me. If you're in danger, run, and I was in danger, so I ran. I ran until my foot hit something and I didn't stop until I was an eyeball away from the liquor cabinet. I'm not going to tell Carrie. She'd chalk it up. Even though I'd tell her I did it as the baby was crying so hard and that it would have happened that way at night or in the middle of the afternoon just the same, she'd chalk it up for a rainy day.

I gave the baby her bottle and she stopped crying. I sat her in her chair and watched her drink and when she was away I mixed myself one, only a little stiffer. When I took a sip, she laid down her bottle and started up.

'Okay,' I said. 'There, there.' But she kept up. I didn't have a story on top of my head, so I kept saying it. 'There, there. There, there.' Like she'd cut her finger a little, or her dog had been run over. There, there.' Then I started listening to myself and I figured I sounded pretty lame. I figured I had to come up with a story.

'All right,' I said. 'I've got one.' She didn't seem too interested. She kept up crying like she didn't want a story. But I knew she did. So I took a sip and started up about all I could think of. 'When I was a kid,' I started off, 'I had a pal called Jim, but everyone called him Bones. I don't know why. I'd tell you if I did. Anyway, Bones and I were firm friends. We would sit by each other at school and leer at the same girls and other stuff you don't need to know about until later. We drank a lot of beer together and we'd do other fine things.'

She was looking at me now, taking it in. She was still crying but it was like a habit. She wasn't setting out to cry any longer.

'Bones was a fun guy. If he was telling this story it would be funny and to the point and everything else. It would be laugh a minute, but that's because Bones was a funny guy and I'm only a god-damned laid-off postal worker.

'Anyway, one time Bones and I went fishing. We lived in this little dive of a town, but it was right on the coast, so you can fish and shoot and other such things. Bones and I would fish a lot, and we knew how to fish. After a while we could read the tide and the weather and knew when to fish and where. We were fine little fishermen.

'So this time we go out to catch some dinner. Bones lives with his mother, and I live with mine. They were fine friends, our mothers, and good sports I guess.

'Well, we weren't fishing two minutes when Bones caught one. It was big. It was as big as you are, honey,' I said. 'And Bones pulled it in with no trouble and then he held it up. It was a big fish, as big as Bones or I had ever caught. It was heavy to lift, as heavy as you, and big. I was awed to look at it.

'Bones kills it straight off, with a stone, and he lays it up on the rocks like it's a big prize. And maybe it was, I don't know. Then we cast again and we can't stop catching them. In half an hour I catch three and so does Bones; and after this I pull in. My mother will love me; three good fish. But Bones baits up and keeps on going. I don't know, maybe he's going to sell them. I really don't know. I lie back and watch Bones. I get a good brown tan there, and for an hour he fishes on. And he keeps on hooking them. Each one he catches he holds up in the air and then lays it up by his first fish, the damn monster-fish, and then he kills them. At the end of the hour and a half Bones has nineteen fish layed out on the rocks, all good ones. Next to my three it is very impressive.'

The baby was drinking again, so I figured I ought to hurry the story along. We had a schedule to meet.

'All right,' I said. 'After the nineteenth fish Bones reels in and fixes up his rod to show he's done. I stand up to look at his fish and, as I say, they're very impressive. I feel inadequate next to Bones and his catch.

'So I say to him, "Are you going to sell them? You'll make a mint." And he would have. But Bones doesn't say a thing. He just smiles. He looks at me and then at his fish and he just smiles. And right then, at the end of that smile, he starts to throw the fish back in, one at a time. Eighteen dead fish he throws back in, and I watch them dive like they're alive, and then just begin to float, making ready to drift up to the top and float on their backs.

'And then I look at Bones, and he's holding that other damned fish, that monster-fish, up in the air in both his hands, staring at it and smiling like he's the god-damned fisherman king.'

The baby was drinking well again, so I left her to it. I went across to the cabinet and fixed another drink. I was wide awake. I'd never felt so awake in my life. Maybe it was the heat. I don't know. I'm not a doctor. It's all I could do to stop from going crazy. Take a drink. It takes the edge off the whole thing. But that's what I do know. That I'd never felt so awake in my life.

I mixed one more and by the time I was back in the kitchen the baby had started up again.

'Okay, honey,' I said. 'This next one's a given, considering. I don't know where my head was.' The baby was making a lot of noise now. That's how she was. She was worse when she was half fed. So I started up.

'Your mother, Carrie, used to have a problem,' I said. 'Before you came along and before I came along too, I guess. But she still had it when I met her, and right up until a while ago. What would happen would be that two or three times a month your mother would get out of bed in the middle of the night and walk. She was a regular no-holds-barred sleepwalker. And I'd find her in the funniest places. Once it was in the garden, at three a.m., wandering around like a genuine greenfingers among the cauliflowers. Another time I caught up with her two hundred yards down the pavement, out for a sunday stroll, her night dress blowing in the wind. It was the funniest thing to wake up in the middle of the night in an empty bed, knowing you had another chase on your hands. It was the funniest feeling.

'Anyway, where we lived in the country, this was fine. But then we were married and we figured we should move to the city. I got a job and Carrie went and studied. But she didn't let up sleepwalking. It got so bad I started locking all the doors and hiding the keys and that worked fine. She'd still walk, but she couldn't go anywhere. I had contained the problem.

'Then one time around Christmas—maybe you were coming by then, I don't know—I got sloppy. This was in the new home up behind the university. It was just before Christmas and hot like this, and we had a few drinks. In fact we had a lot to drink. And after we drank all we had we went to bed, and it just wasn't on my mind to lock the doors at all. I didn't even come close to thinking about it.

'Well, that night, Carrie went walking. Only I didn't wake up at all, not until some samaritan came knocking on my bedroom door. And they took me to her, and I thought she was dead, I truly did. She was lying like this, all flat and still, at the bottom of the stairs. I didn't know what to do, I truly didn't. I just knelt above her, petting her and comforting her, and all the time I'm looking at her ear. Coming out of her ear was a little line of blood, and it was the scariest thing. It was all I could do, stare at that line of blood coming out of her ear, and pet her.'

The baby hadn't finished her bottle, but she was ready to sleep. I could read the signs. I picked her out of her chair as gently as I could, and put her on my shoulder and carried her back to her room.

'Be a goodnight girl, honey,' I whispered to her. 'Be a goodnight girl. There, there.' But she was already asleep. I only said it for luck. I said it every night, and now I said it for luck.

*

I wasn't even close to sleeping. It felt like the middle of the day. So I took my drink and sat on the balcony and watched the fires. They were burning good and the sky was lit red like it was the end of the world. It was almost beautiful. I looked for the old fruit to call out to. I thought I might take him down a drink. It would be hot work, I guess. But as bright as it was, I couldn't see him anywhere, so I let it rest. I'll tell you one thing though. He could stoke a fire as good as anyone, crazy or not. Like I said, if I ever needed a fire lit, he'd be the man. It was the prettiest thing to watch.

CHRIS PRICE

Mix

We were on the rebound
from perfection, piling on the dirt—

a mellotron, the wheezy breath
of old vinyl, character

sounds. We argued over psycho-acoustic
noise optimisation, where

to put the vocals—I wanted walk-in
wardrobe, you favoured aircraft hangar.

Time signatures exercised us into
the small hours. Finally we had to admit

something was wrong
with the voice, the original

performance. Intonation? We thought
we could fix it in the mix

auto-tuned within an inch of its life
to no effect. There was a spike

that wouldn't be softened.
After that you left for London citing

artistic differences. I opted for a cool edit
of the whole performance, released

selected tracks to friends
and family, trashed the backup

sold the gear. I hear you're big
in the clubs over there. Good luck.

JO RANDERSON

I hope my mother will come soon

We were sitting, waiting, in the rain. Mum was late for picking us up, but we weren't worried because Mum was always late. It was just a little bit cold today because of the rain, and also because I didn't have my jumper. Simon had his jumper. But I didn't have mine. I didn't bring it. But don't go thinking that I'm stupid and I forgot it. I'm not stupid. If I was stupid I wouldn't be allowed to choose my own clothes to wear in the mornings, but I can, I can choose anything I want, anything at all from my brown cupboard but not the Barbie-dress because that's only for special occasions, and if I'm not sure if it's a special occasion or not I'm allowed to ask and Dad's not allowed to yell at me for asking because it's not stupid to ask questions, it's smart. It's stupid *not* to ask questions if you don't know something and when people laugh at you, you just smile and rise above it. Because *you* know you're not stupid, and Mum knows you're not stupid so it doesn't matter what anyone else thinks. I'm not stupid. Simon's stupid. He's stupid because Mum still has to help him put his trousers on. But Mum says you're always stupid when you're a baby and only as you get older do you get cleverer and cleverer, and then when you're a grown-up suddenly you become really brainy like the people on TV. But then I guess there must be some point when your brains start to leak out again because old people are stupid too, just like babies, and they can't put on their trousers either. Only no one wants to help old people put their trousers on. They only want to help babies because I'm not sure why but I think maybe because babies look a little bit like dolls but old people don't really look like anything and they are a bit scary because they dribble on you and give you sweets with ants inside them.

I don't really like ants very much.

Also my mother is quite late.

When I got up this morning I looked in my brown cupboard for some clothes and I got my blue trousers, my favourite ones with little motorcycles on them, vvrrmmm, vrrmmmm, they were driving everywhere all over the trousers and one was driving right off the bottom so you could only see the back wheel. Sometimes I check to see if it's driving up the inside leg but it never is. But I always check. Because where else could it go? I can't ever see where the rest of it could be. How come it drove away and just left the back wheel? Mum says maybe it's a ghost motorcycle and you can only see part of it like the Famous Floating Head Lady Ghost. Then she lifts her arms and makes a scary noise and I don't actually find it very funny. I think it's stupid and mean and I'm allowed to go to my room and hide under my blankets if I don't like something. Sometimes I even wear my motorcycle pants to bed even though I get red marks from the zip. I don't care. I like to feel the motorcycles driving all round my legs during the night, and sometimes I try and catch them by turning the lights on suddenly and seeing them all driving but they must be able to know somehow because when the light goes on they're always exactly in the same place exactly as they were even the one that's just a back wheel. Except once when I turned the light on the one that's just a back wheel was gone. I looked everywhere for it in case it had driven somewhere into the blankets but it was totally gone. But then when I was looking on the other side of the trousers, on the other leg at the bottom, *THERE IT WAS*, just exactly the same as it used to be on the other side. *But it had moved legs.* How did it do that? Mum said I was just being silly and that it was a stupid question to ask. I wasn't sure how come that question was stupid but other ones were smart. I think you just have to make a bit of a guess. You have to do a little bit of a figure out in your brain and then you just pretty much have to make a bit of a guess. Because you never know if what you say is going to be smart or dumb.

I think maybe Mum has forgotten us.

Also the rain is starting to feel a bit cold. Simon's okay because he has a jumper. Me, I don't have one. I'm feeling a bit cold and I'm not sure if Mum's remembered to come. Lots of other Mums and Dads are here, but not ours. I'm starting to get a bit worried but I remember what Mum always tells us so I keep just sitting still and don't move. It's not a good idea to move around when you're lost or waiting for someone. You should stay exactly where you are and not move and then Mum will come and find you and everything will be okay. But she didn't say about if it's raining and you don't have a jumper and your little brother's crying a bit. Probably she'll be here soon though. Maybe she'll have drinks and lollies and we'll go to McDonald's. One time I went to McDonald's and a boy spewed up on my Barbie-dress. I wasn't very angry except that my chips went on the ground and no one would buy me some new ones. I didn't think that was very fair.

There's a little ant crawling up the wall beside me but he keeps slipping. I think he finds it a bit hard in the wet. I move a little bit to the side because I don't want him to crawl into my trouser leg, but I don't move very much, only a little bit or else Mum might not be able to find me. I really want Mum to come and find me. When Mum comes and finds you you feel good and you run up at her but not too hard in case you knock her over. She's lovely, Mum is.

She's lovely but you do get angry with her sometimes. I was a little bit angry this morning because she said my motorcycle pants were too dirty and made me put on my brown corduroys. And then since I was wearing my brown corduroys she said I had to wear my brown skivvy, I don't really like wearing all the same colour. It makes me feel like a lizard, one of those ones that changes colour when you put it on different things. Except since I'm in all brown I can't change colour no matter what I'm on. I'm just brown. Although that's not too bad a colour to be since all the buildings are brown. I don't know why they don't make buildings with little motorcycles on them and a little one at the bottom driving off with just its back wheel showing. I would live in a building like that.

I don't know where my mother is.

I would like to go home.

Almost everyone else here is gone. There's just a few kids hanging out on their bikes and they don't mind that it's a bit wet because it's only five minutes the way they ride and then it's warm and drinks and lollies. We don't have bikes yet but we will when we're a bit older and a bit brainier. Simon's still a bit stupid you see. But not me because I can pick my own clothes, anything I want, well almost anything as long as it matches and it's not dirty. But if it's a special occasion I have to wear my Barbie-dress. I know because once I wanted to wear my motorcycle pants and I got thumped. And I wasn't even allowed to hide under the blankets.

I'm starting to feel very cold.

It's not my fault that I don't have a jumper. When I looked out the window it was sunny. I even put my hand out and felt it. It was warm. No one told me it was going to be rainy and cold. Someone should have told me that this morning when I was choosing to take my jumper or not. I'm not stupid. I would have taken my jumper if I knew it was going to be cold. Once you know things, you do them. Otherwise you'd be stupid. When Dad says not to do something, you don't do it. You learn that. Same as you learn not to say anything when the boys put their hands down your top, because they hit you, hard, and it hurts. It's easier to have a hand down your top than a big thump in your guts. I don't really like when I get a big thump in my guts. It kind of hurts me in my body and in my head. I don't really like it.

I wonder if Mum will bring my jumper? She might tell me off for not wearing it. I wasn't being stupid though. It really did seem very warm this morning. I thought I wasn't going to need it. And I didn't need it, all the way to school I didn't need it at all. It was sunny and lovely and fine. And I was glad I didn't have my jumper all big and fat banging around my waist. At school I said to Julie, I'm big enough to choose not to bring my jumper if I don't want to and I didn't bring it today because I'm allowed not to bring it if I don't want to. Julie said, So? She is allowed to say things like that because she is pretty and all the boys want to put their hands down her top. I really like Julie.

Sometimes we go to her house and play, and there are all sorts of dolls and things, not old people dolls but baby ones, and one of them even does real poos when you turn its arm round. Except the poos are pink and they smell like flowers. And when you look in Julie's cupboard (which is pink, not brown) she has all Barbie-dresses. Not any brown corduroys at all. And I asked her if she had any motorcycle trousers but she said, Yuck. Who wants motorcycle trousers? Just then the head of her doll came off accidentally in my hands. I said I was very sorry but she told me to go home now because she was bored of me. She is my best friend in all the world. Except sometimes I hate her. Sometimes I want to punch her in the face and head and put maggots in her eyes.

Simon's crying quite loudly now. I'm a bit embarrassed of him and I don't really know what to do. There's only one other girl waiting and she's a girl that no one likes very much. She has a funny metal thing on her leg and I'm a bit scared she might kick me. When you feel cold, you really do feel cold. All you want is your jumper and going home and hiding under the blankets. If someone even gave me lollies I don't think I would eat them. You're not allowed to eat lollies at school anyway.

I thought that car might be Mum but it was just the maths teacher, if you don't have maths, you don't have anything. You can't fidget in maths class because then it doesn't go into your brain. I've been told off twice today. I was only jiggling my legs because they were shivering but Mr Adams got angry. I had to sit still but the shiver came back. And then when I got asked a question I found that the maths *hadn't* gone in to my brain, even though I wasn't moving at all. So I was stupid *and* cold. Also the boys were very loud today. (Where is my mother?) They weren't better than us at anything but they're louder about what they are good at. And Julie draws a better picture than you, but you like yours more, but it doesn't matter, it doesn't matter because the teacher likes hers. And not yours. And you try hard not to make it matter. You try very hard. But it does. It does matter. And everyone you look at isn't moving, everyone is sitting brown and still, and no one seems to feel cold the way you do, either they have jumpers on or they just can't feel it. But I'm not stupid, I'm *allowed* not to wear a jumper but why did they let me if it makes me feel so freezing, I don't know where my mother is and I really want to go home and no one moves around me so I want to kick them and shake them and I have this funny feeling like my mother might not come but she can't be angry at me for not having a jumper. It's not really my fault because it seemed so warm this morning and no one told me it was going to get so cold so how was I supposed to know and now I start crying, I cry a lot but it's not my fault it's getting dark it's not my fault if I'm stupid. My mother says that a lot.

And the rain is getting colder on my neck and little Simon is crying. All the other kids have gone already. Our Mum is often late but today I have a feeling like she might not come at all.

Please Mum, please be here soon. Please, I want to go home. Please God make my Mum come soon. Please Mum. Please come soon. I really need to go home now, please Mum, please be here soon. Please be here soon. And around me everything is slowly getting darker. I wish that I had brought my jumper. I hope my mother will come soon.

MARG RANGER

Insomnia is a window of opportunity

my father explained,
waking us at 4am
to view the craters of the moon
and Saturn's shifting rings
through his telescope.

Look, yawned my sister.
You can see into the future.

When my brother was a child
he could see right through things.
Once he saw the sun
lighting up the other side
of the world at sunset.

Years later
my sister in Beijing
took an earlier plane
and missed her flight
that crashed into the sea
at Kai Tak.

Listen, my father said.
It's the dawn chorus.

FRANCES SAMUEL

A Memoir

I'll start with the cat:
Annabel, I love you I said.
She was my only wife.
She grew flowers from her ears.
All night I could smell her next to me.
If I ever needed to find her I'd lick my finger
And follow the wind.
Before I was young I crowed like a rooster.
They kept me in the dark.
I could tell it was morning when light
Batted its paws under the door like a kitten.
See what a man is made of said my Father or
Grandfather. I was a teenager then.
Once I could draw a perfect circle
In the middle of a piece of paper.
Afterwards I'd hold it outside
Under rain until it turned blue.
Old po-face they called me
And I'd think of Edgar Allan
And love my cheeks fiercely.
I have always liked Spring best,
Not the clammy palms of Summer,
Or Autumn, which never cleans up after itself.
I can't say I have lived widely or loved thoroughly—
Life began for me an hour ago.
I was in a small room,
Ice in the keyhole.
I reached upwards and found myself
Elbow-deep in flowers.
Annabel, I said, *Annabel*
But the windows became wind
Blew the petals away, stalks

Hanging from the ceiling.
Five minutes have passed since then
I have no idea about my next move.

ALEX SCOBIE

Candles

They burn inwards,
burrowing head down

into the soft columns.
Only their tails are visible,

luminous in the dark,
as they cautiously descend

their tunnels of wax,
lighting their way

like solitary miners
to the bottom of each shaft.

Once there, they find
there is no light, no shaft

to guide them back.

ADAM SHELTON

The Family Album

Yvonne carried Tim into the living room wrapped in a towel. She put him on the floor and unwrapped him with a flourish. Tim made burbling noises and a bubble of spit inflated on his lips and Yvonne beamed at him. Then he crawled across the floor towards the kitchen and a stream of liquid ran out from between his legs. It trickled slowly across the floorboards where the house slumped on its piles and pooled in the loose strands of a rug.

'Jiminy,' said Yvonne. 'Andrew. He's done it again,' she said and Andrew appeared from the kitchen with Barry their lodger at his shoulder.

'My big boy. My tough little nudist,' he said. He threw a tea towel at the puddle on the floor and picked up his son and held him in front of his face. He blew raspberries at Tim and shook him gently so his arms and legs wobbled as if boneless. Tim made baby noises and Andrew said something meaningless in reply.

'You know he does that when you take his clothes off,' he said. 'He loves that. You've got to get his nappies on straight away. Wrap that little piece up.'

'You've got all the answers,' said Yvonne.

'I know my son,' said Andrew.

'You know diddly squat,' said Yvonne.

'I know, I'm a man. I've got balls. I am a man,' said Andrew.

'Learn how to use them properly then little boy. Make something that doesn't wet the floor,' said his wife.

'Jackpot,' said Andrew. He stuck out his arm and then pulled it back quickly towards him as if playing a poker machine. He pivoted on his toes and went back into the kitchen. 'Tea's coming at you,' he said.

Barry knelt down on one knee. He held out his arms towards

Tim, shaking his head from side to side. Yvonne picked Tim off the floor and carried him into the kitchen. Barry stayed down on his knee and pulled fluff off the rug. He was a tall man, nearly forty and never married, still slim and fit, and his eyes held the uncertainty of a schoolboy.

'Baz, Baz, Barry, come and get your tea. Yvonne, my dear, dinner is served,' said Andrew. He ate his chops in his hands like a man playing a harmonica while Yvonne sliced and sliced and sliced her meal. She chewed the meat then put saliva softened pieces in a plastic bowl in front of Tim next to her. Barry put a piece of carrot in Tim's bowl.

'Don't feed him that. He doesn't eat carrot,' Yvonne said. She wiped away a thread of meat that hung from dribble across the front of Tim's face and Barry quietly buried peas in his mashed potato.

'Good stuff,' said Andrew at the end of the meal. 'I'm hot. I'm cooking,' he said.

'Cooking,' said Barry.

Yvonne cleared the table. Her small body moved sharply around the kitchen and Barry, angular like a crane, passed plates over her to the sink. The narrow space between table and sink demanded a practised economy of movement and the two of them moved deftly around the room in silence. Andrew stood at the kitchen door smiling.

'My man Barry,' he said.

When the dishes were done Yvonne picked up her netball bag in the hall. She left Tim with the men and told them not to let him do anything wrong, not to show him any bad habits. She pulled the front door shut and Barry picked Tim up.

'I'm your Uncle Barry,' he said, and his face shone.

'He's your Uncle Barry,' said Andrew. He took Tim from Barry and put him in a baby seat that hung in a door frame from two pieces of elastic. Tim bounced like a tiny Tarzan and the two men sat down to watch the League on TV.

'Big game for the boys tonight,' said Andrew.

'It's going to be,' said Barry.

Men moved like atoms in some strange experiment up and down the TV screen, colliding and bursting through gaps, and jostling in groups and in pairs in fierce bursts of energy. Barry's eyes gleamed and dilated and chased the players around the screen. Neither man spoke, and at times Andrew thumped the side of the couch.

'Uncle Barry,' he said, during the ads in the halftime break. 'Uncle. Barry. How would it be for you to give us some rent, say six months, in advance? How would that be, eh?' he said with a smile. His face was distorted like his slumped house but Barry looked at him with a childlike affection. Yvonne wanted the piles done, and there was no money, and when Andrew had suggested a pile party where everyone brought one pile and helped put it in the ground Yvonne frowed and told him to try Barry for the cash.

'A bit of money for a nice, flat floor, what do you think,' said Andrew.

Barry stretched back on the couch with his hands in a mock pose of power behind his head.

'You can't do without me, Andrew, can you,' he said.

'Barry,' Andrew said. He moved up next to Barry and rubbed his head against Barry's cheek. Then he grabbed him in a hug and held him. 'Barry Baz,' said Andrew. 'Baz. My man Barry.' He pulled Barry off the couch and onto the floor and hugged him. The two men tussled on the rug sucking loudly for breath, laughing and grunting with the effort, and then Andrew pushed Barry flat to the floor. He rolled on top of him and kissed him on the mouth.

'Jesus,' said Barry. 'Andrew. What the fuck was that?'

'We're friends, Barry, aren't we—friends,' Andrew said.

'That's good friends,' said Barry, and Tim giggled from his seat in the door. His legs absorbed the impact of each downward swing and for a short almost illusionary moment at the bottom of each bounce, it looked as if Tim might walk from the door to comfort Barry who lay on the rug, until the elastic pulled him back into the air again.

'Come on, Barry, open up a bit,' said Andrew.

'Get off,' said Barry.

*

'If you were in a spot, Yvonne, what would you do for money?' Barry said. He watched Yvonne cut luncheon from a sausage and put it over cheddar in bread rolls. He squeezed his hands together as she sliced a tomato and put the pieces in the rolls. Then she squirted tomato sauce over the top and closed up the rolls, and passed one over the bench to him.

'Win Lotto,' she replied.

'Come on, what if you had to, to save Andrew or Tim. What'd you do then?'

'I can cook and I know I sew not too bad,' said Yvonne.

'Yes, but what would you do if you had to? I mean, how can anyone tell what's going to happen,' Barry said.

Yvonne stood behind the bench and Barry could see just a yellow woollen torso in the gap between the cupboards attached to the ceiling and the benchtop. He watched Yvonne's hand as it picked up a cup of coffee, then it disappeared behind the cupboards and he listened to her blow and sip, and then swallow the coffee. He stared at her body but its curves were hidden in the folds of her jersey and he tried to imagine the colour of her skin.

'I'm not an evil person,' he said. 'Yvonne. I'm not really an evil person. I've done some silly things sure, but that's all they were.'

'I don't think you're evil. For goodness sakes, why do you say that sort of thing?' Yvonne said. 'Nobody thinks that. What the heck are you talking about?' she said.

'Are we friends?' asked Barry.

The tinny sound of 'Frère Jacques' played in the hall and Andrew answered the door. It's not going to be anyone with encyclopaedias at night or bibles, he thought. Barry heard the door open as he lay on his bed.

'Hey, Donna-baby. You just get right on in here. Big Barry's waiting for you,' said Andrew, smoothly like someone on the TV.

Barry had one leg out the window and the other still in his bedroom when Donna walked in.

'Barry,' said Donna.

'Oh. Hi there Donna, it's you,' said Barry. 'Hello. I didn't hear you arrive.' He pulled himself back inside. 'I think I might have dropped something,' he said.

'You what,' said Donna. She put her handbag on the floor and sat down on Barry's bed.

'What time is it?' said Barry.

'Does it matter?' said Donna.

'I'm bushed,' said Barry.

'Well, good to see you too,' said Donna. Barry sat down on the bed next to her. He stared at his knees but they did not help him and one of his legs began to twitch as if pulled by strings. He looked at Donna and she leaned over towards him.

'I missed you,' she said.

'It is good to see you,' said Barry.

'Do you want to kiss me?' said Donna.

'Of course, I wouldn't miss that,' Barry said in a voice deeper than normal and Donna hugged him and then she kissed him. 'You kiss a lot better than Andrew,' said Barry, and Donna laughed. Barry reached under his bed and pulled out a mauve, plastic-covered photo album. He said his family had been waiting to meet her and he thought tonight it would be nice for Donna to meet them.

'Keep them under the bed, eh. Well. Sir, madam, your son's like an old donkey, but he's not a bad sort of a guy. He's slow and stupid, but he'll do,' said Donna.

'Very nice,' said Barry. Donna turned through the pages of the album. 'Dad, I'd like you to meet my friend, Donna. Donna, this is my father, Bill,' Barry said. 'Call me Buster, Donna, that's what they know me as,' said Barry in a gruff voice.

'Donna. We've heard so much about you from Barry. So many things. It's like we know you already,' Barry said, in a falsetto, pointing to a picture of an elderly woman on the steps of a farm cottage.

'That's very kind,' said Donna.

'Come inside and have a look around. The men can unload the car while we're chatting. It'll do Bill good to carry those bags in,' Barry said.

'Well, okay, I'd love to see the place, thank you,' said Donna, looking at Barry strangely.

'Get those bags, Barry, get 'em inside and we'll get a fire going,' said Barry.

'Showing your age, old man,' Barry said.

'Just showing my experience, Barry,' said Barry, holding up a black and white photo of his father polishing a Vauxhall.

'Barry. I think I get the message. They look like nice people,' Donna said.

'We might look like old fuddies, but we know some things,' Barry squeaked.

'Okay, Barry, calm down. It's okay Barry,' said Donna.

'I don't think she likes us Bill. City girl. All flash and flutter. Give her time, hon, she'll slow down after she's been here a while. Barry, you know how he used to be when he came home to visit after his first couple of times away. Like someone else was in his body, remember that? He used to say he'd been drinking coffee on the train all the way home,' Barry said.

'Yes, very funny. Now give it a miss, eh,' said Donna.

'I don't like her Bill. She's not right for Barry. I mean she's probably a nice girl in her way, but she's not the one for him. Always interrupting. Barry's sensitive. He's a thinker, she'll be too much for him. All her talk and her gloss. Barry needs someone a bit slower. I worry for him, Bill,' said Barry.

'Christmas. Snap out of this. You're slipping Barry,' Donna said.

'Don't talk about our boy like that,' said Barry. He jumped off the bed and climbed out his bedroom window and Donna heard branches snapping off the hydrangea bushes outside as Barry disappeared into the garden.

Andrew lay on his back on his bed staring at the loose flakes of paint that hung from the bedroom ceiling. His arms were crossed behind his head and he moved his bare toes slowly up and down. Late afternoon light settled in the folds of the mesh curtains hanging across the windows. His eyes drifted from flake to flake.

Barry opened the door. He did not knock and he walked quietly up to the bed. He looked at Andrew. Andrew stared at a paint spot in the far corner of the room. Barry looked up at the ceiling but the tattered paint was of no interest to him and he shook Andrew's shoulder.

'I see you,' said Andrew.

'What are you doing?' said Barry.

'Resting,' said Andrew. Barry sat down on the edge of the bed and his weight tipped Andrew towards him.

'You don't look happy,' said Barry.

'I'm resting, not partying,' Andrew said.

'Want to talk about it?' said Barry.

'Do I want to talk about what,' said Andrew. 'I'm resting.'

'Maybe it would help to open up. To get some communication going,' said Barry.

'That's rich, Barry. That's very funny.'

'Jesus, could you ever pull yourself open?' Barry said.

'How's Donna, Barry?' Andrew answered and Barry left the room and Andrew stared at his toes that wagged and jostled now as if they were trying to free themselves from the end of his body. Barry met Yvonne in the hall with Tim and two bags of groceries.

'Here, I'll take those,' said Barry, and to his surprise Yvonne put Tim in his arms, dropped the bags on the floor and went back outside to the car to get the rest of the shopping.

Barry held Tim to his chest. Tim reached up with his arm and put a small finger in Barry's nose. Barry took Tim's hand away from his face and he watched the skin on Tim's arm turn white where he gripped it. He could feel his breath constricted by the baby against his body. Tim smelt like washed towels.

Barry carried Tim into his bedroom and put him on his back on the bed. It was near dark now and Barry with his bedroom light left off was a shapeless form moving around the room. He pulled an overnight bag from his cupboard and filled it with clothes and toilet gear. When there was just a small space left at the top of the bag, Barry squeezed in his photo album. Then he sat down on the bed and waited.

Yvonne came back inside and dropped her next load of shopping on the floor of the hall. She panted a bit and then called Barry. Barry stood up and picked up his bag, and put it over his shoulder.

'Barry, where's Tim?' shouted Yvonne. He picked up Tim and walked over to the window. 'Barry,' Yvonne said.

Barry held Tim out in front of him. He balanced carefully as he put one leg out the window and then shifted his hips so the other leg followed. The hydrangeas at first resisted but then broke under the weight of the man and the baby, and Barry carried Tim away through the garden.

CARL SHUKER

Fugue

The three JETs stand lightly-clothed on the busy street corner in Shibuya on a Tuesday night. It's too hot and they're a little drunk. They've left the post-orientation dinner at a tiny pub in a place called Roppongi that's become rapidly far too claustrophobic, what with the sitting on the floor, the tiny tables, the low roof, the JET vets trading meaningless jokes involving Japanese words that could be names, could be places, or could be just dishes on the menu but mean just as little either way (and all using the letter J either as an adjective or a noun, they're never quite sure).

Two boys and a girl.

They've walked for twenty-some minutes now, alongside a seething black expressway into the hills of Shibuya, the couple trailing behind Drew and his map.

Drew says, 'Let's get some vending machine beer, boys and girls. And drink it out on the bloody street. You know why? Be*cause*—'

'Did you hear what that really really black guy whispered to me?' says Sam. 'Way back there?'

'—we *can*.'

'He said, *Topless bar, topless bar.* But he like, whispered it in my ear.'

'No way, mate. No way I'm going in one of those places. They rip you off wholesale,' Drew says. 'Once you go in those places, they can take you for everything you've got. Even foreigners. There's no laws to stop them just saying your beer costs forty thousand yen. Tell them to fuck off and you'll get your arms broken. It's true. Wait till we're drunker.'

'God it's hot,' says Sam.

'We've got eighteen hours, boys and girls,' says Drew. 'Of piss, and *poontang*.'

'I want to go home,' Brigit says.

*

491

It's said the thing with being a JET is everything is all laid on.

That the thing with being a JET is you can come to Japan and not only do you get a shiny new visa, you get a very well-paid job, and a pretty decent apartment.

And also your plane tickets get organised for you, and you get maps, wads of informative unevenly-photocopied material on Japanese customs, food, geography and climate, a two-day orientation of sorts in Tokyo with JETs from participating countries (mostly Australians, English, North Americans, Canadians, New Zealanders) that after the absurdly pompous contract signings is mostly hard and expensive drinking with wasted-looking older JET liaisons all referring to their chopsticks as hashi and trading jaded, incomprehensible witticisms in tiny Japanese pubs you soon find out are called izakayas, plus tickets to your posting, detailed instructions on which trains to take and how to take them, detailed and vehement warnings about getting off your shinkansen in the fifteen seconds the doors stay open lest you overshoot your stop by two hours and between three and six hundred kilometers. And that you get a polite Japanese teacher to meet you at the station of your new town, an orientation in earnest broken English of your new town ('I amu Mista Suzuki,' 'zat isu shurine,' 'zat isu yo locaru Seben-Erebun conbeniencu'), a drive to your new apartment, often completely furnished with futons and TV and aircon and computer so you can either cry yourself to sleep or lie awake all night staring at your first Japanese cockroach on the wall in your new town in relative but alien comfort before you start work in a job which you'll soon find out doesn't matter a jot that you have no desire for or even remotely applicable experience at, *the very next day*.

But on the other hand, 'all laid on' apparently also means your visa, your job and your apartment are inextricably linked. Quit or get fired from your job (really quite hard to do, unless you break your contract or the law in a fairly drastic way, like try and import Ecstasy or molest your students—simple laziness or incompetence usually doesn't quite qualify) and your visa automatically expires. Quit or get fired from your job and your accommodation 'expires' too.

And the other thing: your visa is valid for two days before you get to your job and your contract begins. Then it's valid for the year of your contract with the school. And then, unless you've negotiated an extension via the immensely convoluted bureaucratic channels you'd swear were designed to *discourage* you, your visa expires a couple of days after your contract.

And that's it. If you haven't signed on for another year and you decide not to make your flight out, you're an overstayer, and you better either stay out of sight or take your chances with amnesty.

So it's one way into Japan.

But unfortunately, and with that sinking feeling you get when you realise you might have really missed out on something just through your own lack of cojones, when you see Tokyo, and you see the freedom most foreigners enjoy in Tokyo in your first few days in the city, or more likely when you reflect on what you saw once your mind-numbing routine of 'teaching' 'English' to little kids by standing in the corner occasionally muttering, 'No, my name pronounce is "Smith"', to be greeted with complete bewilderment or embarrassed laughter (every day) starts to tell, you'll realise JET is not Japan. JET is JET. A well-padded cage that, should you decide is not for you, you've also decided to leave the country.

Sam is a U of Manitoba School of Journalism graduate who sometimes likes to exclaim in muddled German when he becomes excited in conversation, and his girlfriend Brigit is a week late and a U of Manitoba Faculty of Fine Arts Photography major who loves to photograph neon: abstractly, close-up. They have been living together for eighteen months, twelve in their last year at school, six largely unemployed, planning and waiting for JET's summer intake. Drew is a commerce graduate from Brisbane or really Toowoomba with a fledgling obsession for olive skin, narrow hips, shining black hair and shy averted eyes. He also has a credit card bill amounting to five thousand Australian dollars after a spring postgrad diploma in fledgling heroin addiction. He's big, but not as big as he once was, and clean, now.

Sam and Brigit made it very clear to their JET liaison at the

Winnipeg information sessions—a smiling, immensely fat man
their age, a JET vet of three years who pulled at the waistline of
his shirt when he laughed, because when he laughs, he moves,
and cotton touching the parts of you that move will always
remind you that they're moving—they made it very clear that
they were very much prepared to be posted in different high
schools, and that separate apartments, even, were acceptable.
The fat young man laughed and said, 'Sure, fellas,' and showed
them how to write their preferences for place on their application
forms, how to list under Questions 20 and 21 their reasons why,
their commitment to each other, their love, their plans for their
future in Japan together.

That night, after hours of hard silence, wrapped up together,
but apart, in a huge feather comforter against the chill ('Fahkink
Vinterpeg,' Sam shouts, first thing in the morning, in winter,
in Winnipeg. It's something, the very-early-morning swearing,
that Brigit had to get used to; she has learned to if not love,
then at least see this as a sign of spirit), they at last made their
decision, together. If they did get posted to different schools, if
they were given separate apartments, the plan would be this:
the money was good enough and the JET-subsidised rents cheap
enough that they could leave one of the apartments mostly
empty, and live together in the other. Without having to inform
JET, or their respective schools, if it came to that. This would
be their secret, in Japan. Which apartment, they would decide
when they saw what was offered. The bigger one, of course. The
nicest one, in the best location, with the best shops, handiest to
the station with the most lines. If the two apartments were close
enough, they could even use one as an office. 'Or a darkroom,'
whispered Brigit. 'It could be so cool.' 'Yes,' said Sam. 'Ve vill
make it verk.' 'Jawohl,' said Brigit, and they had hard, good sex,
and were not scared, or worried, together.

The next day they signed their application forms and in a
few weeks were interviewed and in a few more weeks informed
they had been accepted—placement pending—for the August
intake. They went about selling off old stuff, planning their
packing, half-heartedly learning Japanese phrases (Brigit would
haltingly order a drink with 'Ano, nama biiru hitotsu, onegai

shimasu'; Sam would growl in Deutsch delight, 'Sehr *gut*, Fraülein!'), getting physicals and visa photos, opening fresh new email addresses to replace old spam-stuffed ones (where their JET predecessors' warning emails sat unopened), moving into Brigit's parents' basement from their apartment (where their notifications of placement location arrived and laid on the chill hallway floor, unopened, too), and saying goodbye to Winnipeg friends who had begun to make their choices between babies, careers or more (and more) school.

And they felt free.

This morning, their first day, in Tokyo Station, in August, in 95°F heat and 80% humidity at nine a.m. underground, surrounded by their hand luggage and the hand luggage of seemingly hundreds of other JETs, they learned from a strangely sweatless three-year JET veteran, an intensely thin woman with a clipboard and a permanent sneer that said the three years had been *lonely*, that Sam had been posted to a senior high school in Sapporo City in Hokkaido; and that Brigit had been posted to a junior high school in Fukui City, Fukui Prefecture, Honshu.

Different apartments; different schools; different cities; different prefectures; *different islands*.

They are to leave and part tomorrow.

Drew and Brigit both have cameras, but Brigit isn't taking photos.

It's late now, almost eleven, and in the streets of Shibuya the crowds are thinning out. All three of them have cans of Sapporo from a beer vending machine. They stare around themselves at the narrow shops, the swathes of neon, the stalls jammed in next to each other, some so narrow a person could lean against one wall and touch the other with an outstretched hand. Only a few shops are open at this time, so the chaos seems broken by the dead patches of corrugated garage doors, pitted and billed with peeling signs in kanji. They walk down a gently sloping street littered with cigarette butts, paper cups and burger wrappings, lined by shoestores, HMV, McDonald's, Wendy's, record stores, jewelry stores, ramen stores, Burger

King, Yoshinoya, game arcades six stories high, still howling and clinking, a few kids squatting outside smoking cigarettes, boys laughing shrilly, faces lit blue and orange by their keitais as they read their skymail. They've been drinking steadily for almost six hours and with the heat their faces are sheened with alcoholic sweat and the strange oil that the air and the humidity wring from pores.

When they look up, the sky is a blackgrey pinprick static cushion, too dense, bulging and somehow particulate, or pixellate: millions of points of shades of gray. The sky looks plump, like fine, dark sand recently fluffed, or a dusty charcoal mould. It looks pregnant with something and appears to them in shapes delineated by the tall thin buildings: huge dusty ideograms as foreign as the kanji. Now they see an L of sky, but inverted. Now, as they pass a crossroads, a huge, monolithic K with an extra, broken arm dangling from the K's back. Now, on the street that slopes to Starbucks and the station, a long, but flawed girder of an I sprouting extra stalks pruned close along its length; all studded with orange blooms of streetlamps, like a gigantic rune relieved in ruins, overgrown with marigolds.

Everywhere they hear the far-off hum and rattle and wash of motors.

They keep drinking, buy three more cans apiece from another machine, and stash them in Drew's backpack. Alcohol vending machines close at eleven; another piece of advice from JET.

'How would you describe this place,' murmurs Sam.

'America's deformed little cyberbaby,' Brigit says. Sam looks up at the flatness of her voice.

'It doesn't matter,' Drew says. 'What it can give you is what matters. What you want. What you can get.'

'What time . . .' Sam mutters. Then, 'I forgot. When's your . . . train.'

'My train,' Brigit says. 'It's not a train. It's a . . . bus.'

Drew looks at them both, then turns and wanders away, over towards a shop window.

'I leave at ten in the morning. From . . .' He thinks. 'Shun-juku?'

'You're first then. I leave at twelve.'

'We . . . have to . . . oh, man,' Sam says.

Brigit examines his shoulders, and his neck. She doesn't look at his face. 'We have to just go. That's all. There's no other choice.'

'We . . . They tricked us. They . . . they all but lied, Bridge.' His tone is accusing. 'We could complain. We could go to the embassy.'

'How do we find the embassy? Who can we complain to. It's . . . not going to happen like that. We don't know enough. We have to do what's arranged. They could cancel the visas.'

'We can . . .'

'We don't have enough money, Sam. We can't do anything now.'

'Do you want to go away then? So it's okay then?'

'What we want doesn't matter here, now.'

Sam turns and looks down the street. He watches Drew staring into a blackened shop window. Then straightening, peering down the hill at something. A few doors up from them a garage door rattles closed; another shop shutting up.

'I don't care about anything then,' Sam says. 'None of it will be any good.'

'We'll have holidays. We can travel and visit.'

'We're on different *islands*. We'll have to take trains . . . and . . . *ferries* and things. Why are you being so . . . I don't know . . . so very pragmatic about this. No, it's . . . actually it's more like completely fatalistic, Brigit.'

'Sam.' She's staring away down the hill. 'We're in a place we can't afford to be anything else.'

Sam looks up, to her face, surprised and hurt. But she's staring past him.

'Drew's waving at us.'

Sam doesn't say anything.

'Come on.'

She walks off down the hill and in a moment, he follows.

At the foot of the hill the narrow street abruptly widens and meets a large intersection. Four other streets fan out from this hub, and opposite is Tobu Department store and the Hachiko exit of Shibuya station. Though on this particular street there are few people, the crowds gathered at the islands of sidewalk waiting to cross are dense and clogged. Floodlights throw ovals of light up the huge thighs of two GAP models on a billboard. The unmoving crowds seem to shift and blur in a pulsing, irregular light from something they can't see.

At the bottom of the street, Drew is standing in the gutter, leaning over a small cluttered desk with chrome legs, perched on the edge of the sidewalk. The desktop is sloped like a shrunken lectern. It has a small lamp and is slanted towards Drew. He is peering down at the lectern like an immensely tall lecturer examining his distant notes, the lamp lighting up his crotch like the floodlights do the GAP models. Opposite him, in shadow behind the lamp, a young Japanese boy with shoulder-length hair points, bored, at something on the desk. His hand becomes a white spot for a moment, then recedes.

Brigit walks down the hill and pauses behind Drew. Sam stands out in the street and stares across to Hachiko, at all the cut-and-pasted buildings like the stacked shoeboxes of an immense foster-family.

On the desk, pinned in neat rows, are more than fifty miniature plastic bags of shriveled brownish objects.

Each bag is individually labeled. Drew is staring down, examining the labels closely.

'What's this?' Brigit says.

'LBMs,' he mutters.

'Uh-huh.'

'Little Brown Mushrooms. *Legal* little brown mushrooms.'

Brigit leans down beside him. Each bag is ziplock, and as small as a bag for a collectable coin. Inside, the mushrooms are more a fawn-gray than brown, and thoroughly desiccated. The texture is something like velvet worn to a near-shine. The tiny caps are elongated, puckered and pointed; the stems crooked and crushed-looking. They look unappetising, juiceless, and banal, like the dried corpses of the most childishly drawn generic mushroom shape.

On each small white label a string of kanji, a weight in grams, and on one in maybe every four, a biological name written in rude penciled English.

'They can sell them on the street?'

'It certainly looks like it, doesn't it.'

Drew is absorbed. The Japanese boy opposite him is smoking, bored. He points down at one of the bags and mutters something noncommittal.

'How much?' Drew looks up. This is the most serious Brigit has seen him in the twelve hours they've been thrown together.

The boy thinks. Drags on his cigarette.

Breathes out smoke, and through the clouds, huskily says, 'Sebunsowzanden.'

'Seven?' Drew says, incredulous.

'Uhn.' The boy nods with the sound, the nasal barely voiced; the Japanese assent.

'One gram?'

Brigit laughs and Sam looks over at them.

'Uh. Won guramu,' the boy nods. Brigit looks at the boy's long, clean hair, dyed brown with messy silver streaks. Black eyes in an unnaturally tan face, a nosering, yellow teeth. And a black T-shirt that reads HIP LOCK! IT'S CHEERFUL GIRL MONSTER!

There's something pleased on her face.

'One gram. It's robbery. And they're bloody *le*gal.'

'I still feel kind of . . . criminal though.'

Sam stands beside her.

'You're doing these tonight then, eh,' he says.

'Maybe.'

'Before you . . . The night . . . before we leave.'

'*May*-be,' Brigit says. The *may* drawn out; the high *be* not a question but near a taunt.

'What the hell is wrong with you Brigit?'

'Nothing is wrong. This is Japan, Sam.' She laughs. 'Sam, Japan. Jap Sam. A man. Marzipan jam, Sam.'

He looks from her to the desk, then back to her. She leans down closer to the display. He looks out to the street and grits his teeth.

'That's like a hundred and twenty bucks. Aussie,' Drew says. 'Fuck!'

It sounds harsh and ugly to Sam, like a deep squawk. *Faahk.*

'We can't afford that, Brigit.'

'One?' Drew says to the boy, tapping his chest, then holding up a finger.

The boy nods, bored. Sense of too many fingers, too many times.

'Uh. Won guramu, you.'

'Fa-*ahk*.'

'Don't do it, don't do it,' a voice whispers faux-dramatically behind them.

It's a tall foreign boy with short black hair in a white singlet. Sam can't place the accent. It's placeless. Brigit glances up, sees the black diagonal stripe of a bag strap across the singlet. That's a wifebeater, she thinks, the English name for a singlet.

Drew ignores the foreigner and points to a different bag.

'Seeksowzanden.'

'Fahk.'

'Australian, Canadian, Canadian. He knows you're JET. He's screwing you.' The boy steps up on the curb, leans over and points at a bag and says something in Japanese.

The Japanese boy swats his finger away and hisses a rapid sentence.

The boy laughs, relents.

'I'd walk away. He speaks English, you know.'

The Japanese boy steps out from behind the desk as if to push him.

'Come on, Manabu, give them a break,' he says, and smiles at the boy.

Drew and Brigit and Sam stare at the exchange.

The Japanese boy turns back to them, his bored mask gone, then to the new boy.

'Everyone, go out,' he snaps. 'Closed. Closing.'

The boy laughs, and says, 'Come with me. I'll hook you up.'

At the corner of an alleyway, Drew a little reluctant and a little suspicious but in massive debt, Sam hanging back and Brigit taking charge, the boy sells them three single-gram baggies of mushrooms he produces from his satchel, for just a thousand yen each. His baggies are unmarked, the mushrooms as unassuming as the others.

'They're very good. I know the guy who grows them. He's almost a genius,' the boy says. 'He's the Mao of shrooms.'

'Right,' Drew says. 'Uh-huh.'

He gives Brigit a business card with no business on it.

'Mao-shrooms,' she says. 'I get it. You have long fingers. Michael Edwards.'

'Before I go,' he says. 'Can I ask you some simple little questions? Tell me one thing you know about this place.'

'It's hot,' says Drew.

'Why?' Sam says.

'Just for my own . . . research purposes,' he says.

'We're here to learn about it,' Brigit says. 'You can't know a country unless you live there for a time.'

'Experience is important.'

'Yes.'

'Who are you?' Sam says.

'It feels . . . it feels like a lonely place,' Brigit says.

'How it feels is important.'

'Of course.'

'One thing, then.'

'Okay. It's . . . incredibly vast. And dense. But everything feels . . . used. Too looked-at.'

'What about you,' the boy says to Sam.

'What research?' Sam says. 'Who are you?'

'Come on. Just one thing. Indulge me.'

'I don't in*dulge* drug dealers. You're just trying to make fun of us.'

'Sa-am,' Brigit says.

'Just tell him something,' Drew says. 'This is a good deal.'

'All right then. I know quite a bit about the monument made by the family of a war criminal with Japanese clay and mud from China. It's of Kannon. The Buddhist god of compassion. It's at Atami, to commemorate the Sino-Japanese War dead.'

'*Lonely Planet*, page 201. "Excursions".'

'Fuck you.'

The boy laughs. 'I made that addition. It was . . . fiercely resisted, I think the term would be. And heavily edited.'

'Hey, no, I've got a real one,' Drew says. 'The Japanese make

sashimi out of blowfish. Pufferfish. It's called fugu. And like
two hundred people die every year from eating it. Some of it's
poisonous. They're the only people in the world that eat it. I
wanna try it man. I'm ready.'

'They cook it, too. The u is sometimes almost silent, so it
sounds a little like "foog". Or "hoog". There's a fugu store up
there,' the boy says, pointing up the street. 'If you want to see.'

'How did you know we were JETs? How did you know where
we're from?' Sam says.

The boy dabs his finger at each one of them in turn, as if he's
counting. 'It's written all over your faces. I can read it.'

Before he turns and leaves, he says, 'It's written all over your
eyes.'

The three JETs stand at the end of the alleyway in Shibuya on
their first night in Japan, examining the little baggies in their
hands. It's grown even more humid, the air hot and close, wet
as sticky milk. An odour rises up through manhole lids in the
black, greasy, litter-strewn street: a yellow diarrheal smell like
sulphur. All three of them are sweating heavily. Their faces
glisten in the orange streetlamps and soaking T-shirts hang
taut and darkly on the slopes and bumps of young shoulders.
Another rattle sounds close by; another shop shuts up. It's hard
to draw breath. Drew smokes, but hasn't lit a cigarette since the
air-conditioned bar in Roppongi. To smoke in this air seems
absurd.

'I'm doing mine now,' he says abruptly. 'I'm gonna do the
shrooms now. Fuck it.'

Brigit laughs. 'Fuck it, *maan*,' she says. 'But my beer is flat.'

'You guys are ridiculous,' Sam says. 'These could be
dangerous. Poisonous. God knows.'

'You're going to have a great time in Japan, mate,' Drew says.
'I can just tell.' He reaches into his backpack and pulls out one,
then, dramatically, two, then three cans of Sapporo.

'But they're warm already,' he says, and looks at Brigit.

She looks at him, then at Sam, then back to Drew, and a
helpless grin takes shape, like an amused groan. Like she's
remembering something left behind, and leaving it there.

Drew is nodding, grinning too. He throws a can to Sam.

He catches it. 'Guys,' he says, and breaks off, looking at their grins, starting to smile too. 'No way.'

'Way,' Brigit says. 'Oh, *way*.'

Drew whoops suddenly, punches the air with the baggie in his hand. 'We're gonna get hi-*igh*,' he shouts.

'Let's do it,' Brigit says.

They squat quickly down on the curb at the corner of the alleyway. They open their beers, suck the froth that bursts out, wincing, making noises at the warmth. Drew is suddenly very businesslike. 'Everything is legal,' he mutters, fumbling with the baggie. 'Street beer, mushies. There are no rules.' Brigit watches Drew for clues, and imitating him, pours the contents of the little baggie into her palm. 'There are no rules at all.' In her hand are three whole shriveled mushrooms, one cap and three stalks surrounded by dust and fragments. She picks through them, looks up at Drew. He puts a whole mushroom in his mouth, and staring first at her, then Sam, chews quickly, exaggeratedly, making sticky clicking noises.

Through a mouthful, trying to grin, he mumbles, 'Remember to masticate the head hard and fast, Brigit,' and snorts.

'Jesus,' Sam says, and delicately puts a piece of cap in his mouth. He blinks and puffs his cheeks. 'They taste . . . they taste like *dirt*.'

Brigit imitates Drew, and squatting, facing each other, faces working, jaws clicking, teeth sometimes bared and sipping beer to chase the taste that's more like very lightly perfumed cardboard, the two eat their bagfuls quickly, finishing obsessively, holding the bags up to the streetlamps, flicking them with their fingertips, licking their palms.

Sam is still eating. 'Oh my god they're dis*gusting*,' he splutters.

'Don't you *dare* spit it out, don't you *dare*,' Drew shouts.

'God, he's right,' Brigit says, grimacing, shuddering at the aftertaste. 'Ooh, God, Drew, they're really *awful*.'

'No,' Drew says. 'They're beautiful. Say it with me. They taste beautiful.'

'They taste beautiful.'

'Jesus, God,' Sam says.

'It doesn't work.'

'I can't eat these, I can't.'

'Give them here then, mate,' Drew says. 'I'll eat them.'

'I'll eat them, too,' Brigit says.

'Good on ya,' Drew says. 'Gimme.'

He snatches the bag from Sam.

'Take them. They're foul.'

'Me me,' Brigit says.

Drew pours the remains of the third baggie into his hand, divides the pile, hands her half. They both chew shuddering, laughing, drinking more beer, Sam shaking his head in disgust.

When all the bags are empty, they leave them lying on the street by their empty cans like burst balloons.

And these streets where they weren't raised is where they walk, waiting for the drugs to come on. It's a different kind of tourism now: they seem to stare at the stores and the tall thin buildings with an expectant childlike energy, waiting for them to change. What was a weary trudge has become a light quick step, of a specific mission, a pleasant appointment. They turn corners without dissent or debate. They pass a line of immense, mirrored escalators, emptily turning—four down and four up—into a giant blue neon-lined chamber. It's ignored, or glanced sharply into then away. Their eyes are bright and alert.

Deeper into endless asphalt Shibuya hills; loomed over, darkened. Sam looks back only once, briefly.

Brigit says, 'I need to find a convenience store. Some gum for the taste.'

Drew just nods. They continue up the hill.

'Segafredo,' he reads from a sign. 'What about a drink. Will that do?'

'I need gum.'

'Chewing will help.'

Something has changed between them, even Sam. Like now they hold a shared secret; like now they hold three corners of a laden table.

Segafredo is a two storied cafe, all red and black tile; plastic furniture outside. It's mostly filled with Japanese, but a lot of foreigners, too, especially later in the evenings. Upstairs is nonsmoking. They stop outside, in front of a table of four young foreigners, all different races.

Drew asks a dark, curly-haired girl.

'Do you speak English?'

There's a young white girl with long black hair and a Chinese boy, and a tall pale boy with shaved hair.

It's him that answers. 'Very well thank you, yes.'

'Is there a convenience store round here?'

He turns in his seat and points up the hill. 'Go go go,' he says. 'Then left then left. Hill. Right. Comme ça.'

The Chinese boy laughs at him. 'Oh "very well, thank you". Asshole, Jacques.'

Brigit's staring inside the cafe.

'What,' Sam says.

'That looks like,' she says, and laughs abruptly.

The four at the table look at her. 'Don't,' the Chinese boy says. 'Don't say it.'

'That's Stephen Dorff,' Brigit says, incredulous.

'Holy shit,' Drew says. 'It is.'

He's sitting at a table just inside the doors of Segafredo, ignoring a Japanese girl.

'Don't say anything,' the dark girl says. 'He gets pissed.'

'It's not,' Sam says. 'Is it?'

'Wow,' Drew says, beginning to laugh. 'Oh wow. Japan.'

At the table the Chinese boy is sneering at them.

'Come on,' Sam says. 'It's not. Let's go.'

He takes Brigit by the arm and pulls her with him.

'That's so cool,' Drew says.

'Assholes,' the Chinese boy says loudly as they leave.

For Brigit, suddenly, out on the street, speaking suddenly and silently to herself at the onset of the low dosage, her own voice inside the feeling feeds her this:

what are you really doing here a tiny nauseaworm is asking, turning in its own heat and feces. what do you really want now coiling around the fetus in her womb. do you think he's a strong boy shaking scales off in her arms. how pretty am I the worm is asking pretty enough to stay and stay alone forever ever in the oilyquiet heat?

'Um,' Brigit says.

'Come on,' Sam says. 'Let's go. Come *on*, Brigit.'

'Oh. I feel a little sick, Sam,' she says. 'I feel a little nauseous.'

'Oh shit,' Drew says, beside them, laughing. 'Oh shit that's the first sign. You're gonna be tripping soon mate. Get ready.'

'I need . . . something. I need gum.'

'Are you okay?' Sam says.

'I feel funny, Sam,' she says. 'I feel funny.'

They walk up to the end of the street and turn left at the corner, Brigit following Drew, Sam beside her. The crowds are thick but thinning as the first night in Japan wears on.

Drew glances back past them down the hill, an amused and wearied grin as he sees Brigit's pale face, and then a little twist as a tiny Japanese girl shrieks with laughter right beside him, and quickly in a voice, recognisably his own but utterly accentless, as the shrooms start to come on, he finds he's telling himself:

the deserts near Toowoomba were rolling hills like these for you but why does that come to you now when the real question is do you want to eat them to make you wet or why? what's enough for you are you enough for one who knows you really anymore that's the really simple little question with spines. watch the flanks of thighs go walking its you who are wet and silver inside and they are dry and you should know this feeling this bitter sticky sickness but at home it's a dry heat man a dry heat you know is what makes and made your world and it used to be the awful twilight lie down in awful twilight when the day dies there was nothing left and you wanted to be cool and warm at the same time but that can never be and everytime the thing can never be is really it was always money money money and so many days and ways of sadness and aloneness till you do it again with a hand on a thigh and a sigh and then wet and cool and warm and dry and a line of light is blackness bursting from a hole so familiar but and then like now always always always made you new and weak and that is all that is good

'Ha!' Drew says. 'It's funny.'

He gets no answer.

'They're different aren't they,' he says to himself.

His voice is utterly sad.

'That's the thing with shrooms. They're always, always quite different.'

Past the corner young Japanese girls in smocks are carrying in the boxes of Don Quixote products stacked outside the doors.

A jingle plays, a high girl chorus, 'Don Don Don, Don Quix-o-te-e.'

Outside the big store is a circle of park benches round a grizzled black old tree. They pass it by; a biker astride a huge Yamaha spurs the engine, makes it howl and murmur.

Brigit jumps at the sound, looks back once toward it.

Sam quickens his step and walks up beside her.

'Are you all right? Do you feel okay? Brigit?'

'Yes,' she says sharply, then softer, 'Yeah. Yes. Hold my hand.' She reaches for his hand and holds it tightly, and they walk along the crest of the hill together, behind Drew, who's rubbing the crook of his left arm absently, kneading the dip at the end of a bicep.

They walk the length of the block, then turn and follow Drew up a steep side street. Sam glances up to Brigit's face every few steps because she's frighteningly pale, her eyes wide and staring. Her right hand in his is very dry and is sporadically clutching hard, then soft, relaxed, then pumping his fingers together like she's fighting something painful. Drew is half the steep little block ahead of them and is pausing, checking across the street.

Sam sees the bright pink and yellow and blue of an AM/PM convenience store ahead, layered back into the ground floor of a squat concrete building like a cave. There are kids outside, mostly Japanese but also foreigners, and they form the ragged end of a queue to the club that's further up the hill. Another squat, lopsided-seeming building, the hill forming a violent angle with the last stair of a well that's crammed with people waiting.

'Here we go, Bridge,' Sam says gently. 'We'll get some water here, too.'

'I don't want to go in,' Brigit says. 'I can't go in, Sam.'

'Don't worry,' he says, and smiles. 'I vill get evrysing ve need, Fraülein. Der Deutsche-mark matters not, ja?'

He's close, still holding her hand, speaking quietly, lightly. She's staring eyes wide up the hill, to the queue, and the store. When she turns her head to him and smiles quickly her eyes don't light on his at all.

'Wait here,' he says. 'Don't move. I'll be back.'

He glances down the street and jogs across, through the loose clusters of kids.

Brigit sits shakily on the milky plastic cube of a PARKING sign. She looks for Drew up the street, but the queue is spreading like a spilled thickshake across the black little street and down the hill. He's lost in it, and the sound of the music from the club is a ferocious thumping.

'Drew,' she says quietly. And looks up at the sound of her own voice. 'Sam?'

wormausea wind and lick and furl asks what is this ve haf here zen? mocking him no he's strong don't say that stronger than me because I falter now I falter I don't know if it's better to go to fukuimiguchihonsho so cruel the words in this place and isn't this when you should be kind? but there's decisions to be made and simple little questions have no place when there are decisions to be made don't you don't you mock him evrysing ve need he said the fucking idiot no don't you say that don't the worm turns the worm turns around the little thing that's purple and sad inside her little lie her little secret her stupid stupid little flight no no not sad inside her god no don't let it know and have wise and sad and violet eyes open inside her let it be cool and sleepy there for simple little questions have no answers here is it your heart? is it your heart? is it your heart?

Brigit gasps a little, and stands up unsteadily, one hand on the PARKING sign for balance. She breathes out sharply, strongly pale; her eyes are wide and her mouth is a violent frown. The look is like feigned or exaggerated confusion. Wild confusion; almost horror. As if she had seen something terrible. She stares up the street, across to the AM/PM. She can't see Sam inside. There are too many people to look through.

She staggers once on her way up the street and into the crowd.

At the crest of the hill that she begins to climb the narrow street forks. In the tiny block formed by the splaying streets there is a building, which at its widest point is no wider than two people arms-outstretched, and at its narrowest—where it meets the forked roads directly; there are no sidewalks here—there is a small violent concrete slope. A driveway, going underground into the heart of the hill. A miniature basement garage—Drew had ducked down to look inside as he passed beside the building: at the level of his feet there was the inverted armadillo-shell of the garage-door opener attached to the garage's roof, just four feet away; he could almost reach inside and touch it—for a miniature-seeming office building that, when he dizzily raised his head, he found was more than twenty stories high.

The hills of Shibuya are mined and crusted; the buildings like a porcupine's spines with follicles diving deep beneath. All the surfaces are deceptions; every one is true.

Even deeper beneath, the subway thrums.

Over the crest of the hill, the right hand fork of the road soon meets a major highway. Taxi after taxi shines past; nearing midnight now, and the trains will be stopping soon. There are few other kinds of vehicle on the road. The median strip is a box hedge; the sidewalks cater for only two abreast. There are handrails for busy days. Lining the streets of this area are mostly business premises; anonymous stone and glass lobbies. From the street they're little more than alcoves poured with tile, elevator doors and ashtrays clinging to the walls. Gold kanji glittering in the streetlamps hangs in the air, sprinkled on the windows;

their dark distorted doubles lurk on the walls inside. Nothing stirs but dust and cigarette butts and coffee cups, dancing in sluggish eddies, clattering in the grained marble corners of entranceways. Inches away, inside the thick plate glass that's coated with the air's sediment until it's cleaned early tomorrow morning, huge paintings, Hirsts and Onicas and Savilles and Lyes, hang on the lobby walls under the shadow kanji, great darkened slabs of beautiful money.

Another taxi purrs past, coasting away down the hill towards the 109 Building and Hachiko. The winds that trouble the buildings' occupants in the day when the men head out for lunch—whipping trenchcoats so hard against legs they shuffle like girls in kimono; bursting umbrellas, puncturing them with an audible sound like a gunshot; tearing sunglasses right off— are made by the buildings themselves. In Shinjuku, the Yasuda Kasai-Kaijo Building flares from the fifteenth floor down to disrupt the power of these gusts as they funnel around the skyscrapers. In monsoon season, when the winds come, there is the salaryman with his ruined stalk of plastic and aluminum dangling, his suit sopping, hairpiece askew, shaking his fist at the new elements.

But Shibuya isn't conducive to the new wind. The hills dip and trick it. The hills break it down into tiny frantic squads, quarrelling in corners, turning on one another, reduced to feeble little dervishes like these, scrapping over litter.

So it stays humid.

And in the deep and wet and humid air Drew is down the sidewalk standing outside a restaurant that's not open.

It's not open but the window is dimly lit. His soaked T-shirt and his awestruck face are lit to a silver sheen by a small light inside. The window is narrow, and only the height of Drew. It is blackened glossily from the sidewalk to his waist; an aquarium fills the rest. He's staring into it. The fugu store.

Above it all, the surge and tide and swell of emotion, is the overriding command he gives himself, a cry:

remember this.

First there's the calm shock: fugu do not look like blowfish or pufferfish at all. They are quite reassuringly fishlike. They are bluegray and silverspotted in the tank. Two hand-spans long. More like cartoonish snubnosed cod; not ominous, spiked or worrying. The outside of the tank is stained with a green and white sediment, blurred to streaks of smeared gray where a half-hearted dishcloth has lazily wiped. Once, twice. The floor of the tank is painted aqua with large darker blue spots; faux-deco ocean, on top of which the oxygen supply is a rusting metal box the size of a pencil case. It bubbles calmly from a corrugated pipe. The back of the tank is a faded poster of a white plate turned yellow with age, with bite-sized pieces of opaque, cooked fugu resting by a single sprig of parsley.

Before their future, the fugu float, lit from above by two miniature fluorescent tubes.

Drew stands, staring, stunned.

Beneath the lights one floats on its side; eyes like drops of mercury unblinking; it gasps at the surface. The eyes and lips have crimson linings, rawlooking. It gasps in beats as regular as the bubbling of the oxygen. Open, shut, open shut, breathe, don't breathe, breathe.

Beneath it, four float free in the center of the tank.

The fugu in the center of the tank have fins that are torn and blistered, white and soft from lack of use, weeping ragged holes like pieces bitten out. They sweep slowly through the murky water, pass each other, bump, and push weakly. Their lips are red and tatters hang from them.

Another bumps its head softly in a glassed corner. There are sores around its eyes.

Through the middle of the tank two filaments of transparent material drift. Sometimes the fish float past them, cause them to trace lazy lines along their flanks. The fugu in the corner bumps its soft white snout against the glass and gasps. The lost soul at the surface floats on its side, near death.

Drew stands and stares, his T-shirt adhering moistly to his stomach, lit silverblue by the light of the tank.

The words and remonstrances have given way and he sees only floods.

'Oh my God,' he whispers, without a trace of an accent.

'What's that smell?' Sam says suddenly beside him in thick

Canadian. Then, 'Look at them. They think they're in some ancient sea. They're actually in a box.'

Drew flinches, slowly.

'Makes me want to puke. Where's Brigit?' Holding gum and a bottle of VOLVIC water.

'I . . .' Drew whispers, 'don't . . . *know* . . . you . . .'

Later, they'd find her in a glassed doorway, crying, sobbing. Sam would go to Hokkaido alone and in two months move a Japanese secretary into his apartment. He would learn to speak slowly and clearly, and never fake a German accent. Brigit would bleed the next day and never go to Fukui. In Tokyo she would get a new visa and a new job and a new last name through a friend of Michael Edwards, and move into an apartment in Shimokitazawa with Drew, whose taste for heroin had gone with his Australian accent, and who started to get really thin and found work and visa sponsorship writing for *Tokyo Classified* and who would also swear, once, in hushed, accentless tones to a nodding Michael and to Brigit, that the kitchenhand he glimpsed behind the tank was carrying a sword.

ELIZABETH SMITHER

The Sloth

Nightly on television the sloth
descends part of a tree in his
allotted advertisement slot.

We see part of a profile, a
suggestion of folded claw
and a nose that seems sunk in sleep

honey-fuzzed, like some more energetic
bear caught rifling a hive.
No leaves (for food) appear:

the sloth's between one food source
and the ground: awful dilemma
to go up or down

or simply in a dreamtime pause
and allow natural camouflage
to send flickering signals to the brain

one claw and then one claw, three toes
or two, too slow for image to explain
but only marvel that he moves

lifting a coiling-designed paw
and arm which so logically extends
his desire to hang on

like a fur grappling hook
disguised in such loose vagueness
we forget it and the sloth's purpose

which must be to instruct
in gentle Doomsday frames
how gentle the fall in dreams

how equal the real pauses
and how the sloth measures these
both remembering and forgetting.

C.K. STEAD

Cartoons

8.8.96

Scientists discover
there's been life on Mars
though dead for aeons,
that's to say yonks.

President Bill says
if there's life in space
he wants the United States
to have an input.

Somewhere in Siberia
a bronze statue of Lenin
falls over
and kills a man.

Watch out for the dead!
They leave their traces—
ideas for example
and heavy statues.

12.8.96

A lost tribe is found
in the Manokwari
jungle region
of Irian Jaya.

Pale-skinned and timid
when spoken to
they hide
behind trees.

Mornings they gather
food in the forest
afternoons
they fish their lake.

Maybe they sing
at evening
omba omba
the reports don't say.

Their sentinels
are green parrots
taught to screech
when strangers approach.

13.8.96

Today it's revealed
that ex-Prime Minister
Paul Keating
kept a trampoline

in his back garden
and bounced on it
daily
to ward off cancer.

At the weightless
apogee
of each bounce
he believed

was the nanosecond
when bang!
the malignant cells
were expelled.

26.8.96

Alzheimered
Ronald Reagan
no longer remembers
he was the world's

most powerful man
carrying in a flat case
the codes
to corpse a planet.

All forgetful
he knows however
that Nancy
is his mother.

So why
after his haircut
does she lock him
in his room?

When the big light
goes down
he sits at his window
in pyjamas

hearing the moon
mumble to the hills
its threats
and rumours.

21.9.96

A Catholic Bishop
runs off with
a Mrs McPhee
and sells his story

to the popular press
but the cash is to go
to his teenage son
by a former mistress.

His housekeeper
who used to browse
in his wastepaper basket
says there were others.

Everyone's distressed.
The ailing Pope,
the nervous clergy,
the sad parishioners

of Argyll and the Isles—
even (I think)
I am distressed.
How could it be

we ask one another.
Isn't a handjob
good enough
for the modern priest?

29.9.96

In this state
the dead man rules.
All bow at morning
to the figure in bronze,

all sing at evening
the late leader's song.
Here is the Future
as the Past saw it

and it doesn't work.
In the countryside
peasants and workers
inherit the earth

which is barren.
Evening television
offers 'ten tasty tips
for cooking grass.'

30.9.96

Faber and Faber
the beautiful woman
among publishers
has a stalker.

A disgruntled author
he threatens
by phone and fax
to slash her tyres

and smash her face
if she won't oblige.
It's rumoured
her biggest boyfriends

Hughes, Heaney, Harold
Pinter, and the like
are taking turns
to see her safely home.

1.11.96

After two centuries
of displeasure
Horsham will acknowledge
its famous son.

A sculpture
honouring Shelley,
poet, atheist
and adroit eloper

will be unveiled
in the town square.
Three thousand
gingerbread men

each with a fact-sheet
about his life
have been distributed
to local schools.

BRIAN TURNER

Close of Day, Oturehua

The sun's gone down behind Blackstone Hill
and the nearby pines are still. There's
not a breath in the willows by the Ida,
but we don't need a breeze
to confirm that the world's alive

and full of promise, inspiriting.
Dogs bark and snarl, chains rattle;
my neighbour is calling
for a daft black lab called 'Boy'
to come home *Now*.

The sky is clear as conscience,
tonally pure, and in the paddock
under the hill, cattle are grunting
as if trying to shove mountains aside.

IAN WEDDE

Ballad for Worser Heberley

for the Heberley Family Reunion, Pipitea marae, Easter 1990

1

I remember the pohutukawa's summer crimson
and the smell of two stroke fuel
and the sandflies above the Waikawa mudflats
whose bites as a kid I found cruel.

At night and with gunny-sack muffled oars
when the sandflies were asleep
with a hissing Tilley lamp we'd go fishing
above the seagrass deep

—a-netting for the guarfish there
where the nodding seahorses graze
and the startled flounders all take fright
stirring the muddy haze.

And who cared about the hungry sandflies
when a-codding we would go
my blue-eyed old man Chick Wedde and me
where the Whekenui tides do flow.

It's swift they run by Arapaoa's flanks,
and they run strong and deep,
and the cod-lines that cut the kauri gunwale
reach down to a whaler's sleep.

When the tide was right and the sea was clear
you could see the lines go down
and each line had a bend in it
that told how time turns round.

The line of time bends round my friends
it bends the warp we're in
and where the daylight meets the deep
a whaler's yarns begin.

I feel a weight upon my line
no hapuku is here
but a weight of history swimming up
into the summer air.

Oil about the outboard motor
bedazzles the water's skin
and through the surge of the inward tide
James Heberley's story does begin.

2

In 1830 with a bad Southerly abaft
soon after April Fool's Day
on big John Guard's Waterloo schooner
through Kura-te-au I made my way.

And I was just a sad young bloke
with a sad history at my back
when I ran in on the tide with mad John Guard
to find my life's deep lack.

Seaspray blew over the seaward bluffs
the black rocks ate the foam
my father and my mother were both dead
and I was looking for home.

But what could I see on those saltburned slopes
but the ghosts of my career:
my father a German prisoner from Wittenburg
my grand-dad a privateer

my mother a Dorset woman from Weymouth,
I her first-born child,
and my first master was called Samuel Chilton
whose hard mouth never smiled.

He gave me such a rope-end thrashing
that I left him a second time,
I joined the *Montagu* brig for Newfoundland,
though desertion was reckoned a crime—

and me just a kid with my hands made thick
from the North Sea's icy net,
eyes full of freezing fog off the haddock banks
and the North Sea's bitter sunset.

And master Chilton that said when your mother dies
you can't see her coffin sink
you can only blink at the salt mist
about the far land's brink.

And in the fo'c'sle's seasick haven
where a lamp lit the bulkhead's leak
you'd share your yarn with the foremast crew
your haven you would seek.

Where you came from the rich ate kippers
or if they chose, devilled eggs.
They didn't blow on their freezing paws
they favoured their gouty legs.

And if you pinched an unripe greengage from their tree
they'd see you in the gallows
or if you were dead lucky
wading ashore through Botany Bay shallows.

But I was even luckier, as they say,
those who tell my tale:
they tell how my tale was spliced and bent
about the right whale's tail.

And how poor young James Heberley
fresh from South Ocean's stench
and the foretop's winching burden of blubber
his great good fortune did wrench.

In autumn I came ashore at Te Awaiti
on Arapaoa Island.
'Tangata Whata' the Maori called me—
now 'Worser' Heberley I stand.

'Ai! Tangata whata, haeremai,
haeremai mou te kai!'
Food they gave me, and a name,
in the paataka up high.

My name and my life I owe that place
which soon I made my home.
From that time, when Worser Heberley went forth,
I didn't go alone.

I raised a considerable family there,
with Ngarewa I made my pact:
from him I got my summer place at Anaho,
my home from the bush I hacked.

I summered there in the mild weather
and in autumn I went a-whaling
from the boneyard beach we called Tarwhite
where Colonel Wakefield's *Tory* came sailing.

And I guessed from the moment I saw their rig
that we had best take care:
not the Maori, nor Worser Heberley's mob
stood to gain from this affair.

With fat Dick Barrett I went as pilot
on the *Tory* to Taranaki.
From Pukerangiora and Te Motu descended
Te Atiawa's history—

a history already made bitter once
in the bloody musket wars,
that might be made bitter yet again
for Colonel Wakefield's cause.

Worser Heberley was never a fool
else I'd not have lived that long:
I could see the Colonel meant to do business,
I could hear the gist of his song.

He was singing about the clever cuckoo
that lays her egg elsewhere
and fosters there a monstrous chick
too big for the nest to bear

so the other chicks must be all cast out
for the greedy cuckoo's sake.
The Colonel sang this song I heard
as he watched the *Tory*'s wake

tack up the South Taranaki Bight
with Kapiti falling astern,
and I, James Heberley, stayed close
to see what I could learn.

And what I learned has since been written
in many a history book:
that you'll find little enough of our record there
however hard you look.

3

And now Worser Heberley's story ceases,
I hear his voice no more
though my line still bends by the notched gunwale
as it had done before

when I was just a kid gone fishing
in my old man's clinker boat
and hadn't learned that it's history's tide
that keeps our craft afloat.

And now I see as I look about
in Pipitea marae
at the multitude here assembled
that your line didn't die—

and though old Worser Heberley was right
to fear Colonel Wakefield's song,
he didn't have to worry about the family
which multiplies and grows strong.

I thank you for your kind attention
the while my yarn has run.
I wish you all prosperity and peace.
Now my poem is done.

PETER WELLS

from One of THEM!

It hurts to be in love

'I just don't get Dad,' says Lemmy in the flat tide-out voice he uses when he's thinking about something else. 'I *mean*. I just can't see why he won't get his eyebags surgically removed. They're so *ugly*, and I mean: *ug-leeee!*'

Yes Lemmy I say looking down at *Vogue New Zealand* which lies open on a cushion in front of us. We're doing research on what a face-lift can do for you. I'm fourteen, Lemmy's going on fifteen and he's fat. I don't ever say this to him, I wouldn't dare. He's four foot nothing, human dynamite.

I'm five foot ten and thin. I like to think I'm Audrey Hepburn thin, sort of elegant. When I sit I try to cross my legs over, like I've seen in books.

When people see us together, they laugh. *We just don't care.* We laugh back. At least Lemmy does.

Lemmy's got eyeliner on, just the faintest line, and he's done his hair all spun gold and ironed flat, not a curl in sight and he's borrowed some Stay Firm from Dianne, his sister.

The faint smell fills the air, we breathe it in hungrily, like it's a perfume.

Lemmy wrote my note and I wrote Lemmy's note and we're hiding out back at his place, windows closed, door shut, we keep away from the windows. His mother's not at home, she was taken away. It happened last week. Now I look around the room, thinking this is where it happened.

Outside there's not a person in the street, not a car: nothing. I watch a blackbird spear a drowned worm. Beak slashes it aside, disgusted.

Lemmy's getting bored, I can feel it. Lemmy gets bored a lot, sometimes he does things just to stop being bored.

He goes over to the radiogram. Lemmy doesn't move a facial

muscle as he puts on one of Dianne's records. I relax and wonder what's coming next. The music swells all velvet around us.

> *It hurts to be in love,*
> > *when the only one you love*
> > > *turns out to be*
> > > > *someone*
> > > > > *who's not in love with you*

I look at Lemmy and Lemmy looks at me as the red velvet unrolls all around us and we lie back into it, we loll.

Lemmy lights up a Bold Gold, blows out a stream of smoke. He says: 'You know he's one of *them*?'

He says it slow and husky, soft, like it's not a question really.

I just look at Lemmy, I'm almost frightened, I'm waiting.

> *So I cry a little bit (to be in love)*

'*Him?*' I say soundlessly and I suddenly think of Gene's face on the record cover and I get this overpowering waterfall of feeling that I want to pull his fluffy jersey down, down round his neck, I want to licklicklick and kiss him right under there, where it's warm, it's hot, it's sticky. This shocks me. I see Lemmy looking at me closely now, he's got this cruel look on his face. *Don't laugh at me Lemmy*. Don't. *Please*.

I look back at Lemmy, forcing my eyes to look into his. His eyes are hard.

'That's really disgusting,' I say. 'He must be *really* sick.'

> *And so you*
> > *die a little bit*

'I don't believe you,' I say desperately wanting Lemmy to say it's really true, and I pick up a book, any book, and pretend I'm really interested in it. But as I flick through all I'm thinking about is Gene's fluffy jersey and his soft parted lips. I can feel myself getting red, slowly, like a stain all through me I can't get off. I can hardly breathe now, yet I force myself to go on flicking through the book, like everything's normal. *Normal*. I hate that word. Then I look down and see what I'm holding and it's *a sex book*. Lemmy just looks at me, blows out this cool veil of blue/grey smoke. He's watching me now, real close.

I act like I'm not surprised but my hand has turned dead on me, I can see it down there, a dead gull dried by the wind, eyesocket staring back at me, watching.

'Look at this,' my voice says for me. 'Look!' and I let out a strangled laugh. I wave at him the cover which says: *A Report on Real-Life Sexual Experience*, compiled by Dr Alfred K. Kitchsenburger, PhD(Med)(Hons)(Tuvalu Uni.).

Now I've got Lemmy's attention and he's no longer looking at my face.

He reaches over, snatches the book out of my hand, cruel, so I'm left naked again, with only my face to hide behind and I can't hide what's in my face, I'm not like Lemmy.

Lemmy now rolls over onto his back and, holding his cigarette in this exaggerated stilt-way, starts reading out. He reads in an American accent like *I Love Lucy*.

> *I followed him into the changing room and as he rammed his ten inch black cock into my mouth, I gagged but then I found I liked it and I started. . .*

He stops now, glances over at me. I'm so naked I grab the book off him. He's surprised I'm so violent, I grab the book and I start reading, practically calling it out at the top of my voice, practically singing:

> *And I just got down on my knees there on that dirty floor and started worshipping his prick, with people just outside the door, on their way to work, but, oh, so help me God, the demon of sex was upon me and I couldn't, I just couldn't keep a control of myself!*

Everything's so silent all you can hear is our breathing, a charged duet, and I know I've got to go on reading.

I feel something dismal and confused and magnetised, I can't explain it and I look at Lemmy and Lemmy has this flushed look and then I hear my voice and it stops me. '*I don't believe you Lemmy Stephenson. I just don't believe you.*'

'What?' he says all flat again. He rolls over onto his back and looks up at the ceiling, bored. Then he stubs his cigarette out real slow, he kills it.

'I don't believe you. Gene's not one of *them. He can't be.*'

'Why not.'

He doesn't even look at me.

'You're making it up. Aren't you? Tell me. *I only want to know the truth*,' I say, both knowing I'm lying and I know we're both thinking, *thinking* about this world we've just opened up.

'You made it all up!' I cry out, my voice all dry and full of hurt and Lemmy looks at me suddenly like he really hates me and then he yawns very elaborate and long and slow like he's just heard the most boring thing in all existence and I'm it.

Lemmy acts like he's just suddenly been woken up, from a snooze, he's such a good actor, Lemmy. He acts like he's surprised to see me there, with the sex book in my hand. In fact he acts like he's surprised he's even on planet earth. He didn't plan it.

'Oh . . . sorry,' Lemmy says to me, fanning his fingers over his open mouth, 'Someone must have slipped some librium into my coffee. You were saying . . . ?'And he looks at me, enigmatic.

'*Nothing* Lemmy,' I say all defeated. 'Nothing.'

And then suddenly Lemmy leaps up and goes over to the window out which I can see, just see, a little old woman in a fawn overcoat wheeling her shopping trolley behind her like she can't get away from it and she's been walking for days and days but the trolley is still following her, and won't go away, and she's just about going crazy with exhaustion, *yet she can't stop.*

Lemmy stands behind the net curtains, and he just screams, in this sound so shrill it's like spun sound made sharp and stalactited so like a sliver of glass it enters the flesh, breaks off, can't get out, aims straight for the heart, arrow of hate, sliver of hurt, all scarlet and drenched: Lemmy just opens his mouth and screams out in this high wavering falsetto, outdoing Lucille

Ball, 'I JES' CAN'T KEEP A CONTROL OF MYSELF, SO
HELP ME GOD!'

I crack up and oh Lemmy I say, I'm laughing but I'm actually
frightened, Oh Lemmy, You're such a scream. Such a scream.
And I think. Lemmy. *Don't kill yourself Lemmy.*

I had no idea I was doing wrong. I loved Lemmy. It was only
later I realised it was wrong. *Yet it was necessary.*

I learnt this too, later, after it happened.

All the things I did that were so wrong were also necessary.

A town without pity

'OK,' says Lemmy who's got over being bored, he's suddenly a
fired up crackercaper, he's twenty-tied-together-tomthumbs all
splattering and battering the silence out of the air, beating it up
as the crackers crack, leap, ignite. Tang of gunpowder laces the
air.

I look into Lemmy's face, his long straight nose, his gilded
hair. His eyes glitter, outlined in mascara. Lemmy examines his
nails, carefully, as if for dirt: but I know he's really thinking.

I stand there, wondering what's coming next. I hope he
doesn't notice I've got a pimple coming up, right in the crease
by my nose. Lemmy is very critical of things like that. But
Lemmy is looking right through me, like he's read me cover-
to-cover, I'm Sandra Dee, or Bobby Darin, positively South
Pacific point, corny as Kansas. *No I'm not Lemmy I silently
say: test me.*

This is how it always begins, right from the start: *test me.*

Lemmy jumps up and does his Pete Sinclair imitation.
Happen Inn: 'New Zealand's Own Go-Go Show', The Chooks
inside cages, rockhard beehives and go-go boots: Pete Sinclair
jumps onto the blackwhite screen, like he's a genie just dying to
get out from inside. He's wearing his old old crooked smile and
baked-on hairdo. He turns sideways, sort of Spanish, clacks his
heels, claps his hands together twice, hard, like castanets and
yells out, 'Let's go! (*clap! clap!*) LETS GO!'

When Lemmy does it, it's like he lets you see the joke inside:

and the joke is this: everything in New Zealand is so crumby it's laughable. Once you see the joke you can't stop laughing. This is the trick Lemmy taught me.

So we decide to fan the breeze, as Lemmy says. We escape into town, on the trolley, looking for excitement of which, that day, there is none. Instead it is cool, wet, lead-grey. The sky is all laced down to earth by black powerlines, as if everyone in this town is frightened to let the sky get too high, it might show us up for how small we really are.

We have a cup of coffee in the mezzanine lounge in 246, watching people go up and down on the escalators, but still nothing's happening so Lemmy takes me down to this toilet in a carpark, he takes me in very casually and we have a cigarette and read all the messages and words on the walls. While I am reading them, Lemmy gets out this pen, and, like he's done it before, writes right central and where it can't be missed, 'STICK YR STIFF DALK INTO MY HOT HOLE—(signed) a schoolboy.' Then he writes: 'I am all sexed up and ready.'

Underneath it Lemmy writes that very day, that very hour. I laugh, oh Lemmy I say, you're such a scream.

Lemmy goes deadpan: 'Let's go outside and watch the fun develop.'

We hide behind the concrete pillars and smoke away about five-ten minutes of no-time, when time stops and waits for something next to happen, to push it along again.

While we're waiting, Lemmy goes back to his old point: *Why?*

'Why what?' I say to Lemmy, my heart sinking because I know what he's talking about.

'Why bother?' Lemmy says then, throwing away his cigarette. I watch it roll over and over itself, disgorging ashes and splinters of fire and spark, till it dies. The wind then rocks it back-and-forth, gently, as if to show its emptiness.

He's talking School Cert.

'*What's the use*,' Lemmy says then, his unanswerable question.

What is the use? I don't know, I did once, I thought I did, then Lemmy showed me different.

'I haven't decided yet,' I say to Lemmy, stalling for time, trying to stop him, *lying*.

'I just gotta get outta this dump, Jamie,' Lemmy says, using my name which he hardly ever does—only when it's serious. '*If it's the last thing I ever do . . .*' and his voice dies off into silence in which there is no sound at all, only a distant car horn suffocating. I think about what he means. Yet I know what he means: it's like we're on gas and it's being turned down so low you can hardly breathe any more, you're slowly dying on your feet but you keep on walking. It's like there's all the air in the world in this place but no oxygen.

Oh Lemmy, look at this, I say, then I do an imitation of the Supremes, singing BabyLove, with a mike and everything.

I sing all falsetto. Lemmy looks at me, kind of smiles, a crooked curl of a smile, then Lemmy changes again, quickly. He forgets me. He puts his finger up to his lips.

'I think we got a live one.'

I lean out from behind the pillar very slowly.

A man in cling bermuda shorts gets out of a car slowly, looks both ways, carefully, then, with an almost elaborate casualness, he crosses the road and disappears into the toilet so quickly it's as if he's never been in the road at all.

I know Lemmy has got it wrong. Because this man is like any man you might see on the bus, he's not a pansyfairyqueerhomo, and just because of his ordinariness, I feel my whole flesh burn with the words on the wall *plugholearsecock* and I look at Lemmy *feelspunkdalk* and Lemmy looks through me, he has the same fever I can see.

But Lemmy waits for one second then beckons me from behind the pillar with his finger. It's very like a movie this: we silently move forward to the toilet door beyond which we can hear the slippery silvery sound of the water in the urinal cascading down and there's a kind of great silence, waiting.

I look at Lemmy as he listens. He is so tense his face has turned to metal: only his eyes flash over at me as he decides to enter, occupy this empty cell of silence.

He goes inside there for a moment, creeping in. I suddenly feel alone. I realise where I am. *What if someone who lives up the road sees me?* Then Lemmy tiptoes back, hides. Now his mouth opens wide, and Lemmy lets out his great screaming shriek from behind the wall.

I feel an intense rush of fear and excitement as Lemmy's scream echoes all over the concrete carpark, multiplies, comes together again, crashes and splinters apart. I don't know what to think, I am so excited by what Lemmy has just done.

The man torpedoes out of the toilet, quickly, not turning around, as if his face couldn't be seen, at all costs he must remain anonymous. I see now he is not so handsome, he is frightened. He gets into his car, a grey Morris Minor, registration number CL52043. He accelerates away while I scream out, taking over from Lemmy: 'WeirdoQueerPansyPoufterHomo! You Ought to Be Put Down! You Ought to be Dead!'

He kissed me on the lips till I came, I think.

Serves them right, I say to Lemmy after we've run away and finished screaming and shrieking, when we've slowed down and we realise there is nowhere else to go, that is our excitement for the day.

Serves him right, eh Lemmy, I say, but Lemmy doesn't say anything, doesn't say a word, just walks along all silent and unknown. Then suddenly he looks at me and I am scared. *No Lemmy no. Don't. Please Lemmy, don't laugh at me.*

I Only Want Be With You

This is how we met, in violence.

We were playing tiggy one day, at school. You take the ball and spin it, and brand someone, the ball so wet, heavy and harsh, it hurts. In the game, you could do this to people and they wouldn't know till it hit them. Then everyone laughs. And everyone laughs nervous, so it won't hit them. Everyone is praying it'll be someone else. And when it hits whoever it is—someone with glasses, or fat, or thin—everyone laughs even louder, because it's not them.

This day, I'm dreaming, I'm dreaming about our head prefect who I can see: this prefect, I can't help myself, he's so handsome and each night I have this same dream; the school catches on fire and I rescue the head prefect and then alone, together, *amo amas amat*. Then I hear Lemmy four foot nothing, fatboy with legs so fat they rub together at the knees, and he says very low, whispering in that flat voice I get to know so well, without emphasis, without any emotion: *let's brand the beanpole*. Me. Five foot ten, aged thirteen.

I am fast, too fast: I am the champion sprinter in all the school, I am famous for fastness. So the ball skids past tearing open the air as it goes, hurtling past me, then into the creek.

I run now to get it, I am hot. Behind me I hear over the wet grass the heavy heartbeat poundbash of other footsteps rushing to get the ball so they can brand me again. I know now the ball will be wet: it will sting. But as I bend over the kikuyu forest, in among the stamens and tongues of green, I see this sandwich, just floating so innocent.

It has been luncheon sausage, and the bread, white, has turned into softsoft blotting paper, floating apart gently so it comes to pieces and gently nudges the turd floating beside it.

My fingers close around the sandwich. I pick it up real gentle and careful so it won't fall apart and then I balance the soggy grey mass cupped inside my palm. I feel tendrils of power rushing down my arm, chill, cold as death. Boys shy away, stand still, panting inout inout scarletblood danger. I hold it high now and then I find *fatboy* and he's looking at me now, without an expression, I see this in a quick glimpse, like a photo, then *beanpole* yells to *fatboy* so loud everyone can hear, urgent, as if to catch the real ball with which I'm going to brand him forever, TAKE THIS FATBOY!

The sandwich flies through the air, disintegrating as it whirls, catching in its path all the power from the other boys whose eyes watch entranced, chanting, singing yelling in one rush of breath, an arrow of pleasure it's not them: BRAND HIM BRAND FATBOY BRAND FATBOY.

The sandwich splatters all across Fatboy's face. He stands there with it dripping and dropping, his face that frozen expressionless mask I get to know so well, when I know what it means. At the same time, his whole face, from his neck up, starts going deep bright red—*the stain*. Everyone laughs now, released, relieved it wasn't them that got hit, everyone is secretly pleased too it is fatboy who has this cruel laugh.

But Lemmy is not finished. He picks off a piece of the sandwich and fishes out the scarlet skin of the luncheon sausage and, holding it between his fingers like it's a delicacy, he opens his mouth, looking at Ken Johnston who is lying on the grass laughing with tears forcing through his lids going heeeeehhhhheeehhheehhh, like he's punctured and all his fear is coming out. 'Fatboy got hit,' Ken says over and over again, so glad it's not him. Lemmy goes M . . . MMmmmm! as if it's the Maggi soup ad on TV, and we all stop so still because, just for one second, *we believe it.*

Then Lemmy opens his mouth, drops the luncheon sausage in, and we all go totally quiet watching him and he looks at all of us one by one as if he is remembering our faces for later retribution, and when we are all silent apart from Ken Johnston who is wheezing now, having an asthma attack of tears and nerves and joy, Lemmy finishes eating, licking his fingerpads delicately clean, and when he swallows I swear across the whole football field under that dirtysheet sky, you can hear us all swallow hard and dry, as if we are trying to swallow a lump, a rock, sand, dirt.

When it is all gone, Lemmy just says, *'Tas–ty!'*

Then he walks away from us, on his own, his fat legs rubbing together at the knees.

A few days later we are sitting in Latin class. Lemmy, who usually sits right down the back, quietly takes a seat right behind Ken Johnston. We're waiting for Mr Chisnall, our Latin teacher, to arrive.

Now Ken Johnston has this Brylcreemed swished-back-hairdo he is very proud of. He has an old grey/yellow comb he slips out of his back pocket, sharp as a knife, which he then pulls, luxuriantly, through his hair, so we can appreciate the extra length. This comb always has a thin line of pus in it from grease and dandruff. Normally someone would have said something about it but the fact is Ken Johnston's father has the only swimming pool in our class and *a two-storey house,* and you could tell every time Ken Johnston pulled that comb through his Fabian hairdo he was just thinking about being the only boy in our class with a swimming pool and *who can he invite home for a swim.*

But Ken Johnston is pretty clever, he never actually *says* his father has a swimming pool. He doesn't have to. Every move he makes advertises it, and the way his hair is all sort of elaborately piled up on his head and swished back into a kind of duck's tail says it for him. Ken has a bike with turned up handlebars, which he rides looknohands, and to see him you know all he's thinking about is how to get that beautiful Brylcreemed hairdo home in one piece so he can float it, all reflected, in his swimming pool.

Anyway, we're all waiting for Mr Chisnall to arrive, to bang his books down on the desk with an extra thump and for him to look at us fierce and angry, and begin. Mr Chisnall is a sports hero, he represented NZ in sprinting and it's always as if he's straining at the start line, muscles all tensed, waiting for the gun to go off. We're all making a lot of noise, filling in our freedom with waiting.

Suddenly I notice the others nudging each other and pointing down the front. I look. There is Lemmy looking very very serious and while Ken is putting out on show his native woods ruler and pencil sharpener in the shape of San Francisco Harbour Bridge, Lemmy is very very intently picking something off the back of Ken Johnston's black jersey. It is the way Lemmy is doing it that gradually gets everyone's attention.

He plucks a little piece off like it's gold, just on the tip of Ken Johnston's shoulder, just out of his sight. Lemmy then holds it up in the air, as if he's inspecting it: then suddenly, it turns into a flea, he drops it with a look of distaste on his face, blows it away from him, flicks it as if it might jump back on him.

He starts off slow and concentrated but, bit by bit, he is finding so much of Ken's dandruff that one by one, everyone in the class starts watching.

There is this pure corridor of silence, we all stand down one end and watch Lemmy touching, or rather *not* touching, Ken, so delicate is his whisk. Then Ajax Murphy, who has thick pebble lenses and is just about as unpopular as Lemmy, starts off this hyena laughter, it's as if he can't really control it.

Ken can hear this laughter and he turns around but Lemmy is faster, he's reading his Latin book very seriously, slowly turning the page. The moment Ken turns back, there is Lemmy back doing it, even more exaggerated and *bored*.

Ken starts going red, he can't turn around too quickly or his elaborate hairdo might sort of glide to the side, the fringe'd come unthatched. Besides Ken is so cool he can't move quickly, cool people don't. So he just sort of sits there wanting to die with this big cheese-eating grin on his face every time he turns around, *suddenly*, to find everyone just looking at him and laughing and laughing and Lemmy sitting there so cool and still and flicking over a page, his lips even moving as he reads.

I looked at Lemmy whose face never changed once, though you could tell behind its whiteness beat this fierce rush, and I suddenly thought I want to know you Lemmy Stephenson. I need to know you. *Lemmy please know me.*

Where he goes, I'll follow

'I usually wait till Mum's gone out then I go through her cupboard and use whatever eyeliner I like. I think it's really important to have *eyebrows*. Don't you?'

Lemmy looks at me. He has this way of looking which is to look all over your face like suddenly your face has turned into a great big planet and he's a long way away on the moon gazing at every square inch of it through a telescope.

'You're a runner,' he says, more like an accusation. 'You're the fastest boy in the whole fourth form.'

I can't help it Lemmy, I want to say but we are just getting to know each other, standing by the wiremesh fence high above the swimming pool, Lemmy giving it a good hard vicious kick every so often, so it rattles.

In the background we can see the tall stooped figure of Mr Brakevich, our gym teacher, who Lemmy baptised Mr Shitalot. Mr Shitalot likes to cane a lot, a kind of cloud of unhappiness envelopes him so much that he looks out at everyone, not quite seeing them, but spraying them with hate.

It was his job every year to make sure that any boy who
didn't participate in sport took part in the school marathon,
which was by way of punishment. You had to keep running
till you dropped, over the school farm, up the extinct volcano,
through the creek, avoiding the hidden boulders, with everyone
waiting at the finish tape to see in how much pain you were.
Sport is important at our school. It builds character.

Like Mr Shitalot, who this very moment is pushing into the
chill water the boys who are too slow getting in. He's really
enjoying himself; you can tell, because the creases in his face go
sort of white, and he bites his lip into a sort of grimace, as if he's
laughing to himself inside all the time.

The biggest mistake Mr Shitalot ever made was sending his
son to our school: he was a punching bag within a week and he
stayed that way till he ran away and was brought back. Then
he got sent away to somewhere mysterious. But in that time Mr
Shitalot's son changed. For life. Our school builds character,
you see. It makes us into men, which is what sport is all about.

And this is how Lemmy and I first ended up being together.

We both had letters from our mothers saying we weren't
allowed to swim. I had earaches and Lemmy had a complaint
nobody was allowed to know about. Lemmy told me he was his
mother.

'It makes things so much easier,' Lemmy says airily. 'You just
have to make sure your writing shows confidence,' he adds.

I look at Lemmy and I can tell there's something strange
about Lemmy when he talks about his mother. Or rather when
he *doesn't* talk about his mother. It was like he didn't have one.
But I knew he did.

'I hate running,' I say suddenly. 'I don't even know why I do
it. Or rather I do, I s'pose. It's because,' I say bitterly, though
this vein of bitterness is new to my voice, it is like I was just
finding it by saying it, 'It's because, like, my mother and father
were *so good at sport.*'

I say the last words like they are one word, which they are
in a way. Anyone who went to our grammar school knew that
beinggoodatsport was a single attribute, like truth, or beauty,
or knowledge.

Lemmy gives the fence an extra hard boot. Unlike me, he is wearing orthopedic-heavy shoes and socks, even though it is supposed to be summer. I reckon to myself quietly that he wears them for extra protection. Getting home without being bashed up can sometimes be difficult.

Fence rattles in complaint.

'My father was almost an All Black,' I say, 'and my mother played basketball for Southland and . . .' It was like a catechism stretching back into my childhood.

'*Misses* Stephenson and Caughey!' drifts across the grass. It is Mr Shitalot, suddenly catching us in his spray of acid. The other boys' laughter follows in a curtain. We both straighten up, whipped. 'If you can spare us the time from your hen party, perhaps you can get on *picking up rubbish.* Quicksmart!'

'Yessir,' I call back then feel Lemmy look at me again like I was the planet earth and he was deep inside a crater on the moon, so distant.

I follow Lemmy away from the swimming pool, losing Mr Shitalot and the boys. Lemmy doesn't say anything. We just walk on. Then we are alone, on a playing field down by the school creek, pitted and pitched with volcanic rocks. Lemmy lies back like a beauty queen, stretching himself out comfortably.

'We'll empty one of the bins for our rubbish,' he tells me and yawns elaborately. 'Shitalot's such a mental retard he'll never notice.' He yawns again.

I lie back too, slowly, and watch a radiating sphere grow round the sun. The sky is very white, stretched tight like a drum. A single bird, very high in the sky, changes its direction and flies away from the flock. In the far distance we can hear the occasional roar of Mr Shitalot on his way, as Lemmy says, to his first heart attack. ('And hopefully his last.')

'I'm going to leave New Zealand just as soon as I can,' I say in a tight voice. I am looking up at the sun and thinking how it looked like a giant diamond. I glance at Lemmy who seems ruby-purple, streaked with orange flares of light. I can't see him but I speak. 'I'm going to be a famous dress designer in Paris.' I tell him what I've told no other. 'I'm already doing designs after school for my first collection.'

Lemmy doesn't say a word.

'*Who wants to be a millionaire*,' I sing falsetto. '*I do!*'

Lemmy lets out a croak.

In the distance Mr Shitalot's voice reaches a pitch of intensity approximating insanity.

'Do you know Archie Bumstead?'Lemmy says suddenly.

Before my eyes I see us all in the changing sheds, struggling out of our clothes, trying not to reveal ourselves. It is cold and wet. And there, on the far side of the shed, is Archie, standing completely naked, no towel, nothing; displaying for us all to see his thick long penis softly embedded in a luxurious nest of black pubic hair. Archie Bumstead, who spent all his science lessons drawing pictures of bums, making them into a kind of targetboard, with circles moving concentrically inwards. I gulped. My throat is dry. The sky suddenly races with stars.

'Why?' I ask, trying to blank the screen out. It frightens me, I know it is wrong, very wrong. 'He's horrible.'

'He lives down the road from me.'

Silence.

'What,' I say very faintly, 'Lemmy, what are you going to do when you . . . ?'

'Grow up?' he offers darkly.

I flush scarlet. Lemmy is now sitting up. He has a stone in his hand and he throws it, sharply, at a cow which freezes, turns a startled eye on Lemmy then shambles away. The other animals awkwardly follow.

'Yes but,' I hurry on, 'what are you going to do when you leave school.'

Lemmy looks at me, surprised. He leaves a long pause in which we both look at the flat horizon of small houses all crouched down under the sky, as if the sky is crushing them with its invisible weight. Over by the pool comes a frantic tugging whistle, frayed by the wind, flittering the sound apart till it faded, an echo inside its own emptiness.

'Nothing,' he says, as if it is a matter concluded long ago. '*Nothing*,' he repeats in a lighter voice as he gets up and I struggle to follow him.

'Hey Jamie,' he says to me suddenly. It is the first time

he's called me by my christian name. I hum with pride, with happiness. All five foot ten of me follows along happily behind his four foot nothing, tailing his every step.

'Hey, do you want to go into town this Friday night?'

'I can't,' I say automatically.

'Why not?'

'I'm not allowed.'

'*Ask.*'

I look at Lemmy and Lemmy looks at me.

'OK,' I say. 'I'll ask.'

Lemmy doesn't smile. But he suddenly yells out, like I told you he did, 'Let's *GO!*' and he smacks his hands together so hard a startled flock of sparrows lift up, zigzag in panic and speckle through the heavens. I laugh and laugh like something in me is broke and I say, 'That's right, eh Lemmy? That's *right.*'

DAMIEN WILKINS

Conversion

For weeks after the crash there were threatening phone calls.

She's been prepared for a scar, the voice on the phone said. There will be a scar.

It was the boyfriend's father making the calls.

That's terrible, I said. I'm so sorry.

She hasn't got her mood back, he said.

Her mood?

You caused her to have these headaches all the time, so she's always in a bad mood. She's foul now.

Oh—.

Once she was sweet, not a temper on her. Now she's mad with everyone. She's mad with my son because of what you did out there on that road.

Look.

Look yourself. I know where you live.

By this time I'd usually become silent. I should have put the phone down. Yet I couldn't hang up on the boyfriend's father— how many people did I want to hurt.

Are you listening to me? Imagine being her. Imagine a headache which is with you all day, every minute you have a headache. Can you imagine that? Even from the outside? It gets her in the left temple. I know who you are. She has to comb her hair down because of you.

Please—.

You are responsible for this and I don't hear any contrition in your voice. Do you have a feeling of contrition somewhere?

Yes.

Don't agree so quickly. Do you think these are just words.

I listened to him on four or five occasions, then my father started taking the calls.

Are you trying to threaten my son? said my father.

I'm not trying to *kill* him, said the boyfriend's father.

My son's upset enough.

I've been pointing out his ways to him. Are you, by any chance, religious?

No, said my father, we're Catholics.

I was once in a creative writing workshop when the teacher, Charlie Newman, suddenly told the student whose story we were discussing to get the characters out of the car. Get these people out of the fucking car! he said. The characters were a young couple, as best I can recall, driving down to Florida on vacation. It was going to be a long drive. They'd been in their car for about seven pages already and they hadn't made it out of their own neighbourhood. Charlie Newman was actually a subtle teacher, a funny man with many miles of sentences under his belt, though occasionally he became exasperated enough to say things. This car is driving me fucking nuts, he said.

I had my car crash after drinking perhaps an inch, no, less than that—maybe half an inch, a splash. We'd taken Michael's mother's car out on Saturday night against her express orders. Michael said he felt nauseous from his new prescription glasses and couldn't drive. Ian didn't drive and neither of the girls had licenses. I remember everyone wandered around for a while after the crash. We talked to each other with our heads close together. Claire. Bridget. The police arrived and were startlingly kind. The lovely smell of the police uniforms as murky rain began to fall on us. It was very intimate in those moments, although at first we just sat there—we'd side-swiped another car which had come out of a tunnel after I'd misjudged a Give Way sign—and wondered if we were alive. I looked down at my knee which had hit something, but it was fine, a little sore. Everyone was fine but we were dreaming of the beds in our parents' houses. We'd suddenly become a lot younger. Babies. Michael's mother had gone away for the weekend. Don't use Rosemary, she told him. Rosemary was their nicely maintained old Wolseley. You mean there's a car and keys sitting in your garage and your mother is away for forty-eight hours, Ian said. How will she ever ever know? I said. Next this big guy from the other car was coming around towards us, walking in the middle of the road, shouting, pointing at me and, for a moment, I thought I would have to run him over. They say I actually tried to start the engine again. You, he was saying. You.

Oh, no, said one of the girls in the backseat. Oh, go away.

You. With his finger. Then the guy must have heard something from his own car—his girlfriend moaning—because suddenly he hit his forehead with his hand and said: Oh, my God. He was running back to his car. I thought I'd killed his girlfriend with Michael's mother's car because of a pair of glasses and an inch or less. Michael has never got on with his mother. His mother's sister, Aunt Betty, once said, on meeting me for the first time, Well, they both have nice *faces*.

My son has admitted fault, my father said. (I was listening in on the extension.) What's the point in making him feel worse with these calls?

What's the point? What's the point of any pain?

The boyfriend's father was beginning almost to enjoy these discussions with my father. Now, when I happened to answer the phone, he *asked for* my father.

Pain teaches you, he said. Pain instructs.

I agree with you, said my father.

It tests you. It's put there for a reason.

Yes.

You find out about people when real pain happens.

What they're made of.

What's *behind* them, said the boyfriend's father.

Right.

I'm talking about faith. The strength of faith.

How's the girl? said my father.

Who?

The girl in the accident.

Oh, said the boyfriend's father. Devastated.

She's being tested, said my father. *Instructed*.

Don't use my own words against me, Ken.

You know, you've never said your name. Who am I speaking to?

Andrew, said the boyfriend's father. Andy.

*

Walking home at night from parties or from friend's places, I went
through a period when I couldn't resist trying the doors of cars
parked on the empty streets. I was sick with car door handles,
the interiors of other people's cars. My cousin in Auckland was
a great stealer of cars and pleasure craft. His father had died
under anaesthetic while in hospital for a routine operation. My
father was vastly alive a few streets away and I had no intention
of stealing the cars I felt my way inside. I climbed into a Jaguar
once. The smell of leather, that smell which seems almost like
a taste, as if you're sucking the seats. O Jaguar. The seats were
like beds, the headrests pillows. The instruments on the dash set
into the walnut like they were miniature trophies. I was inside
a mobile hunting lodge—smouldering logs, heavy rugs. In the
glovebox, which was as deep as a filing cabinet, silent as a cave,
I found a big wad of keys. There were perhaps twenty-five keys,
of all sizes, buttoned up in a leather pouch with a brass clip. I
kept that pouch of Jaguar keys for years, until the leather grew
chalky with mould. I must have had in that one wad the keys to
several homes and several holiday homes and to businesses and
lock-ups and private areas—drawers, secret chests. I was always
keeping keys. They were the coins of my adolescence—great
rings of hope.

For some time after the crash, as a passenger in cars, I carried
around with me a stupid and self-regarding fatalism. I was
satisfied not to be driving. I had an awful and false smugness.
Let this other person have the accident. At least it won't be me
that kills us or someone else. I'm in the clear.

Priests drive smallish cars, never saloons or wagons. Non-family
cars. I could never imagine trying the handle of a priest's car
if I came across one at night. They drive automatics mostly—
widower's cars—because the gear lever is a business. Priest's cars
are garaged cars—not because they believe in caring for the cars
but because church properties have large garages. They can't hear
engines, priests. They'd go up hills in fourth and never know.
They forget about the petrol. They can't read temperatures, any

dials. They can't read smoke. They don't know where the full-beam switch is kept. Priests are hopeless parkers. They'll drive around for ages, unmindful of the petrol, looking for a park they can drive straight into. A priest will hit you three times, front and rear, trying to get out of a straight park. They have no vision. They're talking drivers, busy, late-planners, last-minute deciders. I've seen priests pull out into a line of traffic without looking—they think the traffic will *part* for them. At the time of the crash I had a little job servicing the parish car fleet—three widower's cars. I didn't know anything about cars except oil and water. My father got me the job. I checked the oil and water every third day. I drove the cars to the garage to fill them with petrol. I had the windscreens cleaned while I waited. I took the cars to get the dings hammered out, the paintwork retouched. And I drove the old priest, Father Liddell, who was suffering from, among other things, glaucoma, to and from his weekend appointments. He wasn't kindly. He was taciturn and testy and old and he forgot things. He ached—not just in his eyes. Father Liddell winced with every movement he made. He was a pained shadow of something once formidable. I drove him to doctors. Sometimes he was rude to me. He found out I didn't attend a Catholic school. My father didn't trust the Brothers. Father Liddell often mistook me for other people.

Wild, wild boy, he said to me from the back of the car. Wild, ungrateful Archie.

In cars, despite the appearance of speed, life tends to stop. Children know this. No child enjoys a trip of longer than two hours. They know the true motion of their lives has been arrested. The enclosure which has trapped them grows hateful. Its stillness makes them enraged. Here, outside the moving car, thinks the child, is another view which I can do nothing *in*. This is the real nature of car-sickness. It's also of course what Charlie Newman was saying about the car-story. He wanted the windows down, the doors open, air, escape. Some natural velocity. Or incident, happening. Crash this fucking car, he said. I don't care how you do it. Just get them *out* of there.

*

Ken, said the boyfriend's father, I want to ask your advice.

Very well, Andy, said my father.

Wait. Is there someone else on the line?

Is there? said my father.

Yes, I said.

It's my son, Andy.

The one I threatened?

Yes, I said.

How long ago was that accident? Four, five weeks?

Eight and a half, I said.

Really? said Andy.

Yes, I said.

Time heals, said my father.

She left him, said Andy. The girl in the car that night. The one who got hurt. She's gone.

Oh, no, I said.

Packed her bags.

Oh, I said.

But you didn't cause it, said Andy. Ken, your son didn't cause that to happen.

No, said my father.

They were on the rocks. You were just the last big wave that came along.

I'm glad, I said.

She had nothing behind her. Nothing to draw from.

She was revealed then, said my father. Your son found out about her.

He didn't find out a thing. He's never found out anything in his life. Andy cleared his throat. Did I really threaten your son, Ken?

A little, Andy. Yes.

Boy. Thing is that scar wasn't even a scar in the end. One day it just dropped off.

We're relieved, said my father.

Andy's throat made the noise again. Sorry, he coughed.

What's that? said my father.

I was just apologising to your son, Ken.

We appreciate it, Andy.

I'm still not good at admitting my faults.

Maybe if we, you and me, Andy, said my father, can now be left in peace.

I hung up the phone.

They talked about religion for almost an hour. Andy was a convert. My father got few opportunities to speak.

He said once: But we must be allowed temptation, Andy. Temptation is not the problem itself. If we're allowed it, *then* we can resist it. It's the resistance that—

Later on he got to say: That's the Holy Ghost's role though, isn't it.

My father said not to tell the priests about the accident. It would only bring complications. I drove Father Liddell about as usual. I'm going to injure or probably kill you, Father, I thought. We're going to have an accident any day. Will that meanness really be your last act? I hoped that when it happened, Father Liddell would have just done me some unexpected kindness, some surprising good. With that ancient, unforgiving spiritual head behind me, my fatalism was in full flight. I was chauffeur to a holy ghost. We drove to the orthopaedic specialist. The parking was difficult around the consulting rooms. It started to rain. A storm. There was always a painfully slow walk of several hundred metres to the specialist's rooms. At first the weather made it more likely that we'd have our accident. Then, when we failed in that, the downpour made it more likely that Father Liddell would be very sour towards me. He hated the wet. He forgot he was a priest and he forgot who I was. Fuck it, Archie, he said as we tottered through a whipped-up puddle. He started to turn around. I had his tiny arm in my hand, all coat. This way, Father, I said, trying to ease him back on course. But he had a strength. He turned us both around and we began to move back towards the car. The specialist's rooms were in a nice old converted villa which was set back from the road and drowned in big trees. These trees spread to the street. They arched over the footpath, making a dank canopy for us. Leaves fell with the rain. The rain was so heavy it sparked silver against the road. Father Liddell's front foot skidded out a little and I held him more tightly. Let me be, he hissed. Let go of me! I'm older than you. He jerked his arm away and set off without me. I stood under the trees and watched him. Bent over, he moved in a shaky diagonal across the footpath, towards the wrong car. In the afternoon dark the car had its lights on, the engine was running. Father Liddell put out a hand towards it. Perhaps he just wanted to rest. I watched it all in that quick slow-motion familiar to me from the car crash I had not told the priests about. My life had become a series of partially concealed quick slow-motion episodes. I caused things to happen at a disastrous, unnatural speed. Father, I said. Father! He was turning slowly to face me, some terrible utterance on his lips. The car pulled away and Father Liddell fell. He did not fall to his knees first, then crumple neatly, then fold. He fell like a building, with the same astonishing and complete diminishment. There was suddenly less of him on the ground than had been in the air.

On the way home Father Liddell sat quietly in the back of the car. He hated me even more now. His coat, his trousers, his hair, *the side of his face*—all bore the imprint of the slick, treacherous footpath. He wouldn't let me do anything to help him, clean him. He waved his hand in front of him. Drive on, drive on.

The rain was threatening to flood the road. Traffic moved along slowly through the dark water. Blocked drains spilled little rivers down the road. We cruised through a deep wash and I pulled over.

Suddenly Father Liddell spoke: What are you doing?

I'm pumping the brakes, Father, I said.

I can hear you, he said. Why? Why are we stopped here?

I pumped some more. I put the car in Drive and let it go forward a little, then I stepped hard on the brakes.

What are you doing now? said Father Liddell.

I repeated the manoeuvre.

You're not Archie, he said.

No, Father, I said.

I put on the indicator.

What are you doing with me? he said. Father Liddell sounded

frightened. All of us, I thought, are locked in our worlds. What are you going to do with me? he said.

I turned on the demister to clear the back window of Father Liddell's rapid breath and I no longer considered the possibility of an accident. The general state of emergency around us, the caution and courtesy, seemed to be making us safe.

Bless me, Father, I began, for I have sinned.

Stop that, said Father Liddell.

It has been three months since my last—

Stop this car. Do you hear me! I want to get out now. Pull over. Let me out. I don't feel well. Stop the car.

I pulled over.

Okay, Father, we're stopped. I'm sorry.

We sat in silence for several moments. Father Liddell was staring straight ahead, past me and out through the windshield. Who knows what he was seeing? Was the glaucoma a little like trying to look through this windshield, through these waves of water.

Finally he said, Why aren't we moving? Why aren't we going somewhere? Don't be naughty, Archie. Don't be wicked, bubba.

I have no idea where Rosemary, the Wolseley, is, or where Claire, Bridget, Ian or Michael are now. We do not know if the boyfriend is a boyfriend still or who the father now calls for advice. The last thing I heard from the writing workshop was Charlie Newman had been unfairly removed from his teaching position, but that for breaking the conditions of his tenure, the university had to pay him off handsomely. Amen.

FORBES WILLIAMS

from Motel View

. . . slowing down from the highway as you cross the town's only bridge, you might note the abundance of neon as you first enter Main Street, but all too soon you'll be through all that and back out onto the dark highway. There are three sets of traffic lights in Motel View, but they are traffic lights without purpose—Main Street is the only street—and they are always green. Don't bother slowing down.

You'll continue out along the coast for about another five miles until the road rises sharply and to the left: Hunter's Garage corner. It's actually the second of three nasty bends, but it seems to be the one that does the damage, so watch it. In the winter it can be icy and very treacherous.

Once you're past Hunter's Garage you'll be travelling inland, leaving the bay behind you. You'll wind up the hillsides for about another five miles, till you reach the top of View Rise. At the View Rise lookout you'll probably get out of your car and look back down into the brown silted bay, the steep treeless hills that rise out of its sides, the small but distinct mudflats extending back from the tidal reaches. If it's night, though, all you'll really see will be the flashing coloured dots of Motel View. If you've got a good camera (like John) you may well want to try and take a photograph of all that darkness with the little spots of colour. Put your camera just a bit out of focus and the light blots on the photograph like drops of bright paint. It's like Christmas.

Once over View Rise you'll wind down out of the hills. There's a larger town on the inland plain, and it's only a couple of miles down from the Rise that it first blinks into view, the reassuring sight of a town worth stopping in. As your mind shifts to hamburgers and milkshakes you'll quickly forget the wide round bay, the hills, that odd little amusement park place with the wrong name on the map.

Unless you decide to stay. In which case you'll drive gently once down Main Street till you come to the last motel—The View Inn—realising with a mixture of surprise and annoyance that there are no takeaway bars, no dairies, no pubs, and no vacancy at any of the motels. If you're like us (John is driving), you'll probably do a slow careful U-turn, crawl back along Main Street, 'just to check', turn back round again at the bridge, speed up through all the traffic lights, and head on to the next town, which on our map is a thin circle round a fattish dot: symbol, I suppose, of hope. You'll speed out along the coast, and the rest you already know.

Unless you have a flat tyre. Then you'll have to stop. This need not take more than ten irritated minutes of your time, but perhaps you'll light a cigarette (as I do) and wander up the road a bit first, intrigued by this strange, quiet town. If you do, you'll almost immediately get a strong feeling of emptiness, even desolation, as if Motel View is in reality a bizarre ghost town. There'll be no cars, no people, no bicycles, toys, trees, or pets. No life but for a few small shrubs set sparsely upon flat, broad mown lawns advancing to low brick fences, no noise but for the soft bay. Set back on their lawns the low single-storey buildings of motel units, long buildings full of dark windows— like a school really, or a mental institution—and no sign of activity inside them. Just those faithfully flashing lights, giant electric words against the sky, each sign its own distinct style of lettering. It's as if the town is no more than an advertisement.

Once you've walked the length of Main Street, you'll probably begin to notice how cold you are—no breeze, just a still, sharp chill.

Christ it's cold, you'll probably say (as I do), rubbing each arm with the opposite hand. Let's just fix the wheel.

You'll walk quickly back to the car, head down over your crossed arms, trying to remember where your jersey is.

My jersey's in my bag. We'll have to open the boot.

We'll have to open the boot anyway. My mind drifts across the vagaries of changing wheels.

True, I say at last. We will.

If you're travelling with John (as I am) you'll just have to put up with the cold, because even with your jersey on the

555

chill gets in, and he'll want to set up the camera to take long-exposure views of the neon signs. Not having a tripod, he'll use the car roof as a solid base, so you won't be able to change the tyre while he mucks about. I'm not bitter, of course, but we are always stopping in the middle of nowhere so John can take photographs of broken fences, abandoned barns and dead cattle.

I'll go in this place here and see if they've got any food, I say, lighting another cigarette. John struggles with a knob on his camera.

Do you want any food? John's forehead is wrinkled in intense concentration. When he concentrates he grunts, and it takes him nearly thirty seconds of periodic grunting to answer.

What?

I said, do you want any food? Will I buy you some?

Do they sell any?

I don't know! Christ!

Okay, okay, don't get shitty. Something breaks off in his hand. Get me some fruit.

Have you broken your camera? I can hardly disguise my hope.

I don't know. I can't see properly.

Well sit in the car with the door open. It's too dark for a photograph anyway. Aren't you cold?

Red deco letters flash on and off above the car. View Towers. And —a smaller, squarer blue—No Vacancy, flashing less frequently and staying on longer. John won't tell me if he's cold or not, so I shrug and begin walking up the drive. The gravel crunches under my feet.

Like all the other motels, View Towers is set well back on its lawn. It has the same tidy shrubs squatting like gnomes, and the grass smells freshly mown. Everyone I know has a fondness for that smell, as if some primeval instinct deep within our evolutionary past was actually preparing us for the arrival of lawnmowers. The motel itself is also like the others, a low dark building full of windows. As I near it I cut across the lawn, quiet as a cat, to spy in one, see if I can see inside. It certainly does not look like a full motel. The windows are tinted, and the building set far enough back from the road that the flashing signs only reflect back at me. All I can see are a few indistinct shadows, nothing certain. I look into several more windows. It is the same in each one.

A sudden schoolboy panic possesses me, and I run back to the drive. I realise once more how cold I am and walk briskly round the back, following the drive, to the motel office.

The office is weatherboard, seems to hang off its new brick motel as an afterthought, even though it is almost certainly the older building. A bare bulb, sitting over a single step, lights the outside. Hundreds of insects dart round the light, as if an insect world war has at last ended.

Hey, you guys, one imagines insects saying to their families. Hey, you guys! The war's over! Let's go down to the light!

A pale yellow wooden door with a frosted glass window leans unhinged in the doorway. One vertical board has been kicked in at its base, and the glass is cracked in several places. Someone has painted in rough handwriting on the door:

> View Towers—Moteliers
> —Colour Television
> —Bed and Breakfast
> —4 Star Service
> —Credit Cards Accepted
> —No Vacancy

Standing on the step, I take the door with both hands and lift it with care out of the doorway. I carry it before me into the small office and lean it against the wall. The insects follow me in. Their small wings whisper.

The decor is strictly linoleum. The floor, the top and sides of the high counter, all are linoleum-covered; even the wallpaper looks like linoleum. There's a sign on the wall behind the counter that repeats the painted words on the door.

There's nobody in the office, but another doorway behind the counter opens into a smallish living-room. A small colour TV is going, with some kind of sports programme blaring out, and in front of it—with his back to me—is a short man with short curly hair and a sunburnt neck. He is shadow-boxing, swinging from side to side, and growling out an intermittent commentary on some game which seems to be a mixture of the one on TV and his own private boxing match.

Go get him! he shouts, pummelling the aerial with a brutal left haymaker. There! That'll show you, little runt! Get him! Go get him! He struggles to the floor, perhaps retrieving the aerial, though it could be he has it in a headlock.

I stop for a second, unsure what to do. He seems too violently engrossed for me to consider stopping him. There's a buzzer on the counter with 'Press On Arrival' scrawled alongside, and after a moment's hesitation I decide to risk it. I press. There is no noise. I press again, this time holding it down for maybe fifteen seconds.

Finally another man appears in the living room. He is fatter than the boxer, but shorter. He stops for a few seconds to look at the TV, then turns to me, stepping into the office. He is rolling up one sleeve, and he looks at me with narrow eyes.

Wha'd'ya want? he says. We're full. Can't you read English?

Maim the bastard! shouts the other man, back on his feet and waving his arms.

We've got a flat. Is there some food we could buy?

He begins on the other sleeve. There's no garage in Motel View. Nearest garage is Hunter's, few miles down the road.

Have you got any food? You know, a restaurant or something.

Grind his head! Grind his fucking head!

This is a motel sonny. Only meal here is breakfast.

Well can we stay?

Jesus Christ! What the hell are you? Kill him!

We're full. I told you we're full. Can't you hear either?

But there's no one here. I looked in your rooms. The place is empty.

He leans forward, pudgy hands gripping the counter.

Kill him! Kill him! Fucking kill him!

Can't you see we're busy? He has begun on the first sleeve again. Already the second one is unpeeling. It occurs to me he possibly spends his entire life rolling up his sleeves.

Have you honestly got no food?

His face reddens. He is the perfect cartoon bulldog.

You better get out of here, sonny, or there ain't gonna be too much of you left.

KILL HIM!

I back out of the office, my hands up.

Okay, I say, okay. I'm going.

Out in the drive I can feel my heart pounding. Some motel. I realise we'd better get the tyre changed and out of here.

At the car John has given up on his photograph. The ground round the boot is strewn with bags.

You just wouldn't believe the people in there! I say as soon as I get close. No food, that's for sure.

I can't find the jack.

God, I thought the guy was going to do me in! Bloody crazy. There was this other guy fighting the air, and just bloody screaming at the television. I reckon we should get the hell out as fast as we can.

I can't find the jack. It's not in the boot.

Yes it is. Eager to upstage I push past him, start rummaging around in the dark boot. It's in here somewhere.

Could it be in the back seat?

I fumble around. I'm sure it's in here. Haven't we got a torch?

The batteries are flat. I don't think the jack's here.

Of course it's here. Where the hell else would it be? Listen, you should have seen these guys. They were off the edge.

Can you find it?

Not yet, but it's in here. I'm sure it is.

Another five minutes weakens my confidence. The jack isn't in the boot. It isn't in the back seat. Finally I accept reality. We can't change the tyre.

John looks at me seriously. His face is alternately red, blue and purple.

What about the guys in there?

Look, honestly, they were going to beat me up.

Well what about somewhere else?

We look up the street. Vista View. No Vacancy. Lake View.

No Vacancy. Every one is the same. No Vacancy.

But they're all empty. I just don't understand it.

Well, I don't see that we have much choice. And I tell you, it's too cold to sleep in the car.

I start to shiver. The chill is like a hand down my back.

But we have no choice. Like it or not, we're staying in Motel View.

ASHLEIGH YOUNG

Old Car

One dark night, one wall-eyed headlight.
The Cortina carried us out of town
faithful as the moon.

*

The docile oh
of the steering wheel,
the cool frankness of vinyl.
In an old car you are
always driving home.

FAY ZWICKY

Starting over in autumn

Halfway wise when young,
who could foresee their stubborn mysteries,
their presumptions of innocence?

They intended to disappoint nobody.
Who could have warned them?
Who would have listened?

Can they imagine today what nobody knows,
the span of a human breath
coming and going?

He thinks she can.
She hopes he might.

And why, you ask, does the poet
(jotting under the broken angel's wing
at the bottom of the garden) sound off
such lamentatory alarms?

Observe the verdant celebrant in his hot suit.
He's not reading the sorrows of Job
unsuited to such modern occasions.
Is there anything you would like me to say?
He has a gold biro rolled behind his ear
for the record, smiles on the dotted line:
hello my friends
we are gathered . . .

What lasts is what they started with,
the faltering heart and something else.
Nothing won or absolutely lost,

still here imagining a place
where people work and pray and sleep,
the tender rituals of surrender.

Time has changed sides, no longer on theirs.
She almost knows.
He doesn't want to know and doesn't
know he doesn't.

The poet doesn't like those lines.
Forget the poet at the garden's end,
what he knows and can't forget.
He's called today a day like any other.

The earth's still green,
birds hop in the yard in hopeful rain,
the young still wait, gravid with yearning.

Pray for them, their children, and those birds.
Let them attend the grace of candour or whatever
waits behind the soul's clear windows.

Contributors' Notes & Acknowledgements

'Day Out': *Sport* 20, 1998; in *Glorious Things* (Jonathan Cape, 1999) and *Collected Stories* (VUP, 2005); reprinted with permission. 'Peppermint Frogs': *Sport* 21, 1998; in *Collected Stories*; reprinted with permission. **Barbara Anderson** is one of New Zealand's leading contemporary writers, author of eight novels including *Portrait of the Artist's Wife*, winner of the 2003 Wattie Award. Born in 1926, her first book was the 1989 short story collection *I think we should go into the jungle*, which included 'Fast Post' from *Sport* 1.

'The Badder & the Better': *Sport* 28, 2002; in *Nonsense* (VUP, 2003); reprinted with permission. **Nick Ascroft** is the author of two collections of poems, *From the Author of* and *Nonsense*. He is also a Scrabble champion and editor of *Glottis*, and editor of the November 2005 *Landfall*.

'Pa'u-stina': *Sport* 31, 2003; in *Wild Dogs Under My Skirt* (VUP, 2004); reprinted with permission. **Tusiata Avia** was born in Christchurch of Samoan descent in 1966. She is an acclaimed performance poet, and did the VUW MA in Creative Writing in 2002.

'Liver': *Sport* 31, 2003; in *Mātuhi | Needle* (VUP, 2004); reprinted with permission. **Hinemoana Baker** is a writer, musician and radio producer. *Mātuhi* was co-published with The Perceval Press in California, and coincided with the release of her first full-length music CD, *Puāwai*.

'Membrane': *Sport* 21, 1998; in *Bell Tongue* (VUP, 1999); reprinted with permission. **Paola Bilbrough** was born in 1971, grew up in New Zealand and now lives in Australia. She has been a frequent contributor to *Sport*, since debuting in issue 5.

'Why Do Sonnets Have 14 Lines?': *Sport* 24, 2000; previously uncollected; reprinted with permission. **Graham Bishop** is a retired geologist and mountaineer. His books include a collection of poetry and prose, *Poles Apart* (Steele Roberts, 2000), and he has written the biography of the pioneering NZ geologist Alexander McKay.

'Wellington 1955': *Sport* 7, 1991; in *Let's Meet: poems 1985–2000* (Steele Roberts, 2003); reprinted with permission. **Peter Bland** was born in England in 1934, and was a key member of the 1950/60s 'Wellington Group' of poets that included James K. Baxter and Louis Johnson. Two books of poems, *Let's Meet: poems 1985–2000* and *Ports of Call*, were published by Steele Roberts in 2003,

'The Man Dean Went to Photograph': *Sport* 8, 1992; in *How We Met* (VUP, 1995); reprinted with permission. 'Villanelle': *Sport* 28, 2002; in *Summer* (VUP, 2004); reprinted with permission. Made an Arts Foundation Laureate in 2004, and Te Mata Estate New Zealand Poet Laureate 2005–6, **Jenny Bornholdt** is the author of seven books of poems, including *Miss New Zealand: Selected Poems* (VUP, 1997) and *Summer*. Her story 'The China Theory of Life' appeared in *Sport* 1.

'His Father's Shoes': *Sport* 13, 1994; in *Alpha Male* (VUP, 1998; Jonathan Cape, 1999); reprinted with permission. **William Brandt**'s collection of stories *Alpha Male* earned him an MA in Creative Writing at VUW in 1999, the Adam Prize, and the Hubert Church Award for Best First Book of Fiction in the Montana New Zealand Book Awards. He is currently developing a screenplay based on his bestselling novel *The Book of the Film of the Story of My Life* (2002).

'(damaged by water)': *Sport* 17, 1996; in *Lemon* (VUP, 1999); reprinted with permission. 'The Book of Sadness': *Sport* 32, 2004; in *The Year of the Bicycle* (VUP, *forthcoming* 2006); reprinted with permission. **James Brown** is from Palmerston North. He overcame this to become the author of four collections of poetry, including *Go Round Power Please* (Best First Book, 1996 Montana New Zealand Book Awards), and an editor of *Sport* since 1993.

'A Mullet in Luxor': *Sport* 8, 1992; previously uncollected; reprinted with permission. A long-time food writer on *Cuisine* magazine and Wellington's *Evening/Dominion Post*, **David Burton** is also the author of several internationally successful books, including *The Raj at Table* (Faber, 1994) and *La cuisine coloniale* (Hachette Livre, 2002), and the autobiographical *Biography of a Local Palate* (Four Winds Press, 2003).

'What People Want': *Sport* 5, 1990; in *The Hungry Woman* (VUP, 1997); reprinted with permission. **Rachel Bush** lives in Nelson. Her second collection of poems is *The Unfortunate Singer* (VUP, 2002).

'My father's speakers': *Sport* 28, 2002; previously uncollected; reprinted with permission. **Edmund Cake** is better known as a musician, with the band Bressa Creeting Cake, and with his 2004 solo CD *Downtown Puff.*

'The spine gives up its saddest stories': *Sport* 24, 2000; in *Realia* (VUP, 2001); reprinted with permission. **Kate Camp**'s *Unfamiliar Legends of the Stars* won the NZSA Jessie Mackay Award for Best First Book of Poetry in the 1999 Montana NZ Book Awards; her third, *Beauty Sleep*, is published in November 2005.

'Birthday Photograph, 1989': *Sport* 4, 1990; in *Collected Poems 1951–2000* (Picador, 2000); reprinted with permission. **Charles Causley** (1917–2003) was a Cornish poet who combined wide popular success for poems such as 'Timothy Winters' with high critical regard. He was a guest at the 1990 Wellington Writers and Readers Week. His friend Bill Manhire's elegy is in *Lifted* (VUP, 2005).

'The Craters of the Moon': *Sport* 18, 1997; previously uncollected; reprinted with permission. In 2002 **Catherine Chidgey** won Australasia's richest literary prize, The Prize in Modern Letters, and in 2003 she was voted 'Best New Zealand novelist under forty'. Her first novel, *In a Fishbone Church* (VUP, 1997), was a New Zealand bestseller, and her subsequent novels *Golden Deeds* and *The Transformation* have gone on to international success. Catherine edited *Sport*s 24–26, and now lives in Dunedin.

'Big Louis': *Sport* 28, 2002; in the *London Review of Books* (July 2001), *Quarterly Journal of Medicine* (UK) and *Best Australian Essays 2002* (Black Inc); reprinted with permission. **Inga Clendinnen** is a leading Australian writer whose books include the acclaimed memoir *Tiger's Eye* (Text, 2000). She was a guest at the 2002 Wellington Writers and Readers Week.

'Pile Diary': *Sport* 20, 1998; in *Into India* (VUP, 1998); reprinted with permission. 'The Boiler-House': *Sport* 21, 1998; previously uncollected; reprinted with permission. **Geoff Cochrane** was born in 1951 and is the author of several highly regarded novels and collections of poetry and short stories. A frequent contributor to *Sport*, he is interviewed by Damien Wilkins in issue 31.

'An Explanation of Poetry to My Father': *Sport* 25, 2000; as *An Explanation of Poetry to My Father* (Steele Roberts, 2000); reprinted with permission. **Glenn Colquhoun** is a doctor and poet. He won Australasia's richest literary prize, The Prize in Modern Letters, in

2004. His books include *The Art of Walking Upright* (1999) and *Playing God*, which won the Montana New Zealand Book Award for Poetry in 2003. A poem of Glenn's was published on the cover of *Sport* 20.

'Efforts at Burial': *Sport* 22, 1999; previously uncollected; reprinted with permission. **Tim Corballis** was born in 1971 and is the author of three novels: *Below* (VUP, 2001), *Measurement* (2002) and *The Fossil Pits* (2005). He holds the 2005 Creative NZ Berlin Writer's Residency.

'Boys on Islands': *Sport* 3, 1989; 'Alan Preston': *Sport* 32, 2004; both previously uncollected; reprinted with permission. **Nigel Cox** is the author of five novels, including the suppressed-outside-New Zealand *Tarzan Presley* (VUP, 2004), and *Responsibility* (2005). Nigel was a founding editor of *Sport*, and most of his frequent contributions have been essays. He recently returned to New Zealand after five years as Head of Exhibitions at the Jewish Museum, Berlin.

'Investigations at the Public Baths': *Sport* 8, 1992; in *Early Days Yet: New and Collected Poems 1941–1947* (AUP and Carcanet, 1997); reprinted with permission. **Allen Curnow** (1911–2001) was the most significant New Zealand poet of his era. He received many NZ book awards, the Commonwealth Poetry Prize and the Queen's Gold Medal for Poetry. As an editor, Curnow along with Denis Glover and Charles Brasch established the modernist canon in New Zealand writing. His poems appeared in *Sport* eight times, beginning with issue 4.

'Hunger': *Sport* 24, 2000; previously uncollected; reprinted with permission. **Lynn Davidson** is a Wellington writer and frequent contributor to *Sport*. Her books include *Mary Shelley's Window* (Pemmican, 1999) and the novel *Ghost Net* (Otago University Press, 2003). A new poetry collection, *Tender*, is due out soon.

'Blokes can relate to concrete': *Sport* 20, 1998; as 'Concrete' in *Animals Indoors* (VUP, 2000); reprinted with permission. **Stephanie de Montalk** is the author of three books of poems, including *Animals Indoors* (Jessie Mackay Award for Best First Book, 2001 Montana NZ Book Awards) and *Cover Stories* (2005), and *Unquiet World: The Life of Count Geoffrey Potocki de Montalk* (2001; and in Polish translation, 2003). Her essay 'Pain' is the centrepiece of *Sport* 33.

'A Couple of Mongols': *Sport* 10, 1993; in *Stuck Up* (AUP, 1995); reprinted with permission. **John Dolan** is an American writer and academic who was born in 1955 and came to teach at Otago

University in 1993. He has recently been living in Moscow. His last poetry collection is *People With Real Lives Don't Need Landscapes* (AUP, 2003). *Pleasant Hell*, an autobiographical novel, appeared in 2005.

'The Adoration of the Kings': *Sport* 13, 1994; in *Give Me Your Hand* (Macmillan/National Gallery, 1994); reprinted with permission. **Paul Durcan**, born in 1944, is one of the most celebrated Irish poets of our time. He was a guest at the 2004 Wellington Writers and Readers Week. His latest collection of poems is *The Art of Life* (Harvill, 2004).

'The Inhabited Initial': *Sport* 22, 1999; in *The Inhabited Initial* (AUP, 1999); reprinted with permission. Best known for her novels, which include *The Skinny Louie Book* (1993 NZ Book Award for Fiction), **Fiona Farrell** has also published short stories, plays and poetry. Her first *Sport* appearance was 'The Tale of Richard Seddon' in issue 2.

'Only touch me with your eyes': *Sport* 24, 2000; previously uncollected; reprinted with permission. **Laurence Fearnley** was born in 1963 and is the author of four novels, including *Room* (VUP, 2000, shortlisted for the Montana NZ Book Award) and *Butler's Ringlet* (Penguin, 2004). Her story 'The Piper and the Penguin' appeared in *Sport* 20 (1998), and in Bill Manhire's anthology *The Wide White Page: Writers Imagine Antarctica* (VUP, 2004), and she was a 2003 Artist to Antarctica.

'Ophelia': *Sport* 29, 2002; in *The Adulterer's Bible* (VUP, 2003); reprinted with permission. **Cliff Fell** was born in London in 1955 to a New Zealand father and English mother. He came to New Zealand in 1997 and now farms in the Moutere Valley. 'Ophelia' was chosen for *Best New Zealand Poems 2003*, and *The Adulterer's Bible* won the Jessie Mackay Best First Book Award for Poetry in the 2004 Montana New Zealand Book Awards.

'First Sailing': *Sport* 25, 2000; in *Salt Water Creek* (Enitharmon, 2003); reprinted with permission. **Rhian Gallagher** was born in the South Island, did Bill Manhire's creative writing course in 1984, and has lived in London for 15 years, although a return is imminent. *Salt Water Creek* was shortlisted for the Forward Prize for Best First Collection.

'Irene and Gaye': *Sport* 16, 1996; previously uncollected; reprinted with permission. **David Geary** is primarily known as an actor and playwright, whose works include *Lovelock's Dream Run* and *Pack of*

Girls. He has contributed poetry and short fiction to *Sport*, and his collection of linked stories, *A Man of the People*, was published by VUP in 2003.

'To Mrs Bold from Little Gollop': *Sport* 17, 1996; previously uncollected; reprinted with permission. The poems in issue 17 were **Annora Gollop**'s first appearance in print. She lives in Auckland, and has most recently published work in the online magazines *Trout* and *Fugacity*.

'The Email Drought': *Sport* 31, 2003; previously uncollected; reprinted with permission. **Josh Greenberg** came to New Zealand from the US in 2003 on a Fulbright Scholarship to do an MA in Creative Writing at VUW. His novel *A Man Who Eats the Heart* received the Adam Prize, and was published in 2004 by VUP. Josh is back in Grayling, Michigan working as a fishing guide.

'Go Easy, Sweetheart': *Sport* 21, 1998; in *Settler Dreaming* (VUP, 2001) and *The Merino Princess: Selected Poems* (VUP, 2004); reprinted with permission. **Bernadette Hall** is the author of six collections of poems, as well as plays and short fiction. In 2004 she retired from teaching secondary school Latin, moved from Christchurch to Amberley Beach, and was a joint Antarctica New Zealand Artist to Antarctica, with the artist Kathryn Madill. Bernadette has edited *Like Love Poems: Selected Poems*, by her friend the writer and artist Joanna Margaret Paul (1945–2003) (VUP, *forthcoming* 2006).

'Art Can't Smile': *Sport* 32, 2004; previously uncollected; reprinted with permission. **Peter Hall-Jones** was born in Invercargill and now lives in France, where he works in the union movement. 'Art Can't Smile' was originally published as an extract from a novel, but is now to be regarded as a short story. 'Come Here and Think That' was in issue 16, and a new story is in issue 33.

'Mirror Poem': *Sport* 8, 1992; in *Selected Poems* (Bloodaxe, 1997); reprinted with permission. **Josef Hanzlik** was a leading Czechoslovakian poet. He was a guest at the 1992 Wellington Writers and Readers Week. 'Mirror Poem' was translated by Ian and Jarmila Milner. Ian Milner was a New Zealand writer and academic who lived in Prague from the early 1950s until his death in 1991. *Intersecting Lines: The Memoirs of Ian Milner* was edited by Vincent O'Sullivan and published by VUP in 1993.

'*from* The Harbour Poems': *Sport* 2, 1989; in *Small Stories of Devotion* (VUP, 1991) and *Oh There You Are, Tui!: Selected Poems*

(VUP, 2001); reprinted with permission. **Dinah Hawken**'s *It has no sound and is blue* (1987) won the Commonwealth Poetry prize for Best First Book. Dinah teaches a writing and landscape course at the International Institute of Modern Letters at VUW. *Buoyant and Threatened Like Us*, her new book which combines poetry and journal, will be published in 2006.

'Acrid': *Sport* 32, 2004; previously uncollected; reprinted with permission. **Debbie Hill** has three young sons and has lived in South America, Kenya, Uganda, Pakistan, Bangladesh and currently Australia. She did the MA in Creative Writing at VUW with Damien Wilkins in 2004, and completed the collection of stories from which 'Acrid' comes.

'Sometimes I Dream I'm Driving': *Sport* 15, 1995; in *Stonefish* (Huia, 2004); reprinted with permission. **Keri Hulme** won the Booker Prize for *The Bone People* in 1985. Her collection of stories, *Te Kaihau / The Windeater*, signed up by Bill Manhire in 1979, was published by VUP in 1986. Keri contributed 'The Pluperfect Pa-Wa' to *Sport* 1.

'My life when I had a life': *Sport* 32, 2004; previously uncollected; reprinted with permission. **Anna Jackson** was born in 1967 and is the author of three books of poems, most recently *Catullus for Children* (AUP, 2003).

'Binoculars': *Sport* 16, 1996; in *The Sounds* (VUP, 1996); reprinted with permission. 'Saudade': *Sport* 23, 1999; in *Birds of Europe* (VUP, 2000); reprinted with permission. **Andrew Johnston** has been an editor of *Sport* and has contributed many poems through the years. Since 1997 he has lived in Paris where he works on the *International Herald Tribune* and edits www.thepage.name. His fourth collection of poems is forthcoming from VUP in 2006.

'Journey Through a Painted Landscape': *Sport* 6, 1991; previously uncollected; reprinted with permission. **Lloyd Jones** was born in 1955 and is the author of many books, including *The Book of Fame* (Penguin, 2000), a verse-novel about the 1905 All Blacks that won the Deutz Medal for Fiction in the 2001 Montana NZ Book Awards and the Tasmania Pacific Fiction Award. He has contributed short fiction, poetry and essays to *Sport*. From 2002 to 2005 his Four Winds Press published a series of 18 stand-alone essays, by writers including Margaret Mahy, Bill Manhire, Vincent O'Sullivan, Kate Camp, Damien Wilkins, Lydia Wevers, Harry Ricketts, Glenn Colquhoun, David Burton and Peter Wells.

'The Field': *Sport* 20, 1998; in *All Roads Lead to the Sea* (AUP, 1997) and as 'My Mothers Plants' in *Someone Else's Life* (AUP and Bloodaxe, 2003); reprinted with permission. **Kapka Kassabova** was born in Bulgaria in 1973 and arrived in New Zealand via England in 1993. She has published three books of poems and two novels.

'Sunday, Across the Tasman': *Sport* 10, 1993; in *Red Sauce, Whiskey, and Snow* (Farrar, Straus & Giroux, 1995); reprinted with permission. American poet **August Kleinzahler** won the 2004 Griffin Poetry Prize for *The Strange Hours Travellers Keep*. His first visit to Wellington was for the 1992 Writers and Readers Week, and resulted in this poem.

'Afraid': *Sport* 6, 1991; abridged as 'Take as Prescribed' in *Soho Square* 4, edited by Bill Manhire (Bloomsbury, 1991); reprinted with permission. **Elizabeth Knox**'s books include the novel *The Vintner's Luck* (VUP, FSG, Chatto & Windus, 1998), which won the Deutz Medal for Fiction at the 1999 Montana New Zealand Book Awards and the Tasmania Pacific Fiction Prize; *The High Jump: A New Zealand Childhood*, which collects three autobiographical novellas (1889, 1994, 1998), and *Dreamhunter* (HarperCollins and Faber, 2005), part one of a two-book sequence for young adults. A founding editor of *Sport* and frequent contributor of essays, Elizabeth can still sometimes be persuaded to read an especially troublesome submission.

'Grace to the Goodsyard': *Sport* 27, 2001; in *Anything the Landlord Touches* (Giramondo, 2002); reprinted with permission. **Emma Lew** is a notable Australian poet. Born in 1962, her first collection, *The Wild Reply*, was published by Black Pepper Press in 1997. *Anything the Landlord Touches*, her second, won the Judith Wright Calanthe Poetry Prize and the Victoria Premier's C.J. Dennis Prize for Poetry. She first appeared in *Sport* in issue 16 (1996).

'*from* On the Burning Deck': *Sport* 2, 1989; in *The Free World* (VUP and Vintage Australia, 1996); reprinted with permission. **J.H. Macdonald** did the creative writing course at VUW in 1988. The novella 'On the Burning Deck' was his first published fiction, and became the basis of his novel *The Free World*. After some years in Australia, he now lives in Masterton.

'Off the Record': *Sport* 32, 2004; previously uncollected; reprinted with permission. **Samara McDowell** completed an MA in Creative Writing at VUW in 2003. Her story 'Holloway Road' from *Sport* 8 was reprinted in *Wellington: The City in Literature*, edited by Kate Camp (Exisle, 2003).

'Some Folk-singers and a Theologian': *Sport* 17, 1996; 'Not Telling': *Sport* 20, 1998; both previously uncollected; reprinted with permission. **Dennis McEldowney** (1926–2003) was a writer and editor whose books include his memoir of his childhood and successful surgery for a congenital heart condition, *The World Regained* (1957; second edition, AUP, 2001) and *A Press Achieved: The Emergence of Auckland University Press* (2001).

'Convert to You': *Sport* 21, 1998; previously uncollected; reprinted with permission. **Stuart McKenzie** is a Wellington playwright and filmmaker. His feature film, *For Good*, premiered at the New Zealand and Toronto Film Festivals in 2003.

'Marshmallow': *Sport* 20, 1998; in extended form as 'Marshmallow Queen' in *The Bag Lady's Picnic and Other Stories* (Shoal Bay Press, 2001); reprinted with permission. **Frankie McMillan** is a Christchurch-born short story writer. She received a 2004 Todd New Writer's Bursary to write a collection of short stories.

'Map': *Sport* 8, 1992; in *Dunedin; The City in Literature* (Exisle, 2003); reprinted with permission. **Cilla McQueen** has published nine books of poetry, the latest being *Fire Penny* (University of Otago Press, 2005). She is a three-time winner of the New Zealand Book Award for Poetry.

'A Dissolving Ghost': *Sport* 7, 1991; in *A Dissolving Ghost: Essays and More* (VUP, 2000); reprinted with permission. **Margaret Mahy** is one of New Zealand's most celebrated writers. She lives in Governor's Bay with three cats and a woolly black dog. The author of over 150 titles, her awards include a Netherlands Silver Pencil Award, two Carnegie Medals and five Esther Glenn Medals.

'The Poet's Wife': *Sport* 4, 1990; in *South Pacific* (Carcanet, 1994) and *Songs of My Life* (Godwit, 1996)—the same collection under different titles; reprinted with permission. 'My Sunshine': *Sport* 9, 1992; 'Moonlight': *Sport* 15, 1995; both in *My Sunshine* (VUP, 1996); reprinted with permission. **Bill Manhire**'s many books include *Collected Poems* (VUP and Carcanet, 2001); a short memoir, *Under the Influence* (Four Winds Press, 2003); and anthology, *The Wide White Page: Writers Imagine Antarctica* (VUP, 2004); and a new collection of poems, *Lifted* (VUP, 2005). He is the director of the International Institute of Modern Letters at Victoria University of

Wellington. In 1997 he was the inaugural Te Mata New Zealand Poet Laureate, and in 2004 he was the Meridian Energy Katherine Mansfield Memorial Fellow in Menton, France.

'Tunes for Bears to Dance to': *Sport* 3, 1989; 'Mad Hatter Days': *Sport* 21, 1998; both previously uncollected; reprinted with permission. **Owen Marshall** is one of New Zealand's leading writers. Principally celebrated for his short stories, he is also the author of two novels, including the Deutz Medal winner *Harlequin Rex* (Vintage, 2000), and is a notable editor and creative writing teacher as an Adjunct Professor at the University of Canterbury.

'Glaze': *Sport* 2, 1989; in *Dog Fox Field* (Angus & Robertson, 1990) and *New Collected Poems* (Duffy & Snellgove, 2002); reprinted with permission. **Les Murray** is Australia's greatest poet.

'The Run-Off': *Sport* 18, 1997; previously uncollected except for the chapbook *Seven Letters* (Wellington Plains, 1997); reprinted with permission. **Gregory O'Brien** is a poet, essayist, art curator and painter based in Wellington. His recent publications include the catalogue for an acclaimed exhibition at the City Gallery in Wellington, *Rosalie Gascoigne: Plain Air* (City Gallery/VUP, 2004); a book about contemporary New Zealand Art for young people, *Welcome to the South Seas* (AUP, 2004), which won the New Zealand Post Book Award for non-fiction; and a new collection of poems, *Afternoon of an Evening Train* (VUP, 2005).

'Tin Can Island': *Sport* 10, 1993; in *Ornamental Gorse* (VUP, 1994); reprinted with permission. **Chris Orsman**'s *Ornamental Gorse* won the 1995 NZSA Best First Book Award for Poetry. 'The Ice Explorer', published in *Sport* 14 in 1995, became the nucleus of his book-length sequence, *South*, published by VUP in 1996 and in an expanded form by Faber & Faber in 1999. Chris was an inaugural Antarctica New Zealand Artist to Antarctica in 1998, and VUW Writer in Residence in 2002.

'The Child in the Gardens: Winter'; 'Why Biographers Fudge It': *Sport* 29, 2002; in *Nice Morning for It, Adam* (VUP, 2004); reprinted with permission. **Vincent O'Sullivan** has published novels plays, poetry and novels, including the 1994 Montana Award winning novel *Let the River Stand* (Penguin, 1993), and the Montana poetry award winning collections *Seeing You Asked* (VUP, 1998) and *Nice Morning for It, Adam*. He is also a distinguished editor and an Emeritus Professor of English at Victoria University of Wellington.

'Beginnings and Endings': *Sport* 5, 1990; previously uncollected; reprinted with permission. **Bill Pearson** (1922–2002) is known chiefly for his sole novel, *Coal Flat* (1963), and his essay 'Fretful Sleepers', published in *Landfall* in 1952 and collected in *Fretful Sleepers & Other Essays* (Heinemann Educational Books, 1974).

'Not Her Real Name': *Sport* 11, 1993; in *Not Her Real Name and Other Stories* (VUP and Picador, 1996); reprinted with permission. **Emily Perkins'** debut collection of stories won the Hubert Church Award for Best First Book of Fiction and the Geoffrey Faber Award in the UK, and marked her as one of the most distinctive voices in New Zealand fiction. She edited an anthology of new New Zealand fiction, *The Picnic Virgin* (VUP, 1999), and her most recent novel is *The New Girl* (Picador, 2001). She has recently moved back to New Zealand after several years living in London.

'Fire': *Sport* 16, 1996; previously uncollected. **Chris Pigott** has published work in several issues of *Sport*, and was living in Hawera when 'Fire' appeared. We would be glad to hear from him.

'Mix': *Sport* 25, 2000; in *Husk* (AUP, 2002); reprinted with permission. **Chris Price** edited *Landfall* from 1993 to 2000, and now teaches in the International Institute of Modern Letters at VUW. *Husk* won the Jessie Mackay Award for Best First Book of Poetry in the 2003 Montana New Zealand Book Awards.

'I hope my mother will come soon': *Sport* 20, 1998; in *The Spit Children* (VUP, 2000); reprinted with permission. **Jo Randerson** is one of the most gifted writers and performers in contemporary New Zealand theatre. Her second collection of short stories, *The Keys to Hell*, with illustrations by Taika Waititi, was published by VUP in 2004.

'*Insomnia is a window of opportunity*': *Sport* 25, 2000; previously uncollected; reprinted with permission. **Marg Ranger** lives in Wellington, and has published poetry in a variety of periodicals.

'A Memoir': *Sport* 32, 2004; previously uncollected; reprinted with permission. **Frances Samuel** is a young Wellington poet whose work has appeared in several recent issues of *Sport*.

'Candles': *Sport* 19, 1997; previously uncollected; reprinted with permission. **Alex Scobie** (1939–2000) taught Classics at VUW, specialising in ancient fiction and folk narrative, including comics, from 1965 until failing eyesight compelled him to take early retirement in 1989. He first appeared in *Sport* in issue 11.

'The Family Album': *Sport* 14, 1995; previously uncollected; reprinted with permission. **Adam Shelton** lives in Wellington.

'Fugue': *Sport* 28, 2002; in *The Method Actors* (Shoemaker and Hoard, 2005); reprinted with permission. **Carl Shuker** grew up in Timaru, graduated from the University of Canterbury in 1998, and has lived in Tokyo off and on since 1999. He began his novel *The Method Actors* while doing the MA in Creative Writing at VUW in 2001; it was published in the United States in 2005.

'The Sloth': *Sport* 19, 1997; previously uncollected; reprinted with permission. **Elizabeth Smither** is a prolific poet and fiction writer who lives in New Plymouth. She was Te Mata Estate New Zealand Poet Laureate 2001–2002. Her most recent books are the novel *The Sea Between Us* (Penguin, 2003), and the collection of poems *Red Shoes* (Random House, 2003).

'Cartoons': *Sport* 18, 1997; in *The Right Thing* (AUP, 2002); reprinted with permission. **C.K. Stead** is one of New Zealand's most distinguished writers. He taught at Auckland University until he took early retirement to devote himself to writing in 1986. His most recent books are the novel *Mansfield* (Harvill, 2004), and the collection of poems *The Red Tram* (AUP, 2004).

'Close of Day, Oturehua': *Sport* 29, 2002; in *Footfall* (Random House, 2005); reprinted with permission. **Brian Turner** is an unrepentantly regional Otago poet who lives in Oturehua. He was Te Mata Estate New Zealand Poet Laureate 2003–2004. His most recent collections of poems are *Taking Off* (VUP, 2001) and *Footfall*, and his memoir *Somebodies and Nobodies* was published by Vintage in 2002.

'Ballad for Worser Heberley': *Sport* 9, 1992; in *The Drummer* (AUP, 1993); reprinted with permission. The most recent of **Ian Wedde**'s many books are *The Commonplace Odes* (AUP, 2003) and *Making Ends Meet: Essays and Talk 1992–2004* (VUP, 2005). Ian was a member of the conceptual team at Te Papa from 1994 to 2004. Now a freelance writer, he is the 2005 Meridian Energy Katherine Mansfield Memorial Fellow, and has a new collection of poems, *Three Regrets and a Hymn to Beauty* (AUP, 2005).

'*from* One of THEM!': *Sport* 7, 1991; in *Dangerous Desires* (Reed, 1991); reprinted with permission. **Peter Wells** first came to notice as a filmmaker (*A Death in the Family*, 1986; *Desperate Remedies*, 1993). His first book, *Dangerous Desires*, won the New Zealand Book Award for Fiction. His most recent books are a memoir, *Long*

Loop Home (Vintage, 2001), which won a Montana award, and a novel, *Iridescence* (Vintage, 2003). [Lyrics to 'It hurts to be in love' by Howard Greenfield and Helen Miller. © 1964, renewed 1992 Screen Gems-EMI Music Inc. All rights reserved. International copyright secured. Used by permission.]

'Conversion': *Sport* 15, 1995; previously uncollected; reprinted with permission. **Damien Wilkins'** first novel, *The Miserables* (VUP, Harcourt Brace, Faber, 1993) won the New Zealand Book Award for Fiction in 1994. He has published three other novels, a book of stories and a volume of poetry. He teaches creative writing at the International Institute of Modern Letters at Victoria University of Wellington. 'Conversion' contains the seeds of his third novel, *Nineteen Widows Under Ash* (2000).

'*from* Motel View': *Sport* 1, 1988; in *Motel View* (VUP, 1992); reprinted with permission. **Forbes Williams** lives in Dunedin. *Motel View*, one of the most remarkable debuts in New Zealand literature, received the PEN Hubert Church Best First Book Award in 1993.

'Old Car': *Sport* 30, 2003; previously uncollected; reprinted with permission. **Ashleigh Young** grew up near the Waitomo caves and now lives in Wellington. Her poems have appeared in several recent issues of *Sport*.

'Starting over in autumn': *Sport* 7, 1991; in *Poems 1970–1992* (University of Queensland Press, 1993); reprinted with permission. **Fay Zwicky** is a leading Australian poet whose most recent book, *The Gatekeeper's Wife* (Brandl and Schesinger, 1997), won the 1998 WA Premier's Literary Award for Poetry. She was born in 1933 and has a Wellington connection through her father's second cousin Maria Dronke—but Fergus and Elizabeth met her in a lost luggage office in Changi Airport.